OPEN SECRET

FBI JOINT TASK FORCE SERIES (BOOK ONE)

FIONA QUINN

OPEN SECRET

FBI Joint Taskforce

FIONA QUINN

THE WORLD OF INIQUUS

Ubicumque, Quoties. Quidquid

Iniquus - /i'ni/kwus/ our strength is unequalled, our tactics unfair – we stretch the law to its breaking point. We do whatever is necessary to bring the enemy down.

THE LYNX SERIES

Weakest Lynx

Missing Lynx

Chain Lynx

Cuff Lynx

Gulf Lynx

Hyper Lynx

MARRIAGE LYNX

STRIKE FORCE

In Too DEEP

JACK Be Quick

InstiGATOR

UNCOMMON ENEMIES

Wasp

Relic

Deadlock

Thorn

FBI JOINT TASK FORCE

Open Secret

Cold Red

Even Odds

KATE HAMILTON MYSTERIES

Mine

Yours

Ours

CERBERUS TACTICAL K9 TEAM ALPHA

Survival Instinct

Protective Instinct

Defender's Instinct

DELTA FORCE ECHO

Danger Signs

Danger Zone

Danger Close

This list was created in 2021. For an up-to-date list, please visit FionaQuinnBooks.com

If you prefer to read the Iniquus World in chronological order you will find a full list at the end

of this book.

"Things are much more serious: we meddle with your brains, we change your conscience - and you have no clue what to do about it."

— SURKOV.

1

ROWAN

TUESDAY
Brussels, Belgium

ROWAN KENNEDY DIDN'T PARTICULARLY ENJOY FOLLOWING men into bathrooms.

They were tricky spots.

It was impossible to control for the privacy he needed to get his job done.

The slick density of the tiles amplified the noise. And it hurt like hell getting slammed into one of the edges. That had happened to Rowan only once, and it wasn't in the line of duty. It was just some grunt who got the jump on him when he thought Rowan was hitting on his girlfriend at a bar outside of Fort Benning.

But the danger of fighting in a public bathroom was a lesson Rowan wouldn't forget.

He pushed through the heavy men's room door, timing his entrance to follow thirty seconds behind his contact.

He noted that this was the only exit point.

Rowan also noted the two athletic-looking guys hanging out in the hall who seemed attentive to his movements.

Inside, he stepped past the balding man with his hand on the wall, swaying drunkenly in front of the urinal, having trouble with his aim, past the trough of sinks, back toward the stalls. Rowan paced along the bank of doors, his head tipped to the side.

After finding the pair of oxblood leather dress shoes he was looking for, Rowan moved into the stall to the right.

He sat on the toilet, lined up his foot with the partition, and tapped out 3-2-3-4, thinking about the senator from Idaho who got himself arrested for soliciting homosexual sex doing something similar. Rowan would never use this technique in an American airport restroom. He didn't even like using it here. But this was his assignment, so... Tap, tap, tap.

An envelope slid toward him.

Rowan bent to pick it up, quickly fanning through the photos to make sure they would be useful. Yup, these would get the job done. He smiled as he plugged the tiny USB into his phone, sending the digital copies of the physical images back to headquarters. After the green light blinked on, telling him the transmission was complete, Rowan sealed the envelope and tucked it into the breast pocket of his tux.

The guy who'd handed off the photos hadn't left his stall. He was humming a monotone note under his breath. Nerves.

Rowan continued with his subterfuge. He unrolled some

toilet paper, stood, flushed, and counted to five before he exited to wash his hands.

The drunk was gone.

Rowan was alone in the bathroom except for the guy with the tasseled loafers sweating it out in the stall.

As he exited, Rowan noticed the line-backers were still in place as he strode up the hall, moving back toward his date.

Rowan was on a two-man team tonight.

Only the other man was a woman.

Clara.

She seemed pragmatic about her duties. Professional.

She was wearing flats rather than the typical strappy stilettos. Both sides of her evening gown were slit almost to her hips, revealing athletic legs when she'd walked up the steps to the museum.

Her hair was gathered back into a sleek ballerina bun.

While she blended well with the other ladies at the gala, to Rowan, she looked like she could run and fight if need be.

Chances were pretty slim, though, that Clara would need those skills tonight. This was going to be a pretty banal asset shake.

The guy just didn't realize he was an asset yet.

Rowan had met Clara for the first time in the cab when he picked her up outside her hotel, two hours ago.

When Rowan stretched out his hand to introduce himself, she'd batted him away. "No," she'd said. "We have only a few minutes to get used to each other's bodies, so we look like a couple." Her accent had a practiced flatness to it that told Rowan she'd spent a lot of hours with a speech therapist, trying to sound convincingly American. "We can't have any awkwardness between us. We should make out on our way to the museum, don't you think?"

That kind of suggestion was a first for him.

Rowan didn't mind.

"Sure," he'd said. "We can make out on the way." *Do people even say 'make out' anymore?*

As he leaned into the kiss, Clara had moved Rowan's hands to her breasts and ass, letting him know those were part of the terrain he was supposed to familiarize himself with. While she, in return, stroked up and down his erection.

That snarl of traffic wasn't a hardship.

Getting out of the cab and adjusting his clothes was a little awkward.

But she was right. By the time they moved up the museum stairs, Rowan had felt comfortable and automatic as he put his hand on her lower back to guide her and let his palm slide just south of polite, giving her a pat as they joined the line to show their invitation to the guards. Anyone who saw them would never think that they were strangers. And that he'd never know her real name.

Clara was her operational name tonight. Clara Edwards.

As Rowan moved back into the main hall from his task of gathering the compromising photographs in the men's room, he spotted Clara contemplating a statue.

She must have felt his eyes on her because she turned and sent him a questioning brow as he approached.

He smiled. "You look so beautiful tonight. Like a work of art that belongs in a museum."

She put her hand on his shoulder. "You don't look so bad yourself." Clara slid her fingers down to his chest, resting them over the envelope in its concealed pocket, assuring herself that Rowan had been successful. "Do you see anyone you know here?" she asked as her gaze moved around the room.

"Not yet. Let's look around, shall we?"

He took her hand as they walked toward the exhibit hall. Their bodies moving easily together. Rowan was going to have to remember that make-out trick.

There were a lot of people at tonight's gala event.

Brussels was busy this week, hosting diplomats and policy-makers from around the world. Tonight the museum was full of movers and shakers. So, yes, there were people he recognized, from the intelligence world, from the security world, from the political and business worlds.

But he didn't see Sergei Prokhorov, their mark.

There was a small clutch of Americans laughing a little too loudly. They probably didn't realize they were standing in a spot that amplified the acoustics. Their security team did. As Rowan and Clara moved forward, Thorn and Honey—a couple of opera-tives from Iniquus, a for-hire security group—bent their heads and explained the problem.

The security team shuffled their clients to a spot nearer the stairs. It looked like the US diplomatic corps was well covered. If shit hit the fan, he and Clara might have some backup. As Rowan thought that, Thorn caught Rowan's gaze for a nanosec-ond. The connection made.

Rowan experienced some discomfort with the exchange.

Who else was here that might be able to place him? Who might whisper the wrong thing into the right ear? He wondered if that would make his approach tonight more difficult.

Clara turned and tipped her head up. "Sweetheart, look there on the right. Isn't it beautiful? Let's go see the Madonna."

Sergei Prokhorov.

There he was in the gallery to their right, nursing a martini and looking bored with his conversation, standing in front of a Renaissance Madonna.

Clara's face brightened with a smile of recognition. "Sergei," she called with delight as she patted Rowan's arm. "Come, let me introduce you." She disentangled her fingers and quick-stepped over to Sergei with her arms extended.

Okay. Not the way he would have done this. A little more time. A little more attention to detail. But, all right…

Sergei's mouth formed into a plastic half-smile. He stopped blinking. He must have been combing through his memory banks, trying to figure out who this woman was.

The man who was speaking to Sergei saw Clara's approach, lifted his glass in a parting salute, and turned to move away.

Clara grasped Sergei's arms and came up on her toes as she planted three cheek kisses, right-left-right, as was the custom here in Belgium while sliding into the Russian language. "I'm so glad to see you. Here, let me introduce you to my date. This is Robert Baker." She sent a radiant smile his way, then turned back to Prokhorov. "He's an American business consultant focusing on European economic expansion."

Rowan stuck out his hand and smiled as if he were being introduced to one of Clara's good friends. "I'm sorry, I speak English, *et je parle français*. Are you comfortable with either language?"

"English is fine." Sergei focused back on Clara and seemed relaxed enough with this situation. She tucked her hand into the crook of his arm that wasn't holding his drink, pointed, and started walking toward a private corner by the stairs.

Sergei looked over his shoulder, and Rowan saw him make eye contact with his security detail.

Thorn, from his place on the other side of the staircase, registered their approach.

Players were on the field. And Clara seemed to be taking the lead.

So here we go.

"Tell me, how is Irenka?" Clara asked.

Rowan figured that while he was gathering the intel in the bathroom, Clara had been choosing this spot. It was almost as if she hit an X and came to a sudden stop.

"Lovely, thank you for asking. She is with her friends in Paris, shopping."

Clara's gaze shifted to Rowan. "Irenka is Sergei's new wife. She's connected to a prominent oligarch family, the Orlovs. Their money comes from a variety of projects."

Rowan nodded with uplifted brows and pursed lips as if he found that interesting.

"Is Trinka with her, too?" Clara asked Sergei, then turned to Rowan. "That's Irenka's daughter and the favorite granddaughter of Alexander Orlov. Alexander is very powerful and in very tight with the Kremlin."

Sergei gave a frown and a nod. "This is true. My father-in-law is very influential," he told Rowan before turning back to Clara. "Trinka is at home. She has school."

Clara opened Rowan's jacket. "Trinka just started university this fall." She pulled the envelope from his pocket. "Trinka is learning so many new things this year," Clara was saying to Sergei as she focused on the envelope, ripping through the seal.

Rowan shifted his angle to block her actions from Sergei's bodyguard.

When Clara flipped the first picture around for Sergei to see, Rowan's stomach dropped. A young woman lay naked across a bed, her fingers tangled into Sergei's grey curls as he went down on her. Sergei grabbed at the photo, but Clara was too fast.

She dropped her hands down, and when she brought them back up, the photo on top depicted Sergei mounting Trinka from behind, his hairy ass squeezed tight with his thrust.

The bodyguard was on the move.

Rowan couldn't figure out why he'd been at such a distance in the first place. Then Rowan saw the second thug slide forward. Rowan was forming a plan when Honey Honig's seven-foot frame moved into the body guard's path. Honey looked around like he was lost.

Thorn Iverson got in the way of Sergei's number two as he joined Honey.

"Wave off your team, Sergei. Do it now," Rowan commanded under his breath.

"I'm fine," Sergei called out in Russian. "All is fine." He lifted his martini in the air like he was offering a toast.

Honey and Thorn shook hands as if greeting each other and turned to enjoy the modern nude that took up the wall just to Rowan's left but out of earshot. Perceptive. Helpful. Their movements a study in nonchalance, just accidentally getting in the way. Nice.

"What do you want?" Sergei's spittle flew out with his words.

Clara threw her head back and laughed, lightly touching Sergei's sleeve, like they were having fun, then said, "Your phone. And just for the moment."

"I...my phone?"

Clara lifted the photos. "I've actually never seen these. I wonder what else they'll show." She flipped to the next one. Long blonde hair, lips, and a penis. "Oh." She wrinkled her nose as if smelling hot garbage. "Look how thin and scrawny it is— that rat's nest of grey hair." She looked up to catch his gaze. "You have a pathetic dick."

"Why do you want my phone?" Sergei asked.

"Just for a moment," Rowan said. "Pull it out of your pocket. Open the screen."

Clara flipped to the next photo and cocked her head to the

side as she examined the image, disdain pulling at her nostrils.

Sergei did as Rowan asked.

"There we go," Rowan said. "Now pretend to show me something on your screen."

When Rowan leaned in, he attached a cord to the bottom of Sergei's phone, making sure to block what he was doing from view. That cord was already connected to a burner phone in Rowan's tux pocket. Rowan swiped open an app and started to download everything from Sergei's phone to the burner.

The burner phone immediately encrypted the information and sent it via satellite back to the bureau while introducing spyware. Not that Sergei wouldn't know this and toss his phone. But it was too late. That spyware already reached into his open files, into his computer, his email, his social media accounts. He was exposed. Everything about him. From now on. Unless he torched it all down and started fresh.

But whoever did that?

"Just stand there. This won't take too long," Clara said, once again feigning a friendly air. "You can go right back to your training of Trinka." She held up another photo. "It looks like she displeased you, but you're a good disciplinarian."

Rowan focused on the spectrum showing the download, but Clara shoved the picture of Sergei spanking the girl right under Sergei's nose.

She shuffled through the rest of the photos.

Rowan could feel Sergei's security getting uncomfortable and curious.

"Put the photos in the envelope, please, Clara," Rowan said. The light shined green. "Put the envelope away in your purse. Sergei got the message."

The text came through: **Successful download.**

"We're all done." Rowan pulled the cord from the bottom

and handed the cell phone back to Sergei. "It was nice to meet you," he said, clapping Sergei on the back. "I'm sure we'll be running into each other again." He held out his hand to Clara. "Let's go see what they have on the buffet table, darling."

Sergei growled, "You will regret tonight."

And Rowan didn't doubt him for a second.

2

Rowan

Brussels, Belgium

Rowan took Clara's hand and tugged her away. He could feel the fury radiating down her arm. Those photos had obviously pushed her buttons, and Rowan was impressed that she was able to affect such a pleasant face while squeezing his hand until his fingers were bloodless.

Passing Thorn, Honey, and the American diplomats, Rowan was very careful to divert his attention.

It looked like the stars had been aligned tonight.

Mission accomplished.

Rowan had done what he'd come to do. He had shown his face to Sergei Prokhorov. Sergei was confronted with compromising information, was implicitly threatened, and a bounty paid for silence. Sergei had allowed Rowan to take what he wanted, stood beside him, and facilitated Rowan taking it. He and Clara were training their asset. *When we ask, you need to give us what we want. Message delivered.*

Rowan allowed power to surge through his body.

Exchanges like this always reminded Rowan of his tactical studies of the North American Great Plains intertribal wars. Killing wasn't always the goal of a warrior. As a matter of fact, "counting coup" was sometimes considered the braver deed. The warrior would demonstrate his courage by proving his superiority over his enemy, risking his life to touch or strike them.

Humiliation was a fighting tactic.

It was the tactic they had just employed.

Even Clara's making fun of the guy's dick—calling it pathetic—was strategic.

Emotional emasculation.

Their approach had been a necessary psychological attack. Something that couldn't have happened from a distance. The look in Sergei's eyes told Rowan that retribution was coming. Rowan didn't know when or how. Or even if it would be a direct hit on him. Sergei might go after someone else in intelligence. Or maybe a government official. Someone that Sergei and his family had collected kompromat on.

That was something to monitor.

But tonight? Tonight, Rowan would allow himself to feel victorious.

Those thoughts swelled Rowan's head as he and Clara hustled down the marble steps toward a queue of taxis waiting to take the partygoers to their next destinations. Halfway to the bottom, Rowan saw three men walking shoulder to shoulder down the sidewalk. Anyone in their way had to step onto the grass or street.

They ruled those bricks.

One talked into his phone.

All three snarled at Clara and him.

Rowan pivoted, dragging Clara around with him. As he placed his foot to step upward and scurry back where they could get lost in the gala crowd inside, four more goons pushed through the carved wooden doors of the museum. Sergei must have borrowed some enforcers from friends at the party.

They were about to get sandwiched between the two teams.

Rowan twisted again, looking for options.

There was a group of about twenty that buzzed together at the far end of the stairs. They laughed loudly and called jokes to each other, their voices amplified by alcohol. Rowan and Clara entered into their swarm just as the group moved off the steps and walked down the sidewalk.

Rowan pushed Clara in front of him and held onto her elbows as he steered her into the center of their mass, his height giving him the visual advantage. Together, the friends jostled and joked down to the corner of the walkway, turned to walk some more, and then entered into a parking garage.

While Rowan disliked doing ops in men's bathrooms, he *hated* doing them in parking garages.

Their cover group stopped to call their goodnights, shake hands, and cheek kiss. Breaking into couples, they headed off to find their cars.

Rowan slipped his hand to Clara's lower back and tried to walk them nonchalantly toward the elevator bank.

As Rowan swiveled his head and smiled down at her so he could use his peripheral vision, he muttered, "Incoming. Five. Leader's phone to his ear. He's calling shots on a wider op."

Poor choice of idioms, Rowan thought. Hopefully, there would be no shots. No guns.

"Five of them?" Clara asked, elongating her stride. "Two unaccounted for?"

There was an echoing shout.

They'd been spotted.

Rowan grabbed Clara's hand and pulled her behind a delivery van. They bent in two, running along, peeking through the car windows, trying to stay off the bad guys' paths.

The protection team had fanned out and were moving systematically, applying their training.

Suddenly, Clara scooped the front of her dress up over her arm and raced toward the stairs, leaving him behind.

Rowan would have chased after her. The stairs were a good idea. But the gun pointed at his head was a deterrent.

He looked down at the red dot on his chest. Yup, lasers, and silencers, and a second weapon. Awesome.

"Knees," the gun holder said. "Hands!" His voice was thickly accented.

Rowan tapped his ear. "What? What are you saying? Do you speak English? *Anglais, je t'en prie?*"

There was a sudden scream of tires. Then a woman's scream echoed off the concrete walls. High-pitched, it held for longer than probable and was filled with both pain and terror.

Adrenaline dumped into Rowan's system like a bucket of ice water.

God, Clara, what the hell is happening to you?

There was nothing he could do to help her until he helped himself.

A third gunman. A fourth.

A man from behind him kicked the back of Rowan's knee, and he went down hard on the cement.

A black hood was dragged over his head.

This is gonna suck.

Rowan's hands were zip-tied behind him, then the punches landed. Guts, kidneys…he'd be pissing red tomorrow. *If* he got a tomorrow.

While the bag stopped him from seeing what was happening, the bag also helped the knuckles slide. The punches weren't ineffectual, but the impact was less than if they hit and stuck. That last punch to his stomach made puke slick up Rowan's throat. He forced it back down. He'd be damned if he was going to vomit into this bag and have to smell it through the whole ordeal.

Suddenly, there was an engine roar, and he was caught under either arm and hefted to his feet. A click, a chunk, and a push, Rowan lay backward in what he assumed was a trunk. They pulled off his shoes and rolled him.

Rowan found himself in the fetal position in a closed trunk.

Alone.

He wondered what had happened to Clara. He wondered if she were dead, or captured, or if by some miracle she had escaped.

Perhaps that scream earlier hadn't been hers but some other gala-going socialite who saw the botched operation unfurling and had screamed out her distress.

Rowan wanted to think that. He wanted to believe that Clara had reached the elevator bank, got back up to the museum, and called her handler for help.

She had the photos.

He had his phone, but there was nothing on his phone of interest. Everything he downloaded had been encrypted, sent, and wiped. It was a burner, meant to be destroyed after tonight's mission.

With the car in motion, Rowan had to let all of those thoughts go and focus on escaping.

The driver slung the car around the corner, clipping the curb and bouncing Rowan up, knocking his head into the metal roof.

Dazed, Rowan reached under his jacket and spun his belt to the back of his pants where he could manipulate the black box buckle. Sliding his thumbnail along the edge, he toggled the hidden latch. A razor popped out like a lizard's tongue. Rowan pulled the blade out from its hidden compartment, careful not to lose it here in the stuffy darkness.

Rowan needed two things—time and opportunity. Okay, three. He needed some luck.

Pressing the blade between the knuckle of his index finger and his thumb, Rowan sawed at the thick military-style flex cuffs, slicing at his bindings and trying to avoid his artery as the car bounced and popped over the roadway.

Patience was key, and Rowan struggled to calm his system. It would help if he knew what kind of clock was ticking.

If suddenly the car came to a stop, and he was yanked from the trunk and dragged into some hidey-hole building, yeah...he didn't want to think about that. He needed to focus on the places he had control. His breath. His heart rate. And applying a steady pressure as the blade bit millimeter by millimeter into the plastic.

Pop.

There.

He had it.

One hand free, the other still encircled by the tie, Rowan reached up and clawed the bag from his head. The air outside of the bag was only a bit easier to breathe. Slightly more oxygen mixed in with his carbon dioxide exhalent. Maybe a little less dizzying.

Rowan slid the razor back in place and swiveled his belt buckle with its helpful gadgets back to the front of his pants, so if the thugs did pull him out of the trunk, he might be able to keep some tools with him.

They took his shoes. So they'd guessed he came prepared.

Rowan's mind worked on the knot of his situation while his fingers nimbly worked at the knot of rope that entwined his ankles.

Free, he reached out and tugged the glow-in-the-dark pull that hung from the trunk lid. It was there by law—a safety requirement. That no one had sliced this out told Rowan that this event was a surprise to his captors, too. They were probably up front yammering on the phone, trying to pull together a next step.

The acoustics changed as they moved into a tunnel. A tunnel might be a good place to jump and run...

Rowan let the trunk pop up just far enough that he could see what was behind him. A pair of headlights rode half a meter from their bumper. If he were to suddenly pop out, the car's driver behind him would be startled out of their mind. Their limbic system would do one of two things—press down the gas or press down the brake. Maybe press them both down.

If they pressed the gas, he'd get caught between the two vehicles and probably die.

If they stomped the brake, there would be a massive pileup behind them. Rowan would have to run forward. Forward meant he'd have whatever goons were up front chasing after him, and they'd have the benefit of shoes.

And if the driver stomped both pedals? It was probably the first, kill-Rowan-on-impact scenario.

Nope, too risky. He'd have to wait. He lowered the trunk until it clicked—no reason to tip off the bad guys that he had use of his limbs.

While he waited for the acoustics and speed to change once

again, Rowan patted his pockets, looking for his cell phone, but of course, it was gone. If someone tried to open it, there was nothing there to find. Not a GPS locator, not a last number called, nothing.

The car deaccelerated.

Rowan tugged the trunk's catch.

When they slowed to a stop, he peeked out the back. A line of cars idled behind them. They must be at a traffic light.

Rowan let the trunk lid budge up just enough to get his body through the crack. Still grasping the catch string, he dove out the back. He pulled the trunk shut and crouched between the cars. Rowan rose up just enough to see the driver from the car behind him, wide-eyed, shock freezing his features in place.

As Rowan crouch-walked toward the sidewalk, the guy laid on his horn. Others, too, seemed to take up the chorus. Rowan scrambled to hide between parked vehicles on the side of the road, but the pedestrians stopped, their arms thrown wide as if to protect those around them, and gaped.

Okay, this isn't good.

Rowan decided that the mob-squad probably wouldn't open fire on him in the street, so he stood and took off running, slowed by his flapping socks.

The men had bailed from the car and were closing the distance.

Rowan flew down the street, hooked corners, leaped barriers, and still, they came.

Lungs burning, heart-pounding, the stitch in his side wanted to double him over, but Rowan pushed himself hard. If they caught him, they'd kill him. He could feel that decision chasing him up the street.

Up ahead, he watched the light turn yellow. Rowan slung himself around the corner and saw an empty cab. He thought he might be enough steps ahead. Rowan pulled the door open and dove in. He jerked the door shut again, plunged to the floor, and hit the lock.

If he timed it right, their light should be green.

"Hey!" the driver called out.

"A thousand euro to get me out of here," Rowan panted. He didn't have a way to pay the guy a thousand Euros. That detail was something that might suck in the future, Rowan reminded himself. He had plenty of present time suck to deal with.

The cab doors up front clicked as they locked. A fist banged at the window. Angry yelling in a foreign language.

The cabby took off. His voice pitched high. "*Merde*! They have guns."

"Go!" Rowan yelled. "Go! Go! Go!"

The taxi driver floored the pedal, weaving through the traffic at breakneck speed. "Am I heading for the police station?" he gasped after they had put some distance between them and the scene.

Rowan pulled himself to the seat. "No," he said, then rattled off the address of a safe house he had memorized just the day before.

He needed to get back to his team and get a plan together to help Clara.

Sergei had said they would regret this evening.

Right now, Rowan was okay, but Clara might just be in the world of hurt.

3

THURSDAY AFTERNOON
Washington D.C.

OFF-BALANCE, Avery Goodyear pushed her weight onto her high heels and locked her knees. Her lips curled into a tight line as she willed herself not to sprint out the office door. *Focus*, she rebuked herself.

Her boss—head of EverMore, Windsor Shreveport Publishing's label for romance, women's fiction, and chick-lit—George Pratt, crossed his arms over his chest, stretched out his legs, and thumped his feet onto the corner of his desk.

Always a bad sign.

Things never went well after he struck this pose. "Taylor Knapp is in hiding," he said.

"I don't blame him. His last book caused such horrible public backlash, I can't imagine he could show his face anywhere in public without getting beaten up," Avery said, not sure if she should move farther into the room to sit in the guest chair or not. George had positioned the chair precisely so the morning sun would catch his unlucky visitor in the left eye, blinding them. He was following a strategy from a book called *How to Get the Upper Hand and Win*.

Before George was hired by Windsor Shreveport six months ago, he had been a business acquisitions editor for a top-five publisher. One of their competitor publishing houses had read the manuscript for *Get the Upper Hand* first and beaten George to signing the author's name to a contract.

Now the book was on the New York Times Bestsellers List, and all George had to show for his efforts was his present position with Windsor Shreveport, along with newly rearranged furniture and absurd alpha-male poses.

"He's in a secluded location, so he can focus on his manuscript," George said.

"So he can sleep at night without people chanting outside his windows is more like it." Avery slid her hands into her pockets, but that didn't feel right. She pulled them back out. She stood there, awkward and uncertain. Taylor Knapp wasn't in her author queue, thank God. She had nothing to do with him. Wanted nothing to do with him. Why was George bringing him up?

"I think it's a good decision," George said. "Finding quiet and anonymity to get this damned sequel done already."

"Why push him?" Avery asked, holding the sliver-thin hope that Windsor Shreveport Publishing would tear up the Knapp contract and move on to something more...wholesome. Okay, wholesome was too big a stretch. Wholesome didn't sell. Scandal sold. In today's saturated book market, everyone was elbowing for a place. Avery closed her eyes and tried for a deep breath, but her lungs stuck at the halfway point, leaving her breathless. She lifted her gaze and caught George smirking at her.

"Money. That's why." George uncrossed his ankles and came upright, resting his elbows on the arms of his chair, steepling his fingers. Power pose number four. "Controversy makes Windsor Shreveport piles of money, which equals job security. And right now, in this industry, job security is everything." He cocked his head to the side. "Don't you agree? I mean, what would you do, Avery, if you lost this job?" His raised brows folded his skin into four straight lines across his forehead. "Where would your editorial skills take you? Do you know how many book editors are out there trolling the Twittersphere, looking for writers who need editing at two dollars a page and no benefits? Could you make your life work out on that kind of paycheck?"

Avery swallowed past the lump in her throat. George was positioning the sword of Damocles over her head. She'd have to say yes to whatever came next. "Has Taylor Knapp given you an update on his progress?" Avery hoped to delay whatever George was priming here. A rivulet of perspiration formed on her back, trickling down her spine. She wanted to reach back to pull her silk blouse away from her humid skin, but she was afraid to show any signs of anxiety. It would just strengthen George's hand.

"Nope. I'm giving him to you as a gift. The updates are now on you."

Avery stilled, reprocessing George's words, hoping she'd misunderstood. "I'm a romance editor. I don't know anything about science fiction or dystopia."

"Knapp writes video game adaptation. Surely you could adapt for this project." And he winked like he was telling her a good joke.

"I definitely don't know anything about that. How could I possibly edit something like that?"

He cocked his head. "But you know about *romance*?"

Avery worked not to grit her teeth.

"Fiction is fiction." George shrugged. "Wheedle something out of him." George picked up his pen and jabbed it toward Avery, punctuating his instructions. "An outline, a first chapter, anything you can get. I want something on my desk yesterday."

Pen jabbing. Power move number nine. Disdain bubbled in Avery's stomach. *He's turning himself into a caricature.*

Her cell phone buzzed against Avery's thigh. She pulled it from her pocket and tapped it off without checking the readout. "Me? But…" Avery moved behind the chair, using it as a shield against all the ramifications of this conversation. "Please, I'm really opposed to this whole project. Maybe the intern would like to get this on his resume?" Avery threw out the Hail Mary with little hope of success. George looked too smug right now to be generous.

"You. Knapp insists you're the only person he'll talk to."

"But I've never met him."

"He wants to work with a woman. You're all we've got. So you're it."

George's PA came over the speaker announcing George's wife was on line one.

He reached for the receiver and pointed at the guest seat.

Avery dragged the chair away from the window and sat down to wait. She checked the number that had called. Lola. Shoot. Her best friend wouldn't call her at work unless Avery's mom was acting up again.

One crisis at a time. Being thrown into the Taylor Knapp three-ring circus certainly felt like a crisis. His last book was so inflammatory that Avery had received hundreds of nasty e-mails from strangers, telling her that she'd damned her soul to hell by her involvement with Knapp's novel.

And she hadn't been involved at all.

What would happen now that she was going to be in charge of this project? Avery needed to stay as anonymous as possible. She'd need to get a new phone number right away, an unlisted one.

George banged the receiver onto its cradle. He wasn't wearing his Titan of the Literary World mask anymore. Stress constricted the muscles around his eyes, making them seem small and too deeply set. He paused. "You should know that my wife found an old photo from back when we dated. Luckily, you were wearing that big floppy hat of yours. She asked if it was you. I said no. She thinks we met here at the office after I signed on with Windsor Shreveport. And she will never know anything different." George paused and considered Avery. "If she shows up here with the picture and asks you about it, you will deny it's you."

"George, we had this discussion. We stopped dating when I graduated from grad school. That was years before you even knew her. I'm not sure why this is an issue."

"Right, well, I want to be clear. You need to be very careful and stick to our story. If she brings up the conference in London last Christmas when we—" he stopped and winked, "became reacquainted, that's okay. But since then, I was married, *and* I became your boss. You are now my underling. And that's it as far as she's concerned." He stood up, stretching to his full looming height of five feet seven inches—move number thirteen, *How to Get the Upper Hand and Win*.

Avery would have liked to laugh at the absurdity of his affectations, but this wasn't funny *at all*.

She didn't like to be blackmailed and manipulated. What did

she have to say to the man's wife anyway? Okay, back in the day, George had looked like a blond Tom Cruise, but that resemblance had faded over time along with his hairline. Now, he was just a pompous ass who could barely eke out a mildly satisfying orgasm. And that was before he was married and gained a twenty-pound spare tire. Really, Mrs. George Pratt had nothing to worry about from Avery.

"Obviously, I want you to keep on working here," he continued. "I don't want anything to make that feel impossible."

"It's not a problem, I assure you." Avery stood, so they were eye to eye. She wanted this meeting to be over already, but she sensed there was more bad news to come. "As far as I'm concerned, our history started here at Windsor Shreveport when they hired you on last April." Avery's voice sounded strong and a little bored. She couldn't have pitched her tone any better if she'd practiced in a mirror beforehand.

"Good then." George slid a piece of paper toward her. "As a reminder that projects are contractually protected, this is a copy of your NDA. That's your signature." He tapped it twice. "Immediate dismissal from the company, and a million-dollar fine if you break this. You can also anticipate being blackballed industrywide. I'm reminding you that if you say anything about what goes on within Windsor Shreveport beyond the name of the author you're working with, it would be a detriment to your future. You are prohibited from speaking with anyone about the Taylor Knapp project—until the publicity department has made something public, that is."

Avery swallowed. "I can't imagine wanting to associate my name with Taylor Knapp's in any way, shape, or form. I don't want to be associated with this project. I don't want my name on anything to do with this project. No putting my name on news releases, no 'thank yous' at the back of the book."

George moved the top sheet and tapped the second one in the pile. "This is Taylor Knapp's e-mail. I want you to get in touch with him. Immediately. Use your feminine wiles." He waved his hand up and down to take in her body.

Avery stood there, wide-eyed and disbelieving.

"Do whatever you have to do to manipulate that book out of his brain and onto a computer."

She went to snatch up the paper, but George held it in place on the desktop with a firm hand. "Avery, you also need to clear your calendar for next week. I've had my PA send you the itinerary. I need you to fly to New York with me. It'll be just the two of us from this office."

Avery watched the smile slowly spread across George's face. He would have seemed handsome, except she knew his character too well. She now saw him through the filter of their shared history. Avery pulled the paper out from under his hand. "I'm going to take the Simpson manuscript home and read for the rest of the day." She spun to move toward the door.

"Oh, and Avery?" George called.

Avery stilled but didn't turn toward his voice.

"Burn that damned hat."

4

Avery

Thursday Afternoon
Washington D.C.

Avery strode across the parking lot, trying to get as much distance between her and George as she could, as fast as possible. The sun blazed down on her head, and she yanked her suit jacket off, seeking relief from the humidity. It was fall, for heaven's sake. The leaves should be changing colors. She should be looking forward to pumpkin spiced lattes and wrapping up in fleece.

Fall was usually her favorite time of year.

This extended heat, now becoming more the norm, was just upping Avery's frustration.

When she went to check her phone for the weather, Avery remembered she hadn't called Lola back from earlier. *Funny how*

*having your career threatened can move your brain cells from
one crisis to another.*

Avery opened her car door and let the heat swell out while
she pressed number two on her quick dial.

"Holy Mary and Joseph, thank the Heavens you called.
You've got to get home now. And I mean right now," Lola said
in a single breath.

Avery slid under the wheel, with the phone squeezed
between her jaw and shoulder, as she tugged the door shut and
pressed the ignition button.

The air conditioning belched out heat, and Avery's long
blonde hair caught in the sweat on her neck. "You'd better give
me the bullet points, so I'm ready when I get there."

The car's Bluetooth picked up the call, and Avery listened to
Lola's voice, spiced by her Latina heritage, through the car's
speaker system.

Lola always sounded like there was a private joke entwined
in her words. "Let's see. Father Pat is on his way. The police are
climbing out of their car. Your newest caregiver, Sally-what's-
her-name, is sitting on your porch in tears. And one of your
neighbors is starting a petition drive to get your mother removed
from the house for Home Owners Association noise violations."

"So, Mom is doing well then." Avery paused and strained to
hear the background noises. "Are there chickens in the mix?"
Avery pulled out of the parking spot and clicked on her right
blinker.

"What? No. No chickens. Why?"

Avery pulled out onto the tree-lined street in Washington
D.C., heading for the highway and Falls Church. "It sounds like
someone's trying to strangle the whole flock."

"Nope, it's your mom." There was a long pause. "I think
that's supposed to be Ave Maria." The screeching reached a

crescendo. "Sally says your mom thinks the Devil stole her vocal cords. Now your mom's in an all-out battle to show the old Devil he didn't win."

———————

AVERY INCHED her car past the police cruiser and the ambulance. Father Pat sat in his sedan with the engine still running, his head leaning against the headrest, his eyes closed. The uniformed men stood in the shade of her broad-limbed tulip tree.

Pulling into the empty drive, Avery realized Sally had left. She wondered if the newest adult sitter had already decided this assignment was too big.

Would Sally show up to work the next day?

One problem at a time.

Avery opened her car door slowly, not quite ready to throw herself into whatever brouhaha her mom had stirred up.

Lola sat on the porch, looking thoroughly amused. "Your mom won't open the door, and I decided not to use the key until you got here. She's pretty confused."

Avery nodded. A tension headache thrummed behind her eyes. As she reached the top step, the door popped open.

"Avery Grace, thank goodness you're home. What a day I've had."

Avery watched the first responders gathering up their equipment to head inside.

"Mom, how are you feeling?"

"I'm fine. Why?"

Avery lifted her hand to wave at the paramedics. "I've got this. Thank you so much for coming," she called as she watched them striding as a group toward her, their cases in hand.

They stopped, seeming uncertain, then nodded and moved to

their vehicles, leaving one guy behind to approach and have Avery sign the requisite paperwork.

By now, Avery knew the drill.

"Mom, Lola came to help you. Why didn't you let her in?" Avery turned her mother around and moved her into the house where the air conditioning provided some relief.

"Lola Santiago? She didn't come here."

Avery pointed over at Lola, who plopped onto the couch. "This is Lola, Mom."

"No, it's not," Ginny Goodyear scolded. "You are not Lola Santiago. *You* are an imposter. Did you come with the bad men?"

"What bad men, Mom?"

"The ones who are watching the house." She turned and pointed a menacing finger at Lola, whose eyes glittered with merriment. "You can't fool me. You are not Lola. You don't even look like her mother. Her mother is beautiful."

"Mom." Avery's voice strained to sound patient. "Lola's last name is Zelkova now. Did you get confused when Sally told you Mrs. Zelkova was at the door?"

The doorbell chimed, and Avery answered it to find Father Pat standing red-faced on her stoop. He had a gallon jug of holy water in his hand, still in its Giant Foods grocery bag.

"Your mom called me and said the Devil was here. Shall I look around and see if I can find him?"

Ginny jumped forward and grabbed the priest's hand. "Would you? I think he went away, but if you could make sure."

Father Pat smiled weakly and shuffled toward the back of the house.

Ginny's face shifted from grateful parishioner to an angry mother who wasn't having the wool pulled over her eyes as she turned on Lola. "This floozy is an imposter, I tell you. She's just wearing a Lola disguise, but I see through you, you floozy! You can't come and take my house from me."

Lola's designer dress; her long jet-black hair, cut into face-framing layers; and her manicured nails gave her the air of a society belle. There was nothing floozy about Lola Zelkova. "Mom, look at her. This is Lola. She has her own house. She doesn't need yours. She lives there with her five kids."

Ginny's gaze narrowed on Lola. "Five children? Do you know who any of the fathers are?"

"Mom!"

5

ROWAN

THURSDAY EVENING
Alexandria Virginia

CLIMBING STIFFLY from the back of the Lyft parked at the front of his Alexandria home, Rowan promised himself a scotch and time in front of the TV, just chillin' with some ice packs.

The one piece of good news was that he was the only one bumped and bruised from the night at the gala.

Clara was fine.

She'd gotten away from the man who was chasing her.

The scream Rowan had heard in the parking garage when he was taken captive, as it turned out, wasn't a woman's at all. And now, Rowan knew what a man sounded like when he was stabbed in the dick.

Rowan was sincerely grateful that he and Clara were allies.

The Lyft driver had already popped the trunk and was hefting out his suitcases and duffle bag.

If only he knew the size of the arsenal, I carry in there. He might not have let me in his car.

"Thanks, man." Rowan reached for the suitcase handles and strap of his bag. "I left you a good review and a tip."

With a wave, the guy headed on to his next fare.

Rowan stood at the end of his drive, where Jodie's car blocked the sidewalk up to the house.

Her being here should make him smile. He should be glad he wasn't coming home to an empty house.

But the truth was, Rowan wished she wasn't there.

He stopped by the mailbox to give himself a little time to figure out why he felt so indifferent.

He and Jodie had been dating for almost three years now. She checked all the boxes for life-companion—well, she had when they first went out. She was still smart and attractive, but over time, the charming and funny had kind of slid to the wayside, for both of them, like it was too much effort to maintain. The good-conversations part had turned more to grunts of acknowledgment. The caring and nurturing had become canceled plans. Both of them had kind of given up, their relationship more about habit than anything else.

And now, things were just in a holding pattern until someone made an exit move.

He was going to make the move.

Not today. Today, he was going to smile and be pleasant. Sometime this weekend, he'd have the conversation and wish her good things in her future.

And he'd mean it. He wanted her to be happy.

He wanted them both to be.

Just not happy together.

Happy apart.

God, I need a scotch.

The mailbox was empty. Jodie must have brought the letters in. With his duffel slung over his shoulder and a pull handle in each hand, he hefted the luggage into the air to carry them across the lawn to the top of the sidewalk.

He wondered if he should feel some remorse, some guilt, for the taxi cab make-out session with Clara and decided that there was nothing to feel guilty about. He had no affection for Clara, no desire to see her again. And Jodie was well aware that he had to pose as a couple on occasion. She'd said she was okay with that as long as he kept his pants zipped, which he had.

The door opened. "Home again, home again, jiggery jig."

"I see you started drinking without me."

"Captain Morgan's been keeping me company while I waited for you." She lifted her half-full glass. Diet Coke and Captain, what she drank when she was going for the buzz and not the nuance.

She wasn't slurring. That was good.

"Sorry, my flight was delayed." He hitched the suitcases up higher and climbed the porch steps, trying not to wince.

Jodie moved back into the hallway, giving him room to maneuver. "So—how long do you think you'll stick around this time?" she asked.

"I leave out again Tuesday." He deposited his load at the bottom of the stairs; he'd take them up to his bedroom later. Rowan headed to the kitchen.

Jodie looked like she was revved up for a fight, and walking away from her to take that hot shower he'd promised himself would only escalate things.

When he ended their relationship, he didn't want it to be with angry words that popped out of an exhausted brain. Jodie deserved better than that. There was no way he was going to turn a bad day on the job into a fight, punishing her when she wasn't the reason Rowan was maxed out.

"Where'd you go?" Jodie asked, following him into the kitchen.

He noticed she didn't mention his bruised face. She'd learned over time that he could never say anything other than "I'm fine" to her questions and concerns.

It had been a long time since she'd asked.

Not that he got beaten up *every* time he was in the field.

Rowan actually tried to avoid such encounters.

Reaching out for the bottle of single malt, Rowan thought twice about that choice and dropped his hand. Both of them drinking might be a bad combination. He could still taste the survival hormones in his saliva from getting dumped in the back of the car trunk, headed somewhere for an uncomfortable chat about who and what he knew. And there was also the flavor of the anticipated bullet of silence to the back of the head.

He opened the fridge. It was empty but for a bottle of hot sauce and some cocktail onions. "You know I can't tell you where I go." He opened the freezer. There was a lone freezer-burnt waffle laying at the bottom and three of the bags of peas he used therapeutically. He pulled them out and knocked them on the counter to release the clumps.

She followed him to the den, where Rowan sat on the couch, resting the pea bags on each knee, another on his shoulder.

"This is how it would always be, isn't it? You get called away. I get the last of what's in your fridge." She gestured toward the kitchen.

Well, at least that explained the empty fridge.

"I ate everything in your freezer too."

Rowan nodded. From the tiredness and just a touch of bile in her voice, he'd bet that she'd come to the same conclusion as he had when he was standing by his mailbox.

Only, she had decided the time was ripe.

This smelled like a breakup.

Rowan let his gaze slip back toward the kitchen, now regretting that he hadn't poured himself that scotch.

"I let your plants die."

He nodded.

"I'm keeping your cat."

So here we go.

"This is the way you live your life, and this is the relationship you expect me to have. It seems awfully convenient for you."

"Convenient?" Rowan tipped his head. "That's probably a term I wouldn't attach to any part of my life."

"All right," she slurs, "but for clarity's sake. I've tried this for a few years now. Your job doesn't lend itself well to long-term relationships...to having a family."

She stood next to the table under the window.

Rowan noticed the thick metal candlestick holder beside her hand. Not that he expected her to pick it up and wail on him with it, but his job taught him to check for weapons of opportunity and emotions that might make someone want to use them.

"You told me you wanted kids." She flipped her hair out of her face. The move she made when she was pissed and trying to hold it together.

"I do."

"But you won't make changes—take another job, for example, in order to have that?" Her mouth had drawn into a pucker like she was locking back the words she really wanted to say to him.

"My job is important to creating a safe world for my future children."

"So you say. But maybe you could apply your importance in a way that would lend itself to a stronger commitment. Marriage, those children…"

Rowan didn't know what to say. Yes, he wanted that—a strong marriage, children, a happy home life to balance the shit-show he trudged through day in and day out.

"I thought you would—I've always thought you would—change your assignment, change your department, change *something*. But now, I realize that change would require something else."

He shifted the peas to the other shoulder.

"*Someone* else." She gave a strange plastic smile that was more like a grimace. "I'm not her. She's not me. I'm not *the* one."

Rowan just sat there. She was right. She simply wasn't *the* one. That was it in a nutshell. It was so clear, now that she'd spelled it out. No blame or shame, just the wrong size.

"Yeah, I thought so." Her finger traced around the top of her half-filled glass that she'd set on the table. "So I'm going to make this simple. Like I said, I've taken custody of the cat. He likes me better than you anyway and always has. And he's used to living at my place. I've gone through your things and taken everything of mine back to my apartment. I thought it was for the sake of ease, now I realize that I knew this was it." She lifted her glass to her lips and drained it down.

Rowan wondered how much she'd drunk and if he should let her on the road. Liquored up and emotional was a dangerous driving combination.

"Call it a gut feeling. I packed up some things of yours I

liked too. If you want to arm wrestle for them back, I'm up for it." She lifted her chin to a pugnacious tilt. She wanted a fight.

Rowan said nothing. He absolutely *did not* want that fight. Not to keep her and not to let her go. He gave her a shake of his head and a shrug, feeling the muscles in his neck scream at the move. He worked to keep the wince off his face, lest she interpreted it as a verbal blow that landed. That would just egg this on.

"You probably won't miss those things anyway. You're hardly ever around. Okay, then." Jodie reached into her pocket and slammed something metallic onto the table. "Here's your key. I know you'll just change the locks in the morning anyway. You just sit there with your bags of peas. I'll see myself out."

"Jodie—"

She stopped mid-stride and braced.

He felt her fill with hope as if she had thought this ultimatum might bring her a different outcome. That he'd beg her to stay and promise her that he'd change.

He realized the tone of his voice might have given her that impression.

That hadn't been his intention.

The thickness had to do with fatigue and physical pain, not emotion. While he should probably feel bereft at this moment, he was surprised that all he felt was...a kind of relief. The pop of air when a top finally comes off the jar, the vacuum seal broken.

"Jodie," he tried again. "I wish you every happiness."

When she slammed the door behind her, it shook the whole house.

6

   Thursday Night
   Falls Church, Virginia

LOLA CALLED JUST as Avery shut the door behind Father Pat. Lola had a knack for timing. "Well? Everything back under control?"

"Is it ever?" Avery picked up the gallon of water Father Pat had left on her coffee table and walked toward the kitchen. "I gave mom a sedative while she was saying the rosary with Father Pat. I think he was grateful."

"Yeah? Why do you say that?"

"He left the holy water as a parting gift." Avery looked around to find someplace to store the jug. "Hey, do you know if you need to refrigerate water after it's been blessed?"

"I would. I mean, it might be strong enough to cast out demons and all, but I don't think it'll kill bacteria."

Avery opened the fridge and put the container at the back,

behind the orange juice and salad dressing. She reached for the bottle of wine sitting on the counter. "Thank you for today. You know I love you and all you do. I'm racking up quite a debt. If I ever have kids, I'll owe you my firstborn."

"No, thank you, I've already reached my kid quota." Lola laughed. "I think your mom's a hoot. Life would be boring without her to jazz things up a bit. Was that pop the sound of you pulling a wine cork?"

"After the day I've had, I wish I had something stronger." Avery let the Merlot glug into her glass until it brimmed. "Looks like I'm headed to New York, just me and George."

A gasp came over the speaker. "No!"

Avery bent to slurp some wine, so she could lift the glass without spilling. "And better yet, guess who they positioned as the babysitter for Taylor Knapp and the newest dystopian garbage conspiracy thriller?"

"You?" Shock brightened Lola's voice. "Put the wine away. Just go ahead and pour yourself a glass of the holy water. You can't do that. Can you? I mean, they can't make you take on that assignment, can they?"

"Swear you will tell no one that I'm on that project. I was reminded of my NDA, and they'll send me a million-dollar invoice with my pink slip if I disclose anything at all."

"Holy…what? I have to sit down. Are you serious right now? You aren't pulling my leg?"

"George let me know that a job in this business is a precious commodity in this day and age." Avery swirled her glass and sniffed the wine appreciatively.

"Oh no, he didn't."

"Yup. Since I've never read Knapp's book, I put it on my agenda for tonight. I need to know exactly what I'm getting myself into." Avery opened the cupboard and gazed at the supper possibilities. Cooking felt like more effort than she could muster at that moment. Even chewing seemed beyond her. She eyed the chocolate cake sitting on the counter.

"Lola!"

"You know your brother-in-law will tell you that you're going to hell. He'll have prayer circles going around the clock."

"Hush, I don't want to talk about it. I'm going to focus on the cake you left. Actually, I'm going to hang up now to eat the entire thing for dinner. You're the absolute best. Love you."

"I love you, too. But Avery, I'm not kidding around here. This is serious. This project is dangerous. Fine that you told me. But *do not* tell anyone else. I'm really worried. I mean, the last editor ended up quitting his job and moving his family away. Don't you remember all of that? Can't you go up the hierarchy and say that this isn't what you're trained to do? You don't know how to develop this kind of book?"

"Knapp is insisting on a woman. I'm the only one, other than the PAs and a couple of older women in HR, that has the right attributes."

"Surely that's illegal."

"I can't risk anything right now. I just need to put my head down, press forward, get this wrapped up. Then I'll follow up with a good romance, where it is absolutely predictable, and there's always a happily ever after."

"There's nothing happy about this. I'm so sorry."

After saying good-bye, Avery cut herself a sizeable hunk of cake. Avery gathered her wine glass and moved to the dining room. She set her dinner on the table by her laptop. She picked up her Kindle and searched Taylor Knapp to download a copy of his work. Pushing the 'read now' button made her jaw clench.

Manipulated.

Used.

Miserable.

Words strung together like pearls on a necklace, wrapping around her throat and making her choke as she swallowed a sip of wine.

Avery put the Kindle to the side and hefted a forkful of cake. "Only Lola could make a cake this sinful," she said to the empty room.

Her mother's resonant snores rumbled their way down the stairs.

Avery scrolled through the happy chatter on her Facebook newsfeed. It was depressing to see all of those clever chin-up-and-carry-on quotations. Everyone was out having fun. Yummy food. Luscious looking cocktails. Fabulous vacations.

Avery clicked over to Twitter.

All she needed was a little distraction from reality.

A moment of respite.

Two new people now followed her on Twitter. One was a dentist in Idaho, one a life coach. She didn't know either name and wondered why they'd follow her randomly. Maybe Twitter's algorithms had suggested her for some reason or another. Avery didn't understand how any of that worked.

She moved to 'notifications' where she saw she was tagged into a thread with some fellow writers. She scraped the last of the icing off her plate and looked toward the kitchen. Should she get another slice? She clicked in and read through the thread.

Scribbler: Sorry for the autocorrects. I'm on my phone. My computer crashed. Here's your life lesson: Back your stuff up.

IndieBound: Oh, no! You lost everything? The computer repair place can't retrieve it?

Scribbler: It caught on fire. So, I'm guessing no.

A_Very: Did you at least have a copy of your WIP?

DBennet: What's a WIP?

A_Very: Work in progress.

Scribbler: Yeah, every night, I email my work to myself—poor man's copyright.

A_Very: Well, at least you have that. Sorry about the fire.

IndieBound: Mercury's retrograde. The stars just weren't aligned right.

Scribbler: Mercury. Good. I can live with that. It'll pass. There was a little old lady throwing curses on the train this morning. I thought maybe some of the evil eye stuck to me. I've been wearing a garlic necklace ever since.

IndieBound: What did you do to deserve getting cursed?

A_Very: Garlic necklaces are for vampires, not the evil eye.

YUP, another piece of cake was just what the doctor ordered. And another glass of wine. Avery thanked goodness for her high metabolism, and a trainer who kicked her butt, or this slice of cake would probably induce more guilt than it was worth.

Avery leaned the wedge of chocolaty decadence onto her plate, sending Lola a silent *bless you!*

When she sat back in her place at the head of the table, she saw @Row_man was online.

ROW_MAN: For future reference, what do I use in such a circumstance as evil-eye curses if not garlic?

AVERY CLICKED on Row_man's icon and wondered, once again, if the photo was actually his photo or a stock photo he'd bought on one of those websites. In this icon, he had a yummy kind of face that was part movie lead man, part nice guy at the office.

His hair was just long enough to wrap her fingers in, messy —like he'd just been having fun in bed.

But mostly, Avery liked his eyes. They were kind and intelligent, with maybe a shadow of sadness behind them. Avery wondered what could have happened that seemed to haunt him.

This image was definitely worthy of using as main character fodder.

And if Avery hadn't taken a hiatus from her own writing, she might just make him into a romance hero.

He'd laugh if she told him that.

Avery stared at his Twitter handle, Row_man, and wondered what his real name was. Something that conjured manly capabilities coupled with a warm, genuine heart. Tristan, maybe. Or Brock.

She was objectifying the guy.

"It's not like I'll ever actually meet him," Avery mumbled against the rim of her wine glass. "I can make believe all I want."

In the photo, he looked remarkably like a younger Gerard Butler during the time Butler was training for his movie *300*. That was assuming this was really him in his banner image, sculling in front of the Jefferson Memorial at sunset.

Avery took a bite of cake and licked the icing from her lips. Nah. These were probably some online stock photos.

Of course, she didn't mind imagining it was really him, and his muscles truly looked like that.

Avery decided she'd much rather go to bed tonight with a romance novel, maybe even romantic suspense and Row_man's image in her mind, than read the Taylor Knapp book.

She could work remotely tomorrow and put skimming the first Knapp book on her agenda, hanging out in a coffee shop or the library. The farther she stayed from the office, the safer she'd be from surprises, like today.

The cure for evil eye if not garlic…maybe some of that holy water she had in her fridge.

Row_man had been a favorite on Twitter since she'd first joined a few years ago. She'd enjoyed the banter. He was funny. And insightful. He wrote, but unlike many people who followed her, he wasn't looking for lubricant to slide into the publishing industry, not that she advertised where she worked. In her bio, she'd just listed "Editor at a major publishing house."

He wrote for himself and didn't have any desire to publish. He said it was a way to pass the time waiting in airports. A way to process through things that he was up against in his job. He'd never said what his job was. She'd never asked. She liked to keep Twitter folks securely in the virtual world. But Avery got the sense, from the excerpts of his surprisingly well-written pieces that he'd sent to her over his ShareTogetherApp, that he was ex-military and now did something for the government and having to do with security.

Riding high on the intoxicating effects of her wine and a wave of dopamine from the chocolate cake, Avery clicked on the action bar beside his name and selected Direct Messages.

A_Very: So, tell me the truth. Is that your picture in your icon and banner?

Row_man: Sadly, so.

HE COULD BE LYING to her.

. . .

A_VERY: It's a very handsome picture.

AVERY BLUSHED HOTLY as she hit the enter key but was oddly empowered at the same time. In the real world, she'd never say such a thing to someone she wasn't dating.

ROW_MAN: Well, thank you. I wish I knew what you looked like —unless, of course, you're actually a cartoon, in which case, I apologize.

SHE SMILED, feeling flirty. "Why didn't I try this before?" she asked her empty plate, then pushed it to the side.

A_VERY: I'll trade you. My selfie with a clock for your selfie with a clock.

OKAY, that was taking things too far. This is what happened when you lived in the fictional world. You tended to think in terms of plot points and story arcs. That kind of remark would be the thing Avery would put in a margin for an author to contemplate. Not an actual thing someone would do. In a book-world, the character would never give up something for nothing. And if she wanted to see what he really looked like, she'd have to do the same. *Books don't work like the real-world.* Ach! What if he said yes? She smoothed both hands over her hair and bit at her lips to bring out their color. Did she have time to run upstairs for a quick freshen-up?

. . .

Row_MAN: I'll show you mine if you show me yours? That sounds like the exact indecent proposal I got when I was in grammar school.

A_Very: What happened?

Row_man: I became very aware girls and boys have different plumbing systems, and I got paddled. Well worth it, though. I'd love to see what you look like. But let's hold off on the exchange for now. I was in a car accident Tuesday night, and I'm a little banged up.

A_Very: What?

A_Very: I'm so sorry! Are you okay?

A_Very: What happened?!?!

AVERY CLUTCHED her hand around her neck, wondering why she felt so panicked. Especially now that he'd declined to show her in real-time what he looked like. He was just some anonymous guy. Or gal.

She shouldn't feel this concerned.

And that concerned her.

It was ridiculous, in fact, to conjure any emotion for someone who might well be making up some story so that Avery wouldn't discover that he was an eighty-five-year-old toothless grandfather who relieved his boredom by playing on that new-fangled Internet thingy.

She decided she might ask again someday, and then she'd assume the worst. After all, Twitter was all about the disposability of humanity. Mute. Block. Move on.

. . .

ROW_MAN: I didn't really see what was going on. I was in a blind spot. I was on foot when I got knocked around a bit. I was in the back of some guy's car where he couldn't see me. Nothing's broken. Not much in the way of blood. I've got some frozen peas on my bruises. I should be shipshape in a few days. Then we can do the exchange. Or maybe we could even Skype?

AVERY'S EYELIDS HELD WIDE. *Skype*?

ROW_MAN: Before I ask you to Skype with me, maybe I should introduce myself. I'm Rowan Kennedy.

DID Avery want to let go of her own anonymity and tell him her name?

It was a pretty unusual name.

It would be easy to look her up. That reminded Avery that she needed to take steps to make herself into a ghost. If anyone found out that she was on the Taylor Knapp project, things could get bad. Very bad. She'd start by locking her Twitter account.

As she opened the settings feature to make the security changes, the snores from upstairs turned into gagging.

Avery raced up the stairs and flicked on the light. "Mom?"

_____

7

ROWAN

FRIDAY MORNING
Washington D.C.

ROWAN SHOWED his badge as he made his way through the checkpoint at FBI Headquarters.

His friend Lisa stood against the wall; Rowan saw her right away. Anxiety tightened her facial muscles. His own brow furrowed in response. "Hey, are you okay?" he asked as he approached. "I got your text."

She squinted as her scrutiny ranged over his face.

"It's not as bad as it looks." He laughed. "As it turns out, black bags do a hell of a job of softening the blows."

"Don't kid about this shit," she said, crossing her arms over her chest.

"It's the job. You know what the job is. You knew me when I

was a Ranger, and this was an everyday thing. Now, it's only every other month or so. It's a good gig for an old man. What's the 'I've got to talk to you ASAP' text about?"

"Hey, Rowan." Lisa's supervisor, James Miles' voice, pulled Rowan's attention around.

"James." He held out his hand.

He gripped Rowan's hand in a shake. "Lisa's going to be talking to some folks from the Hill in ten minutes. These people have the ears of some big wigs connected to funding. Cyber is their first stop today. I'm hoping for more *dinero* to focus on our disinformation problem. Would you be willing to give us a few minutes at the beginning of the meeting? I think you can tie this into a bigger picture for them. Lisa's going to be presenting. It would really help her out."

Rowan looked over at Lisa to see if she really needed to be helped out.

"Ten minutes?" She cocked her head to the side. "You could help me make one of my points about the ever-expanding scope. I'm focusing on Taylor Knapp as my example." She turned her focus on Miles. "We need to get him out pretty quickly. He has a fire to douse, so let's call a coffee break right after he freaks them out with what's going on."

Miles clapped Rowan on the shoulder with a nod and walked off.

"Do I really have a fire to put out?" Rowan asked, thinking that before he did this, he'd need an Advil and a stronger cup of coffee.

"First, I'm sorry about you and Jodie. She wasn't my favorite. She was a bit of a stick up the ass kind of person, and I never could see how you two worked, but that's not really for me to judge."

Rowan stilled. He'd broken up with Jodie last night. How in

the world could Lisa be mentioning it twelve hours later? Rowan brushed a hand over his face. "What did she do?"

"Jodie doxxed you. She put up a tweet." Lisa lifted her phone to show him a screen capture.

Rowan read: *Well, that's three years down the toilet. I'm drinking heavily tonight. Tomorrow, I burn all the shit that reminds me of my mistakes. Thanks for nothing, @Row_man, or since you're always at work @Dark_Matters.*

Rowan stared at it, stunned. Fear shot through his system.

"She deleted it first thing this morning," Lisa said. "Probably as soon as the Alka-Seltzer kicked in, and she realized what she'd done."

As soon as his heart started to beat again, Rowan muttered, "Too late."

8

ROWAN

FRIDAY MORNING
Washington D.C.

"THANK you all for coming today. I'm Special Agent James Miles. I think most of us know each other, but let's make a round of the table. Just your name, affiliation, and role, if you can." He turned to his right to get the ball rolling.

They progressed around the table. A dozen names were offered, representatives from the Pentagon, White House, and Congress, a lot of suits and brass.

Rowan sat to Miles's left, last in line. "Rowan Kennedy, FBI, Eastern Europe."

Miles gave Rowan a nod then turned to the rest of the room. "We'll begin with information from Special Agents Griffin and Kennedy. Special Agent Kennedy is coming in from the field."

There was a shift of unease as the people at the table came to the understanding that his bruised face was probably the result of what happened in the field, and so the real dangers weren't just a cognitive understanding but were physically evident.

Lisa stood and moved behind her chair, pushing it in. "Again, I'm Special Agent Lisa Griffin, cyber."

Rowan and Lisa had known each other for a long time. They had each other's backs.

Lisa had been cyber support for Rowan's Ranger unit, and after retiring from the military, they'd both found new careers in the world of intelligence and counterintelligence. But the thing that had kept their friendship solidly in place was their writing.

Both of them found fiction to be a good valve for releasing pressure. They wrote for themselves; they shared their writing with friends; they'd both gained from A_Very's editorial eye.

Sometimes, though, their writing was more realistic than might be palatable for someone who hadn't experienced a ground war. So, when they were describing the kinds of scenes that their psyches wanted out on paper, rather than swirling through their nervous systems, Rowan and Lisa shared those stories with each other.

"My expertise is in computer gaming, smartphone apps, and their applications as communications devices for crime and terrorist organizations." Lisa reached in front of Rowan to snag the computer remote and changed the photo on the large screen behind her head. Up came the art for the video game *The Unrest.*

"I tell people that I play video games for a living," she said. "Which is true. But the reason I play games is to track terrorist and criminal behaviors."

Rowan watched the group. Their interest was piqued, but they were pretty confused.

"Video games are an easy means of communication and

building alliances that our intelligence communities cannot track," Lisa explained. "If a criminal or terrorist wants to communicate via a video game, it's almost impossible to trace by any of our signals intelligence agencies. Signals intelligence is the term for government monitoring, intercepting, and interpreting communications. This is done by the military and also by our alphabets, including NSA, CIA, and here at the FBI. The problem here is that if our normal means of communication gathering doesn't pick up an exchange, then our enemies become invisible. And right now, we just don't know how to thwart them."

"Slow it down," a man in a gray suit said. "Some of us are dinosaurs who didn't grow up with the computer. When I was a kid, I played Mrs. Pacman. None of this blood and guts deal that I see my grandkids playing. How in the heck could a terrorist use a video game to communicate?"

Lisa rested her hands on the back of her chair. "It started with low-tech gaming consoles. Many of those games allowed gamers to play with their friends remotely. My brother, for example, plays with our nieces and nephews while he's on base in Germany, and they're here in America. It keeps them connected. Other gamers enjoy the competition and the ability to interact with folks from all over the world. The games are fun. And the games naturally feed a part of the brain that makes us want to play more. Gamers often spend hours a day in these worlds." She lifted her finger to focus everyone on the Knapp game from a PowerPoint presentation showing on the screen.

"I was doing a simulation game once on the computer that had to do with animal populations," an easily identifiable White House staffer said. "If I left the game to get something to eat or what have you, when I got back, there was no water, or there were too many predators. I remember playing that darned game all night, trying to keep my video game hippos alive." He stopped and chuckled. "I got a case of carpal tunnel from it. That game grabbed me by my emotions and wouldn't let go. The devil it was. I tossed it in the trash and won't go near that kind of thing again. Addictive. Whatever you were saying, Special Agent Griffin, about feeding that part of my brain, you aren't kidding."

"Yes, sir. And while I threw that information into the pot. It might have been too early in our discussion. Let me redirect our talk back to communications. As I was saying, the games are a more secure means of communicating than encrypted phones, texts, or emails. At first, gamers could send messages back and forth to each other through the game. Now, as the gaming systems have advanced, players can do things besides sending messages. You can now chat through the game, for example. The FBI, the NSA, the CIA, among other alphabet organizations, and the military, have infiltrated online games where there were terrorist meetups. In those meetups, the game was being played, and the terrorists were discussing strategies and cell movements."

"This is common then?" the colonel asked. "We probably need people to play games all day and watch for this."

"Yes, sir, that is much of what I do," Lisa said. "And even the Army, sir, though you may not be aware, has gamers. Their public-facing function is to play in international gaming competitions as a recruiting tool. But that's public-facing. The Army doesn't let folks know that they're trying to monitor our enemies."

The colonel tapped his pen aggressively on a pad of paper.

"You said terrorist meetups," a suit said. "I'm guessing that they decide on a time, and, wherever they are in the world, they can all get on their gaming platform and play video games together."

"Exactly," Lisa said. "They all collectively join a multiplayer game, and then they might do something like, instead of shooting the bad guys, they'll focus the shots on a wall to spell out words with the bullet holes."

"Within the game."

"Yes, Colonel."

"So anything, coins, bullets, whatever thing they can manipulate in a game can be used as a method of writing words," the colonel said. "No one could figure out how they're passing the information."

"Unless they are an accepted member and are playing that game at the same time," Lisa said, "that's right. Our signals intelligence simply can't find, collect, or stop it. But now, things are evolving. And we see another terror use for video games…widespread social unrest. Groups who have anti-American sentiments are now discovering that they can use video games to create cells of violent activists. Backing up a step, a simple definition of terror is when an ideology uses violence to change society."

"And why are you at this meeting?" The colonel turned steely eyes on Rowan.

"Sir, I work between Washington D.C. and Eastern Europe as a legal attaché," he said, standing. "I am specifically involved with following and understanding the functions of crime families that operated in the former Soviet Union. These crime groups are thriving in countries around the world, including the United States. Their criminal enterprises are thought to cost the US hundreds of millions of dollars in losses each year."

Rowan's jaw was still swollen and stiff. He worked at projecting his voice and enunciating so people could follow him. But he really wanted to keep his portion of sharing to a minimum. The ache seemed to intensify with each sentence.

"These crime family groups no longer conform to the typical

structure one would think of when it comes to Russian mob activity," he said. "They are now divided into cells of operation. These cells function independently of each other, each with their own task, but the cells have overarching goals."

"Why did they shift to this new organizational model?" a suit asked.

"When the cells operate independently, there is limited connection to members of the entire organization, and this protects high-level figures," Rowan said.

"So they're functioning like terror cells," the suit concluded.

"In many ways, yes. They've been working with those the US has identified as terrorists for a long time now, and I'm sure that they picked up on those techniques that have helped keep the terror networks functioning. This includes the secret communication systems, which Special Agent Griffin is speaking about." Rowan adjusted his tie and cleared his throat. "This leads me to the mission that I just returned from. It concerns one of the crime families based out of Bulgaria. They are connected by marriage to the Russian Orlovs and the Slovakian Zoric families, both of whom have been in the news lately."

There was a shifting of bodies in their chairs as tension rose in the room.

"What we know is that this Bulgarian family is launching a campaign in the United States geared to intensify the 'us-them' narrative that we've seen an increase since our last national presidential cycle. The goal is to foment hate and hate crimes. It is this family's objective to weaponize social media, producing the most damage to a unified United States citizenry over the longest period of time possible. Taylor Knapp's work that Lisa is using as an example is supported by this particular crime family."

"And you've seen them up and functioning?" a woman asked.

"Yes, ma'am," Rowan responded. "In the news today, you'll see that Facebook took down four channels. These channels were micro-targeted toward the millennial consumer and had tens of millions of hits. The pages pushed their agendas through posts on these channels. The pages didn't disclose that they were owned by the Russian government. The company was registered in Germany by Fast Forward. Fast Forward is also the company that produces the Taylor Knapp video games that Special Agent Griffin is discussing. This is important. Truly." He paused and let his gaze sweep the room for dramatic effect. "We are fighting a new kind of war. We know how to put bullets on a target. How to drop bombs from the sky. But here? This? The target is ideas, and you can't just shoot them down." He turned. "Special Agent Griffin, can you put a sharper point on this idea? Tell them why Taylor Knapp is so dangerous."

9

Rowan

Friday
　FBI Headquarters, Washington D.C.

"Terror attacks are useful," Lisa said. "But they don't really change behaviors, not for long anyway. Propaganda, on the other hand, changes hearts and minds. Case in point, the Taylor Knapp video game." She pointed up at the picture of *The Unrest*. "Taylor Knapp was a nobody three years ago. He is a coder and game developer. His game came out, and he married three components: a video game, ideological music, and a compelling narrative in the form of an action-adventure novel. All three became wildly popular and vastly divisive. The novel hit the New York Times list for fifteen weeks straight. It's a new genre of science fiction called 'video game adaptation,' and it's huge with the teen population."

"Who are in their formative years," a suit said. "This is looking bleak."

When Lisa looked at Rowan, he said, "Knapp's work was discovered by Russian interests. They saw that this layered program—game, music, novel—was exactly the kind of thing they were looking for to drive the 'us-them' narratives."

"You keep saying, 'us-them.'" The colonel scowled. "Give me an example."

Rowan sat down.

"Let's look at some themes from the first Taylor Knapp game and novel." Lisa looked up at the screen as she flipped through her slides. The bullet points came up:

—Pro-Israel v. Anti-Semitism
  —Black rights to safety/equality v. white supremacy
  —Common sense gun laws v. 2nd Amendment, guns without restrictions

"Now, let's take a look at a picture." She flipped to a new slide and used a laser pointer to highlight the items she was calling out. "This first picture is of a black man being beaten at a rally by a group of white men." She clicked the fob to move to the next photo. "A picture of a man driving through a group of counter-protesters, killing a female." She moved to the next image. "This photo is from a recent rally. You all recognize it from the newspapers. There are the tiki torches bought in the outdoor section of their local hardware store. The white males who are marching obviously came up with a unifying dress code. If you look at all of the faces in these photos and the aggressors in the previous two photographs I showed you, every single one of them has been identified by the FBI. Every single one of them plays the Taylor Knapp game."

"And that's creating this atmosphere of hate violence?" a suit asked.

"The identified individuals don't play the video game a little. They play for hours each day. While there is some psychological literature that supports violent video games leading to violence, this game is a new and potent tactic that we're still trying to understand. In Taylor Knapp's video game, called *The Unrest*, the more the gamer creates conflict in the population and in the government, the more points they get. You cannot advance in this game without causing unrest. *The Uprising*, by the way, is the name of the game that's about to be released."

Lisa flipped to the cover art for *The Uprising*. "We see that many of these themes from the first book have been debated in the public sphere, and they no longer have the same kind of punch, no pun intended."

A hand raised. "The developers are trying to create anarchy?"

"The developers are trying to create sales," Miles said.

"Right." Lisa flipped to another slide of bullet points. "Controversy equals free publicity. While that can be leveraged by folks working in a market system, we also have those with Russian interests paying close attention. They want to use issues that are already here, already creating problems, then they want to blow them up. Again, no pun intended." She grimaced, and her face pinked up a bit.

"Special Agent Kennedy has been keeping an eye on this in Eastern Europe," Miles said, "where bot farms are making pop culture their vehicle for disruption through the 'us-them' narratives."

"Special Agent Kennedy," Lisa said, "can you go over this next slide?"

Rowan stood again. "The music score for *The Uprising* is already out and quickly becoming popular. What we anticipate in the themes in *The Uprising,* the second video in a series, based on what is gaining sway on social media, are the following." He turned to the screen and read off:

—ENVIRONMENT IS on the precipice v. climate change is a hoax/scam

    —Women's equality/respect/safety v. toxic masculinity

    —Immigration v. Populism

    —Vaxxers v. anti-vaxxers

"OKAY, good. They didn't dive into pro-life versus choice." Came a sarcastic voice behind his back.

"I'm assuming they have to save some themes for the next game," Lisa said in all seriousness.

"My guess is that *The Uprising* will be about doomsday scenarios," Rowan continued. "Which player has the resources? How can they keep the distribution to a select few? That kind of thing. Another speculation is that in order to win, you have to amass those resources and allow photoreal video characters to die, taking the 'us-them' equation to the next level. And I believe these photoreal characters will be sympathetic, as in they could be your neighbors or colleagues, and you have to destroy them to advance."

"I was struck by your using the word 'photoreal.' Is that particularly important here?"

"It helps emotionally train a player for a real-life scenario. We use them in our training," the colonel said.

"We know from brain science that the mind can't distinguish

between real and not real," Rowan explained. "That's why special forces operators, elite athletes, and others are taught to visualize before an important event. As the player moves through the game, a person makes choices. They see their avatar—which is their symbol for themselves—move through a scenario to an outcome. This trains the brain. To have that same outcome in the real world, of course, you'd also have to train your body to be able to function that way. But visualization registers in the brain as real."

"Photoreal plus the hours a day that Special Agent Griffin mentioned seems very potent, then." This woman hadn't stopped clutching her throat since she first asked a question, a body language tell that she felt personally and imminently threatened.

"The more photoreal the experience, the better the brain can integrate that training," Rowan explained. "The more the brain will believe and behave according to the training. And these gamers are training for long periods each day, pulled in, and rewarded with the hormone dopamine, among others. It's like a chemical addiction."

"And there's nothing that can be done with the various social media platforms to shut this down if it's being used as a Russian attack?" a congressional aid asked.

"We're a country of free speech," Miles said. "Our enemies use our strengths as well as our weaknesses against us."

"It might be cheaper just to pay this Knapp guy a significant sum not to produce these games. Has anyone approached him yet?" a man in a black suit asked.

"We don't know who he is," Lisa said. "Taylor Knapp isn't the guy's real name."

"Are you serious right now? The intel community can't figure out who a game designer is?" a White House staffer exploded indignantly. "There have to be contracts—"

"To get to those contracts, we need warrants," Prescott explained. "To get a warrant, we need a crime. This is all legal."

"Free speech is why this country is great," the colonel said. "It's a judo move. Use your adversaries' strengths against them."

"Okay, let me see if I can't run this down for you," Lisa said. "Because it's best that you know just how difficult our situation is. The Russian-affiliated bots have information, both hacked and purchased through conventional means, that targets American consumer audiences such as those who use various social media platforms. The bots send messages, articles, and memes to United States citizens to solidify their already-held belief systems and to make them feel that those beliefs—whatever they are—are under attack.

No one moved. The listeners seemed to be holding their breath.

"That is what a bot does," Lisa continued. "It creates social unrest by pushing people's buttons." She flipped back to the picture of *The Unrest*. "Taylor Knapp's products *The Uprising* and *The Unrest* are examples of video games that are being used by post-Soviet countries to foment anger and controversy in America. Taylor Knapp's works are prototypes of social engineering that do a number of things. First," Lisa ticked off on her fingers, "they help solidify and entrench gamers in their personal ideology and belief systems. Second, they train the player to be angry and afraid. Third, it teaches the player that they will be rewarded for violent action. And fourth, it helps those of like minds communicate completely anonymously."

"So groups like the ones who stormed through city streets with tiki torches," the colonel growled, "chanting that they will not be replaced, have a community of like-minded agitators and a means of communication to plot action in a way that is not discoverable by our intelligence agencies?"

The room fell into silence as people processed this information.

"These Taylor Knapp games," the White House staffer asked, "what are we doing to stop them from planting seeds of discord in our society?"

Rowan replied, "There's an unusual synergy between Knapp and the troll farms, a natural symbiosis."

The colonel's hand formed into a fist. "So we nip this in the bud."

"This is a new kind of warfare," Miles said. "We're behind the curve. We're running to catch up. Money. Manpower. And a will. We lack all three. We *need* all three." Miles's gaze traveled around the table, focusing on the stakeholders who weren't already involved in solving this crisis. "We need you to go back and work with your people and help them to understand. This is getting away from us fast."

He let his words hang there until they began to sink in.

10

FRIDAY MORNING
  Falls Church, Virginia

RUMMAGING IN THE CLOSET, Avery reached in and pulled out a pink shift. "Do you like this one, Mom?"

"I don't like clothes at all. Why wear them? They're imprac-tical." Ginny shook an agitated hand, speckled with age spots. The loose skin of her upper arms jiggled with the gesture. "You have to put the darned things on, move them out of the way to use the bathroom, clean them, hang them. Just a bother if you ask me. No. I don't like clothes at all."

"Well, Fanny and her family are coming over, and you can't be naked for that." Moving away from the closet, Avery reached into a drawer and pulled out a pair of underpants and a bra. She turned and stacked them on the bed next to where her mom sat, wrapped in a towel. Ginny had combed her damp shoulder-length hair—now sparse and grey—straight back and pushed the strands behind her ears.

"I don't want her here." Ginny's glare stabbed Avery in the back as Avery was once again digging through the closet, looking for her mom's matching shoes.

"Now, why not?" Avery didn't want them here either. She squatted, holding one beige sandal and one black flat. Either would do if she could find a match.

"Is she bringing those bastards here with her?"

"Mom, please. Those are your grandchildren you're talking about." Avery tossed the shoes back in the closet and crawled over to pull out the house slippers she spotted under the bed. Her mom could go casual for the morning. Avery would look for the shoes if Fanny was willing to take their mom somewhere. Anywhere. And give Avery a little peace and quiet. "Stop calling them bastards."

"What am I supposed to call them? They're bastards. Fanny wasn't married in a Catholic church. In the eyes of the Lord, Baptist churches don't count."

"Mom, her husband is a preacher." Avery worked hard to keep the exasperation out of her voice. "Of course, she got married in his church. It was a legal wedding. They're married. There are no bastards. These are your grandkids." Avery's patience was wearing thin as she got up off the floor. They'd had this conversation so often that Avery dreamed it sometimes.

The bell rang, and Avery turned to go downstairs and answer the door. She stopped to look back. "Mom, get dressed, please, and come down to visit."

Ginny stuck her tongue out at Avery.

Avery raised a stern finger. "And be on your best behavior while they're here. Don't make a row."

Ginny stood up, causing the towel to drop, grabbed her bra, turned her back to her daughter, and bent in half to fasten it behind her back, mooning Avery in the process.

THEY SAT IN THE DEN, each of the adults individually occupied.

Avery was making her way through the first Knapp novel, *The Unrest,* on her Kindle, trying to get a feel for the tropes in this new genre, jotting notes on a pad.

The two boys ripped up Avery's magazines, making them into paper airplanes that they would let fly through the air, landing hither and yon. Rather than pick them up and launch them again, the boys tore more pages out and folded new planes.

Avery watched the recipe for the chocolate mousse, she'd wanted to try, turn into the next projectile.

This one landed in her mom's lap, but her mother didn't seem to notice. Ginny was muttering under her breath, "Strawberries in the garden, warmed by the sun's rays," as she rocked herself. "Sitting, and picking, and eating one after the other." She stopped and pounded a fist into her chest as a string of barking coughs erupted.

Avery moved over to her, placing a protective hand on her mom's shoulder. "Are you okay?" She turned to her sister. "Fanny, could you get Mom some water?"

Fanny put her finger on the bright image in her magazine where she left off reading. "It's *Stephanie*, and you're already up."

Avery's mouth pressed into a tight line as she moved toward

the kitchen. Her brother-in-law stood and followed her through the door. As Avery fished in the cupboard for a glass, he leaned a hip against the counter and crossed his arms over his chest. Power move number twelve, George's go-to position, Avery thought as she prepared herself for some kind of scolding.

She moved to the sink.

"Avery, I have a burden pressing on my heart." This was Curtis's concerned preacher voice—the one he deployed when he saw a sin coming on. "The Lord, our God, has asked me to lay this at your feet."

Avery's hand stilled on the tap; the glass hovered mid-air.

"You work for Windsor Shreveport Publishing. We were informed today that Taylor Knapp's second book is being prepared for print."

She filled the glass.

"I believe that you have a role to play in this."

How could he know? Avery composed her face in a studied blank before she shut off the water and turned his way.

"You could be a weapon against Satan's tool coming to fruition."

Avery glared at her brother-in-law. "I'm definitely the wrong tool for that job. Are you asking me to confront management about their publishing the Knapp book? If I say anything to anyone, I'd be risking my employment, Curtis. In case it isn't abundantly obvious to you, my work is how I keep a roof over my head. And how I pay for Mom's daycare. It's how we eat and have electricity."

"I'm not asking you to leave your employment. But you have to see you are in the unique position to be an instrument for Christ." He went to the table and pulled out a chair, the metal legs scraping against both the tile and her nerves. "You can help shepherd this wayward lamb back to righteousness." He caught her gaze, his eyes filled with moral conviction. "Satan, the great enemy, is causing mischief and damaging souls. You have to intervene on the side of Jesus Christ, our Lord. The anti-Semitic narrative in his last book, *The Unrest,* created a dangerous atmosphere here in America, an environment of distrust by the peoples of Israel. They must know we are firmly in their corner. That we support them with our hearts and our might."

He hadn't heard a single word she'd said.

"Think on the Old Testament Genesis 12:1-3 and God's promise to Abraham. 'I will make you into a great nation… I will bless those who bless you, I will curse those who treat you with contempt, and all the peoples of the earth will be blessed through you.'" He tapped his fingertips on the table. "And John 4:22 from the New Testament. In those words, the salvation of the Jews is affirmed. We must reject anti-Israeli activities in the United States, and in this case, in the popular literary culture. We must reject, reject, *reject* any activities that attack Israel."

"I reject them. I want nothing to do with Taylor Knapp. I am equally appalled by the anti-Semitic themes that I'm reading in Knapp's book."

"Inaction is the same as action! If you are not dynamically opposed, then you are propagating Taylor Knapp's sins."

Avery blinked.

"You *must* act to stop the next book from going to print."

"As if I have that kind of power," Avery scoffed. "I'm a romance project manager. I edit love stories."

"You can do something. You probably have more power than you think," Curtis insisted.

"I do what I'm told to do, period. If I fail to do as I'm told, I will be fired. I have no backup plan for Mom or for me. I need my insurance. I need my paycheck. This is a dumpster fire, and I refuse to martyr myself over the flames. Is that why you came here this morning? When you called and found me at home, it's because Mom's caregiver had car trouble. Someone has to stay with Mom twenty-four seven. You get that, right? She can't be left alone?"

"Yes."

"And when you found out I was here, you didn't come to see Mom. You said the kids had off of school and that they wanted to visit. But that's an outright lie. It's a sin to lie, Curtis."

"We try to bring the boys to see their grandmother as often as we can."

Avery rolled her eyes so hard she thought maybe she could see the gray matter in her brain.

"This is, I believe, God's hand. He allowed for all things to align so that I might speak with you this morning." Curtis tipped his head back and scrutinized her with what Avery assumed was a great deal of sanctimoniousness and loathing.

She didn't like his word choices or demeanor, but as far as this project went, she agreed, it shouldn't go forward. As far as her being a righteous warrior and the person with the power to stop it, that was laughable.

"This is indeed a critical time when dangerous forces are mounting up against the nation of Israel. We must pray for peace in Jerusalem. Romans 1:6 'God's power for salvation to everyone who believes, first to the Jew then the Gentile.'"

"That's fine, Curtis. I'll pray for Jerusalem. But let's be practical here for a moment. This is a bigger conversation that we really need to have. And I'm just going to circle it around to refocus you on my minute to minute issues. I have an obligation, an oath I took to my father on his death bed, to protect my mom and keep her home for as long as I can."

"A generous oath, Avery. You will be blessed in the Hereafter."

"Okay. But let me tell you that there are days when I don't think I can cope anymore. You could help. Fanny could help."

"Your father had life insurance." Curtis scowled. "Hire more help. I don't understand the problem."

Avery spread her arms out and rested her hands on the counter, borrowing from George's book of stupid alpha-moves. "Mom's got a little money in the bank, and it's helping me afford Sally to come and stay here during the day. Mom's money is dwindling fast. And by that, I mean this is probably the last year I can make her funds stretch. Then what? What am I going to do?" She lifted a brow. "And you're asking me to get fired. Do you honestly think that my losing my job will stop this project? Let me answer that for you. No. No, it won't. I am easily replaced in this job market. *So* easily replaced that they would have someone sitting at my desk before the seat cools from the heat of my ass."

"Avery, please. Language!"

"Curtis, *listen* to me. If I intervene for God to try to stop this book from going to print, Windsor Shreveport will fire me. *Fired.* Do you know what kind of job I could get after I was fired? None. Zero. Zilch. I'm over-qualified to be hired in a low-wage job, and people are scrambling to find any kind of work in my field. You're asking me to become destitute."

"I am not. No." He shook his head to emphasize his words. "And if you were to lose your job, preventing this book from going to print, the Lord would provide for you. You must believe that."

"Must I?" Acrid laughter slicked up Avery's throat.

Curtis raised his chin. "I would give you a job if it came to it."

"As what? Your secretary?"

"Part-time secretary. We don't have a full-time opening."

"Are you hearing yourself?" Avery slammed her fist on the counter. "If I lose my job, then you get Mom. You get that, right?"

Curtis blanched. "Your mother," he stammered out, "does better with you than with us. She feels her Catholic background... She feels that I... She would be happier..." Color rose in his cheeks as he puffed them out, then let his exhale hiss between his teeth, staring over Avery's shoulder at the wall.

"Maybe you can see I'm stuck and out of options? Windsor Shreveport isn't my dream job, especially now, believe me. But I can't police the world. I'm going to have to believe that since God is the maker of Heaven and Earth, if any smiting needed to be done, then God could aim his lightning bolt and sit back laughing after it strikes Taylor Knapp down."

Avery watched anger brighten Curtis's pale blue eyes.

"Avery, be careful what you say." He pitched his voice low, biting out each word. "Your soul is already tainted by your association with the Devil's book. Don't add to the sin by presuming God would have a sense of humor."

"Give me a viable option, hell, give me a quasi-viable option, and I'll take it."

"I don't want you to suffer the wrath of God. I don't want your soul to fall into perdition," Curtis shouted.

In response, Ginny's cracked screech of a voice rose in the den with an operatic *Gloria in Excelsis Deo*.

"Thanks," Avery bit out, looking toward the den. "That's bound to last for the next five hours." She picked up the kitchen towel and swiped it across the counter. She lifted her chin to read the clock. "It's almost lunchtime now, so you're heading home to do as you please. Meanwhile, I'm living my purgatory." The cloth dangled from her clenched fist as Avery pointed to the cacophony in the other room. "Don't you think?"

Curtis stared at the table. An internal argument seemed to churn in his brain. Avery was too tired to deal with him. She grabbed up the glass of water and went to her mom, hoping to distract her with something to drink and nip a singing marathon in the bud.

Avery found her sister gathering the boys for their departure. A fake smile spread across Fanny's face. Her eyebrows lifted with nervous energy. "Gotta go," she said brightly, as she shoved her magazine into her purse and bee-lined for the door.

Avery caught her sister by the sleeve. "Listen, Fanny."

"*Stephanie*," she hissed.

Avery rolled her eyes. "Whatever. I have to fly to New York next week for three nights. You'll need to pick up Mom and have her stay with you overnight. It's Wednesday, Thursday, and Friday nights that I'll be gone. Since Sally isn't working today, she said she'd work that Saturday."

Panic flashed across Fanny's face.

"My flight should be back in time to be here before Sally clocks out on Saturday. But I'll call you with a heads up if my flight gets delayed." Avery pushed up against the wall as her nephews barrelled out the door.

"Can't there be another arrangement?" Fanny laced her fingers, holding them under her chin as she begged. "Can't we hire someone for the night shifts, so she can stay at your house?"

"Sure, if you can pay for it. It's time-and-a-half, and my budget is stretched to breaking now."

"But you don't understand. The last time she stayed with us, she sprinkled holy water around the doorframes like a scene from *The Exorcist*. Then the next night, Curtis found her in the boys' room, standing on a chair reciting the rosary and trying to cast the demons out. He had to pull her bodily out of their room. I was down in the kitchen drinking the cooking sherry to get through it."

Avery folded her arms. "Not my problem."

11

Friday afternoon

Washington D.C. FBI satellite office.

Arms outstretched, Rowan stood patiently while the guard ran a wand over his suit and checked his credentials.

His colleague, Deputy Assistant Director Amanda Frost, waited for him on the other side of the checkpoint. "Thanks for coming on short notice." They moved together to the elevator. Their footsteps echoed in the empty hallway.

"Slow day?" Rowan asked.

"A lot of folks are at one of the offices for a presentation." She tapped the button to call an elevator. "How was your flight back stateside? You look like shit, by the way."

Rowan chuckled. "The flight home was uneventful, thankfully."

As the doors slid open, they stepped on to the elevator. Rowan was glad they had it all to themselves. "I have some bad news."

"Let's hear it," Frost said, jabbing the nine button.

"Jodie and I broke it off."

"Oh, I'm sorry about that." A frown of concern formed on her brow.

"Yeah, that's not the bad news."

"Oh shit," she whispered, leaning her hips against the elevator wall and crossing her arms over her chest.

"Jodie posted a tweet, tying my personal Rowman Twitter account that I use to talk with writers about craft and so forth, to my Dark Matters account. She was drunk and angry. She erased it. But the damage is done."

"Maybe not. How fast did she get it down? Right away?"

"Next morning. Lisa Griffin saw it and told me. When I checked the Dark Matters account, I was blocked by a good number of people I had been following."

"Wait, I don't understand." She came back to her feet as the elevator bounced to a stop. "Did you say you were FBI on the Rowman account? Why would Dark Matters followers worry about you and your writing buddies?"

Rowan held the door for Frost, then they started down the hall. "I didn't identify my job as FBI anywhere. But it had a banner picture of me sculling in D.C. And Jodie said that Dark Matters was my work account. Since the Dark Matters IP address is in Bulgaria, the D.C. photos were a pretty big tell that I wasn't who I said I was. I suspended both accounts to give myself time to make a plan."

She put her hand on the conference room doorknob and stalled. "Shit. That took years to build."

"I was afraid something might happen—some hacker with a

high skillset could trace the account back to me, or what have you, so I built a parallel persona. Fornicate. It's spelled f-o-r-n-i-c-then, the number eight.

"Nice." She rolled her eyes.

Rowan shifted on his feet. "I was trying to appeal to a certain kind of target."

"Understood."

A man came up behind them and paused. Frost moved back from the door to stand at the corner of the corridor. Rowan followed her over and lowered his voice. "Fornic8 never spoke to Dark Matters. And is fairly quiet. But that account has been helpful to the participants, so it still has good standing. It routes through a computer in Poland. The IP will read Poland."

"So all is not lost?" she asked.

"All? No. Too much? Yes. I mean, I've lost relationships that Fornic8 doesn't have."

"I'm really sorry. How did Jodie even know about this account?"

He scrubbed both hands over his face and leaned backward as he remembered that fight. "I was working from home during that big snowstorm last year." He focused back on Frost. "Jodie saw it over my shoulder and asked about it, thinking I might be catfishing or having an affair. I explained it was a work account, she wasn't quite convinced, so I showed her the followers list, which was long. It was full of symbols, flags, and men. She seemed convinced, and the subject was dropped. And I had hoped forgotten. I thought it was safer than having her go in and friend folks to spy on me."

"She'd do that?"

"Who knows. This job makes me suspicious as hell. I always wonder about people's motivations and try to predict possible outcomes. In my personal life, I try to check that to some degree, bring my alert level down to a more reasonable zone."

"In other words, you didn't predict Jodie would doxx you."

"She respects the work even if she doesn't respect me."

"On the train this morning, I read how the El Paso Zoo will name a cockroach after your ex and then feed it to the meerkats. That could have felt satisfying and not destroyed an FBI op."

"If only Jodie knew that was a possibility." He offered what he hoped was a wry smile. "It might have saved the account." The truth was, he had a headache brewing. There was nothing funny about this situation.

Frost slid her hands into her pockets. "And you told everyone who needs to know?"

"Now that I've told you? Yes."

"All right, nothing to be done about that now. Before we just blow it up, though, I'd like us to get some others involved and strategize. It could be that we can come up with a cover story. They'd make you jump through hoops to get back into their good graces. It would mean that we had to give up something big to convince them. We'll have to weigh this." She glanced over her shoulder at the meeting room door. "The information you got off Sergei's phone is being processed. They're combing through his computer files, all of it. I have nothing to tell you in that regard. I asked you to come here to meet this guy who will be speaking. I think he'll be an interesting person to have in your back pocket. The lecture is going to seem elementary to you. Bear with it. You're here for the connection."

Rowan nodded.

"You won't be called on. You won't be introduced. If someone tries to engage you, wave them off."

"Got it."

Frost pushed through the door and held it wide for him.

Rowan wended his way past knees and chairs to the back corner of the room and took a seat without making eye contact on his way.

He huddled into the corner, still seething about having to wipe two of his Twitter accounts. Not only did it set him back years with his work, but it also ruined what he thought of as a positive in his life—the support of his writing community.

He still had Lisa.

He didn't want to lose A_Very.

Rowan was oddly unsettled by how much the possibility of that loss was affecting him. Up until now, when curiosity about A_Very filled his thoughts, he'd pushed those thoughts out of his mind. But now that he wasn't in a relationship, he was free to think about her past the anonymity of a Twitter handle.

He'd known that Lisa had met A_Very in person and had pointedly not asked Lisa a single thing about it, not even A_Very's real name. Somehow, he'd felt like asking for information was invading A_Very's privacy. It felt like some form of doxxing. But now that Rowan was single, he could see... He could test the water...

Every few minutes, from the moment he suspended the account, he thought about her. He didn't know who she was or how to contact her other than through Twitter. He had to admit to himself that he'd developed strong feelings about her. A strong connection. Which was ridiculous. She was a cartoon avatar on a Twitter account. She could be anyone. She might not like men. She might be too young or too old or...too many things.

But none of that rang true to Rowan.

He believed she was genuine.

And kind.

With a big enough heart to help writers hone their craft.

He believed she had a sense of humor and playfulness that he enjoyed.

As he sat here in yet another meeting about the evolution and impact of cyber connectivity, he felt the press of what he knew about Sergei Prokhorov and felt genuinely afraid for the future.

Rowan had lain awake long nights trying to figure a way out of the dystopia he thought the world community was headed for. If people didn't get off the computer and into real life with real person to person relationships, they were all doomed.

He and A_Very had a Twitter relationship.

That wasn't good enough. He needed to meet her in real life and see if what he experienced on Twitter was his brain filling in the blanks to meet some need he had or if what he was feeling was the real deal. In the time it took this guy to make his way up to the lectern to stand next to Frost, Rowan had convinced himself that meeting A_Very in the flesh was his step toward the exact thing he thought the world needed—face to face connectivity and less cyber.

Lisa could tell A_Very that he was using a new Twitter name. He pulled out his phone and sent Lisa a quick text.

Once they were reconnected, Rowan could take the next step forward.

"Good afternoon, everyone," Deputy Assistant Director Frost said from the lectern. "I know this is probably your last meeting of the day. The hour is late, and the room overly warm, so there are coffee and doughnuts with extra sugar up here to pump your system. Why don't you help yourselves as we get going? Bathrooms are out the door to the right and up the hall. Take your first left. Please don't wait for a break. There will be none. Move about to the refreshments or to use the facilities or take calls as need be. Just with as little disruptions as possible if you please."

There was a general shift in the room as people settled in to listen.

Rowan was back on the ramifications of the Twitter debacle, and the more he thought about it, the more his blood boiled. A short little tweet and his work was blown out of the water. Maybe Frost was right; maybe there was a way to right this ship. Maybe Lisa could help. She might be able to get into the networks and see what they were saying. If he could come up with a good enough cover story, he might be able to turn the Dark Matters account back on, and bitch about some slime ball who was trying to make waves. Post something threatening that would just skim under the Twitter police bots. Something about come after me with your attacks, and I'll demolish you or some such crap. Better that he locked it all down. Yeah, he'd talk to Lisa about it.

The speaker cleared his throat. "I'm Ethan Terry. Today, I'm here to talk to you about the role that mainstream media plays in the Cyberwars or vice versa."

The picture of a gorgeous woman appeared on the screen. "Meet Tania. She tweets an average of a hundred and fifty times a day and now has a Twitter following of over two hundred thousand." He scrolled through some posts of her eating out and hanging with friends. "With a show of hands, who believes Tania is a real person?"

Half the hands went up.

"How many of you think that Tania is a social media marketing account. That an agency hired a model for a week or so, they staged photoshoots of her with her dog, her ice cream, her walk on the beach," he flipped through the photos, "her being sick, her singing into a hairbrush, jumping on her bed in panties and a man's shirt. Hands?"

Almost all of the hands went up this time.

"Does it matter?" Ethan asked.

"That depends on what she does with this account," someone said.

Ethan pointed at the person who said that and nodded his head. He changed the image to a screengrab from a computer —*Find an Influencer*. Step One: Browse through hundreds of accounts in our Influencer Shop. Choose by category, follower size, niche. Step Two: Load your influencers into your cart. Once you've made your purchase, Step Three: Upload your picture or video and fill out the form.

"So Tania was a low-level influencer. But it looks like she's signed on with some click farms and some bot farms, and they have boosted her cred. She's making a lot more money for her posts now. 'She,'" Ethan stopped to do air quotes around the word, "is probably someone sitting in a cubicle somewhere developing several accounts. If this is true, that's what we call a 'sockpuppet.'"

He put up a cartoon of a sock puppet. People offered up the required chuckle.

"Now, many of you know how bot networks and sockpuppets make divisive materials go viral. It just takes a few bucks and an influencer. Tania's account, which is listed as having an educated audience of twenty to thirty-year-olds, is a good choice."

A hand went up. "Isn't that easy to track? Can't we tell when someone is paying an influencer to, well, influence? Can't we just find some mechanism to expose this ruse in real-time, so consumers don't accept this as fact but understand it's fiction?"

"Like a verifiability stamp? How would that work?" the person next to him asked.

Ethan shook his head. "Usually, influencer purchases don't require anything that associated them with the buyer."

"Money trail?" he asked.

"Bitcoin," the guy behind him said.

"Right, so we have an influencer who is trying to make a story go viral." He flipped to another picture of the woman. "When Tania tweets that photo out, the algorithms at Twitter lift the story up. Twitter gamifies the tweet by rewarding users who share the content. They get extra points for sharing emotionally charged content and for sharing it quickly. When a story goes viral on Twitter, it sets an agenda for journalists. And that's our topic for today: 'Pseudo Events and Mainstream News,'" he read off his next slide. "Emotion is the name of the game. A journalist's job is to present both sides of a story, even when there isn't a 'both sides' to present. In fact, to make a story into a story, it needs two components—something to report on and a debate. Journalists emphasize the us-them of a subject matter. Our studies—and I'm waiting for your coffee to kick in before I pull out my stats and graphs."

He paused so a chuckle could run through the room.

"Our studies demonstrate how journalists are rewarded by provoking the us-them narrative because their articles are picked up and discussed. I'll give you an example—a reporter goes up to a politician and asks them a question. The politician answers. They go up to another politician in the same party, ask the same question, and get a different answer. Now the reporter has something to report and will make it a debate by saying something like 'a rift is forming in the party.' The more emotionally charged they can make that rift sound, the better. Even if there is no rift."

"Stick to the talking points," someone shouted.

"Exactly," Ethan said. "That's why they developed talking points so that the journalists couldn't develop pseudo-events. In the cyber age, reporters need the emotional component to drive the Internet algorithms so that their work can be seen. It's built into the structure."

"Are you going to discuss the algorithms and filter bubbles? How social media filters people, so they only hear from and interact with those who are like-minded?" the woman directly in front of Rowan asked.

"Yes, I'll be touching on that. But for now, let's stay here on the concept of artificial newsworthiness."

Rowan knew all this. He fought this in his day to day work. He knew, for example, that a cartful of influencers had already been purchased, and they'd pushed the first song for Taylor Knapp's *The Uprising*. As soon as the influencers pushed the videos of the band playing, Sergei's bot farm started to spread its menace. Some of the bots thought this was marvelous. Other bots thought that the new song was terrible racist rhetoric. The people who were working at the bot farm would sit in a circle, and one after the other, pick a side and push it, fighting with each other, using emotional language, quickly and emphatically entering into an argument. Boom! Up the algorithms it went, and the song ended up in the mainstream media being mentioned on EntertainmentPM that evening as newsworthy. Cheap. Easy. Effective.

That was just the start of what was to come when the video game dropped and then the novel.

Sergei Prokhorov's bots had learned a lot since *The Unrest,* Taylor Knapp's last game, was released. From the chatter Rowan had been following, this upcoming campaign was based on much better data. Rowan couldn't figure out where they were getting their data and how they knew what they knew about micro-targeting the players.

The Russian bots used this micro-targeting to bring violence to American streets. Rowan needed to stay out in front of this. He needed to find a way to shut it down before more innocent people were run down and killed or gunned down in their yoga studios.

Foreign influence creating domestic terror.

A new brand of terror.

A terror that started with a spark in an American citizen, that fire was fanned with the fear and anger of like-minded Americans in their artificial communities and then blown into an inferno by our enemies abroad.

A conflagration that could wipe out the united part of the United States of America.

12

AVERY

FRIDAY EVENING
Falls Church, Va.

THE SOUND of hymns filled the air, but only the stray high note filtered through the ear protection Avery wore as she frosted her cake. Her mother had been singing since Fanny, and her family had left.

Her phone vibrated in her back pocket, and Avery pulled one side of the muffs free so she could hear her friend. "Hi, Lola."

"I called to see if you wanted company, but I can hear your mom's feeling musical. So I'll just ask how your day was instead."

"Can't blame you." Avery licked the side of her icing spatula, smearing chocolate across her cheek.

"So what started her up?"

"Fanny was here. She came by with her family. The kids had the day off school."

"Blessed Joseph. Did Curtis try to convert her again?"

"Not this time." Avery opened the cupboard and pulled out a wine glass and a dessert plate, which were stored side by side for convenience's sake. "This time, it was my soul on the precipice."

"Yours? Why? What did you do?"

"Oh, you know the usual—first I broke Old Testament law. I wore a cotton polyester blend. I got a tattoo. I served shellfish for lunch. Then I admitted I worked on a Sunday."

"Four sins. And I bet your hair is uncovered."

"Yep. If I'm heading for hell," Avery cut a giant piece of cake and plunked in on her plate, then shoved the cutlery drawer shut with her hip, "might as well go all the way." She shoveled up a bite of cake as a high note sounded overhead and held long and sharp in the air. "Curtis doesn't like that my publishing house is working on the Taylor Knapp project. He thinks I should find a way to tank it."

"Are you kidding me? That's self-sabotage." Her friend's voice bristled with indignation. "Wait. Did you tell them that it's your project?"

"Of course not. I'm not a masochist. Besides, NDAs and million-dollar fines help me keep my lips sealed tight. But Curtis says I'm an instrument of the Lord," Avery continued, walking to the dining room.

"As long as the instrument isn't a drum, and he's trying to bang you."

"Lolly, that's gross. Don't say shit like that to me." Avery set her cake and wine on the table. "*Ew*, now I have to go wash my mouth out with vodka."

Lola snorted. "Yup, me too. Better make mine a double. Ach. Kid's got a bloody nose. I'll call you tomorrow."

Avery sat down, pulling the sound canceling muffs back into place. She opened her laptop, took a deep and satisfying slurp of wine, then draped a napkin across her lap. Avery was re-tweeting a haiku when a smile crossed her lips.

LisaWrites was in her message box telling her Rowan's account got hacked. She said that he was going to follow Avery as LeGit.

Avery tapped on her followers and followed Rowan back, and now here he was in her direct message folder.

LeGit: Hello. Thanks for the follow back. I'm checking in on you. We were chatting, then you suddenly disappeared. I got your message, "Sorry about that. Life. TTYL." It got me worried. Can you let me know you're okay?

AVERY GRINNED. And drummed her fingers on the table. What should she say?

A_Very: I'm okay. Thank you for asking.

Lame.

She sent him a smiley face emoticon.
Double lame.

A_Very: I'm glad Lisa told me about your new account. So sorry you got hacked!

LeGit: Yeah, well, I'm sure it will work itself out eventually.

Until then, I'll just talk to a couple of people as LeGit. I was going to pick the Dead Kennedys, but that was taken.

AVERY HAD NOTICED THAT. He followed two people, to be precise. Rowan followed her and Lisa. Lisa was in a serious relationship with her long-time girlfriend. Rowan and Lisa had been friends for a lot longer than Avery had known either of them. It must mean something that Lisa had specifically contacted her and told her to follow Rowan. It must mean *something* that she was the only other person that Rowan even tried to follow with this new account. And he'd said he wanted to Skype. That, too, must mean something, right? Maybe it meant that Rowan was interested in her as more than a Twitter-pal?

A_VERY: I follow the Dead Kennedys already. When I'm in the right mood, I like their music. But even so, that's kind of...I don't know...seems like it's giving fate the raspberry.

LeGit: Which I would never do.

A_Very: Besides the hacking, how is your day going?

LeGit: The day was passable. I just got home from the gym. You? How is your day treating you?

A_Very: Better now.

LeGit: Why? Something happen earlier?

A_Very: Oh, my sister was over with her two boys.

LeGit: Got a bit rowdy, did they?

A_Very: They are, IMHO, over-fed & over-indulged. But no, they weren't the problem. It's my sister, Fanny. I'm traveling next week for work, and I need her to keep my mother during the nights after her caregiver is done for the day. My mother has health issues and can be difficult, so Fanny's not excited to take on the extra duties.

LeGit: Fanny, is that a nickname for Stephanie? Or your polite way of calling her an a**?

A_Very: Ha! Yeah, a bit of both. She hates that I still use her childhood nickname. But I can be passive-aggressive when I don't have any other weapons.

TOO MUCH INFORMATION? Too weird to announce? No. That should be okay. This was sister-dynamic. But he may not have sisters or have that kind of dynamic in his family…

LEGIT: Forewarned. A_Very, is that really Avery? A nickname? A clever Twitter handle from an inside joke that I don't understand?

SHOULD she tell him her real name? Why was she worried? They'd been tweeting for years. The guy (probably a guy) wasn't trying to get her to send money to him in Africa or catfish her. If he was, he was the most patient cat-fisherman in the world. Rowan was fun and interesting, and kind. You don't fake that over time. Meanness is impatient. You learn someone is mean-hearted pretty quickly. Unless they're psychopaths, and they're grooming you.

Thoughts like that were a consequence of being in the book-writing industry. Her mind always wandered down the darkest path. Even in romances, it can't be just butterflies and kissy faces. Things have to go badly. Very badly. Or it just wasn't a story worth telling.

. . .

A_Very: My name is Avery Goodyear. And before you ask, yes, it's the real deal. My dad insisted on it. When I was born, he pronounced that it was going to be A. Very. Good. Year. That's his humor.

LeGit: That's awesome! What a great name/great story. Does he live nearby?

A_Very: He passed away two years ago. So... Yeah. I miss him. We were buds.

LeGit: I'm so sorry. I remember that now. You posted a few years back. That's rough.

A_Very: My turn. Is Rowan Kennedy your real name?

LeGit: Why do you ask if that's my real name?

A_Very: I Googled you.

LeGit: Wanted to see if I had any arrest warrants?

A_Very: Just to see…I don't know. I was snooping.

LeGit: The Internet age.

A_Very: There's nothing out there. Not even a LinkedIn account. No way I could see if we have anyone in common other than Twitter.

LeGit: So, you could get the scuttlebutt?

A_Very: Just being nosey.

LeGit: I'm learning a lot here. Passive-aggressive, nosey…

A_Very: Since I've outed myself as nosey, I'll go ahead and ask, how old are you?

LeGit: 31, you?

A_Very: I'm about to turn 33. My Jesus year.

LeGit: Close in age, then. What does that mean, a Jesus year?

A_Very: Jesus was sacrificed on the cross in his thirty-third year. My brother-in-law, who is a preacher, believes that in everyone's thirty-third year, they should reflect on the sacrifices and suffering of Jesus, and…that's a whole kettle of fish. And a poorly chosen idiom.

LeGit: This is nice, visiting one on one in the direct messages. I'm enjoying talking with you.

A_Very: Well, thank you. I have to get off in a second, though. I have to contact my new author.

LeGit: A new project? Who are you working with?

A_Very: I can't tell you.

LeGit: Big secret, huh?

A_Very: Million-dollar secret.

LeGit: Seriously? How is that?

A_Very: I signed an NDA. If my lips unseal, my financial future is toast.

LeGit: Where do you work? That sounds hardcore. I know you're an editor—but I didn't know romance editors had to be that secretive. Your job is pretty cutthroat, huh?

A_Very: I'm with Windsor Shreveport. Normally not. With certain projects, yes. With this one, to be honest, I'm thrilled I have an NDA.

LeGit: Now I'm intrigued.

A_Very: I showed you mine, now you show me yours.

LeGit: What?

LeGit: Oh, what do I do? I work for the FBI.

A_Very: And you think I work in a cutthroat industry?

LeGit: Thankfully, my job is fairly sedate.

A_Very: Can you share more? What do you do for them? Throw flashbang and break down doors?

LeGit: That's the SWAT team. No. I'm a foreign attaché. I shake a lot of hands. I mostly work in Eastern Europe. I'm home in the States right now.

A_Very: Interesting. I'm afraid I don't know much about the international crime world. I guess that's a good thing. But somehow, I thought it was the CIA who did stuff overseas, and the FBI did stuff on US soil.

LeGit: Sort of. The CIA is an intelligence-gathering entity, and the FBI is law enforcement. Overseas, it's the FBI's job to gather information, run down leads, what have you, and share them with our colleagues in the United States, so they can bring suspects to trial.

A_Very: There's that TV show, "Quantico." Quantico is south of where I live. Did you do your training there? How did you get into the FBI?

LeGit: I got in by taking one step then another down the path, not knowing it would lead here in the end. I went to West Point, then became a Ranger, got out and did some grad work, got my Ph.D.

A_Very: Brains and brawn.

LeGit: Brawn?

A_Very: Is that a picture of you sculling? That picture was taken at one of my favorite picnic places.

LeGit: Yeah, that was me a very long time ago when I was leaving the military. A journo was taking pictures, and he sent it to me. I liked it. You live in D.C.?

A_Very: That's where I work. I live in Falls Church. Ph.D. in what?

LeGit: Media, Culture, and International Affairs.

A_Very: Sooo…you're a doctor of propaganda?

LeGit: Exactly.

A_Very: Right time, right place. That's our zeitgeist, isn't it? Then Ph.D. to FBI?

LeGit: I was recruited while I was writing my dissertation. After training, I went to the FBI National Academy, which sounds America-centred, but it's a place where thought leaders from around the world train together. Our objective was to learn from each other and build friendships.

A_Very: Okay, that doesn't sound too cloak and dagger-like. That sounds more like statistics and coffee in a boardroom.

LeGit: You sound like you were worried about me :)

A_Very: I think of you as a friend even if we haven't met. I don't like to imagine you in situations like you see in the movies. Getting held at gunpoint. Running through the city streets with the bad guys at your heels. The danger of trusting the wrong person to do the right thing at the right time…

LeGit: Yeah, fiction doesn't really represent this job very well. I'm sorry to say, I have an overseas conference call to get to.

A_Very: Go. It's time for my author anyway.

LeGit: Avery?

A_Very: Yes?

LeGit: I bet you're shoveling chocolate cake in your mouth as fast as you can.

A_Very: Ach! How did you know that?

LeGit: Well, I know from your chocolatoholic tweets that you use it to self-medicate. And when you typed about the author, I could feel the stress attached to those words. Just breathe. Everything's going to be fine. I'll be here later if you want to talk it out.

13

AVERY

LYING ON HER BED, Avery let the cool breeze from the air conditioning vent waft over her. Surely, it was about time for Mother Nature to turn down the temperatures. Avery wanted the comfort of her hoody and the crackle of a bonfire on a crisp, cloudless night under the stars. A mug of hot chocolate. A strong arm around her shoulder, pulling her in to cuddle. Quiet. Lots of quiet.

Outside, a full moon backlit the pine trees. Like dancers, they swayed gracefully in the wind. Avery watched them, hoping their movements would hypnotize her and she could fall asleep.

She hated sleeping on her back, but this was the only position that would allow Avery to wear the noise-canceling headphones. Otherwise, her chance of drifting off was practically nil. Avery made a mental note to call her mom's doctor during office hours and see if she could do anything about her mom's medications.

This singing had to stop.

The flashing light on her cell phone inched into Avery's awareness. She glanced at the clock. In the wee hours of the morning, this was either a mistaken drunk dial or an emergency. As that thought slicked through her mind, she ripped off the earmuffs and swiped her screen.

"Hello?" she gasped.

"For Christ's freaking sake, can't you make her be quiet?"

Avery cleared her throat. "Excuse me?"

"It's Matt Harlow, next door. I know you're having a bad time with your mom and all. I sympathize, really I do. But you have to understand how well we can hear her over here, especially with the wind driving every *freaking* note toward our kid's nursery. We had to move the baby in with us. We can't sleep through this. You have to do something."

"Oh, Mr. Harlow, I'm so sorry. I had no idea you could hear her. I…" Avery couldn't tell the man she'd take care of it. If she had a way to take care of it, she'd be sleeping right now herself. Once her mom started singing, Avery just had to wait her out. "I'm so sorry." She finished lamely. Tears burned the corners of her eyes. "I'll do everything I can. I'm going to try to get her to the doctor again. She's…well, that's too much information. I'm doing my best."

"Seriously. Take care of this. I'll be generous and give you ten minutes. After that, I'm calling the cops—disturbing the peace. Noise ordinances do exist, you know."

"I do know, Mr. Harlow. I can't tell you how sorry I am."

"My buddy on the police force says I don't have to put up

with this ongoing shit. Seriously, shut it up, or I'm making the call. Do you want your mom to spend the night in jail?"

"Mr. Harlow, you have been so kind to call me first. I'll do everything in my power to—"

"At this point, gag her. I need some sleep. My wife *needs* some sleep."

"Yes. Immediately, Mr. Harlow. I'll find a way to get her settled right now. Okay?"

The crashing sound of a receiver slamming down on its base made Avery jump. She stood there with her phone in hand, trying to figure out a strategy for keeping the police out of this.

Maybe she could get her mom in the car and drive her around for a while.

She had ten minutes.

Avery ran to her mom's room and flicked on the overhead light, laying her phone on the highboy, upright so she could find it quickly if she needed to call an ambulance. The hospital and its costs were preferable to the police coming and the imagined bail and lawyer bills.

When Avery cut on the light, it startled them both into wide-eyed stares.

The shock of the sudden glare was enough to make Ginny close her mouth. The last note of *Adeste Fideles* hung in the air.

"Mom. What are you doing? Why aren't you sleeping?"

Her mother stared at Avery. Opening her mouth wide, Ginny sucked in a breath.

Avery leaped forward, slapping a hand across her mother's mouth. "Don't you dare open your mouth. Do you hear me? Stop. Don't you dare sing another note."

Ginny clawed Avery's hand away. "Avery Grace Goodyear, how dare you manhandle me?"

Avery released her mother and spun around, looking for a

plan, trying to get control of the anxiety and anger pumping through her veins.

Her mom was not responsible; it was a disease. Hate the illness—not her mother, Avery tried to reason with herself.

"Mom, I'm sorry. Right now, I need you to tell me why you aren't sleeping." Avery moved to the highboy, where Ginny kept her medications.

She examined the prescription contraption that separated the pills by date and time. When the time came to take the medication, a bell sounded, and the compartment popped open. That way, Ginny wouldn't forget how many tablets she'd taken and OD. Again.

All of the opened boxes were empty.

"Mom, you took your sleeping pills, didn't you?"

"Yes." Ginny pulled her sheet in front of her and looked at the floor.

Avery watched her mother carefully. "Mom, did you take your sleeping pill tonight?"

Ginny cast innocent eyes at Avery. "Yes. I took a shower, dressed in this gown, took my pills with a glass of water. Then, I said my rosary."

Avery expelled an exhausted sigh.

"Mom, why didn't you take your pills?" Avery tried to modulate her voice to sound as friendly and supportive as possible. She picked up the wastebasket and searched through the debris. She opened the drawer of Ginny's nightstand. "Mom, we need to find your pills. Where did you put them?"

Ginny slid to the end of the bed and put her hands flat on either side of her. "Avery Grace, don't you sass me. I told you, I took the pills."

"Get up."

"What? No. Leave my room this instant."

Avery reached for her mother's wrists, planted a foot on the bed for leverage, and pulled. "Get up!"

With Ginny standing beside her, Avery lifted the corner of the mattress. There lay a dozen or so pills—blue, white, yellow, and two-tone. Avery scraped them onto her hand and held them under Ginny's nose.

"What is this? What did you do, Mom? No wonder you've been off your rocker. You haven't been taking your medications."

Ginny shook a defiant finger in Avery's face. "Who are you to tell me, your mother, what to do?"

"I'll tell you who I am. I'm the daughter who's keeping you out of a jail cell tonight." Avery moved to the bureau, where she put down the jumble of drugs. She picked out two of the little white ones and advanced toward her mother. "Here you go, open up."

Ginny sealed her lips in a tight pucker.

Avery reached for her mom's jaw, but Ginny twisted her head to the side.

"I swear to God, Mom, you're going to take these pills and go to sleep if I have to sit on you and force them down your throat."

"Why?" Ginny's voice trembled with emotion. Fear and sadness filled her eyes. "Why are you brutalizing me? Why are you helping them?"

"Helping who?"

"Sally and the others. They're trying to kill me, Avery. They want me dead. Then they won't report it. They'll shove my body into the deep freezer downstairs and leave me there, frozen like a human ice cube."

"What?" Avery scanned her mother's face and only saw conviction there.

"They want my money, Avery, my social security check. Once I'm dead, they can keep taking it for the next thirty years without anyone knowing the difference. Unless we lose electricity. Then maybe my body would stink, and the neighbors would call the police to figure out what the smell was."

Avery stood there flabbergasted as she listened to her mother unfold her delusions.

Ginny had laced her fingers and held them in front of her face like a beggar. "But then I saw the delivery man bringing the box, and I asked Sally what was in it. She fessed up and said it was a generator. So now I know they're prepared to keep my body frozen even if the electricity goes out."

"Mom, no one wants you dead." Avery pushed away the whisper that she would feel relief without the burden of her mom's illness. But being unburdened by the trials of her mother's illness didn't mean that Avery wished anything bad for her mom.

Avery remembered her dad in his last moments alive. He lay in the hospital, crying, pleading, and pulling from her the promise she would take care of her mom—keep her out of an institution for as long as humanly possible. Avery focused on the pills lying on her palm, and she thought she was getting to the end of her strength. She just wasn't sure if she had hit the mark yet where her dad would agree she had done her very best. Avery desperately wished her dad had been clearer about her oath's parameters when he had asked her for this sacrifice.

"I'm not going to prison for the rest of my life for the chance at sixteen hundred a month of social security money split with your caregivers."

"Not you, Avery. Sally and the others. They're plotting. I know it. And they're stealing my clothes, too. My things. My things are all disappearing."

The tension behind Avery's temples beat a palpable rhythm.

"Okay, Mom. We need to talk about this sometime. But right now, it's too early in the morning. I need to get some sleep."

"Well, go on ahead, then. You're the one who barged in here and put the light on."

"Take your pills, and we'll both get some rest."

"No!" Ginny put her fists up as if to punch Avery.

Avery lunged forward, grasped Ginny's face at the tender spot where the upper and lower jaws came together, and squeezed. It was the same move her mom used on her when Avery was a little girl and refused to have her mouth washed out with soap. It worked like a charm. Ginny's mouth popped open.

Sweating and shaking, Avery shoved the pills down the back of Ginny's throat then released her.

Ginny was sobbing when Avery handed her the glass of water.

"Now get in bed, Mom. Don't you dare open your mouth— not one single note until breakfast, do you hear me?"

Her mother nodded, her childlike eyes filled with hurt.

Shutting off the light, Avery moved down the stairs. She'd need to ask the doctor if she could have a shot for her mother instead of the pills. Something liquid that she could mix into her hot tea. Something easier.

In the kitchen, Avery lifted the lid off the cake plate and considered the last piece of Devil's Food. If she continued to self-medicate with cake like this, she was going to be an elephant no matter how hard she pushed herself at the gym.

She opened the lid on her laptop, checked her email. Nothing in her inbox from Taylor, darn him. She sent him a reminder.

Chapter Outlines

. . .

HELLO TAYLOR,

I THINK that you're probably very busy working on your manuscript. It's probably too time-consuming to ask you for the information I requested in our last email exchange.

HOW ABOUT A BRIEF CHAT?
I can come to you immediately, leaving out as soon as I know where you are. I just need to make travel arrangements.

LOOKING FORWARD TO IT!
Avery Goodyear

SHE PRESSED SEND, thinking that if Taylor happened to be in Paris, that wouldn't be a hardship. Maybe she could even get out of going to New York with George. Surely, from all of his angst, he would deem Knapp the more important focus.

Avery flipped to her Facebook feed. Scrolling through the duck faces and delicious-looking food photos of people who were out enjoying their lives over this past weekend sapped Avery's reserves. She worked hard on not feeling bitter.

Her mail pinged.

RE: Chapter Outlines

Avery, don't you need your beauty sleep? Hope my missing your deadline isn't what's keeping you up.

I've rented a house in Warrenton, Virginia. Off the beaten track, but near the Rappahannock and awesome horse country. It's just boring enough to keep my fingers tapping at the computer. Later in the morning, when normal people are awake, my band will be here, checking out the game component of The Uprising project that is featuring their music.

Come on. Why not?

Culver's Farm off of Old Waterloo.

T.

AVERY STARED AT THE SCREEN.

Warrenton was only an hour away. At least she wouldn't need to fly out of town.

An hour's drive into the country was manageable.

Nice even.

It occurred to Avery that there were only snippets of her day that were bearable—stuck in bumper to bumper traffic while listening to music, talking to Lolly, and Tweeting with Rowan. She rubbed the heels of her palms into her eyes.

What a pitiful excuse for a life.

14

AVERY

MONDAY
Warrenton, Virginia

THE OLD-FASHIONED FARMHOUSE had been beautifully refurbished. The high ceilings and intricate crown molding, the polished wooden floors, were backdrops for lush modern furnishings and art.

Avery wandered into the house, back toward the kitchen, following behind the woman who had opened the door with an "Oh, hey, you actually came." She'd turned and headed toward the back of the house, slinging an "I'm still drinking my first cup of coffee. Want some?" over her shoulder.

"Sure," Avery called. After her neighbor had phoned, Avery hadn't been able to fall asleep. The anxiety that sparked her nerves was too bright to allow her to rest.

Another cup of coffee might just help.

Of course, Avery was already nervous and twitchy, so she wasn't sure about adding caffeine to the mix. What Avery needed was a slice of chocolate cake. She knew she was an addict. She knew that was her mental health crutch. But she'd tried the counseling-pharmaceutical path, and that dampened her creativity to the point that she couldn't function at work. That was the time she'd given up her own writing and hadn't picked it back up.

Writing would wait. *Hopefully.* She'd just churn stories through her brain, and someday she'd have the time and the quiet to write them all down. Uninterrupted.

Avery was perched on a red cushioned stool in the bright yellow kitchen.

The woman placed a mug in front of her on the countertop and pushed a tray with sweetener options and cream over.

Out the window, across the manicured lawn, a horse was munching grass behind a barbed-wire fence. Avery dragged her attention from the picturesque scene to glance back down the hall, then over to the woman who was fixing her coffee. "I'm Avery Goodyear from Windsor Shreveport."

"I know who you are," the woman said, then sipped her coffee.

"I'm sorry. I'm uhm…here to talk to Taylor Knapp?"

"Uh-huh," the woman said.

Avery looked around to the hallway again. "I'm wondering if you could let him know I'm here."

"He knows," she said. "Or at least, I know. I go by the pen name Taylor Knapp. You can call me Taylor."

"Oh!" Avery said.

George had definitely used male pronouns. George must never have met Taylor. Avery wasn't sure this woman wasn't pulling her leg. She didn't look like a gamer. Not that Avery had a specific idea of what a gamer should look like.

"Surprise," Taylor said.

"I…assumed," Avery said lamely.

"Oh, I meant for you to. In the gaming industry, women are treated like shit. If you think I'm a guy, I'm brilliant. If you knew I was a woman? You'd drag me through the mud and spit on me. Then you'd kick me while I was down. I tried that route, and it sucked," she said, dumping a spoonful of sweetener into her mug. "Yeah, things have been much easier since I started pretending to be a guy."

"I'm sorry," Avery whispered.

They were both quiet.

After another sip of coffee, Avery asked, "Is that why you wanted a female editor?"

"I didn't have any standing to ask for what I wanted with the first book. Now, they'll do just about anything to drag a sequel out of me." She chuckled. "I figured I could use that power to lift another woman up."

Is that what Taylor was doing by getting Avery involved? Lifting her up?

"Also, Fast Forward, my video production company, told me to request you."

"They told you my name specifically, not just to ask for a woman?" Avery settled her mug on its saucer.

"Yeah, your name specifically. Why?"

Avery lifted her gaze to meet Taylor's eye. "It's just that you're listed as a science fiction author with video game adaptation. I'm a romance editor. I'll be hard-pressed to help you with your content editing. The voice, the rhythm, the tropes, and characters, this project isn't something I should be working on."

Taylor shrugged.

"Would you like me to help you find a more appropriate editor?" Avery slid her hands to her lap and crossed her fingers hard.

"Nope. I was told to request you. I'm good."

"All right," Avery said, lifting her hands back to the counter, not at all surprised that the finger crossing hadn't worked. By rule, it never did. But Avery still tried, just in case there was any chance at a change in luck. "I'm wondering if you need a sounding board to bounce some ideas off so the project can move forward."

"Are you familiar with my work?"

"I read *The Unrest.* I didn't enjoy the themes that you presented. I was surprised by the quality of your writing. The writing is actually incredibly good."

Taylor laughed big loud guffaws.

Avery studied the young woman in front of her. Maybe ten years her junior, but light years ahead in the infamy and fortune categories. Avery reached her fingers up under her glasses and rubbed her eyes. She hated wearing glasses, but this morning her eyes were too tired to wear her contacts. She was exhausted and really, truly, deeply didn't want to be having this conversation.

Avery spun her mug in her hands, feeling the radiant warmth through the ceramic. "Your work made me think of the phrase, w*ild Abyss.*"

Taylor's eyes shifted up, and her lips moved as she mouthed the words to herself. "That's from Milton's *Paradise Lost.*"

"Right." Avery nodded. She pulled out her phone and scrolled to the page she'd pasted into a memo. "The whole quote goes—"

"Into this wild Abyss/ The womb of Nature," Taylor recited. "and perhaps her grave—/ Of neither sea, nor shore, nor air, nor fire,/ But all these in their pregnant causes mixed/ Confusedly, and which thus must ever fight,/ Unless the Almighty Maker them ordain/ His dark materials to create more worlds, --/ Into this wild Abyss the wary Fiend/ Stood on the brink of Hell and looked a while,/ Pondering his voyage..." Taylor took a sip of coffee. "You're right. That's exactly what I wrote—pregnant pauses, personal confusion, standing on the brink of hell, and a fight that will never be solved. It's the human condition. Really astute of you." Her gaze was far away, and she nodded her head, then focused again on Avery. "I hadn't put that together before. But that quote there pretty much embodies my work."

Avery stared at Taylor, then slid her phone back into her pocket.

"Wild Abyss," Taylor repeated. "Not everyone's mind would jump to Milton."

"Do you have a lot of poetry at the tip of your tongue like that?" Avery asked.

"That? Yes. My mother thought I had a gift with words at an early age. Ever since I was five years old, I had to memorize a poem a week. And then she'd put the name on an index card. On Sundays, she would have me recite the poem I had just learned, plus those she selected at random from the pile so I could keep them fresh. Or as she would explain it, move the poems from my prefrontal lobe through my hippocampus and encode them into the various places in my cortex."

"Ah," Avery said. "Well, that helps me to understand the language you chose."

"Epic, don't you think?" She wiggled her brows.

"That seems like a lot of work to keep that many poems so easily accessible."

Taylor shrugged. "I didn't think it was such a big deal. Once

I've seen words written down, they go right in." She tapped her forehead. "Sort of like a cloth cleaning up a spill."

"Do you remember your very first poem?"

"Sure, it was 'Wynken, Blyken and Nod' by Eugene Field. We worked on it all week. Mom made it into a game." Taylor shrugged. "I thought it was fun."

"Your mom had you do fifty-odd poems a year, and by the time you had been doing this for a decade, you could easily pull five hundred poems forward as you wished?"

"Pretty much. Though at some point in middle school, I refused to do it anymore, so I didn't memorize five hundred poems. By that time, I preferred Lego robots and coding. But I think the poetry made a permanent impression. Codes can be a kind of poetry. Math done right is elegant. When I think about my games, I think about heroic works and try to capture the expanse and humanity of it all."

"Video games and coding is not part of my world. I'm sorry. I don't have any frame of reference. I'm only managing this project because you requested me."

An explosion of voices burst from a room down the hall.

"That's the band that makes the music for my games. Come on, I'll introduce you, and you can watch them play *The Unrest*. Then I'll show you something that I think you'll find very interesting.

———

AVERY DIDN'T THINK she could stand this much longer.

The smell of sweat and testosterone filled the air.

The men were intense as they moved through the scenes. Spurting blood, shoot 'em ups, and anger. The photoreal men that looked like poster boys for the Aryan race were in the streets hunting for stereotypes of those in marginalized communities. If they were discovered, they were chased, there was a brutal fight. The winner, when he emerged from the dust, was rewarded with enthusiastic sex in an alleyway from an overly stylized woman in barely-there clothing.

The grunts that the band members made as they egged on this newest coital celebration was just too uncomfortable for her. Avery simply couldn't believe that epic-poetry-spouting Taylor developed this game.

Avery stood and left the room, stopping at the bathroom where she relieved herself, washed her face, and checked her phone. She had no bars here.

When she exited, Taylor was standing in the hall, leaning against the wall. She waved at Avery to follow her, and they moved outside, walking toward the horse.

"I am tired of two things about men," Taylor said.

Avery was still in a state of shock from what she'd witnessed in the video game. No wonder Curtis had wanted to find a way to stop the next book from release.

"I'm tired of working with them and socializing with them. I prefer the company of horses. This is Goose." She chirruped, and Goose came over to eat a sugar cube that Taylor placed on her open palm.

"Female game designers are harassed unmercifully. I had a good friend that attempted suicide from all of the shit she got blown back on her. She left the field and became a graphic artist. She hates it, but what are you going to do?" Taylor shrugged. "And on the social side of things, you think you're going out with a nice guy, and, as you get to know him, you realized he was really a male chauvinist pig."

"Your experience doesn't seem to be reflected in the game that I just watched," Avery said, trying to choose her words carefully. They needed to work as a team. Avery's job depended on her successfully managing this book. And that meant getting some words on a page.

Taylor ignored Avery's comment. "One night, after yet another horrible date, I thought, you know what I want to design? A game that helps people know who it is they're dealing with."

"Like a psychological test, like a personality test?"

"The idea is that in a game, a designer normally gives the player a vocabulary, and they build a level of fluency. The player learns what the characters can and can't do and what objects will and won't do. They enter the world and learn to navigate the new terrain. But, I asked myself, what if I built a game the other way around? What if the player's terrain was of their own design? What if I build a game that learned the players' vocabulary, and the game learned the individual's fluency using machine learning and artificial intelligence?"

"I…" Avery shook her head. Not her bailiwick. She'd just have to try to figure this out as Taylor spoke. "If I hear you right, you're saying that in this game, if you were a misogynist," she lifted her hand toward the house to indicate the band members playing the game inside, "for example, you would develop female characters within the world that had a certain look, and you could manipulate them. The game learned how the player wanted the women to look and behave."

Taylor grinned. Her brows popped up and fell back into place.

"So in there," Avery focused on the house, "the game had really objectified kinds of bodies. Women were offered up as a reward, or as a barter, or gift."

"Yup, that's how those guys developed their women characters. They're pigs. After you saw them playing that game, would you date any of them?"

"Uhm, no," Avery said.

"Now, watch me play that same game." She pulled out her phone. The landscape was serene. Children were laughing. Women were of various sizes, shapes, and colors. "In my game, I'm rewarded with chocolate and massages. My goal is to pop the bubbles. The repetition with no competition or other level to reach is hypnotic and soothing. When I get anxious, I play ten minutes of this, and I'm much more centered and comfortable."

"Nice!" Avery laughed as she watched. "But these seem like completely separate games. Why don't we hear about this side of your game?"

"Simple. Few people who play *The Unrest* develop their world in this direction. And too, this is low drama. I mean, it's a woman taking a walk, seeing pretty things, popping bubbles, and eating chocolate. Where's the controversy there? The thing that powers attention is angst. Attention gets sales. Those purchases are made by people who enjoy the idea of the drama. Therefore, *The Unrest* is played by people who create the kinds of worlds that you saw being played."

"Why did you call it Unrest if a bubble chocolate world was available?"

"You cannot advance in this game without causing unrest."

"With chocolate?" Avery's brow creased.

"Ah, but I said you could not *advance* in this game without causing unrest."

"And in your bubble-chocolate-kumbaya-world, you have no desire to advance."

"Exactly." She grinned.

"And your novel?" Avery asked.

"My novels don't offer as wide a range of options because

they can't. It's still a novel and still has to hit the tropes of the given genre. But I still developed the plot to reflect a world of the readers' own making to some degree. While the bubbles and chocolate scenario wasn't available, whatever the reader's mind-set, the book will support that world-view. The book is designed so that it is read through whatever lens the reader sees through. I got a lot of pushback when it came out because the book was racist and anti-Semitic. If you are racist or anti-Semitic, you will understand the characters in the book to share your racist point of view. And the reader will come to understand that they live in a world of 'us versus them.' That's where the controversy of my work lies. That's where people's emotions live. It's what feeds their brains. Humans are animals that thrive on conflict."

"Us-them. Huh." Avery was unsettled by these concepts, and she had to admit, perhaps they were a little too philosophic for her to grasp. But there was more to this. Avery could feel that she was dipping her hand into a very deep well. And she'd admit that something about what she was learning today frightened her in a way that went beyond clinging to her job. "I have another question."

"Shoot," Taylor said. "Or don't shoot. You build your world on your own paradigms."

"How does the game know."

Taylor scratched her brow. "Know what?"

"What's going on, how to mirror the player."

"Easy. And I'm going to remind you of your NDA."

"Yes, of course." Avery swept her hand through the air.

"The game is connected to the user's digital platform. All user data collected in the past, present, and future helps to build the framework of the player's world. Once that frame is in place, then the choices that the players make refine that data."

"Wait, what data?"

"From Internet use."

"Like search engine histories from your computer? Your phone?"

"Exactly." Taylor paused. "Social media…" Taylor made an odd kind of bemused tweak of her lips. "Ha! I wonder where you've been and what you've done to have your face make that expression."

Avery wasn't going to admit that she got a wash of fear like when she read *1984* or *The Handmaid's Tale* back in high school. Instead, she said, "I'm an editor. As I edit books, I have to fact check my author's work. If they're doing a romantic suspense, for example, I might look up information about hiding bodies and decomposition, I might look up various religious groups or cultures, even stuff about bombs and terrorists. I think that your game would be pretty confused by my online activity. But data is more than that, isn't it?"

"More than the sites you've been on? Sure. The game has one of those permissions that are found on almost all apps. They can access your contacts lists and learn from those. It can look at your photos, your GPS, read your email and texts. When you function on the Internet, you are an open book. Big Brother is watching you and compiling your data. This game simply uses that information and artificial intelligence in a new way."

"Its job is to provide a mirror for the person playing, so others can see what they're really like."

"And save themselves some heartache."

Avery felt the need to run as far and as fast as she could. She checked her watch. "I have to get back to the office. I'm so glad that I was able to meet you in person. Listen, I need something back from you by Saturday, okay? Seriously, my job is on the line if I don't get something from you, and if I get fired, you'll be working with a guy. There are no other female senior editors to manage your project."

"Okay, I'll get you something."

As they walked back toward the house, the trepidation Avery felt run through her body was almost palpable.

15

MONDAY AFTERNOON
   Washington D.C.

AVERY HAD THOUGHT when she got back to the office and told George she'd had a face to face with Taylor that he'd be beaming. She'd thought when she told him she'd gotten a promise from Taylor, she'd have something on Saturday, the day Avery was coming home from the conference in New York, would be soon enough.

She was wrong.

George had called her—*commanded her*—to come to his office. And as soon as she shut the door, George began to unspool.

That was a half-hour ago.

Now, Avery sat immobile, poised tight as a spring, ready to

eject herself from George's office. Her hands and feet tingled with electricity while her nervous system processed the unfolding scene. George was scaring the bejeezus out of her. She couldn't remember the last time her scalp prickled with fear.

She had never seen George this unhinged before, despite their history.

With unblinking eyes, Avery tracked George as he prowled five steps and then retraced his path.

Back and forth.

Back and forth.

His face fired a brilliant red hue, deepening to a purple across his throat. His arms went from clasped behind his back to fists shaking in the air—the calisthenics of the overwrought.

In George's impassioned speech, his words leapfrogged one another, making them incoherent.

All Avery could do was wait and hope the blaze would cool.

It was taking a long time.

"Reasonably, George, you just handed me the assignment last week, and Knapp was already contractually three months late with the manuscript," Avery said. "I reached out electronically, then I went to physically visit. Knapp is clear about my expectations. I anticipate a good amount of work to be handed to me by the time I get back from New York. But I can't realistically imagine the manuscript being complete before Thanksgiving."

George stared out the window. He didn't turn his head or respond.

"I suggest you push the publishing date forward. This timeline is too short, given our present situation."

"What in the hell is wrong with you?" George balled his hands into fists and swung, stiff-limbed toward her.

Avery shook her head.

"I need that manuscript." Spittle sprayed the air, leaving a strand dangling from his lips.

Avery didn't move. Words failed her.

"Have you any clue what's at stake here?" He batted the phone from his desk. It hit the wall with a deadly thud, leaving a dent behind. "Our heads are on the collective chopping block. You get that, right?"

"I'm not sure I know what you want me to do here." The tone of her voice came as a shock to Avery. She sounded composed and reasonable, extremely professional, and not at all like the chewed-up-and-spat-out-piece-of-garbage feelings poisoning her insides. "I can't make the words come out of Taylor's head, through his fingers, and onto the screen." Since obviously George had no idea that Taylor was a woman, Avery had decided not to disabuse him of his assumptions. Avery felt somehow that Taylor and she both gained some protection from the subterfuge. "There is only so much someone can do from the outside."

George stalked around his desk.

Avery jumped up and circled to the back of her seat, using it as a barrier between them.

He grasped the arms of the chair, put a knee on the seat, leaning within an inch of Avery's nose. "I don't care what you have to do." His voice had dropped to a menacing whisper. "I don't give a shit if you have to move in with him and babysit his every move. He has a contract. He owes us a book." With each staccato word, vehemence ramped up George's volume. "And you will hand me that book." George raised himself to stand. "Or so help me…" He was up on his tiptoes with an arm over his head, pointing a finger like a weapon down at her head. Reflexively, Avery ducked.

"George, I have my mother," she whispered.

"Then take your mother with you as you move in next to Knapp and monitor his every move. There are no more jobs open in publishing. No matter what we've accomplished in our careers, if we fail to deliver the Taylor Knapp book and get fired —and make no mistake, we *will* be fired—our careers are over. *Over.* This will *not* happen. You will hand me the manuscript, and it will be the best manuscript Windsor Shreveport has ever touched. Do I make myself clear?"

"I understand you want me to go babysit Taylor. I'm not in a personal position to pack up and head there for an arbitrary amount of time. Quite frankly, George, I think you've lost your mind. I'm glad to strategize with you. But I will not stand here one more second and have you threaten me. I promise you if this continues, I'm walking out the door, heading to HR, and filing an abuse report." Avery's mind stood back and watched with awe. She couldn't believe she sounded so solid and strong when this whole time, all she had wanted was to curl up in the corner and whimper like a beaten dog. She was so tired.

But look at her; she was doing great.

George stilled.

Avery wondered if she had, over the months and years she had known him, by degrees, ceded power to him to the point that George thought this kind of behavior was acceptable. Somehow, she held herself responsible for his tirade.

"You said you were there today. It can't be far away. You figure it out. I want Knapp's babysitting to start the moment we get back from New York. I want you to monitor his progress. I want reports. I want a manuscript in the next month ready for your content edits. And you go back again tomorrow. You put him in a chair. You tie him there if you have to."

Avery opened her mouth.

George's hand came up like a stop sign. "Not a single word. Get out."

Avery walked from the room with as much poise as she could muster. When she got to her office, she was shaking violently. She yanked her purse from the desk drawer and pulled out her compact to inspect her neck. Splotchy red welts ran all the way down her chest. Avery slung her purse over her shoulder and headed to the pharmacy for an antihistamine, hoping it would calm the hives.

16

AVERY

MONDAY EVENING
Falls Church, Virginia

PARKED IN HER DRIVEWAY, Avery called her sister Fanny. She might as well get this over with out of earshot of her mother. Neither of them was going to be happy with this turn of events. Oh, well.

When the call connected, all Avery could hear was background noise. "Fanny?"

"Hang on. I'll get my mom," one of her nephews huffed rudely.

Avery took another slug of Benadryl, paying no heed to the dosage warning on the label, as she resisted scratching. She wanted to peel her skin off and throw it out the window. Avery blasted the air-conditioning. It offered her a modicum of relief.

"Why are you calling?" Fanny sounded put out.

Avery felt a sudden wave of satisfaction flow through her, knowing she was about to dump her mom-burden squarely onto Fanny's lap. "I'm just giving you a heads up. That the day I get home from New York, I have to turn around and head out of town again. I don't know when I'll be back. It's probably for the rest of the month. Mom will be with you."

"Wait. What? You don't know when you're coming home?" Fanny's voice squeaked out. "But Mom…"

"Is your responsibility." Avery tried hard to keep the glee from her voice. She suddenly felt vengeful for having shouldered the cost and the responsibility for the last two years, almost completely alone. Fanny got the husband, her own home, children, and the freedom to come and go as she pleased, spend her money on what she chose. Those jealous thoughts churned angrily through Avery and seemed to suck all the air from the car. She climbed out, panting, her nails ripping at her blotchy, itchy skin.

Fanny went off like a volcano. But Avery had been through one too many of these tirades today, so she just said, "Bye." And hung up.

She made a second phone call. "Lolly, how would you feel about getting rip-roaring drunk tonight?"

AVERY STOOD at the kitchen counter, wiping tears from her eyes that she blamed on the onion she was cutting.

"Are you going to tell me what happened?" Lola asked.

"In a minute. Let's start with you. How was your day?"

"Fine. The kids were all in school. My mother came over in her full OCD-mood. So I needed to leave the house while she sterilized everything." Lola took the chocolate cake out of its bakery box and positioned it on the cake stand.

"God, you're lucky. I have to pay Sally extra to run the vacuum or dust the furniture."

"Mom would come over and do your house too, but Ginny scares her to death. Mom thinks delusion is contagious."

"But she watches the kids all the time, so you can come be with me."

"Yeah, well, she thinks it's contagious after you're fifty, so I have a few more years."

"What did you do while she cleaned, go shopping?"

"I went to confession." Lola poured Chardonnay into their tulip glasses.

Avery stopped mid-chop and held Lola's gaze.

Lola's eyes lit up with laughter. She winked at Avery. "Bless me, Father Pat, for I have sinned." She chuckled.

Avery slid the onions onto a plate and moved to the sink to rinse the cutting board. "Lola, I tell you, you're going to be the death of that man. What did you tell him this time? You couldn't very well say you like it best when your husband ties you up and uses the whip. Andre is out of town, and Father knows it."

"You're right." Lola swirled the wine in her glass, then took a long swig. "So I took my copy of *Fifty Shades of Grey* with me and read some of the passages."

"Lolly, you didn't. Stop." Avery lifted her wine, breathed in the crisp, clean scent before taking a sip.

"I was paraphrasing this bit about vibrating eggs and butt plugs, and Father Pat stops me and says, 'Wait, my dear, I didn't catch that last part. What exactly is 'rimming'?"

Avery sputtered as the wine went up her nose. She gasped and doubled over, laughing. "Lolly, you didn't." She crouched down to the floor. "Oh God, you're going to make me pee. I know you're just pulling my leg, but I can actually visualize you doing that."

Lola looked at her friend with a grin and wiggled her brows. "All right, girlfriend. Now that I've made you laugh, you owe me an explanation for this drunken girls'-night-in." All levity wiped from her face. "I'm thinking it must be pretty bad."

Avery stood and drew in a deep breath before telling Lola as briefly as possible about her trip to see Taylor and the following encounter with George. "And that was my day."

Lola just listened, standing at the sink, peeling shrimp, letting Avery vent.

Even after Avery stopped talking, Lola silently worked through the pile of shrimp, scraped the shells into the trash, and slid the board into the sink. "You're going to end up in the hospital." She raised her brow and tucked her chin. "Or maybe the nut house from all this hoo-hah. What crawled up George's ass? He's a pig, and I never liked you dating him, but he was never abusive."

Avery pursed her lips.

"Okay, he's not clear about his sexual boundaries when it comes to you. But you have to admit this tirade is pretty far out there."

"The founding father, Joseph Shreveport himself, called and chewed George a new one. Everyone's losing their minds over this darned book. And it all comes down on me finding a way to get a manuscript from Taylor."

Lola processed that then said, "Okay, on the bright side, having to babysit Taylor will give you a break from your mom for a while. You'll get some sleep. Maybe after this is done, Fanny and Curtis will understand what you go through day in and day out, and they might help a little more."

Avery nodded; the hives sparked on her neck.

Lola moved the shrimp to the frying pan. "Okay. Let's change the subject. Let's talk about this guy, Rowan Kennedy, FBI. He wants to Skype with you?" She paused and laughed. "Oh, that's a very pretty shade of pink you're blushing."

"That's not a blush. That's hives." Avery reached out and grabbed a tomato to cut for the salad. "But about Skyping with Rowan, I'm on the fence. I actually don't think I'm going to do that."

Lola turned to Avery. "Why?"

"Well, his picture looks exactly like Gerard Butler."

"And that would stop you?"

"I asked him if it was his real picture."

"And?"

"He said yes."

Lola moved the pasta pot to the stove and lit the burner. "And?"

"Look at my life, Lola, I'm not that lucky. Aside from you, I only have certifiably crazy people filling my freak-show of an existence."

Turning to push her hip into the counter, Lola pursed her lips. "What are the chances he is who he says he is?"

"If you look at my life-line, not that good. He could be some grossly over-weight, Hawaiian-shirt-wearing, balding-with-a-comb-over, retiree in upstate New York."

"Or he could live in Australia," Lola offered, "trolling the Internet for vulnerable women, enticing them into sordid cybersex relationships that they videotape and then sell on amateur porn sites."

Avery took another swig from her wine glass. "He could be a woman."

"He could be ninety-two, toothless, with a colostomy bag, needing someone to push his wheelchair."

"*Ew!*" Avery scrunched her nose.

"Let's find out!" Lola switched off the flames and dashed to the dining room. "See if he's there."

Avery shot Lola a dubious look, but it was missed on Lola, who had already made her way to the dining room, sat down, and was pulling up Avery's Twitter account as Avery followed behind.

A_VERY – Rowan, are you around?

"WHY AM I DOING THIS, LOLLY?"

"We need some proof about who he really is. I'm laying money on the nursing-home guy needing someone to smuggle cigarettes into him, so he can suck the smoke in through his trach-tube."

Suddenly, Avery felt green. Maybe she didn't want to find out the truth. Maybe living in her little fantasy world was just fine, thank you very much. Why rock the boat when she was clinging to the side of it for dear life? She played that thought through her head again. It seemed true.

Shit.

Avery leaned heavily on Lola as her cornerstone, the person who supported the structure of her existence. If something, somehow, pulled Lola away from her, everything in her world would collapse.

But Rowan. Rowan was hope. Hope for what? She wondered, and then the trickle of comprehension came to her, and all of the air left her lungs. She hoped Rowan would pull her out of the water onto that metaphorical boat, and they could sail into the sunset. That is, after all, how romance books worked.

And that was the world her brain inhabited most hours of the day.

Lola sat quietly as the cogs whirred in her friend's mind, giving her the space and time to work through whatever it was she'd latched on to.

Avery clawed at the welts on her chest. This fantasy about Rowan was not healthy, and she knew it. She was not the heroine of a romance novel plot arc. This was real-life, and real-life just didn't work that way.

LeGit: Hey there.

Lola pulled the computer away and typed.

A_Very: Let's do a real-time selfie exchange. Include a clock. Ready? Set? Go!
  LeGit: Okay.

Avery pulled the computer back to see what Lola had typed. Her eyes grew wide. Why the heck had she told Lola that she'd proposed this to Rowan? "You didn't even say 'Hi, how was your day?'!" Avery called back to Lola as she dashed up to her room, pulled on a turtle neck to hide the hives, brushed her hair manically, swiped on some bright red lipstick, and ran back down the stairs.

Lola was obviously amused at Avery's panic. She got up from the chair in front of the computer and let Avery slip into place.

Reaching out, Lola unceremoniously tugged Avery's shirt smooth over her bust and arranged her hair. Once Lola approved, Avery, clicked the computer camera button.

"Um—not a good look for you, Avery," Lola said, leaning over the laptop. "You need to take it again. Think something less panicky. Puppies. Think puppies."

Seven shots later, with Lola's teasing, Avery's face had let go of the manic energy and had softened into a gentle smile that crinkled the corners of her eyes. She posted it up on Twitter direct messages before she lost the nerve.

A_Very – Tada!

Rowan had already posted his picture. He was at a table near a dark window. Behind him, she could see a tidy kitchen. And there was Rowan smiling at her from a poorly lit room, wearing a running tank that exposed his gym-hardened shoulders. A clock radio sat behind him; it read 8:12. Avery glanced at her watch; it was now 8:18.

This was his actual picture.

"Holy Mother Mary." Lola grabbed the corners of the laptop and turned it toward her. "He is freaking gorgeous. Look at those shoulders. Look at that smile."

Avery pulled the screen back in her direction and drank in Rowan's image. His tousled brown hair was short enough to be clean-cut and long enough to be unruly. It hung a little damp. Avery looked out the window, seeing that it was still raining. Maybe he'd just dashed into his house. Maybe he'd just gotten out of the shower. Avery's imagination flashed to a picture of him naked, except for the soap bubbles, standing under a showerhead, and her body responded, making her feel warm and tingly.

Manicured stubble made Rowan look fashionably edgy. But it was his eyes that transfixed Avery. They reminded her of the ocean—bluish-green with flecks of white and thoughtfully deep. Intelligence. She read a hint of mirth. The crooked smile he offered up had her smiling back. Avery felt the compulsion to lean forward and kiss his lips. She might have done it if Lola wasn't sitting next to her, mouth hanging open.

Avery flipped out of the full-screen shot back to Twitter. Rowan had not replied.

Lola sat back, watching her friend. "Well, isn't *this* a revelation?"

Her hands clasped in her lap, Avery waited. Still nothing from Rowan. Shit. Avery looked at her empty wine glass but knew that drinking another would take her from a buzz to sloppy. "We're Twitter pals. That's it," Avery said. But she knew that wasn't true.

Rowan had become something pretty darned significant in her life.

LeGit: Avery, I'm stunned. I thought you were probably very pretty, but in my mind, it was more like Bonnie Hunt-wholesomeness.

A_Very: You don't think I look wholesome? Bonnie Hunt is who my sister looks like.

LeGit: Uhm wholesome? No.

Lola grabbed the keyboard. A_Very: What then?

. . .

"LOLA, stop it. He's going to think I'm fishing for compliments."

LEGIT: You are breath-taking. I had no idea. I don't want to type in messages.

LeGit: Would you like to have that Skype conversation we've talked about?

DUMBFOUNDED. It was the only word to describe Avery at that moment.

Lola reached over and shook Avery's shoulder. "He wants to Skype. How awesome is that?"

Avery turned a blank face to Lola.

"Your mom's fully sedated. She won't bother you."

Avery said nothing.

"Look, I'll hide out of the picture. If it gets too bad, you signal out of his view, and I'll call you. You can say you have to go."

Avery nodded and put her hands on the keys. "I've been drinking a lot of wine and Benadryl. Am I slurring my words?"

"Not that you'd notice," Lola encouraged her.

"If I start to make a fool of myself, you'll intervene. You'll pretend to come in, and you'll stop me, right?"

The corner of Lola's mouth came up. "Why are you stressing about this?"

"I like him as a Twitter-friend. I like how easy we are together. Skype..." Avery held up her hands and spread her fingers. "It could go well, or it could be a disaster, or it could be kind of flat. No matter what it is, our relationship will be different. We'll never be able to go back to what we had earlier in the evening. It's changed. What if Skyping is awful, and then our friendship collapses?"

"Holy Mary, you have it worse than I thought," Lola said.

"I don't," Avery countered. "He's a *Twitter*-friend."

"Prove it," Lola challenged.

17

Rowan

Monday Night
Alexandria, Virginia

Rowan sent Avery a smile. He hoped Avery sensed the warmth that fuelled that smile. When the Skype image filled his screen, she'd seemed pretty nervous. As they spoke, Rowan watched for body language tells and was glad to see that she was growing more comfortable.

Avery wouldn't be nervous if she didn't care what he thought, Rowan told himself. That was good. He wasn't the only one that had feelings sparking. He wiped damp palms down his pants. He, in fact, cared quite a lot about what Avery thought of him, and he was working hard at not working too hard and being obnoxious as he tried to make a good impression.

It was first date kind of nervousness, and that's why he was smiling. She felt something between them too.

And he liked that.

He also liked that they'd already moved their conversation to the point where they were checking on each other's relationship statuses. It felt good to say he was single. Not that Rowan wanted to stay single, but he wasn't entangled, free to date. Free to get to know Avery.

He'd listened as Avery explained that it had been a while since she'd been in a relationship. Her mother's health made things problematic. Rowen understood that she was laying it out for him from the get-go. If he wanted a relationship with her, it would be complicated.

Well, same for him. His job being his job and all.

She was now telling him her breakup story from the last guy she'd dated.

"Anyway, I was standing there in a bog with mud up to my hips and a leech sucking at my neck when I decided that was enough. I'm not sure if or how they ever dragged his truck out of there."

"Big truck?" Rowan asked.

Her brow flicked with amusement. "*Massive* tailpipe."

"Compensating?"

She held up a pinkie, and he winced. "I don't know if this will win me any points," he said, "but I drive a Volt."

She did it again. She sent laughing eyes over to the side of the room.

"You keep looking off to the left. I'm guessing that we have a chaperone."

"We do. My best friend Lola is here with me."

When Avery said that, no one moved into the camera view, so Rowan called out, "Hey, Lola. I've heard about you over the years. You're the one who torments poor Father Pat?"

"Oh, he loves it. Father Pat is the priest who baptized both Avery and me, performed our first communions. He's family. You know, I've heard a lot about you, too, over the years."

That meant Avery was talking about him. And it also meant that what Avery was saying hadn't thrown up any best-friend to the rescue vibes. At least he wasn't getting that from Lola's tone. He'd lay bets Lola was hoping that things went well here. That she was an ally. "Thank you for helping Avery to feel safe by being here."

"Absolutely," the voice called, warm and jovial.

Rowan would also bet good money that these friends had hit the bottle before Avery got on Twitter.

"You know what would really make Avery feel safe?" Lola asked.

Avery shot a wide-eyed, shut-up look her friend's way.

"If you showed her your FBI ID badge. That way, she knows you're not just a pretty face making up shit."

Rowan blushed. Pretty face, huh? "My ID badge? OK sure. It's upstairs. Give me a second."

After he stood and left the computer screen, he paused for a moment out of the camera's view. He could hear Avery say, "Lola, how could you?"

"He understands. Here I've given him the chance to prove he's a good guy. You won't have any worries that he's not who he says. No one wants to think they're being catfished."

Rowan wanted to call out, "I'm not catfishing you!" but he jogged up the stairs instead.

Lola was the dragon at the gate that he'd have to go through to have any chance with Avery. If Lola had a hoop that needed jumping, Rowan wanted to jump through it.

After all, Lola knew Avery, knew her history and what she'd need to feel safe. Lola setting up an obstacle course for him to navigate was actually really helpful. It meant that he could prove himself in all the relevant ways he needed to prove himself to be a worthy man for Avery. And with that thought, Rowan realized that was *exactly* what he wanted to be.

First proof required? That he was who he said he was and not some hound dog making up credentials to impress the lady while really working at a box store and living in his mom's basement.

He sat back in his seat and opened the badge wallet, holding it up to the camera lens. The top was his picture—albeit taken a few years before, with a clean-shaven chin and a tighter haircut —and his signature. There was a certificate and expiration date, and there was his badge.

"Can you read it okay?" he asked.

"Yes, thank you." Avery sounded mortified by her friend's antics.

He grinned as he closed the wallet and laid it on the table.

"That was nice of you," Lola called out.

"I'm glad that we could make Avery feel safer."

"All right," Lola said. "Now that I know she's in the hands of an upstanding citizen, I'm going to scoot on. I need to make lunches and get them in the fridge for the morning. Avery, I'm going to let myself out."

"But you didn't eat dinner."

"I'll eat a sandwich at home. Love you."

Avery's focus was on her friend. "Love you, too. Bye."

Rowan had passed the dragon test, and he was elated.

Alone, Avery and Rowan sat in silence, looking at each other. It was surprising how comfortable this silence was.

Avery tipped her head to the side. "Hey Mr. FBI-man, are you assessing me? Have you been reading my face instead of listening to my words?"

"It becomes an innate skill set. I can't say that I turned that off for this conversation."

"It seems an unfair advantage." She offered up the sexiest little pout Rowan thought he'd ever seen. His body stirred in response.

"Can you use your FBI skills in other ways, too? For example, can you find out things about me on the computer? Did you research me?" Then her face flamed red. "Wow. That sounded egotistical. Like you are interested enough in me that you'd want to do something like that." Her eyes wouldn't land on his.

Rowan found her discomfiture charming. He was used to working with hard people, asking hard questions. By his standards, what she'd just asked was a data point that needed to be addressed. Her sensibilities were softer. She *felt* things and hadn't cornered off her emotions. In his career, Rowan had found emotions inconvenient to getting a job done. The same for most of his friends and colleagues. Even for Jodie and her job as a business executive.

Rowan was rather stunned by Avery's blush. Happily so.

"Looking things up for personal reasons is against Bureau policy." Rowan put his hand to his chest. "It's also against my personal policy."

Her face changed. Some thought. Some vulnerability. A fear. This time he absolutely did *not* like what he saw. "Tell me," he said, his voice sounded too gruff and demanding, but he saw in her look that she felt endangered. And whatever it was that caused that look, Rowan wanted to go after it. He cleared his throat. "Excuse me," he said and cleared his throat again. Taking a swig of water to show her that what she'd just heard was not him turning all "alpha" on her, as Jodie would call it. He noticed that as he thought of Jodie right now, it had nothing to do with their past intimate relationship but more about her finger-wagging and lessons learned.

So he took another swig of water before he said, "Just now, that look on your face, would you share the thoughts behind it? You suddenly seem upset."

"This conversation took me back to…" She paused to think. "I had an uncomfortable meeting this morning. I was listening to someone talk about data gathering and artificial intelligence." She looked up to her right, remembering. When she looked back, she had rolled her lips in. "I'm having an existential crisis. This might not be a good day to talk to me."

"I think it's an excellent day to talk to you," Rowan countered. "I've been trained in crisis management." He chuckled to take some of the sharp energy out of the air. He wished he was there with her. His protective instincts revved.

"Okay." She knotted her hands and rested her chin on them.

"What's going on?"

"Sometimes, I feel overwhelmed by technology. Things are changing so fast. It makes me anxious. Just this morning, I was thinking about novels I had read in high school—*1984* and the *Handmaid's Tale*. They frightened me when I read them. Now, I feel like they're coming to fruition. Artificial intelligence and the Internet and all of this connectivity are helping us move toward things that can be positive, like our meeting and being able to see each other." She offered up a little smile. "But I'm becoming aware of how things can turn dystopian very quickly." She paused, but Rowan said nothing. "I like things to be quiet and neat. For people to care about each other and to be kind. I would prefer to wear rose-colored glasses as I look at the world. My job, after all, is about hearts and flowers and the power of love. But it feels to me, especially today, that the world is getting dirtier, nastier, more vicious. And very soon, most assuredly, it's going to get worse."

Rowan sat quietly, nodding to show he was focused on her words.

"There are plenty of people like me out there, who are pawns getting pushed around the board as if we have no say and no volition of our own." She took a deep breath and swallowed, then tucked her chin down. "Circumstances…"

Rowan waited. Interrogation 101: If someone was talking, shut the hell up and listen. Avery hadn't offered up any clarifying information, and he had no clue what they were talking about. But there were worrisome themes. And because of where she worked, Rowan's mind leaped to Taylor Knapp. "Avery, can I ask where this is stemming from? Is this something that happened with work?

"I would say that the chaos in my head is a reflection of my externals—unlike the author that I'm working with who wants the externals to reflect what's in everyone's head."

Rowan's brow creased. "I'm not following."

"And I can't talk about it. I want to, believe me. I think this is so wrong. I think people should know what's happening. But…" Again, with the shake of her head, the little sigh, the angst tightening the skin around her eyes.

"So this has something to do with this specific author?" He was taking mental notes. He'd have to parse through this after they were done talking. Rowan recognized he had Knapp on his mind, but this sure sounded like Avery had a connection, and she didn't like it. Or, she could be talking about something else—her mother, for example. But no, that couldn't be right. Why wouldn't she be able to talk about that? He decided to throw a thought at the wall and see if it stuck. "If you know of a crime, we can protect you. There are whistle-blower statutes."

"Whistle-blower?" She stilled her fingers to her lips. "What do those statutes cover?"

"On a basic level, if you know of something illegal or unethical, and you tell the authorities, then the laws prevent you from being fired or punished."

"Oh. Well, I guess if everyone *agrees* to what's happening, then it's not unethical or illegal." She caught his eye. She smiled. "You're trying to read my expressions. You're in FBI mode, aren't you?"

He was indeed one hundred percent in FBI mode. Avery knew something about something. And she wasn't going to share.

What needed to happen now was for Rowan to stop asking for this to be a one-sided conversation. He needed to put some skin in the game. Build mutual trust. Expose something private. And that wasn't something Rowan liked to do. "As to the face reading, that's not an FBI thing, though sure, they fine-tuned things for me. But I grew up with an alcoholic father. The mean kind. I learned to read faces as a survival skill from an early age."

Her face went slack with sorrow. Her eyes glazed with tears.

Rowan swallowed past the lump in his throat, trying to force down the unexpected and unfamiliar emotions that Avery conjured with her sympathy. She had enough emotions she was juggling, so he wanted to wipe those tears away. "And I'm grateful that I have that skill, even if I'm not grateful for the means by which I learned. It serves me well as I serve my country."

She nodded.

"I'm not sure what you're grappling with, but here it is—there are bad people out there who want to do whatever they want to do, whenever they want to do it. We can't have that. My job is to stop them."

"I thought you shook hands for a living and made connections. You told me you were safe." Accusatory. Worried.

It was interesting to be on the other end of someone's genuine concern. He both wanted to rebuff it and revel in it. "No matter what your job, there's risk. Though probably less risk for someone in your job than someone in mine." He paused. Did he want to march over this bridge? "Windsor Shreveport." He stopped to weigh his words since he had apparently already made a decision. If Avery knew something about Taylor Knapp, Avery could be in a very dangerous situation, and he needed to know if she was okay. "The name of your publishing house came up in a meeting I was in. Our mutual friend Lisa was there."

"LisaWrites from Twitter?"

"Yeah, she's a special agent for cyber. I've known her from back in my Army days."

"Small world. We had coffee once, she and I. I like her."

"Lisa's a good friend to have. She's a big gamer. Big science fiction reader. She said that the *Uprising* video game is about to release and that the book will soon follow. Do you know anything about that project?" He held his breath.

There was a flash. Something moved across her face. He'd seen that look before. It was the same look that was on Clara's face when they were trapped in the garage, and she had the compromising photos in her purse.

Avery was in some kind of danger.

"Avery, you know I work between the United States and Europe. But if you ever felt you needed help, you could tell me. If you felt unsafe. If you knew something about some things and needed a sounding board…"

Her shoulders shifted as she rubbed her hands up and down her thighs, a self-comforting gesture. Her eyes scanned left, then right, then left. She wasn't focusing on him. He'd hit on something.

He wondered…but before that thought formed, he reminded himself she was a romance editor, and no matter his concerns, would never be in danger of getting rolled up in the pro-Russian cesspool that surrounded Taylor Knapp.

Would she?

He sensed Avery pulling herself back from him. The warm bubble that had surrounded them during the Skype session burst.

The chill set in.

He'd blown it.

And he wasn't willing to let that happen. He dove straight in, head first. "Avery, I'd like to take you out for dinner. Unfortunately, I'm leaving out of town tomorrow afternoon." He stopped and smiled. He let that smile come from his eyes, not just his mouth, so she'd know it was genuine. "You're in Falls Church. I live near you, in Arlington. Maybe I could meet you for coffee in the morning?

"I'm sorry." She glanced down at her lap and back up, a sign of disappointment. "I have an early morning meeting with one of my authors." She pursed her lips, a signal that she didn't like this author. "Wednesday, I'm heading out of town, too. There's a convention up in New York."

"New York City?"

She cocked her head. "Yes."

"I'm not trying to stalk you." Rowan chuckled, feeling that fortune was on his side in this. "But I happen to have meetings up there this week. I'll be at the FBI Headquarters on Broadway, which is walking distance to Little Italy. Do you like Italian food? I don't want to push, but New York is as good a place to meet as Washington. I'd really like to meet you in person, Avery."

18

Rowan

<small>Monday night</small>
Alexandria, Virginia

<small>The screen went dark.</small>

He couldn't believe it.

He just couldn't believe his luck. She'd said yes.

Whew. He blew out a breath. Haha! He sat there and grinned at the blank screen.

Slapping his hands on his thighs, he jumped up and ran up the stairs—barely registering the residual pain from the Brussel's attack—to pull on his running shoes.

Avery had said a lot of things that he wanted to mull over on his run. Her saying yes to their meeting being a really important one. But other things jangled his nerves. The beginning stuff was the usual laundry list. Are you available for my affections? Are you receptive to my affections? He'd gotten past the castle gates of the best friend. And both he and Avery understood that as thirty-somethings, they both had lives that they were leading, careers, personal obligations.

Check. Check, and check. Housekeeping done.

Then there was that weird heaviness that Avery allowed to surface.

Rowan pulled his shoelaces tight and wrapped them into a bow that he triple tied—a habit from his high school cross-country running days.

Something other than her mother and her normal life had thrown Avery into an existential crisis. He needed to review those words. And he needed to figure out if he *really* thought they might be tied to Taylor Knapp.

He scooted down the stairs, pulling his lanyard—with his key and ID—over his head, tucking it inside his sweatshirt. He moved out the front door, stopping long enough to check that it was locked, then glanced up and down the road.

The night was dark. Clouds hung low, wrapping blanket-like around the roofs and treetops. The street lamps glow reflected off the slick surface of the pavement, still wet from the earlier rain.

Besides a random barking dog, the neighborhood was still and silent. Most people were already in bed, clocks set to ring their early morning alarms.

Rowan decided he'd run down past the Methodist church to the park trail that led around the back, past the graveyard, then around the pond, finishing the circuit by rounding up the back-side of the neighborhood. It was almost exactly a six-mile path and would take him a little less than an hour.

He jogged in place, then used the porch rail to do his stretches. Rowan's body was stiff from the beating. The run would probably help him shake that off. Rowan tugged a beanie in place to keep his head and ears warm and set off at a practiced pace.

By the time he left the neighborhood, Rowan's limbs were warm, and his stride was comfortable. He didn't try to push any thought-agendas. He let his mind churn past the hurly-burly thoughts, the chaotic thoughts, the pick-me pick-me thoughts. He watched them pop up, and he watched them fade away.

The meditation of the road.

This was Rowan's way of dealing with stress.

Getting centered.

Or, as his team leader used to say, getting his head on straight.

Right now, the thing he needed to get straight, the place that wobbled for him in the conversation with Avery, was this convergence of his job and his personal life.

He liked those things in two separate pockets.

He had no proof that there was a convergence other than the gnawing in his gut.

The reason for Avery's existential crisis was still tucked away. She didn't want to show it to him yet. Or ever. It might just be one of those days when things felt bleak, and she'd be okay tomorrow after a good night's sleep. He held that thought through a few strides before he rejected it. Something pretty serious had happened. And it had happened today—this morning.

"There are plenty of people like me out there," Avery had said, "who are pawns getting pushed around the board as if we have no say and no volition of our own. Circumstances."

A pawn getting pushed on the board because of circumstances...

God, she was beautiful.

And smart.

And tender.

Those lips. Rowan had been talking about Little Italy and having dinner, but what he'd been focused on were her lips, how they'd taste. How they'd feel pressed against his.

Rowan's body stirred at the thought. "Down, boy," Rowan said as he left the pavement and the ambient street lights and moved to the dirt path.

It would take his eyes a couple of minutes to adjust, but Rowan had excellent night vision. It had served him well in his career.

An owl hooted from the distant trees.

The fog hung in streamers off the limbs.

Eerie.

Rowan was aiming for the massive oak. Just before he got there, the path would dog leg to the left and circle behind the church's graveyard. The sound of his breath and the pounding of his footsteps filled Rowan's ears, and then he thought he heard something else.

The moist wind carried a hum of conversation toward him.

He slowed his gait.

Maybe it was some local teens out late, trying to get space and autonomy from their parents.

Then, there was a flash of a red beam that tapped the ground just ahead of his feet, and Rowan knew that wasn't a group of teens. That was a laser sight, seeking a target.

Or, it was someone with a laser cat toy out messing around.

Low probability on that one.

After being shoved in the trunk of a car and driven around Brussels, Rowan was in no mood to find out who had a laser out and if it was attached to a rifle. He shifted his body to a low combat silhouette. Bent knees, balanced on the balls of his feet, he was ready to dive off the X.

Rowan tracked the laser as it searched along the air, looking for something solid to illuminate as it passed over the grave-stones. When the light swung his way, Rowan threw himself onto the wet grass underneath the beam.

"Nothing?" The voice carried his way. "Here, let me see that. I could swear I heard his footsteps. He can't have passed here yet."

Not a cat toy. They were looking for someone without sending out a flashlight beam. Were they looking for him specifi-cally, or was this a random drug deal he'd walked into?

The red light swept over the graves again.

Rowan was glad he'd decided he didn't need his high visi-bility running gear tonight since he'd mostly be off the street. Still, he needed cover. And he needed to see who these guys were. Count heads.

Or not. Maybe just get the heck out of here and get the PD involved in sorting this out. He didn't have his badge on him. Or a gun.

On his elbows, head low, Rowan lizard crawled toward the woods, due south of the voices.

"Dan said Kennedy left his house fifteen minutes ago. He should be here by now."

"Don't use real names. Say Delta Five."

Alrighty then. Definitely not random. They were lying in wait for him. At least they weren't speaking Bulgarian. Though having Sergei ID him, gather intel on him, and place a crew on site so quickly seemed a stretch.

If Sergei had ID'd him, he'd never be able to go home again.

Talk about an existential crisis, Avery.

They weren't modulating their voices as low as they had a moment ago. The red light was off. That spoke to the level of their training. If they were the real deal, they would be silent. Of course, you didn't need a whole lot of training when you had numbers on your side.

That they were waiting to ambush him outside of his house might be telling.

A hit squad would come in the middle of the night like a draft through the cracks of the door. They'd pull a plastic bag over his head until he was done struggling, then melt his body in an acid bath, letting the residue go down the drain. Then they'd bleach everything clean and slip out before the birds began their morning songs.

Of course, that they wanted to find Rowan off his property—away from his security system and home-court advantage—probably meant they wanted him alive. That they picked his jog when he'd be physically tired and probably without a weapon made sense.

Rowan was reticent to let them take him alive.

Sometimes dead was just better.

He had a knife. He always had a knife.

He had a phone, but it would light up and give him away if he tried to call for help. At least he'd put it on airplane mode, no risk of it suddenly buzzing and giving his position away.

They thought they had the jump on him. But the surprise belonged to him. That might be his best asset.

Rowan pressed silently forward, slow and steady.

Hiding was his best advantage.

Big, fat, friendly trees were his best advantage.

He'd almost dragged himself to the tree line.

"He left his property fifteen minutes ago." A normal tone of voice came over someone's radio. They needed to turn their volume down, stick an earbud in their ear.

"Fifteen minutes?" someone whispered. "He should be here."

Someone had been watching him and timing him. The mile

and a half from house to the park that abutted the church property did indeed take him less than thirteen minutes. That was his every-day jog time no matter where he did his daily run. If he was in a race, he could shave that down from seven miles an hour to a pace of a little better than nine. If there was something chasing his ass, then he might even be able to shave a little more off that.

But adrenaline can do that for you.

Radio static was followed by, "Delta Three. Where is he? He must not have his phone. He's not showing up."

"Delta Two. Even so, you should have him by now."

"Delta Three. I'm *telling* you he hasn't come through."

"Yes, he has. I watched him leave the road. I'm Delta Two."

Okay, their radio skills sucked.

That was information.

Rowan had to acknowledge that his own skills also sucked. He was obviously too predictable. They knew he'd jog, and they knew where. They had placed a crew out here. Of course, they could have crews set in each direction coming out of his house. And that felt right to Rowan. He had to plan as if these weren't the only guys lying in wait. These were just the lucky guys who would get action from being posted in the right direction. Maybe build up some points with whoever had an ax to grind. They thought he didn't have his phone. Later, he'd have to figure out what that could mean. He'd have to figure out a lot of things.

"Delta Eight. I'm positioned at the corner of Billings and Turnbull. He's not to me." That must be the guy at the next trailhead, where Rowan would hit pavement again on the other side of the pond. If it had been Rowan planning this operation, that pond was where he'd lay the trap. Fewer opportunities for escape.

They were tactically weak. That was more information. And so was number eight.

Delta Eight?

Eight was a lot. Rowan didn't want to take on eight. Or one. He just wanted to finish his jog, pack for New York, go to bed, and with any luck, have an excellent dream about Avery.

"Delta One. You're sweeping?"

"Delta Three. I'm sweeping!"

Rowan watched the light move across the gravestones left to right, right to the left. He wanted to catch one of them and make them talk. He needed to understand just when and why he'd been targeted. If he could figure out how to do that and not get dead or rolled up in the process, that would be good.

"Delta One. I'm coming up the back. I'll see if he didn't have a heart attack and keel over between here and there."

Rowan drew himself up along a thick trunk opposite the guys with poor radio discipline. He focused on the shape of this man striding up the trail. That was the tango he wanted to take down. The head of their spear. Delta One. If he could trap *that* guy, Rowan could get answers.

This was the time for Rowan to get his body under control, slow his breathing and his heartbeat, and make a plan.

The Delta One guy moved forward, and a red laser beam danced across his black pants. "It's me, fool. We're at the thirty-minute mark. We've missed our opportunity for tonight."

"We *got* to get him before morning!"

19

ROWAN

MONDAY NIGHT
Alexandria Virginia

SNAKING his way through the trees, Rowan moved toward the road. Blade in hand, he wanted a look at their vehicles. Get a license plate.

A dog was going ballistic in the house up ahead.

The group of hostiles—male, military-age—formed a single unit of dark shadows as they made their way to the road. It wasn't exactly a wedge formation. Some of those guys were spooked and bunching up tight on the next guy's heels—ten of them.

Weekend warriors strapped with weapons.

With less than a teaspoonful of skills of the men in Brussels.

Had those been Sergei Prokhorov's men, Rowan would be back in a car trunk.

The hostiles gathered at the edge of the road, whispering into their comms.

Under the parking lot light at the church, Rowan could just make out three cars parked nose out over by the shed. When the tail lights popped on, and they powered down the road, Rowan would take a video. He couldn't get it from this angle, though.

Rowan bent in two and sprinted toward the church, then stood at the wall, peering around the corner.

Rowan closed his blade and slid the knife clasp onto his waistband, ready to pull and flick open if needed. He reached into his pocket for his phone and got ready to get the pictures.

A surprised intake of breath spun Rowan around. A form hovered just there behind him, mouth open.

Adrenaline dumps can make you freeze in place like a statue.

Freeze sucked. Rowan knew that personally. That moment when the brain stutters…

Sandwiched between the hostile's hands was the unmistakable shadow of a gun tricked out with a suppressor and laser.

New guy. So now they were up to eleven head. He was probably jogging in from his position farther down the trail.

As Rowan processed that information, his body was acting from training. He dropped his phone to clear his hands as he grabbed the top of the gun, gripping the slide so the guy couldn't shoot, and pushed it away from where it was aimed at Rowan's chest. Rowan slammed his knee into the guy's groin to steal the air that was going to form the call for help.

Just as Rowan swung a follow-up fist into the guy's jaw, the held back scream of discovery slid past the pain. "Here!"

It was loud, and it carried. So did the *oof* that sounded as the guy's head cracked into the corner of the brick building. The tango crumpled to the ground.

Rowan picked up his phone and quickly snapped the guy's picture, front, and profile.

Now Rowan had a knife and a gun as he moved behind the church and into the graveyard to find cover. Rowan didn't want to use a gun, especially this gun, a .40 caliber from the heft of it. Depending on the bullet in the chamber, it could tear through the walls of a house. It could speed through the woods. Any bullet that wasn't precisely on target meant that his neighbors were endangered.

Unlike the silent shots that made spy thrillers on TV so exciting, there wasn't actually something called a silencer. The most you could do was suppress the volume of the gunfire. The noise would still drag everyone awake. People would be scrambling to pull their own weapons from their bedside tables and out of their safes. If this was Afghanistan, the sound of gunfire could turn into a battle for survival, and the chances of him coming out of this shitstorm whole and healthy would be pretty much nil.

Good thing I'm home safe and sound in my neighborhood in Arlington, Rowan thought wryly.

In a low crouch, Rowan slunk between the tallest gravestones.

A *pew* sounded, and at the same time, a chunk of marble exploded upward near Rowan's shoulder.

Rowan dove to the ground.

He hoped the sound of that shot and the barking dog got a good Samaritan to pick up their phone. A few sirens would clear this place out nice and fast.

The clouds moved off the moon, and from where Rowan lay, he saw a human shape, not twenty feet, and three gravestones away.

To hell with it, Rowan thought as he framed the shadow in the glow-in-the-dark sights. Rowan wasn't going to shoot anyone in the back, though. "Hey buddy, you looking for me?"

"He's here!" the guy yelled, then came the *pew* as Rowan acquired the target and put a double-tap in the guy's chest.

Rowan squat ran toward the guy to make sure he'd taken this tango out of the game. He reached down and touched his chest. Heavy plates. Did they think he'd be jogging with an AK?

The tango was probably just knocked out from the impact, not killed. He just might get his opportunity to have his question and answer session after all.

Rowan fumbled his phone out and snapped the pictures before he snatched up the guy's gun. Problem was, Rowan had nowhere to put it. The elastic on his jogging pants wasn't going to hold the weight. After another quick pat-down for weapons, Rowan grabbed the guy's radio, using his mouth to twist the knob, turning the volume off.

Rowan scanned left then right, deciding his path.

Beyond, lights flashed on in the neighborhood. *Stay inside your damned houses. Get your kids down.* He sent the mental command through the wind. He wouldn't head that way. He needed to draw any gunfire away from the houses.

Rowan crouched behind the tombstone as a door on the church popped open. A man's form stood silhouetted by the interior light. He was about Rowan's height. About Rowan's coloring. And was wearing clothes that, in a panicked mind, could be jogging clothes.

Rowan rose to sprint for the door when he saw figures rounding the corner of the church. *Shit.* "Get in! Lock the door! Get down!" Rowan yelled. "Call 911!"

So he gave up his position.

A gun in each hand, his knife in his waistband, Rowan took

off, zig-zagging toward the tree line. If they were to shoot at him, those bullets put kids at risk. Where he'd go to keep everyone safe, he hadn't a clue.

He stopped at the dumpster, took a knee, drew a bead on the front guy chasing him, and pulled the trigger in one fluid motion.

Rowan didn't aim center mass. Since one of the tangos had body armor, they probably all had body armor. Rowan wanted spurting blood and screaming pain. *That* would spook a novice crew.

Pew. Pew.

And then the scream.

And the jostling confusion.

And the sirens. Lots of sirens.

Panic.

Garbled commands.

Grunts.

Rowan had a pretty good idea of how this would unfold. It sounded like it was taking a normal trajectory, but that didn't mean that as soon as he got his shot off that Rowan didn't haul ass off his X and make his way deeper into the tree line and safety to wait for the police.

He'd approach the authorities with an introductory phone call to their commander first.

He had knocked a guy out and shot two other men.

He was the aggressor with weapons in his possession.

And Rowan had no desire to get locked up in the pokey tonight.

20

TUESDAY MORNING
Warrenton, Virginia

AVERY PUT her to-go cup of coffee into her cup holder as she motored toward Taylor's house. She was listening to George over the Bluetooth. It was really just too darn early for George to be this angry. Windsor and Shreveport, the publishing house owners, must be really riding him hard. Her sympathy meter was set on low.

His snarls rose from the speakerphone as Avery clicked on her turn signal and rounded past the barn with its peeling white paint and sagging doors. She took a right at the fork.

"Since I'm almost to the house now," she said with an even tone, "I'm not sure, outside of teleporting, how you think I can get there any faster. Please remember, I'm the editor, not the writer. I can't make the manuscript show up out of thin air. You're confusing me with Hermione Granger."

"Listen to me—"

"Before you say anything else, this is about the location I lose cell service. If I lose you, it's because I'm—" and then she pressed end.

It wasn't far from the truth. Cell service out here was nil. That was probably a feature, not a bug for Taylor.

Avery rested her phone on her lap. She was thinking about Rowan. Something about him was unsettling her. She'd gone to bed right after their talk and woken up an hour later in a panic, terrified for his safety. She couldn't figure out why.

He pressed between the leaves of her thoughts like a bookmark.

Here was her place.

At the next red light, she sent Rowan a text. He'd given her his number last night, and she realized she hadn't given her number in return. In her mind, it was a good enough excuse to reach out.

Avery - **Good morning. This is Avery. Now you have my number.**

Rowan - **Thank you. I was just thinking about you. Want to Skype tonight? Nine?**

Avery - **Okay. Hey, an odd question, I know, but is everything okay?**

A CAR behind her tooted its horn, and Avery realized the light was green.

At the church, she pulled into the parking lot to read his response.

. . .

ROWAN – **Things have been a little tense since we talked. Some people were fighting in my neighborhood last night. Not the norm here. Police were making their presence known, so I didn't get much sleep. Then I got a call from my uncle. My dad is in the hospital out in Sacramento. Something kidney related. Meeting now. Talk to you tonight.** :)

IT WAS good that they were going to talk again. For many reasons. But mainly because she might have more information about this project, and Avery could ask better questions, even if she couldn't tell Rowan anything from her end.

Ever since the Skype conversation last night, Avery had been mulling the concept of whistleblower. Rowan must have picked up something in her words or her inflection since he'd even brought it up and asked if she was okay. If an author had given Avery this present scenario in a manuscript, it wouldn't make it through content editing. Avery would be leaving comments like. "I need more. This doesn't rise to the level of threat we need here."

But Avery *felt* threatened.

Like the ground was shifting under her feet.

Like she didn't understand the rules, and invisible hands held the remote.

Like she was living in an alternative universe, and the idea of being in control of even one's own thoughts and emotions was an illusion.

Maybe this was how things worked now.

Or, maybe ethics and laws simply hadn't been developed to counter this yet.

What was "this"?

Avery couldn't even define it.

She had other things to do besides babysit Taylor Knapp. Other projects on her plate. But here she was, pulling onto the long dirt drive toward Taylor's farmhouse because…Avery wasn't exactly sure about the why. She wanted to say it was her civic duty, but that was a bizarre thought.

The "because" is that my name is going to be associated with this thing. And as much as I disagree with my brother-in-law on a daily basis, Curtis was right about this; Taylor's project was morally wrong. Even if Taylor herself thought she was some kind of white knight exposing the evil underbelly of the nation.

I guess there are worse things than being starving and homeless on the street with your bat shit crazy mother, Avery thought as she popped her car door open.

She made her way up the front walk. The lights in the house were off. Avery checked her watch. It was the same time as when she arrived yesterday. But who knew? Maybe Taylor had been burning the midnight oil typing out her story.

When she reached the door, Avery mashed her index finger onto the illuminated button to ring the bell.

After a long moment, the door opened. Taylor, dressed in over-sized pajama bottoms and a ratty T-shirt, pressed her lips together and rolled her eyes, stepping out of the way for Avery to enter. "I don't have anything for you."

"Nothing? You did nothing yesterday after I left? Not a single word?" Avery stood momentarily blinded after moving from the bright morning sun into the dark hallway.

"I'm still waiting." Taylor brushed past her. "Come on."

Dutifully, Avery followed toward the back of the house. "I don't understand."

"Which is fine. Look, you said Saturday, right?" They were in the kitchen, and Taylor moved to the coffee maker. Avery had probably pulled the woman out of bed.

"You said you needed my outline by Saturday, so get off my ass. I'll have it by then." She reached up to grab the bag of coffee grounds. "You'll have something by then."

"Perhaps you'd like a sounding board." Avery climbed onto the same stool she'd sat on just yesterday morning at this same time. "We can talk, and I can type notes."

"Want a cup of coffee? You've got bags under your eyes."

"Yeah, well, work is stressful right now."

"Because of me?"

"Because of the industry changes. Yes to the coffee, thank you." How was she going to get Taylor to give her information to possibly talk to Rowan about when she didn't even know what information she was looking for? "You slid in just before things started to get really bad. Good for you. How exactly did you land on Windsor Shreveport? Who's your agent?"

"Oh, I don't have one of those." Taylor reached for two mugs.

Avery frowned. "We don't take unsolicited manuscripts. We wouldn't consider you without representation."

Taylor turned, mugs in hand. "I know Inge Prokhorov. She's the wife of Patrick Windsor."

"Our founding partner."

"Yeah, so she gave Patrick my MS, and Windsor Shreveport offered me the contract." She took the carafe to the sink to get water.

"Nice!" *Lame.* "How is it that you ended up with this pen name? Did Ms. Prokhorov suggest it?"

"My agent suggested it."

"I thought you just said you didn't have an agent."

"I *had* an agent. I just didn't have an agent who was effective. I got this gig on my own. It probably had nothing to do with his capabilities. I give him kudos for even signing a female. He was trying to pitch my ideas for games to the industry where there's a huge bias against women."

They sat in silence until the coffee pot dinged.

Taylor filled their mugs and brought them to the counter. She pushed the tray with sweeteners toward Avery and pulled a carton of half-and-half from the fridge, and held it out.

"Thanks," Avery said, accepting it. "This agent you had, did he pitch anything under the Taylor Knapp pen name that caught on?"

"Different pen name, Tyler Krill, and yes. I had a contract and developed a game, but just before release, the project got pulled. It got some pretty big public outcry."

"That stopped production?" Okay, that was hopeful. Maybe the same thing would happen with this project. "What was the genre of game?"

"It was an active shooter game. There are a ton out there. This one was called *School Shooter*." She doctored her coffee without catching Avery's eye.

"You were training people how to go in and shoot up schools?"

She shrugged. "It's topical. It's relevant. I hoped that it would advance the conversation about what was acceptable about guns in society. I hoped it would show people what it was like to be inside a situation like that—something beyond what you get on the news. I wanted to make it visceral and frightening." Her eyebrows popped. "We have that with war games. You can play and understand, to some extent, the dynamics of battles. Why not show people what the kids are going through in school? Sometimes you have to stir the pot so you can see what you're dealing with at the bottom."

The white knight exposing the shadowed underbelly of the dragon again.

Taylor took a sip of her coffee. "And it can go both ways if you train people to shoot up a school, you also teach people how to get out. Like the game "Oregon Trail" teaches you to boil your water and only drink coffee, or you get cholera and die. You either learn from your mistakes, or there are consequences. I'm allowing people to see their mistaken thought processes by playing a game. It's a way to suppress real-world tragedies. People have the capacity to learn and grow."

"Or they can become entrenched and possibly even radicalized," Avery countered.

"Someone who is open to being radicalized can be radicalized. Like I said before, that's just stirring the pot and getting the chunks off the bottom so we can see them."

Avery wanted to keep pushing down that trail, but she was afraid to push too hard and end their conversation. There were so many things she wanted to know. A talented CIA heroine would circle. She should circle. It worked in books.

"It's interesting what you said about women in your industry. I'm amazed that any woman would want to swim against a riptide like that."

Taylor took another sip. "There are oh so many reasons a woman like me would try. I could ask you the same. How is it that you're the only female senior editor at Windsor Shreveport? Inge doesn't like that very much. I'm sure that's why she told me to request you."

"I thought you said Fast Forward told you to use me."

"I met Inge through Fast Forward. Fast Forward introduced me to Inge when they suggested adding the book and music. So if you're being precise—as I know editors like to be—Inge said to request you, and Fast Forward agreed you'd be best."

"Ms. Prokhorov gave you my name. That's interesting. You make really good coffee, by the way."

"Not at all bitter?" Taylor smirked from behind the rim of her mug.

"Funny." Avery set her cup on the saucer. "You were telling me about the connection—how it was that you got your first contract. Connectivity is so fascinating, especially with the International production you have going on. Did you get to travel to Europe? Is that where you met Ms. Prokhorov? She's from Bulgaria, I think. I would so love to travel there. I read once about their roses. The best in the world. And they have a rose celebration that's on my bucket list."

"I've never traveled."

"How did you get to work with Fast Forward?"

She pressed her lips tight and took in a deep breath. "A friend."

"Someone we have in common?" Avery smiled. "What's your friend's name?"

"I can't tell you that."

Avery canted her head. "NDA?"

"No. But since you have an NDA, I guess I can tell you this much. She's—she's a friend of mine who's here past her visa. If anyone found out my friend is here, she would be deported. Going home would be very dangerous for her."

"Wow." Avery leaned forward. "I'm so sorry that she's found herself in this dilemma. Why is she in danger at home? Couldn't she apply for asylum? Maybe I can get a lawyer's name…"

"I don't know about asylum. I'm guessing that she's too worried that it will be denied, and then she'll have no control over the outcome or next step. She's from Russia—well, she's Russian by birth. She grew up in the United States from the time she was a baby up until high school. Her dad's job here was done. But when she moved to Russia, she didn't like it at all. She's basically American, after all. She came back for University, hoping to figure out a way to stay here or maybe move to Canada. One night she got a call from her mom that her dad was picked up by the police. That was a few years ago when she and I were living together. No one's seen him since. It's been really hard on her. My friend believes that if she were to go home, she might be used as a tool."

"Wait, your friend is from Russia? I thought Inge was Bulgarian."

"Yeah, I don't know how Ka—my friend and Inge met."

Avery looked at her lap. "Poor thing." She sighed, then focused on Taylor again. "I can't even imagine being in her position. I can certainly understand the choices she's making. But if anyone had the wherewithal to help, it would be Inge Prokhorov. This must be the best decision under difficult circumstances. Is your friend a game designer too?"

"No. She's working under the table now, picking up random jobs. She seems to be doing okay. I help her as much as I can. When I was visiting her, and I told her my idea for *The Unrest*, she told me that for a grand, she would put together the research notes for me. She said she'd need a couple of months. I didn't really have a thousand dollars laying around at the time. But I borrowed it from my aunt. And so my friend made rent and ate. And it was money well spent."

"How did she know how to do that? Put together the research notes, I mean."

"She majored in anthropology and minored in women's studies at the University of Michigan."

"Ah." Avery got up and walked toward the coffee pot. "Do you mind if I help myself to another cup of coffee?"

"That's cool. I'll take some too. My brain still isn't fully awake."

"She gave you the file, and it was helpful." Avery hoped to get the rest of that story.

"A few months later, I got a file. She's the one who thought that this should be a three-pronged approach—music, game, novel. I came up with the plot for my book based on her notes. While I would expect those to be good—she's really quite brilliant, a straight-A student—I was really elated by the ideas that she had for the game."

Avery poured the coffee into Taylor's mug. "But she's not a game designer."

"We were roommates at the university. From my talking through different projects with her."

Avery set the pot back on the plate quietly and moved back to her stool while Taylor talked.

"I guess she was paying closer attention than I thought she was. To be honest, I thought I was boring the stuffing out of her talking about coding and such. But her notes were fantastic. She had even developed gaming rings." Taylor was becoming more animated now that she was talking about something she enjoyed. She was using more facial expressions and miming the information with her hands. "In each ring, the player learns a little more. In the first ring, for example, you might learn what capabilities your character has—run, jump, etcetera. In the next, they might learn to shoot. Then they learn to breach walls, then they learn to seek out a prize. See? It's all about learning. Each circle, there's a learning component that includes success and failure. Failure is often where the character learns the most and can use those lessons to advance quickly. For *The Unrest,* the player is learning the game, and more importantly, the game is learning from the player."

"You knew from the get-go that you would harvest data from the players to help the machine learn them better? Or quicker?"

"What I had imagined was much more simplistic than what I was able to achieve with my team at Fast Forward. Ka—uhm, my friend's boyfriend is working on his artificial intelligence Ph.D., and she included code in the notes to show me how the game could tap into the mass of data that was already out there and available for microtargeting."

"Very cool. Where's he working on his Ph.D.? I hear MIT has an excellent program and Stanford."

"No." She shook her head. "He's not in the United States. He's working out of Germany. I ended up using his connections to get the contract with Fast Forward. They do production out of Berlin."

"Your university roommate's boyfriend. And it was your roommate who also knew Inge Prokhorov. Your friend is really well connected for someone living under the radar."

21

ROWAN

TUESDAY MORNING
Washington D.C.

"AND THEY AMBUSHED you while you were running by a church?" Frost's brows were pulled tight. "That seems sacrilegious."

"I've written out the communications that I overheard, as close as I could recall. The hostiles were talking about my running pace. Here's the thing, I've been gone for the last month. They had to know I was home. They also had to know my running habits to know my speed."

"You're FBI. You shouldn't have public-facing habits."

"Understood. However, there are only two directions I can go out of my house to jog. Granted, I don't jog from my house if I'm able to go elsewhere. But I run every day that I can. If it's late, and I'm home, I run in one of two possible directions. Someone with a pair of cheap binoculars… Anyway, Monday, as you recall, it rained, so it was late when I got my run in. They could probably figure that out by checking a weather app for when the rain would stop."

"All right. How would they know you were home, and how would they know your routes?"

"I'm pretty sure it's my running app. It's the only app I have on my phone. I use the same one I had in Afghanistan when we got in trouble for the searchable heat map that lit up our base. Someone who hacked my account could see my running history, locations, times, all of it."

"You were hacked? Did you give the phone over to tech?"

Rowan lifted his new phone. "Brand new. I don't know if I was hacked. It seems improbable, but forensics should be able to tell me. I'm waiting for the report. Also, when I dropped the first two guys, I took their pictures. I didn't mention the photos to the PD. But they're also trying to run down those IDs."

She leaned back in her captain's chair. "Any chance in your mind that this is connected to Sergei Prokhorov?

A tick started under his right eye. "Too soon. Too sloppy."

She nodded.

"These guys might have had military concepts, but they didn't have the body mechanics smoothed out. In my mind, I could see them playing first-person shooter scenarios, not real-life training. One guy froze when I turned on him."

"Amateur then," she said.

"My read. The second contact, the guy leveled his gun, had his laser on my heart, but didn't pull the trigger. I dropped him with two shots to the plate."

"And one guy had two penetrating shots to the leg, according to the report I got in my inbox," said. "But like a terrorist unit, they scooped up their wounded. No one was left behind?"

"Nope."

"The guns you confiscated were registered?"

"Nope."

"You have a good alarm system on your house?"

"I do. But I have no idea what their goals were. When no one shot at me, I thought they might want to take me hostage."

"One interpretation. Another might be that they wanted to kill you, and when push came to shove, they couldn't follow through." The springs on her chair complained as Frost leaned forward and picked up her pen, scribbling on a pad resting beside her water bottle. "I'll reach out for a copy of PD forensics. Maybe we can get a fingerprint ID."

"They're expecting the call. I talked to the detective this morning. They found blood and brass. One of the gravestones took a hit. So far, the hostiles haven't taken their injured to a local hospital."

"No one wants to die of a festering gunshot wound. At least the leg guy's going to show up, sooner or later." She lifted her brow for emphasis. "Next on my list, did you talk to Jodie about her tweet and tell her to lay off?"

"Jodie's not answering her phone."

She nodded. "Okay. I may send someone around to have a little chat with her off the record."

Rowan nodded.

"We're going to have you pack up and head back out. We have an op spinning up that needs your expertise. And I know it's soon, but we need to twist Sergei Prokhorov's arm again. We've received some sensitive information from our friend John Green in the CIA field station. You're the one that Sergei will talk to."

"It's going to be harder this time."

"It's going to be impossible," she conceded.

"What's the plan? When do you want me to go? I can ditch New York." God, he hoped he didn't need to ditch New York and miss his opportunity to meet Avery.

"Sergei switched out his electronics devices, but the spyware is doing its job. He's planning to go to Paris to an art event with his wife. We're getting you tickets and a date."

"Clara?"

A slow smile slid across Frost's face. "I read her field notes. That's quite a get-to-know-you tactic she has. She spoke highly of your skillsets." Frost tipped her head, laughter in her eyes. "And even mentioned that we might want to consider using you as a raven."

"Sex for intel? Yeah, I'm not that guy."

A knock sounded at the door.

"Come in," Frost called. "To answer your question about Clara, no, not this time."

"When do I leave?" He looked up as Special Agent Steve Finley and Special Agent in Charge Damian Prescott filed into the conference room.

"We're waiting for some pieces to fall in place," she said. "Gentlemen." She waved them toward the empty seats. "Perfect timing. I was about to get to my next topic."

"Taylor Knapp," Rowan said.

"Taylor Knapp." Frost nodded.

"Taylor Knapp," the task force leader, Prescott, repeated as more of the team streamed in the door. They moved to the back of the room, finding their seats around the conference table.

Frost's gaze went from face to face. We're waiting for one more before we start our meeting.

"Did you tell Rowan he doesn't get to play with Clara on this mission?" Prescott asked Frost.

"She's quite an interesting character," Frost said, taking her seat at the head of the table.

Prescott plunked his briefcase onto the polished wood next to her, then swung his head toward Rowan. "What did you think of working with her, Clara Edwards?"

"Fearless, which has its good points, and its bad points," Rowan said.

Finley chuckled. "Yeah, we heard about the knife incident. The local news said the guy was mugged, and when he handed over his wallet, he was stabbed. You'll be happy to know the surgeons were able to reattach his dick, and he'll be getting physical therapy to make sure it's working all right."

"Speaking of doctors, I assumed you went through medical?" Prescott squinted at Rowan's face. The bruises were healing. They'd progressed to the bile-yellow and green end of the damage spectrum. "Everything checks out?"

"I'm cleared for fieldwork." Rowan took a chair to his left. "Ice packs and time."

"Sergei Prokhorov shouldn't have had that many people on his protection team." Prescott settled into the leather captain's chair. "Seven, you said?"

Rowan nodded. "In the garage, yes. Inside the museum, I only counted two. When Clara and I made contact with Sergei, Iniquus was in the room. I recognized Panther Force's Honey Honig and Thorn Iverson doing close protection for some American big wigs. At one point, things started to get interesting with Sergei's men. Thorn and Honey staged an intercept, preventing Sergei's security from interfering with the cell phone download. I'm wondering if Panther Force didn't pick up on what Sergei did after Clara and I took off."

"I have a meeting at Iniquus later today. I'll see if those two are available for a debrief." Prescott made notes on a pad: Honey and Thorn, he underlined their names.

"I've partnered with Honey and his colleagues before." Special Agent Brandon Carmichael opened his laptop. "It was a positive. Iniquus does good work. They stay in their lane," he said as he booted up, "and don't take public credit or interact with the media. It helps when the silver-backed apes aren't thumping their chests and maybe letting go of some details that shouldn't be out there."

"It's interesting that they should come up in this conversation," Prescott said. "We're finalizing a contract. In the case of trying to run down the Prokhorov connection to the communities that are elevating hate crimes, Iniquus would have more latitude with what and how they gather information. They can go in directions that the FBI itself can't go." He leaned back in his chair. "Right now, we're spinning wheels, trying to figure out the synergy of the Taylor Knapp bourgeoning empire, the increase in public hate speech, and the sheer numbers that are joining into dangerous cliques and behaviors. We can see it." He rapped his knuckles on the table. "We just don't understand it. It's sucking manpower that we need focused on solving crimes that have already been committed. And so, to that end, I have a meeting set up. A strategy session with Iniquus command." He pointed at Rowan. "You and Finley will be leading that collaboration. All public-facing events outside of arrests—if we can make solid cases—will be performed by them, so if there's blowback, it's on them and not us. And more importantly, not on the government."

Rowan nodded.

Carmichael looked over at Finley. "You've got an eye-twitch over Iniquus."

"Good group," Finley said, his voice tight. "They pulled us out of the Zoric cesspool."

Special Agent Chet Talbott shot a glance at Prescott. "But we didn't contract that, did we?"

"No. A civilian, Lacey Stewart, hired them," Finley said. "They did their 'we're special forces, we got this' thing."

"They had it, though, right?" Talbott asked.

Rowan didn't think Talbott was being a jerk. He wasn't from their office and probably just didn't understand that Lacey Stewart had been Finley's asset, and Finley had almost gotten her killed. Oh, and he'd fallen in love with her, hoping to marry her after the case was wrapped up. But Lacey fell in love with the Iniquus guy who saved her from the terrorist's bullet. Finley was nursing a broken heart while he was holding his new position as a desk jockey instead of being out in the field where he wanted to be. All in all, it sucked for Finley. But the arrests of almost an entire branch of the Zoric family was huge for the FBI. And Iniquus took zero credit.

Talbott's brow creased. "Or was that a bluff?"

"Oh, they had it all right," Carmichael said. "Solved the crime, gave us the evidence we needed for conviction, found the bomb, and the icing on the cake was their operative got the girl." He slapped Finley on the shoulder, gave him a squeeze and a locker room shake.

Finley didn't rise to the bait, but Rowan could see he'd clamped his teeth down tight, making the muscles in his jaw bulge.

Sensitive topic.

"Speaking of losing the girl." Finley's voice was sincere. "I hear you and Jodie called it quits. Sorry about that, man."

News traveled fast…

"It was a long time coming. I'm comfortable with this turn of events." Rowan wasn't going to bring up the effects on his Twitter accounts here. That work wasn't part of this task force.

"Yeah?" Talbott asked. "Have someone else in the wings?"

Avery flashed through his mind. There was something about her that was warm and calming. Something about her made him feel centered when the world was whirling around him. "Time will tell," he said, now that he was free to take their friendship to a new level.

"Hey guys, before Peterson gets here and the meeting gets going," Carmichael spun his computer around, "I wanted to show you this."

There was an image of a children's board game. The writing on the box was in the Cyrillic alphabet.

"What does it say?" Talbott asked.

"Our Guys in Salisbury," Rowan said.

Talbot leaned forward to see better. "Are those guys in hazmat suits at the end of the game?"

"Yup," Carmichael responded. "The children start playing at the image of the Salisbury Cathedral where the real-life Russian agents poisoned their defector. They play the game and get to the end, which apparently requires hazmat suits for survival."

"This is…what is this?" Prescott pulled the laptop closer. "Is it really a game they're selling in Russia? An Internet meme?"

"Real deal," Carmichael said.

"That's messed up." Rowan stretched his legs out under the table to ease the ache in his knee caps.

"I brought this in," Carmichael said, "because I thought it might be interesting in light of this new tack they're taking in political gamesmanship. As Kennedy's been reporting, The Bot Farmer of Bulgaria, Sergei Prokhorov, is planting new seeds of discord, hoping to harvest US civil unrest to ingratiate himself with his Russian father-in-law."

"Yeah, well, if Sergei doesn't become very cooperative, very fast," Rowan said, "his father-in-law will see some intimate images that'll put Sergei's health at risk. He might end up with a Salisbury Cathedral incident of his own."

"Got the goods, huh?" Carmichael stretched out his fist for a tap. "Kudos, man."

22

ROWAN

WASHINGTON DC
Tuesday

"SORRY ABOUT THAT," Peterson said as he rushed into the room. "My meeting just let out."

"Okay, gentlemen, enough gab." Frost sat tall in her chair, taking control of the room. "We're here to talk about domestic hate speech, Russian-connected bots, and the fomentation of violence, especially as it pertains to Taylor Knapp." She looked at Finley, who was over at the fridge, grabbing a bottle of water. "Finley?"

Finley worked domestic terror.

He turned. "We're watching insular groups light up about a new video game, *The Uprising,* that's going to be released next month. We're looking for communications where the participants are taking their chatter from constitutionally protected speech into conspiracy to commit acts of terror. It's big. And getting bigger." Finley rounded on a chair and sat down. "It's like watching the ocean suck the water off the beaches, so it has enough volume and capacity to crash onto the ground with a destructive power unimaginable."

"That was rather poetic of you, Finley," Frost said. "Data shows that when *The Unrest* launched, there was an uptick in hate crimes by thirteen percent nationwide. In the last two years, data says that hate crimes are up thirty percent after an eight-year period of decline. People have ended up in hospitals, and they've ended up dead. All from Knapp's work? Obviously not. How much impact did Knapp's work have?" She tipped her head left then right as if weighing the idea. "The jury's still out. It's certainly made for an enabling environment."

"If civil unrest is the guy's goal, surely he learned a hell of a lot in the time between projects," Prescott said. "AI has improved. FBI domestic terror funding for domestic terror training and intervention programs has been defunded by our present administration. We're working on fumes. And to switch metaphors, the domestic terror hot spots are bursting into flame, and there are just too many of them. We simply don't have the firefighters or the equipment to put them out."

Rowan rubbed his thumb into his chin. "Do you all think Knapp's books and games are the brainchild of a single person?"

"To be honest, no." Frost reached for her bottle of water. "Hey everyone, Finley's already found his way over there, but if any of you need water, help yourselves. They're in the fridge." She lifted her bottle toward the bar fridge beside the credenza.

Rowan stood. "I think it's a writing team of social scientists, propagandists, skilled as hell. I could write a dissertation on the first novel. Look at this." He moved to the whiteboard and grabbed up a marker, and started scribbling.

He tapped the board where he'd written: **Christian pro-Israel v. Anti-Semitism.** "Call this I/S"

Black rights to safety/equality v. white supremacy. "B/W"

Common sense gun laws v. 2nd Amendment, guns without restrictions "G/R, Okay?"

The others nodded.

"Eight basic permutations. I get that I'm simplifying this." He lifted his brow and tucked his chin as he checked in, making sure they were all on the same page. "But just as a quick look at the lenses someone could wear as they read this novel, we have…" His pen raced down the board drawing combinations like a Mendel genetics experiment. "There are eight main views. Pro-Israel, anti-racist, gun enthusiasts is one permutation. See?" Then he tapped another combination. "Anti-Semitic, racist, gun restriction." He rotated his pen in the air. "Eight basic points of view. With this information, I read through the book eight more times. Each time I read it in the character, or mindset, if you will, of one of these permutations." He tapped the board. "Each of the eight times I read the book, my position was supported. If I was an anti-Semitic, racist, pro-gun guy, my understanding of how the world was ordered was more deeply entrenched. But it was equally validated if I was a pro-Israel, racist, gun-restriction guy." He snapped the top on the marker. "And that right there is either *mad genius* IQ, or it's a dedicated team of social scientists who engineered this platform as a weapon against the United States."

"I'm laying money on the team approach," Prescott said.

"And you think this author—team, what have you—is

directly connected to Sergei Prokhorov and his propaganda farms?" Frost asked.

"I do." Rowan moved back to the chair. "I've been tracing the bot activity for a while now. Bulgaria and the Philippines."

"The best way to get the dots connected is through the Windsor Shreveport contract and work backward to Sergei Prokhorov." Frost took in a deep breath and sighed out. "Signals intelligence tells me that they have no information on this."

"How is that possible, unless—" Finley started.

"We know that the game is played as a collaboration, and communications devices are embedded within. That means they're untraceable through our normal signals intelligence," Frost said.

"These groups are getting higher-tech every day." Rowan came back to his seat. "Special Agent Lisa Griffin was in here last week showing me that there was a game that had a trash can in one of the scenes. You could get your character to pick things out of the trash can, balled up paper, for example. Some communications devices can be laying there in plain sight, and no one would know. Griffin happened to figure it out on a lark. In the game, she pulled a ball of paper out of the trash, had her animated character smooth it out, and there was a topo of where our troops were hunkered down in Syria. The unit got moved stat."

"And things like that make Taylor Knapp, and the groups that form through playing his games, into ghosts." Frost planted flat hands on the tabletop. "We're trying to find informants inside Windsor Shreveport."

"They have million-dollar guns held to their heads," Finley said. "It's going to be hard to find someone who will talk."

Rowan doodled on his pad. "What happens if we had someone inside? What could we do to protect them?"

Finley leaned forward, excited. "We'd bring them in, talk to them in a safe room. Let them know there's no way anyone would find out. Do you know someone?"

Rowan looked at Frost; their gaze held. "I do," he said slowly. "We're dating. I'm not turning her into my asset. Certainly not in something as messy and dangerous as this." Rowan looked pointedly at Finley. Finley's girlfriend almost died when he was using her to stop a crime ring. The post-Soviet Union crime ring families don't mess around. When someone gets in their way, that someone gets removed from the picture, sometimes viciously so.

Of course, if Avery cooperated, she'd be considered an asset. Which gave her some legal cover and had the potential to help her if things took a criminal turn.

There was a lot to weigh.

"That's fast, man," Prescott said. "You jumped right back on the horse? Jodie doxxed you just a few days ago when you broke up."

"Okay, dating is a stretch," Rowan said. "We have plans for a first date. I've known her for a few years. I'm not going down the road of making someone I care about into my asset," he repeated. He wished he hadn't brought this up, but if things unfolded, and he hadn't mentioned it, life could get tricky. For one thing, if he hadn't been forthright, he might be cut out of the need-to-know loop, and that meant he wouldn't have information that would help him keep Avery safe. Should she need to be kept safe.

He looked around at the faces. To them, national security superseded the chance at a relationship. Or the safety of a single individual. "Look, Lisa knows this person, as well. Let me talk to Special Agent Griffin and get a plan together to feel this individual out. Just see if she doesn't know the general area where the truffles are buried, and we can bring in a pig to sniff them out."

"And that metaphor, gentlemen, is what happens when you spend too much time on the other side of the Atlantic." Carmichael chuckled.

Frost maintained her focus on Rowan. "Do you think this individual knows something that would be helpful?"

"We were talking about work last night," Rowan said. "She brought up morality and was asking about whistleblower laws. But we all know what happens to whistleblowers. They are the best of the best, the ones with the straight moral code, and they're the ones that get smashed. Every time." He sent his gaze around the room to make sure everyone was paying attention when he said this, "I don't want that to happen to this woman. She has a lot on the line. Not just her, but she has a dependent mother."

"We don't know what she might be blowing that whistle about, right? Do you think she might know specifics about Taylor Knapp?" Prescott pressed. "Maybe she's on that project?"

"She's not in that genre of writing, so I'm just not sure. Maybe she heard industry rumor or could tell us who's on the project team, help us focus on the right targets."

"All right," Frost said. "I need you to make that happen, Kennedy. Team, if this route produces intel, we need to develop a next step, so we can act swiftly. Time is of the essence. As you all know… this bomb is ticking."

"Say we can get to Taylor Knapp himself—or the person who is posing as an author with this pen name—how do you think we engage this person to get him talking without him knowing he's talking?" Prescott asked.

Finley looked up at the ceiling. "What if we made talking to us something elite?"

Frost focused over on him. "Like what? What are you thinking?"

"What if the FBI is developing their own Red Cell?"

23

AVERY

TUESDAY NIGHT
Falls Church, Virginia

"WHATEVER THEY PUT in those shots is a pure miracle," Lola said from the hallway.

"Mom's asleep?"

"Yup. But since it's early, I just gave her the dosage that's supposed to help her calm down. You'll need to give her the regular dose later so she can sleep tonight."

"Okay, thank you." Avery was perched on her toilet. Lola had already given her a pedicure and manicure, and now there was a pot of hot wax warming in the sink. Avery was wondering if a little bit of one of her mother's shots wouldn't help this next step in Lola's process of "making Avery presentable."

As if reading Avery's mind, Lola said, "Look. If things are

going well with your mom, you might leave a little bit of medication in the syringe, you know? I'll buy them off you. There are some nights at my house when I want to drug the entire congress of baboons who've taken up residence there."

"Flying from your chandeliers and eating all the bananas in one sitting?" Avery smiled.

"You've been to my house. You know what they're like. Anyway, think about it. It could mean some extra income."

Lola stirred the wax with a wooden stick, testing the consistency. "Ready?" she asked. "Lift your arm. I'll start there."

Lola slicked the melted sugar wax onto Avery's underarm, pressed a cotton strip, counted 3,2,1, then ripped it off in one quick movement.

Avery gasped at the pain then turned her head to look at her bleeding underarm. "Ouch! Holy hell, Lolly, that hurt. How in the world did I let you talk me into this?"

"You must be in love." Lola batted her eyelashes. "There is no other reason for a woman to jerk hundreds of hairs out of her skin other than to ensnare a man's heart. Hold up your other arm."

Avery reluctantly lifted her hand in the air while Lola smeared on the hot goo. "You do this all the time, Lolly, and you've been married forever."

"Right, well, ensnared is one thing. Keeping them entangled is another."

"Entangled in what?"

"My bedsheets." Lola winked. "Deep breath in."

"Ah ah ah ah. God. Are we done?"

"Moustache and eyebrows next."

"I don't have a mustache!"

"Oh yeah? What do you call that?" Lola held up a hand mirror.

"I call it natural. And I call it blonde so no one can see."

"New Yorkers don't go for hippies. And people *can* see it. Roll your lips in."

Avery clutched the rim of the toilet lid where she sat being torture-groomed. She wouldn't have tolerated any of this if she weren't so stressed out about what Rowan would think when he saw her in person. "Oh, thank goodness. Done," Avery said as Lola tossed a cloth strip into the overflowing trash bin.

"Not so fast, young lady. I haven't finished. Legs and bikini line. Not a Brazilian, mind you—that takes a professional. I'm just cleaning things up a bit."

"Why would you need to? Bikini line? Seriously, Lolly, there's no need for that. No one's going to see down there. I swear."

"Hmmm. Maybe you'll get lucky." Lola held up a finger. "Not George, mind you. Lean back and put your foot on the tub. I went to the store and bought you some pretty little under-things as a birthday gift, and we don't want you looking like an unweeded garden."

"I'm going to be gone for a few days. What kind of girl do you think I am?"

"I think you're the kind of girl who hasn't gotten any game in almost a year now. You know," she said, then stopped as she blew on the stick to cool the wax, "you have to exercise things down there, blood flow and muscle tone. If you don't hit the sheets regularly, your bladder drops down in your pelvis, and you start to pee yourself. Then you have to wear a diaper for the rest of your life. Use it or lose it, is what the article said."

"That's… Okay, that's a solid reason to have sex, I'd say. Protecting the function of my lady parts and all."

"So you were asking what kind of girl I thought you were. Besides a girl who's about to need Depends because she doesn't do the deed enough to keep things toned and happy, I also think you're the kind of girl who's been disappointed by her ex's sad lack of skill." She reached over, skimmed the goop onto Avery's calf, and rubbed the cloth into place. "And the kind of girl who's been chatting up a gorgeous guy with a panty-dropping smile." She waggled her eyebrows and ripped.

Avery screamed, her hand clamped tightly over her mouth.

Lola ignored the tears that sprang to Avery's eyes and dipped the stick back in the pot. "And you said he plays guitar." She slathered on another thin layer of wax. "So he must have dexterity in those fingers." She smiled conspiratorially at Avery as she rubbed the next strip then ripped.

"*Agh!*"

"I think you're the kind of girl who deserves a good time."

Avery thought she was the kind of girl who deserved a brandy.

Wrapped in her terry cloth robe, Avery stood in the driveway, hugging Lola tightly. "You're the best friend any girl could ever want." She laid a loud, smacking kiss on Lola's cheek.

Lola hugged Avery hard. "Stop. You're going to make me all weepy. Now that you're headed out of town, what am I going to do without you and your mom to break up my day?" Lola pulled back to look Avery in the eye. "It means I'm going to have to hang out with the baboons." She smiled her soft motherly smile.

Avery suddenly longed for her own baboons to cuddle and smile about. Her mind flickered to Rowan. And she wondered… Avery quickly shook herself free from the thought. That was dangerous ground to tread. She had never even met the man in person.

Now she was going to meet the man.

Waving at Lola's car as it backed from her driveway, Avery knew there was no way she was going to pull a happily-ever-after from her present scenario. Happy endings belonged to other people's storylines. Better to nip any other fantasies in the bud. This was real life, not a manuscript she was editing.

Avery checked her watch. Rowan had said nine o'clock. He was having a rough day with a parent, too. His dad was in the hospital. He didn't expound, but Avery saw emotions sowed into his words that reminded Avery of her own ambivalence. Or maybe she was doing what Taylor had talked about. She saw everything through her own lens. Maybe Rowan was scared and heartbroken and not ambivalent at all. Maybe they had repaired their relationship despite the fact that his dad had been a mean drunk in Rowan's youth. Perhaps his dad had gotten help and patched things up.

Her mom was beyond that. They'd never patch or mend. This was as good as it was going to get.

Avery had a duty to her mom. She loved her mom. But her mom wasn't the kind of mom Avery had always longed for.

She walked back inside to go, get ready. Ten more minutes, then she and Rowan would Skype. Avery would have to dim the lights now that her mouth was clown red from Lola's waxing.

And then, selfishly, she thought, I hope that, despite his dad, we still get to meet in New York.

24

AVERY

TUESDAY NIGHT
Falls Church, Virginia

THE SKYPE CALL CONNECTED IMMEDIATELY.

"Hi, there." Avery lowered her eyelashes as a flush warmed her cheeks. Suddenly shy, she fidgeted, her hands in her lap.

"Hey." Rowan's smile was more a greeting than happiness. He looked worried. But that made sense, his dad and all.

Avery raised her gaze to take in his image. A long silence followed. "You look tired. Was your flight to New York, okay? Is that where you are now?"

"Yeah, I'm at my hotel." He held up the computer and rotated it around for her to see.

"Swanky."

"I'm not sure how this worked out. Usually, the bureau pays

for rooms you share with the cockroaches. But I'm happy to take it." He sat back down at the table and adjusted the computer screen.

"How are you?" Concern infused her voice.

"I'm a little off-balance, to be honest."

"If you're not up to a conversation right now, I understand." Avery leaned forward. "Though I hope this is okay. I'd like to be here for you."

"This is good, thank you." He jostled his chair around and positioned his elbows on the tabletop.

"I don't want to pry, but would you like to talk about what happened? How is your father?"

"No news is good news on the dad front. If he calls *me*, I'll know things are getting bad." He smiled, and it took any sting out of the words. "He's private by nature."

Avery tipped her head thoughtfully. "Like father like son?"

"Oh, no." Rowan chuckled. "No, this apple fell far from the tree. I am nothing like my father. And he would enthusiastically concur with me saying that."

"Yes, I…you told me he drank, and he was mean. I didn't mean to imply… I can't see you being either a drunk or mean." Avery bit at her lip, trying to figure out how to get out of the hole she'd just dug. "So you're more like your mom? I don't think you've ever mentioned her in your tweets."

"Well, nothing to reveal there. I haven't seen her in over a decade." His words were matter-of-fact and held no emotional load. "She took off with a work colleague on a business trip, which was actually her moving out and moving on—to Spain to be exact."

"Wow. That must have been a shock."

"For my dad, perhaps. I was away at West Point, and I hadn't grown out of my teenage narcissistic stage then. As long as it didn't affect me directly, it didn't matter." He shrugged. "Besides, she wasn't your normal cake-baking, kiss-you-good-night kind of mom. She was more of the drama-making, vodka-swilling kind. She and dad were greeted as friends at the local ABC store."

It seemed to Avery that Rowan's tight-lipped half-smile punctuated the end of his sharing about his parents. "I had a difficult day today. It looks like you did too."

Canting her head, Avery asked, "How did you know?"

Rowan rubbed his index finger at the corner of his mouth. "You have a little chocolate icing, just there."

Ha, she'd grabbed a little piece of cake to calm her before the Skype date. Avery scrubbed at the indicated spot with her fingers then pushed her face closer to the camera.

"Yeah, you've got it. So what happened?"

"My mother." Avery's mouth twitched. "When my dad was dying, he asked me to move home and look after my mom, who is not well. And she's having a bad day today."

"Does your sister Fanny help out?"

"Fanny…" Avery began, but she saw Rowan focus over her shoulder. Turning her head to see what had caught his attention, she saw her mom standing behind her. She was dressed in mismatched church clothes with a shower cap arranged at a jaunty angle on her head.

"Avery, those men are outside watching the house, again. You need to brush your hair and go out and talk to them. Tell them we don't like them here."

"Mom." She turned back to Rowan. "Let me Skype you back in a few minutes."

"It's fine," Rowan said as Ginny moved up behind Avery, a hairbrush in her hand. She dropped the bristles onto Avery's scalp and yanked.

Avery drew her shoulders up to her ears, turtling her head as best she could to deal with the pain. "Mom, that hurts. Please stop." Avery reached out to end the Skype call, but Ginny smacked her hand.

"Don't touch that," her mother said.

As Ginny took another swipe through her hair, Avery reached again for the laptop. A second smack landed. Avery jerked her hand back, wincing.

"Avery," Rowan said. "I'm going to go make myself a snack. You do what you need to do, and I'll be here when you're ready." Rowan got up and disappeared from view.

"Mom." Avery strained for patience. "There is no one outside. Please stop hurting me."

Ginny's voice drowned out Avery's words with a sonorous *Lumen Christi.*

Avery stood up, took her mother's hand, and pulled her upstairs to the master bedroom. There, she gave her mom the night time dose of medicine that would help her sleep until morning.

Her mother was still singing when Avery closed the door and bolted it from the outside. It was sometimes her only option when her mother lost touch with reality.

Avery looked at her watch. It could take twenty minutes or so for the meds to kick in.

She slugged her way to her own bedroom, where she stopped in front of the mirror to check her hair. After applying some gloss and brushing blusher over her cheeks to mask her wan complexion, Avery blinked at her image in the mirror. She was stalling going back downstairs. *Okay, so now he knows, so what? He's a pen pal, and he works far, far away.*

On the way back to the dining room, Avery stopped in the kitchen to pour herself a cup of tea from the now tepid pot. She slid onto the chair in front of the computer, watching Rowan's face focused on some task. When she placed the cup and saucer on the table, the rattle caught his attention.

"Everything okay?" he asked, swiveling to face the screen.

"Everything is normal." Avery rubbed her fingers back and forth across her forehead. "Is that okay? I guess it has to be. What are you doing?"

"Doodling is all." Rowan held up the picture of a caged bird.

Avery thought it was an apt metaphor for her situation. "Lovely," she said.

"Do you want to talk about it?"

"Nothing to say, really. It is what it is."

Rowan nodded. "Your mother has dementia?"

"No. She's just crazy." Avery thought, yup, that's the nail in the coffin of what might have been something more. "It's not genetic. When Mom was pregnant with my brother, she was on bed rest and developed a blood clot that led to a stroke. She lost the baby, which I guess didn't help things. Or maybe it was for the better, who knows." God, she was tired. All of her energy just drained right out of her. She desperately wanted to go to sleep. "The brain damage from Mom's stroke resulted in psychosis."

"Delusions."

"And paranoia, like when she said there are men watching the house. Though that one is new."

"How new?" Rowan asked.

Avery had to think about that. "Last few days. Not long. If it's not that, then it's that her caregiver wants to kill her and steal her social security check. It wasn't always this bad. She was okay. Not great. But okay, before my father got sick. They discovered stage four pancreatic cancer, and Dad died that same month. Mom's doctors say that the increase in her symptoms is caused by the stress of losing him."

"Is her medication helpful?"

"When I can get her to take them. She thinks we're trying to poison her. I have these new shots that are easier for me to work with. The pills… Sometimes, I literally have to force them down her throat." *TMI.* It didn't matter. He was gone anyway. "I feel like the bad guy. And as I have learned over the last two days, who the bad guy is depends entirely on where your feet are planted. For many who are looking at me, judging me, I'm the bad guy."

Rowan sat silently.

"Do you want to hang up now? You don't have to follow through with dinner in New York."

"What are you talking about?"

"I'd understand if you'd rather not…uhm, meet, or anything." *Lame.*

"Because I got to see the kind of stress you're dealing with?" He leaned forward, his face filling her screen. His eyes were so intelligent and kind.

"It's a complication. I've lost most of my friends over this." She shrugged. "It's okay." She offered up a smile. "Really. I understand."

She needed to just let this go.

Let Rowan go.

She closed her eyes.

"Please stop. Avery, look at me."

She lifted her lashes and looked him in the eye, gripping at the seat of the chair, bracing herself.

"Nothing has changed between us except that today you learned that my home life wasn't Norman Rockwell, and I learned even more deeply what a strong and amazing person you are."

Tears sprang to Avery's eyes. She looked away and batted her lids to quell them.

"The singing stopped. Does that mean your mom's asleep?"

"The medication kicked in. Yes, asleep."

"Then take a deep breath," he said. "Let that all go. I wanted to ask you about something."

25

AVERY

WEDNESDAY EVENING
New York City

TODAY HAD BEEN SURPRISINGLY NICE.

Avery woke up, grabbed her suitcase, kissed her mom good-bye, and left the house without any falderol. The ride to the airport had been uneventful, her flight short, her hotel room comfortable. Today's sessions had been fun. Lots of old friends. Lots of hugs and smiles.

But in Avery's life, nice rarely lasted long.

George corralled Avery into an alcove at the convention hotel. They had just finished up listening to pitch sessions followed by an open bar meet and greet.

Avery wished he wasn't standing so close.

"I'm getting pushback from the production departments.

Shreveport is hellbent on bringing out the Knapp book on schedule. He's rabid about it. I told him you'd met with Taylor in person. He didn't believe me. You did meet with him, didn't you? I swear to God if you lied to me."

"Have you met Taylor Knapp?" Avery's back was pressed against the wall as she tried to gain distance. "Do you know who this is? I mean, beyond a name."

"No. And I don't need to. I was told to assign it to you. That came from Windsor himself. But I have all the pressure of getting this project accomplished."

"This is dangerous stuff. But you know that from the fallout with Taylor's first book. And I have the impression that what Taylor is cooking up pushes things far beyond what happened with the last book. It's as if that last book was testing the waters. Something's going on here, George. Seriously. I think we're being used in someone's game."

"The only thing that's going on here is we're going to make money. *Big money*. That protects everyone's job. Yours and mine. It's a tentative time, Avery. You're getting this done, and getting this done right, can protect a lot of people's livelihoods." He put his hand on the wall above Avery's shoulder, caging her there.

"No pressure."

"Just be professional," he said. "Just do what you do."

"Turn a blind eye." She tried to take a step to the side.

He put his other hand to the wall, stopping her. "Not a blind eye. A critical eye. An editorial eye. Find every single wayward comma. Find all the plot holes and the pacing issues. But don't rock the boat on the themes that Taylor wants to put forth. He's a genius! He can read his audience like they're tea leaves."

"Like he has a lot of data that would help him hit the right psychological buttons."

"Exactly." He lifted his hands in the air, shaking his fists. "Brilliant!"

Avery took advantage of the move (number twenty-seven in the alpha-ape how to win book), side-stepping out of his reach, then moving quickly toward the elevators, seeking the privacy of her room.

George wheeled around and quickened his pace to catch up with her.

Adjusting the shoulder strap on her briefcase, Avery waited with the pool of convention-goers waiting for the next car going up. George stood right behind her back.

Now that the day was over, his cologne smelled sickly-sweet and stale, exciting her gag reflex. Avery moved away from him, trying to cover the move as a shift of balance. The bell dinged, and the doors slid open.

George placed a possessive hand on her lower back as he shepherded her in.

Avery tensed at his touch.

They squeezed into the crowd and turned toward the closing door. George's hot breath whispered in her ear. "You know, it's kind of a shame we had to go through the pretense about booking two rooms."

Avery shot a glance over her shoulder. "It's not happening."

He chuckled. "No?"

They moved to the side as people arrived at their floors. The pushing jumbled her into George's arms as he steadied her. Avery let her breath hiss between her teeth. This was probably the longest elevator ride in the history of elevator rides.

Finally, on the ninth floor, they both exited.

George propelled Avery down the corridor by the elbow.

She stopped abruptly to face him. Pitching her voice, so her words didn't carry into any of the other rooms, she pulled her briefcase between them. "I'm serious. It's not happening ever again. Clear?"

"Sure. But then again, I've heard that from you before, haven't I?" He sent her an audacious wink, and Avery wanted to smack the smugness right off his face. She glared disdain at him and moved up the hallway. George's laughter following after her.

In her room, *finally* alone, Avery kicked off her high heels and stripped off her suit pants. She headed straight to the shower, where she let the pulse of hot water loosen her muscles. Her thoughts trailed back to the time before her old boss moved on to greener pastures. Avery had liked her job—traveling to other cities, meeting famous authors and those still in the fingers-crossed stage of the publishing game. It had always felt more like a party than work.

But the industry had changed. There was unrest, a feeling of endangerment as if the publishing dinosaurs were going extinct. Everyone, it seemed, was clinging to their jobs by their finger-nails. People were scared. At the cocktail reception, it made them talk too loud and drink too much. It was all the more apparent to Avery since she'd abstained.

The pervasive undercurrent of stress was not Avery's alone.

But it added to Avery's tension headache.

She stepped out of the shower, wrapped a towel around herself, and wandered into her room. At least she would sleep this week; that was worth the trip right there. She wondered if she should give Fanny a call to check and see how things were going.

Just as she was talking herself out of making that call, her phone played Barry Manilow's *Copacabana*. "Hi, Lolly."

"Hey there. I need to talk to an adult right now, or my head's going to explode."

"Rough day with the kids?"

"I have them each in a corner. They've been there long enough the little ones have curled into balls and fallen asleep. But they're alive."

"Good to know." Avery picked up the room service card that encouraged her to circle what she wanted to be brought up for breakfast and to be hung on her outer doorknob by midnight. She glanced down the offerings of oatmeal and Greek yogurt with fruit, then tossed it onto the bed beside her.

"Sounds like your day was no better than mine. I think maybe Mercury's retrograde or something."

"Something." Avery stretched out her legs and took a long swig from her bottle of water.

"No good manuscripts being pushed under your nose?"

"Nothing new. Everything is same old, same old. Rename the characters and tell the identical story."

"Hmm. Well, since you have nothing interesting to say about your day, let's get right to it. George's not playing nice?"

"Too nice and too hovering. He wants me to sleep with him."

"I've met his wife. I'd bet you anything he's not getting any, and he's remembering how you rocked his world when you did have that one-for-the-road, one-night stand just before he walked to the altar."

"It was a mistake. A great big, depressing, I-lost-my-damned-sanity mistake."

"Still, you weren't married when you two boinked, so Jesus says you're a slut."

"Gosh. Thanks." Avery laughed, feeling the tension start to ebb.

"Now listen, if you start to fall prey to George in New York, remember, the Bible didn't make any stipulations about using the back door."

"Lolly!" Avery gasped in mock horror.

"And I know for sure because I asked Father Pat."

"You know that man is going to have an aneurism and die, and it will all be on your conscience."

"Oh, he loves it. I'm not sure he understands all of it, but he schedules extra time for me at the confessional."

"Well, that's one sin I won't have to confess. No worries about me ever sleeping with George again. *Ever.* No matter what the Bible allows for.*"

"Good because I didn't listen to you scream in my ear yesterday to get you all sexified for George. I'm team Rowan. I so hope everything's going to work out tonight with you two. You deserve a nice guy. Someone who treats you like you should be treated. Do you have a condom in your purse?"

"Right now, there's no way I could have a relationship. I have Mom. And no, of course I don't have a condom in my purse."

"Someone who loves you would help you with that burden." Lola's voice had just a touch of pity in it. If it came from anyone else, Avery would have been offended. But she knew her best friend was speaking from their long history and mutual devotion.

"Yeah, well, if he loved me, and then this situation happened, I might agree. But who in his right mind would wade into my pool of crazy?" Avery cleared her throat.

"When does Rowan pick you up?"

"We're having a late dinner. He's still in meetings." She stopped to check the clock. "I have a half-hour to get myself ready. I told one of my romance writers I'd meet her for a drink at her hotel. It's just up the street from the FBI Headquarters, and I thought it would be better if I met Rowan over there."

"That's cautious of you."

"I'm an editor. I live in a world of plot twists."

"Be open to the possibility that those twists could be good

ones. I liked Rowan's reactions on Skype the other day. His voice is all warm and sexy. You're going to go, relax, and enjoy. This is about having some fun. Can you use this half-hour to lighten up a little? Eat some chocolate. When you get home, I want details."

26

ROWAN

New York City

HE'D ARRIVED EARLIER than intended. His Lyft driver was damned aggressive. Rowan wouldn't mind, except he knew that Avery was having drinks with one of her authors, and he didn't want to interrupt her work. Mixing her private life with her career life might be uncomfortable. And meeting Avery in person for the first time was bound to feel a bit awkward.

Rowan didn't like that he was empty-handed. He'd considered bringing her flowers, but with nowhere to put them, she'd be dragging around a wilting bouquet all night.

Maybe he could send some flowers to her room tomorrow.

Rowan had gone back to his hotel and changed into a pair of jeans and a button-down shirt. He wanted to take Avery somewhere relaxed with zero pressure. A suit felt like it would make things too stiff and formal.

Was he overthinking this?

His Ranger brothers would bust his balls if they could see this playing out. Okay, he was nervous. The good kind. The expectant kind. It had been a long time since he'd felt this way.

Rowan got out of the car and nodded to the bellhop, who pulled open the giant brass and glass door for him. He took a moment at the entrance to scan, mapping the room—a habit.

Walking farther into the lobby, he spotted her.

Avery stood in a small group of women. She had her back to him. But he knew it was her by the way his heart skipped a beat before it raced in his chest. He stepped forward, standing under the opulent dome ceiling, and blew a long breath from between his lips.

The woman opposite Avery looked straight at him when he did that. She put up her hand to fan her face as she made some comment about him.

The group unwound to turn and look.

Rowan slid his fingers into his front pockets and rocked back on his heels.

That's when Avery caught his eye. The look held. His breath held. The world stopped.

She blinked and smiled, and with a little bounce, she stretched out her hand toward the group. She turned her head to say something to them but didn't break eye contact with him. Then she rushed, laughing, straight toward him, and he held out his arms to catch her up and spin her around. A grin stretched wide across his face.

It was heady.

It was unexpected.

It was magic.

With her hands resting on his shoulders, he set her down. He saw it dawn on Avery what she'd just done. Her face turned pink. Self-recrimination moved into her eyes. And he wouldn't let it. He wanted that moment to be exactly what it was—a slice of time when nothing was held back. It had been so natural. He wanted that. So he bent his head and kissed her.

Warm and soft. Sweet, like warm cherries under a summer sun. That was the kiss that clinched it for him. Gone. He was gone. "Hi, Avery," he said, his lips just brushing against hers.

"Hi, Rowan."

As Rowan laced his fingers with Avery's, he straightened back up and glanced over at the women in her group, who were clapping and cheering and making a ruckus. "One more kiss. One more kiss," they chanted.

"They've been drinking since noon," Avery said.

Rowan wrapped his free arm around her waist and, dipping her back, kissed her again, long and satisfying, her arms tight around him, her body melting against his. "Still," he moved his mouth to her ear to whisper, "I don't mind obliging them."

"Chivalrous of you." She laughed as he brought her back to standing.

"Isn't it?" He dropped a kiss on her nose. She was a lot more petite than he'd expected. He stood a good six inches taller than she was, and she was in heels. Her body was curvy and toned. Her long blond hair fell in soft curls to her breasts. Her breasts... yeah, he needed to move his mind to cleaner thoughts. "Are you ready to go, or do you still have work to do? I can wait in the lobby."

Avery waved at the group. "Nope. They're too sauced to do anything meaningful work-wise." She looked up at him and smiled. "I'm ready when you are."

He was ready all right.

Man, was he ready.

But she probably wasn't thinking the same thoughts he was.

They walked out the doors into the night air.

"You're in heels. Should we walk, or shall I hail a cab?"

"The temperature is perfect. I'd prefer walking if you don't mind," Avery said.

Hand in hand, they started up Broadway to Worth Street toward Little Italy. He'd called and made sure that his favorite restaurant had a private table set aside for him. Avery stopped and rested her head on his bicep and looked up at the FBI Headquarters building. "This is where you were today?"

"Some of today," Rowan said.

"I've been in there before. I have a T-shirt to prove it."

They set off walking again. "I can't imagine a circumstance that would put you in that building."

"Propaganda, Dr. Kennedy."

"Okay, you've got my attention." They paused, then crossed the street.

"The FBI likes to help writers write stories that shine the Bureau in their best possible light. To that end, the FBI wants to influence writers to put out books with a positive spin. Every year, there's this big writer's convention here in New York City. The day before, the FBI hosts an all-day class full of shock and awe." She used her free hand to waggle spirit fingers. "It's very impressive."

"Sounds like a great time."

"Ha. The one time I did the class, I learned that I am most certainly not built to be a spy. You know when you watch a movie, and you think I could do that. That's how I'd be. Well," she reached across to lay her hand on Rowan's chest, "not you. You do that kind of thing in reality." She dropped her hand again, and Rowan wanted it back—the warmth of her hand on his heart.

"What happened?"

"We had to do a background check before we went. And we were told that we couldn't bring our phones in or any weapons. So that's all fine. I don't have a gun or anything. I had some pepper spray, and I left that back at my hotel. I didn't really think things through."

"Uh-oh."

"I was standing in line to have my purse go on the belt for the x-ray machine, and I started inventorying the things I had with me, like my credit card knife."

"What's that?"

"Oh, it's the size and shape of a credit card. I carry it in my wallet for opening boxes and what have you. It folds origami-like to become a very sharp blade, like a razor. It's handy."

He nodded.

"I had a Leatherman and a Swiss Army knife. And there was one other thing that I'm drawing a blank on. Anyway, four things that would get me in trouble. I go to the guard at the door and tell him the problem."

"He said get rid of them or don't come in."

"Exactly. I asked if he could hold them somewhere for me, and that was a no. Could I put them in the trash and dig them out later? That was a no. It was like two hundred dollars' worth of—"

"Weapons."

"*Tools* I had in my purse."

"Why were you carrying a Leatherman?"

"One of the wheels on my suitcase kept coming loose. I needed a larger Philips head than I had on my Swiss Army."

"And why did you need a Swiss Army?"

"Corkscrew for my wine."

"Okay, so you have all this contraband. What did you end up doing with it?"

"The guard said I could try to leave it outside somewhere, so that's what I did. I crossed Broadway, and I was looking for somewhere I could hide the stuff. And there was nowhere. So I started thinking like a heroine in a novel. Where would a female protagonist hide this stuff? If I was a spy and had to leave something for someone else in one of those dead drop thingies, how would I do it?"

He was grinning hard. "How did you do it?"

"Badly." Avery grimaced. "I saw a bin. You know the bins, the kind where they leave rental property newspapers?"

"Like those?" Rowan pointed over at the three periodical boxes lined up next to the public mail drop.

"Exactly. There weren't enough papers in there that I felt confident that they wouldn't all be picked up, then someone would get my tools. So I went around behind it. I was concealed from view from the street by the UPS truck. And I thought I was pretty slick as I squatted down behind the thing. It wasn't all that heavy. I pushed it with my shoulder just enough that I could slide everything under, then I stood back up. There's this ring of New Yorkers staring at me. I brushed off my hands and walked on as if nothing had happened."

Rowan had stopped in place and turned to listen to Avery, chuckling under his breath.

"I went back into the FBI Headquarters. The guard looks at me. I give him a thumbs-up, get in line, go through the check, get escorted up to the class, sit down, and that's when I started to sweat."

"What? Why? You thought one of those people just went up behind you and stole your tools?"

"No! No, I thought they'd go look, see the weapons and call

the police. The police would come, the bystanders would point to the FBI Headquarters, and at any minute, the NYPD would swarm into the conference room and arrest me in front of all my colleagues."

"Why?"

"I don't know. Maybe it's against the law for someone to leave knives in the streets. And then it got worse. I thought, oh no! There I was hiding something under an object in front of the FBI Headquarters. They might think it was a bomb! They might have watched me on their security cameras and think that I was a terrorist. They might even cordon off the road and evacuate the block and have a robot out there looking to see what was planted on the street corner. And I'd never know to go explain because there were no phones and no windows in our room. The FBI agents were going to arrest me."

"For what?"

"Making them worried and using precious taxpayer dollars on a bomb robot. Snarling traffic and inconveniencing the citizens by hiding weapons on the street."

Rowan was laughing so hard he could hardly stand up. Avery didn't seem to mind. She was smiling back at him. He lifted her hand to his lips and kissed it, then held her hand to his heart until he stopped laughing. "You are so right. You should never try to be a spy. You're just too tender for that life." He pulled her hand and got them walking again. "Are you hungry? We're not far now."

Avery looked up the road then focused back on Rowan. "Can I be honest?"

"Always."

"I'm not really in the mood to be in a restaurant right now. I'm an introvert by nature, and I've been around a lot of people today."

"But you still have to eat."

She stood still, her gaze held his, and he thought maybe the hunger in her eyes could be his imagination. Or a reflection of his own emotions. Rowan looked up the road again. Should he? "My hotel is just past where I was taking you for dinner. We could go there and order room service. Would you rather do that?"

27

AVERY

WEDNESDAY NIGHT
New York City

"HE SAID WHAT NOW?" Rowan had his arm around Avery and was mostly holding her up as she leaned into him, laughing. They had been laughing from the point where she told him her ridiculous FBI story all the way up the road.

It was hard to walk and laugh at the same time. Their progress was measured in inches and feet. People along the way picked up on their mood, grinning and chuckling along with them as they passed.

It was so cathartic to laugh this way.

A stranger in a busy city, Avery couldn't care less what folks thought of her, so she threw her head back and laughed loud and hard when Rowan told her about the time he had to steal a camel and ride it out into the desert with no idea what he was doing, his legs wrapped tightly around the camel hump and holding on for dear life.

By the time he'd finished the story, she was gripping at the stitch in her side.

They'd made it, drunk on hilarity, to his hotel, and into the elevator.

He had asked her about what kinds of pick-up lines men had used on her. So she was telling him about her trip to Cancun and the guy in the tiki hut.

"He said, 'Do you want to pet my leezhard?'" She affected a deep-voiced foreign accent.

The elevator door slid open, and they stumbled into the hallway.

"I'm standing there trying to figure out if he's saying what I think he's saying or if maybe someone had taught him an English phrase that he was mangling. He was so earnest and expectant. 'I'd like to show you my leezhard," she said with the feigned accent low and intimate. "'I want you to touch heem.'" She bobbled her eyebrows like a cartoon Casanova. "'I promise you, you'll like it very much."

"No, he didn't," Rowan gasped as they walked up the hallway to his room.

"Yeah, then he reaches into the leg pocket on his camo pants and pulls out a bearded dragon and sets it on his shoulder. 'This eeze my drinking partner. I call heem Smaug.'"

"An actual lizard in his pocket?" Rowan swiped his card across the lock and got a green light. He pushed the door wide for Avery to go in first. "Not a really bad pick up line?"

She stepped inside then turned, her eyes crinkled with mirth. "An actual lizard."

Rowan followed behind and shut the door, watching her take

up a position, leaning back against the wall and looking up at him.

The mood shifted.

Both together, like a well-choreographed dance. Their laughter fell away to a quiet intensity that an author would write something like, "she looked at him with longing." No. "She looked at him with hunger in her eyes." More. "She looked at him and tried to telegraph, 'rip my clothes off me, take me to your bed, and make me cross-eyed with orgasms!'" Avery chuckled. Yeah, well. The truth was the truth, she thought. *I wouldn't mind that at all.*

Rowan stepped forward and brushed the hair from her cheek.

She focused on the warmth in his eyes and drank him in. Avery wanted this picture to stay with her forever. The way he looked at her, she was beautiful. The way he looked at her, she was respected.

Avery had never experienced this level of trust and freedom with someone in her life.

This picture, this moment, she wanted to put it in a bottle and hang it on a golden chain around her neck, under her blouse against her heart, so she could lift it up and breathe it in like a heady perfume when she needed joy.

Rowan moved his gaze from her eyes to her mouth. He grasped her chin and stroked his thumb over her lips. His breath caught then released. He looked back in her eyes again. "You're astonishing."

One side of her mouth quirked into a smiling question.

"Twitter doesn't come close to doing you justice. Doing your sense of humor justice." He laced his fingers with hers and led her forward. "Twitter funny is nothing like real-life Avery funny."

Avery got the sense that he was trying to wrangle his

thoughts to something gentlemanly. She couldn't say she appreciated it. There was a time for being a gentleman, and there was a time to drop a girl's panties. Right now, she would rather Rowan rip her clothes off.

She was warm and tingling. She had a desperate need to feel his weight between her legs. To have him sliding in and out of her, bringing her relief.

Avery stepped farther into the room.

A king-sized bed. A table with two chairs to the side by the window. A lowboy with its coffee pot, sitting opposite the bed.

He stood there behind her. Their fingers laced. He seemed to be waiting for a signal, maybe to see where she wanted to settle in.

Avery turned and reached for his other hand and laced those fingers, too.

She leaned back against the wall and slowly lifted her chin as she closed her eyes.

Rowan's lips found hers with a nip and a lick that had her opening her mouth for his tongue to play. This wasn't the soft kisses from the bar earlier. This was hunger.

Rowan dragged her hands up the wall and pinned them over her head, holding her there as his body pressed into her. She could feel the strength of his chest and thighs.

She completely trusted him.

It was heady stuff to have someone so smart and handsome look at her the way Rowan had looked at her from the moment their eyes had caught. Oh, there he is, she'd thought in the bar and had raced into his arms like she'd always been there like that was her place in this world. And that's how this felt. Perfectly right.

Lost.

She was lost in their kiss.

Couldn't get enough of this kiss.

He released her hands and swept her up in his arms. He took the three steps to the bed, where he laid her down.

Yes! she thought. *Now*!

But he stopped, stood, and took a step back. She could see in his eyes, he was wrestling with himself. Avery imagined that he thought he was moving too fast. When for her, it wasn't nearly fast enough. Her gaze skimmed his body, stopping on the bulge in his jeans where his hard-on pressed against his zipper.

A flood of hormones swirled through her veins.

Avery curled her legs under her as she came to kneeling on the bed. There was nothing coy about the look she was sending him. She had tucked her chin and looked at him with smoldering eyes. She reached down and slowly, slowly unbuttoned her blouse.

Rowan's body tensed as he watched her. He stepped to the end of the bed, settling his hips against the low boy.

Slipping her silk blouse from one shoulder, then the other, her breasts rounded out of a frame of violet lace. She let the blouse fall to the side, then swept her hands under her breasts, lifting them and pressing them together, stroking her thumbs along the tops, down around her hardened nipples.

Rowan curled his fingers into the edge of the low boy and licked his lips.

Avery reached behind her as she unbuttoned her skirt, unzipped the zipper, and pulled it over her head. She was wearing silky panties in the same deep purple and stockings held in place around her legs by lacey elastic.

She glided higher in the bed and lay back on the pillows, letting her long curls form a halo around her head. "Your turn," she said.

A slow smile slid across Rowan's face. He unbuttoned one cuff, then the other.

Avery desperately wanted to reach into her panties and bring herself some relief. Watching him slowly unbutton his shirt, seeing the strength of his pecks, the washer board ridges on his abdomen, she was drunk on desire.

He tugged the tail of his shirt from his jeans, slid the shirt off, and cast it aside.

The lights were dim, but they didn't hide the bruises that ran up and down his side.

He'd been in the accident.

The bruise on his face hadn't looked so bad. Avery hoped this wasn't going to cause him pain. And she hoped it didn't stop him from making love to her. Because right now, she was feeling frantic to get him inside her.

Rowan moved to the end of the bed, popping the top of his jeans, dragging down the zipper. His cock bulged out.

Avery reached out her hands, welcoming him into her arms. But he crawled onto the bed and stopped.

Kneeling at her feet, he reached for her ankle, dragging her toward him.

Off came her first high heel. Her second.

She moaned and closed her eyes.

He pulled her a little further down until she had a leg on either side of him. He caressed her calf with the silky stocking. His fingers danced along the top where the lace stopped, and her skin was ultrasensitive. Rowan smiled knowingly, lasciviously, when her body shuddered.

He bent and licked along the top of her stocking, then curled his fingers into the top of the band and slowly dragged the stocking down to her ankle. He let his thumbnail graze over her instep as he pulled it off and watched as her muscles tensed.

She was so sensitive, so turned on, that she was growing a little panicky, angry even, that he was down there smiling when she just wanted him in her.

He lifted her foot to his lips and kissed her just below the ankle, working his way up to her knee. When he got to her thigh, his kisses turned to little licks. The higher up he moved, the more she wriggled, her eyes squeezed shut, her fingers tangled in her hair.

He stopped when he reached the top, just shy of her panties.

She lifted her head and looked at him. She growled her displeasure that he'd stopped. Then, dropped her head back down, frustrated.

Rowan chuckled.

"Patience," he said.

He removed the stocking from her other leg in similar fashion, but this time, when he licked up her thigh, Avery was grinding her hips at him. Rowan blew warm air over the moist trail he'd laid.

He kissed her belly, her neck, her lips. His weight was on his elbows as he hovered over her.

"Avery," he said.

She opened her eyes.

"What are we doing?"

She blinked. Hopefully, they were going to fuck each other's brains out. What did he mean, "what were they doing?"

"I need to know what you want to happen here. You, all splayed out in front of me like this. It's probably good if I check-in."

She rested her hands on his biceps. "Responsible even."

"What do you want me to do? When do you want me to stop?"

"Stop after we've orgasmed. Maybe after we've orgasmed a few times."

His smile. She wanted to live in the light of that smile.

He looked toward the bathroom and back to her.

"Is that okay?" she asked as she wrapped her legs around him, squeezing his hips between her thighs.

"More than okay."

"Now it's your turn." She batted her eyelashes at him. "Why don't you tell me what you want *me* to do?"

He pushed back to his heels and held his chin as he studied her. "Are you wet for me, Avery?" He lifted his brow and waited for her answer.

"Desperately so."

He nodded. "All right then." He reached up and drew her panties down her legs. "I want to watch you play with yourself. I need to get a condom from the other room, and I want to make sure you'll keep yourself nice and warm for me while I'm gone."

28

ROWAN

THURSDAY MORNING
New York City

THE ROOM WAS JUST bright enough to see the form and shape of the furnishings. Rowan couldn't remember sleeping so deeply or so well. Thunder rumbled. Rain pattered hypnotically against the window.

He'd come awake at five, the way he always did and had lain there for the past fifteen minutes reveling in the moment.

Avery's breath tickled his chest. Her little sighs brought a smile to his lips. He loved the warmth and weight of her thigh as she tangled her legs with his.

And though he didn't want to break the spell, he'd promised Avery that he'd have her back to her hotel by six.

Rowan combed his fingers through her hair to wake her.

Tipping back her head, Avery blinked her lashes open and smiled before she moved her hand to his throbbing dick. She turned her face toward the clock. "I wish you'd woken me sooner."

He pressed a kiss into her hair. "You needed some sleep. I promise to make up for it tonight."

Without an ounce of modesty, Avery climbed from under the covers and made her way to the bathroom. "Is it okay if I shower first?"

Rowan's phone buzzed. "Yes," he said, seeing that Lisa was on the screen. "I need to take this."

The door clicked shut.

"Lisa?"

"I'm at your house," she said.

"What do you mean you're at my house. I'm in New York."

"Yeah, I get that. The alarm company called me when Jodie didn't answer. I'm standing here with the DCPD."

"Wait. What? I'm sorry. I just woke up. The DCPD?"

"When your alarm goes off, your company calls Jodie first."

Rowan scrubbed a hand over his face. "Yeah, since I'm almost always out of town. You're—"

"Second on the list."

"I'm sorry about that. Thank you for going over so early. Is everything okay there?"

"Not so much. The alarm was set to silent mode. Apparently, it was already signaling the alarm service, but you know, they don't call the police right away. They call—"

"The people on my list."

"By the time I got over here, the P.D. was in here."

"Sorry, no coffee in me yet. How did the P.D. get there before you did?"

"One of your neighbors took their dog for a walk. The dog

was off lead, and he ran across your yard and into your open front door. The neighbor followed to catch their dog and called the cops."

"But why?"

"It looks like Jodie's pretty angry."

"What?" Rowan came to his feet. Jodie had eaten everything out of his fridge, had taken the cat, and doxxed him on Twitter. Those were things he could imagine Jodie doing. Breaking into his house made no sense. "Jodie gave me back my key. Jodie wasn't in my house. What are you seeing? Why do you think it's her?"

"Your drawers are emptied out. Your cushions slashed. It looks like someone was looking for something, and they were shaking your house hard. Or they were trying to make a point of how pissed off they were."

"But *Jodie*?"

"I'm going to send you some photos."

After a moment, Rowen heard pings as his texts dropped. He opened them and couldn't wrap his brain around what he was seeing. Along the walls in his hall, blue spray paint spelled out a bunch of cuss words.

"Well, Dr. Kennedy, you know the human brain pretty well. Is it at all possible it was Jodie?"

"I suppose... She cusses like a sailor, but this is a stretch of my imagination. I'd never imagined her doing something like this."

"It is kind of a coincidence that you had some squad of idiots trying to ambush you and then have this happen. Your car's not here, so I guess even the lowest common denominator could tell you weren't home."

"I told Jodie I was going out of town on Tuesday. Look, I can't come home right now. As a matter of fact, I was going to call you later today and ask you to come up here. I need you to talk to Avery."

"About what?"

...

"About Windsor Shreveport? About Taylor Knapp?"

...

"Well, damn. Is there a reason why this can't wait for her to come back to D.C.?"

"A few. The biggest two are; first, she's off her turf, away from her norms. This might be a good time to broach a change. Second, when she's in D.C., she's tied up at work, and with her mother, she can't get free to come meet us or speak privately."

"All right," Lisa said. "Let's start here. What should I do about your house? Should I tell the DCPD about Jodie? Do you want her picked up for questioning?"

The water in the shower turned off.

"No. No. Let's keep that between us. I'll need a police report for the insurance. Other than that, just lock the house up and try to find out who my neighbor was with the dog, so I can send them some doggy biscuits or something. I'll work on figuring this out later."

"All done," Avery called as she left the bathroom.

"Is that Avery?" Lisa asked.

"Yes."

"In your room at five in the morning?" Lisa laughed. "No wonder you don't seem to give a shit that your ex is a psycho and destroyed almost everything you own. I bet you're too mellow from last night's workout."

"Lisa—" There was a warning in his voice.

"Okay, real quick then. I can't make it up there today. I can come tomorrow."

"Hey, Avery. Lisa's on the phone."

"At five in the morning?"

"We were in the military together. Old habits die hard. She says she's coming up to New York tomorrow, is there time in your schedule that we can meet her for drinks or something?"

"That's my last night in town." She paused. "Sure. I have to be at the convention during the day." She was wrapped in a towel that barely covered from breast to thigh as she leaned against the wall. "But I can do what I want at night."

When she winked at him, Rowan's mind went blank as his blood rushed southward, and his dick stiffened with a raging hard-on.

There he stood, naked in his hotel room with work-Lisa on the phone at his ear as she stood in his house that was probably wrecked by his ex, Jodie, all while sexy-as-hell Avery stood licking her lips as she looked at his dick.

It was one of the more bizarre moments of his life.

29

AVERY

THURSDAY NOON
New York City

WHEN SHE CHECKED HER PHONE, she had four calls from Lola. Lola was probably frantic because Avery hadn't called to give her any details about Rowan, and more importantly, assure her that Rowan wasn't some serial killer who had her tied up in a slum warehouse outside the city.

Avery read romance, and Lola read Stephen King.

She moved to the corner to call and relieve her friend's anxiety. And maybe dish a few of the delicious details about just how amazing Rowan was, how they seemed to fit together like a hand in a glove.

She quick dialed. "Hi, Lolly. I had my phone in airplane mode while I was lecturing. Sorry I didn't call earlier."

"It's fine. Well, it's almost fine. It'll be fine soon. I'm heading over to the Giant Foods grocery store now."

A frown crossed Avery's forehead. "Okay. Um, I don't think I need anything."

"Sally didn't call you?"

Darn it!

Avery made her way toward the next ballroom for her talk. "What's Mom done now?"

"Ginny went missing for about an hour. The police found her, though."

Avery pulled her convention schedule out of her pocket and checked. She needed Ballroom C. "Sally called the police, but didn't call me?"

"No, the police found Ginny all on their own."

Avery leaned against the wall. Her hand came up to cover her eyes. "Is Mom under arrest?" she whispered into the phone. "What did she do?"

"Not under arrest, no. Giant Foods doesn't want that kind of publicity." Laughter danced through Lola's reply.

Avery felt the blood drain from her face. "What did she do, Lolly?" Avery's hand moved to her throat. She sank onto a nearby chair.

"Well, the best I can tell from what the very lovely Officer Thibodaux said is that your mom thinks her babysitters are trying to poison her. She says she hasn't eaten for days because they're all trying to kill her, freeze her, and take her social security check."

"Oh, God." Avery got up and moved with the press of convention-goers, swarming through the hall.

"Apparently, they're also stealing all of your mom's clothes because she…" Lola broke off talking. She was laughing too hard to make her words understood.

"Lolly, please. Please. Lolly, stop. What about Mom's clothes?"

"Well, she isn't wearing any. She walked into Giant Foods stark naked except for her bedroom slippers and was strolling up and down the aisles putting things in her cart."

Avery lapsed into stunned silence. She pulled the phone away from her ear and stared at it.

"Are you there? Are you all right?"

Avery put the phone back to her ear. "Fine. Go on."

"The manager called the police. The police called an ambulance. Your mom called me. I tried to call Sally. This is sounding a lot like the 'There Was a Crooked Man' nursery rhyme. Sally didn't answer, so I went to your house and let her out of the basement."

"What? You let Sally out of the basement?"

"She went down to do a load of clothes, and your mom put a chair under the knob. Sally couldn't get back out. Anyway, after I freed Sally, I gathered up some clothes for your mom, and I'm heading to the store now."

Avery imagined the grin on Lolly's face. "I'm glad you're having fun."

"Oh, Avery, lighten up. It is what it is. This is what's going on for your mom. There's no changing it, so you have to reframe. She's not upset, so why are you upset? I'll get her dressed and take her back to your place."

"Completely naked?"

"No, she had her slippers. Remember? But yes, otherwise, she was sporting her birthday suit."

"I...I have no words," Avery stammered out. "What am I going to do with her?"

"Look, I'm pulling into the parking lot now. I'm taking her

back to Sally and making sure your mom's okay. I just wanted to ease your mind if you'd gotten any other calls."

"Lolly, thank you. Thank you for doing this for me. I truly appreciate you."

"Are you kidding? This is a good time—now if you asked me to change your mom's diapers at some point—yeah, *then* you'd owe me."

"No, really. This is beyond the pale. It's one thing to have this happening in my house. But it's affecting my neighbors. It's affecting people who are just trying to go get their bread and toilet paper unmolested at the store. It's affecting you and your family." Avery raised her hand and dropped it. "Even Father Pat. And Sally. Can you imagine having her job? I don't pay her enough. I *can't* pay her enough. I'm done." She shook her head, feeling the full weight of the defeat. "My dad had no idea it was going to be like this."

"Okay, I don't disagree with you. I've actually thought this almost from the point when you made your promise. But it wasn't for me to make that call. You needed to come to this decision on your own."

"Yeah, I'm sorry it took so long. Sometimes I feel like a garbage friend to you."

"Okay, you're going to stop the self-flagellation right now. The church hasn't condoned that for centuries. What's your next step?"

She walked into the ballroom and stood next to the back wall. "I guess while Mom's staying with Curtis and Fanny, I'll have to find some place to take her where she'll get the constant care she needs. Someplace that can do a better job of keeping her safe. She locked Sally in the basement? Dear God."

"*Please welcome our speaker, Avery Goodyear, senior romance editor with Windsor Shreveport!*"

"They announced me. Lolly, bless you. I'll talk to you tonight."

Avery put her phone back on airplane mode, affected a semblance of a smile, and walked up to the lectern.

30

Rowan

Thursday Afternoon
FBI Headquarters, New York City

"Thank you," Rowan said and stood. "This is supposed to be rather informal. We wanted to bring some dynamics to your attention. These might be new concepts, and we want to make sure you understand, so please ask questions as Special Agent Gonzales, and I proceed. I am Special Agent Rowan Kennedy. My job is to help the FBI gather information from Eastern Europe that we need to stop international criminal activity. My colleague, Special Agent Miguel Gonzales, works on cybersecurity and data collection."

Frowns all around.

Angst it was.

People who didn't play with technology on a daily basis

often got this look before a talk. The vocabulary was difficult, the technology advanced quickly. If you had a handle on things yesterday, you'd have lost your grasp by today. Rowan got it. But anxious people couldn't absorb information.

On the screen was the ShareTogetherApp logo.

"Per my introduction, I'm an attaché in Eastern Europe, monitoring crime families. One of the ways that the crime families have been communicating under the radar is through the ShareTogetherApp. The way this app operates makes it extremely difficult to track communications by the NSA and other signals intelligence, both foreign and domestic. That's the first danger I wanted to tell you about. Second, the ShareTogetherApp is now contacting its users—by the way," he paused and looked around the room so his point would get the focus it needed, "there are approximately nine hundred million people who use that app—the ShareTogetherApp is now contacting their users and letting them know that their personal information and communications, while encrypted, are still hackable unless they turn on their security key."

Lisa and Rowan both used the ShareTogetherApp for their writing files. Lisa had given him the heads up right away about the security breach, and Rowan had already checked his security key. Though, hacking into his account would only show writing files badly in need of editing, so he hadn't been worried about it.

A suit leaned forward, a deep frown making a wedge between his brows. "Our office uses the ShareTogetherApp, we were told that the information we were sending was encrypted end to end. And now you're saying it's hackable?"

Rowan nodded. "Very."

"Shit," he muttered, sitting back.

"But there's a security key you can turn on. Ask your IT to help you with that," Gonzales said.

"We don't have that app," another suit said. "What is it? Nine hundred *million* people use it, and they might have been hacked?"

"For those of you who are unfamiliar with ShareTogether-App," Rowan explained. "It allows smartphone users to send texts, files, and images via the Internet. Unfortunately, this has proven to be a pretty big security hole that was exploited by criminals and other rogue players. The most concerning part of this, for the purposes of this round table, is not the criminal hacking piece, but that the ShareTogetherApp accumulated their user's data through this app and sold this data on the open market. While this information is meant to help marketing algorithms find and target the best potential customers, unfortunately, this same information can be used by others to target propaganda. The ShareTogetherApp doesn't discern end use of the data, they only care about the sale."

"In plain speak," a woman said, "everyone who uses this app had data about them hacked and or collected, and it was sold to the highest bidder. Is that right?"

"Yes, ma'am," he said.

"And you work in East Europe," she continued, turning to Rowan. "How do you tie into this app?"

"We have information that has led us to conclude that six months ago, a Bulgarian bot farm purchased data from ShareTogetherApp with money that was funneled through a Russian oligarch. We believe that the Bulgarian crime family who made the purchase will be exploiting this data to micro-target United States citizens with their propaganda and disinformation campaigns."

There were a lot of emotions floating around the table. Emotions almost always led to bad decisions. The more they could keep this to fact-finding and dissemination, the better the chance that the Monday morning quarterbacks would let the professionals do their jobs unimpeded, or better yet, fully funded.

"I want you to hold these two thoughts for a moment. A. Hackers and rogue players have advanced marketing data on a wide swath of people living within the US, and B. Rogue players can communicate without our intelligence knowing about it."

"Wait," a suit said. "If we can't track it, then we don't know about it. If we don't know about it, we can't thwart it. That danger is catastrophic."

Rowan looked the man in the eye. "Exactly."

31

AVERY

THURSDAY EVENING
New York City

PACING BACK and forth across her hotel room floor, dressed in her bra and panties, Avery had her phone pressed to her ear. "I called to thank you again."

"It's all good," Lola said. "Your sister showed up and took your Mom back to her house. Sally said she'd had enough for one day."

"I don't blame her one iota. How did Sally get locked in the basement? There's no lock on that door. I think I missed that part of the story. Or I blocked it out."

"Your mom shoved a chair under the doorknob."

"That's not something I've seen Mom do before. Is Sally okay?"

"She's fine. Sally said she'll keep her phone on her at all times from here on."

"Why did mom do that to Sally?"

"Ginny said she didn't. She said it was the bad men that snuck in who did it. Then they were looking in your drawers. After they left, your mom got hungry and went to the store."

"Oh."

"Okay, enough about your mom. Everything's fine. Fine-ish. Let's talk about you. I want you to jump right to the end of the night with Rowan because that's always the point that is the most telling." The clatter of pans and water running in a sink was the backdrop behind Lola's voice.

"Rowan insisted that he see me back to my hotel safely this morning. And he asked to see me again tonight. He texted that there's a gallery exhibit he thinks I'll like, and they're doing a wine reception with classical guitar."

"I'm looking into my magic mirror and foresee lots of finger strumming in your near future."

Avery sighed.

"I heard that. Didn't you like him in person? Why do you sound stressed? I thought he would have worked that out of your system with your bedsheet aerobics."

"He told me he's heading back overseas soon. If you could see me right now, you'd see that I'm freaking out. He's going to be in harm's way. I know he said he shakes hands for a living, but his body is all bruised up."

"He was in that car accident, right?

"That might be part of the story. It isn't the whole story. A car accident doesn't leave bruises like that. Fists leave bruises like that." Avery wrapped her hand around her throat. "I'm so afraid for him."

"Holy Mary and Joseph, you're in love," Lola shrieked.

"You're in *love*. Oh, I'm so happy for you. This is wonderful. Well, not wonderful that he works on the other side of the Atlantic. And, yeah. The whole harm's way thing is pretty bad. But you *love* him."

"I think I might." Avery sank onto the bed. "Oh, God. I need to…breathe. I need to…not pass out." She stuck her head between her legs.

"It's been a while since you fell in love with a guy. Senior year in college, in fact. This is *supposed* to feel like butterflies and rainbows."

"Feels more like angina and an asthma attack, to be honest."

"So maybe as we age, we interpret things differently."

"What am I going to do, Lola? This has disaster written all over it. He told me that he *just* broke up with his long-term girlfriend."

"Lie down on your bed. Close your eyes. And without thinking, tell me what you want right now."

Avery fell back across the bed, her lids squeezed tight. "To be back in Rowan's arms where everything is safe and good."

"Ah. See? Not so hard. What time are you seeing him tonight?"

"I have a half-hour. I was trying to decide on a dress to wear. I have that cream-colored silk with the flowers at the hem. I have that green dress with a low neckline."

"Do red. I saw in an article the other day about psych studies that show when a man sees a woman wearing the color red, his mind goes straight to thinking about sex."

"What do they think when they see green?"

"Sex." Lola's laughter bubbled through the receiver. "I can't imagine a man who isn't constantly thinking about sex. I honestly don't think it matters what you wear."

AVERY HAD DECIDED on the cream dress with the flowers at the hem. It had a retro-romantic feel to it. She had planned to wear it to the Romance Award Dinner tonight, but real-life romance was so much better than book romance. Even if it did mean that the butterflies in her stomach were high on crack and making her nauseated with the violence of their fluttering wings.

It would be better once she saw Rowan.

Once she was touching him, everything would be okay.

She was supposed to meet him at the FBI building. The gallery was within walking distance.

She took the elevator to the lobby. George stood there, drink in hand. He was making his way through the crowd to her when she turned and walked straight out the front doors, a smile on her lips.

Outside, the city air was pregnant with moisture. It hung thick and heavy. She looked up at the gray clouds swirling between the skyscrapers. The doorman asked her if she wanted a taxi, then stepped out in the street to hail one for her.

Avery waited next to the wall, the wind whipping at her skirt, and that made her feel heroine-like. Feminine. Pretty, even.

The doorman was successful and popped open the taxi door for her, held out his hand, and assisted her as she slid in. He bowed and shut the door. Avery gave the Broadway address, and off they motored.

Avery – **En route, see you in ten minutes or so. Traffic is moving apace.**

Rowan – **My meeting should wrap up here soon. Can I meet you in the lobby?**

Avery – **:)**

Rowan – **No weapons allowed past security. I imagine you'd get stopped. I'm the only one who gets to frisk you.**

32

Rowan

Thursday
New York City

They started up the street. Rowan was shifting gears from the doomsday briefing he'd just given to a pleasant evening with a gorgeous woman. He hoped the walk would help him get his head clear. The only problem was that, from what Avery had been saying lately about her assignment at work, she—very innocently, and probably naively—might be one of the cogs driving the disinformation machine that was ripening hatred in America.

Date-Avery and Endangered-Avery were hard to separate out.

If she had *anything* to do with Taylor Knapp, things could turn ugly. He was afraid for her. She absolutely didn't need any more shit piled on her plate.

Lisa was coming in tomorrow, and maybe this could all get cleared up.

There she had stood, heads turned her way as his fellow special agents made their way through the lobby. She looked like a movie heroine in her simple retro-dress. He'd tucked her hand into his elbow and pushed the door wide. He'd kiss her hello once they were a little more private.

"You're okay walking in those heels?" he'd asked as they stepped to the sidewalk.

"You seem to be overly worried about my wearing heels and being able to walk. You asked about them yesterday."

"I wore heels once," Rowan said.

"I can't even imagine the circumstances. Were you undercover?"

"I lost a bet." He grinned down at her. "I had to wear them from the time I got up until I went to bed. There was a list of activities that needed doing."

"Like what?"

"Grocery shopping, I had to walk across a park on the grass, I gave a speech, the things a woman would do on an everyday basis, balanced on those things."

"You lost the bet to a woman?"

"Yep."

"What did you discover?"

"That if I had to wear heels, I would sit in one place and never get up. My feet, my knees, my back, I would rather do a day of Ranger training than ever try that again." He looked up and held out his hand. "It's starting to sprinkle. I'll get a cab." He reached his hand out to flag a taxi.

Everyone on the sidewalk around them stuck their hands out.

If you were driving a cab in New York City at that moment, you were suddenly occupied.

"Let's just walk a little faster. We must be almost there," Avery suggested.

Rowan looked down at her heels again and decided that he'd let her set the pace while he kept his eye out for an open cab.

She was athletic; he'd give her that. He gripped her hand tighter in case she were to trip.

Suddenly, the skies opened up, and the rain dropped like a downturned bucket. One second they were dry, the next minute soaked to the bone.

There was no overhang here; the doorways were crammed with people diving out of the deluge.

Rowan looked down, and Avery's dress had become transparent as it clung to her skin. The soft pink lace of her bra and panties, her tight nipples, the mound of her pubic hair was all visible as if she'd just disrobed and stood there naked in the streets.

She looked down when he did and gasped. Rowan spun her up against him and waved a cab down, using his body to offer her some modesty.

As the taxi pulled up, he saw there was an older woman in the back seat, waving him in.

He opened the door and put Avery in the back seat, then climbed into the front next to the driver before spinning around.

"I saw what happened. You poor thing," the grandmotherly woman said in a thick Brooklyn accent, *tsk*ing her tongue. Even though it was in the seventies before the rain suddenly plunged the temperature, the woman was wrapped in a brown sable coat. "Where are you going? We'll drop you there."

"Just a few blocks. Thank you, ma'am." Rowan gave his hotel address, and they sped off, throwing up a splash of muddy water as the taxi left the curb.

The old lady reached out and patted Avery's hand as Avery

shivered in the back seat, one arm crossing over her breasts, shielding them from the curious looks the cabby was sneaking in his rear-view mirror.

Rowan fixed on him pointedly, a snarl on his lips. It was a message. The man needed to focus elsewhere.

When they pulled up to the hotel, the rain was still dumping from the sky. Rowan pushed a twenty-dollar bill toward the cabby.

Avery reached out and squeezed the woman's hand, chattering out, "I'm so grateful. Thank you for your kindness," in her soft, lightly-southern accent.

The woman smiled and gave her a nod. "Go get warm and dry before you catch pneumonia."

Rowan pulled her door open and hustled Avery into the building, then over to the elevator.

They were both streaming, sopping wet.

Avery curled into Rowan's arms and vibrated.

Once they hit his floor, he moved her quickly into his room and right in the bathroom, where he bent to plug the drain and start the hot water running.

Avery's shaking fingers fussed at the back of her dress.

"Please," he said.

She turned and gathered her long hair to the side.

Rowan released the button and unzipped her. When she reached to peel the dress off, Rowan stopped her hand. "Let me. I want to take care of you."

She looked at him in the mirror.

"Please?"

She nodded and shivered. He didn't undress her delicately. He didn't stop to kiss and fondle her. He wanted her in that tub, soaking in hot water. Her lips were turning blue, and she had chill bumps on her arms and legs.

He held her hand as she stepped in and sank down in a tight tuck in the water. "That was unexpected," she chattered. "What a lovely woman. I hope that a wonderful magical surprise comes her way."

"Instant karma?" Rowan asked, pulling off his tie and unbuttoning his shirt.

"The good kind of instant karma. You look mighty sexy, Special Agent Kennedy, with your white shirt plastered to your pecs and your badge at your hip. I'm going to remember this scene for a future novel."

Rowan laughed as he pulled off the rest of his clothes, glad that his dick was getting hard so he didn't have the infamy of cold shrinkage. He'd been in SERE training—survival, evasion, resistance, escape—after long days with blaring music and strobe lighting, they'd taken them out of their cages and lined the team up, spraying them with freezing cold water. His dick had crawled up into the warmth of his abdomen to nestle in when they brought in a pack of women to point and laugh. It had been pretty humiliating. And that's how he knew the impact of Clara telling Sergei, with her lip curled in disdain, that he had a pathetic penis.

Yeah, male egos could be fragile about things like that.

He stepped to the back of the tub and climbed in, straightening out his legs on either side of Avery, letting her rest back against him.

They cuddled there, not saying anything. The quiet was comforting, peaceful.

He combed his fingers through the wet strands of her hair and braided them into a rope. He cupped warm water over her breasts and shoulders. She leaned up and kissed him. Her kiss felt contented.

"We need to talk about us," Rowan said after a while. "I care for you very much. I want to see where this might go. I see a future for us. I want to know if that's what you're feeling too."

She nodded.

"I can feel you thinking about complications. You have a very busy mind, Avery." He kissed the top of her head and went back to cupping up the water to keep her warm.

"You said you're leaving."

"I'm gone a lot. I can talk to you most days. We can video chat even if I'm gone."

"And some days not…because you're on a mission of some kind."

"Mission…well, I'm working. And I don't have nine to five hours. And there's the time zone issue."

"And the worrying about your issues." She turned to her side, so her ear was to his heart. He knew she was looking at the bruises along his ribs. Her fingers traced over the colors now starting to fade. "You aren't allowed to explain things like this to me, are you? I'm not allowed to know where you are, am I? In effect, there's always going to be a big chunk of your life that I'll know nothing about."

"There's that. That's exactly right."

"How long do you go away? Days? Weeks?"

"It can be months. If I'm gone for a stretch like that, you could come for long weekends where I meet you in a different country. That might be problematic for you because of your mom. Maybe your sister could help."

"After today, that's going to have to change. I'm just not capable of keeping her safe unless I board up her window and lock her in her room."

Rowan wrapped his arms around her and tucked her under his chin. "What happened today?"

"Can we not talk about my mom right now? I'm trying to

pretend that isn't part of my life this week. I was really trying to remember what it was like to be me the way I was before my dad got sick."

"We can hold off talking about it while you're in New York, but when you get home, will you tell me?" He tipped his head to the side to see her eyes.

"Sure." She sighed, and he felt her lashes flutter against his skin as she closed her eyes, turned, kissed his chest, then nestled back in.

Her body had tensed.

Rowan kept cupping up the water and rubbing his hand over her skin in a steady rhythm until she let that tension go.

"We were talking about dating," he said. "And I was explaining that my job is very much like being in the military. I get sent overseas. I get called in when there's a matter that needs my attention, which sometimes interrupts plans. Often those are important plans. I miss things that shouldn't be missed, like birthdays and special events. As you pointed out, like special ops for the military, I can't tell you anything about anything. That part of my life is a closed book." Then he thought about Clara and decided Avery needed as clear a picture as he could draw, even if it frightened her off. "There are times when I need to pose as part of a couple. And in those cases, I need to act the part."

"So you'll hold hands with another woman?"

"Yes."

"Kiss them?"

"Yes."

"Have sex with them?" Her voice tightened, and Rowan knew that was her line in the sand. Up until now, she'd weighed and accepted.

"So far, no. And I can't imagine that. I really can't. If it ever did happen, I would tell you. I might not be able to tell you why, but for your health's sake, and because I feel it's the moral thing to do, I would tell you, you'd never have to wonder."

She said nothing.

"But I've never even come close."

"How close?"

"Petting."

She sucked in some air. Held it. Pressed it out through pursed lips.

"Rarely. And I'd tell you that too."

She said nothing.

"All the issues with my job have proven unsupportable in my past relationships. I want to be fair to you and tell you, it's been hard on me and on the women I've dated."

"Did you love these women? Did they love you?"

Rowan considered that. That was certainly an interesting question.

"Love might have helped. I think, if I were to be honest, I dated women who had the qualities that I thought were important in a life partner. I want to be married. I want kids."

"How many kids?"

"Four."

She moved her hand to wrap his waist. "Four is a lot."

"Or it's just right."

She didn't answer.

"I think I was kind of looking for a woman like one might hire an employee."

She tipped her head back to look at him.

He dropped a kiss onto her nose. "That sounded colder than the truth. I was here in America for short bursts of time. I was looking for my life's partner. I didn't have time to mess around, so I figured out what I thought was important, and then I looked for chemistry."

"But I asked if you loved them."

"No, I've never been in love before now."

She leaned further back and looked at him with eyes held wide.

"The kiss in the lobby after you threw yourself into my arms."

She nodded. Her eyes were still wide and unblinking.

"We've talked as friends for years. I've sought your input and insight for years. I've respected and enjoyed you as a person for years. And then, there you were."

"All your boxes ticked?"

"Stop. I wasn't thinking in those terms. Instead of chemistry to a relationship, this was a relationship that turned out to be full-on chemistry. Don't you think?"

33

ROWAN

FRIDAY MORNING
New York City

ROWAN WATCHED Avery in the glow of the clock readout. He loved her face. He loved how angelic she looked in her sleep, loved her smiles, loved when her brow creased and her gaze grew thoughtful and serious. He loved watching her come. Loved her.

He loved her.

This was what it was like.

It was glorious, and it was terrifying. He was thinking about her work with Windsor Shreveport, and he was thinking that Lisa was coming into town to make Avery an asset to help them identify Taylor Knapp.

Avery needed to cooperate for the country's safety and for her own safety.

These fringe groups of wackos were getting more and more emboldened. Just last week, a man ran down almost a dozen women in his white van *just* because they were *women*, and he was angry at women as a group because they had turned him down for sex.

It wasn't a religious group.

It wasn't a political ideology.

It was a man who thought that women were mean because he wasn't getting laid. So, he plowed down random women, killing them to show his displeasure in his circumstances. This was a whole new kind of risk.

His phone vibrated on the bedside table.

Rowan reached for it before it woke Avery.

Lisa.

"I'm here."

"Where's here?" Rowan whispered.

"Here at your hotel."

"Lisa, it's two a.m."

"Which is why I called, and I'm not pounding on your door."

He slid from under Avery. "I'm coming down now."

He pulled on his gym outfit and kissed Avery on the shoulder, whispering, "I have to go talk to someone in the lobby. I'll be back up soon."

Avery lifted her head to see the clock. "Now? What is it?" She rolled toward him. "Is everything okay?"

"Yeah, yeah. Just work. Sometimes there are things that are too sensitive to send electronically, and we have to communicate in person."

"At two in the morning?"

"I'll be back," he said and left, checking that the door locked behind him.

He took the elevator. His heart pounding. Lisa wasn't supposed to get here until tonight. Two in the morning was cause for alarm.

She was standing in front of the elevator bank, back to the wall. "Hey, sorry."

"No." He grabbed her elbow and moved her toward the empty breakfast room. They sat at a table in the dark.

"It wasn't Jodie in your house," Lisa said.

"It would be hard to imagine it was. But how do you know it wasn't her? Did you two talk?"

"I went by her place. Her neighbor said she went on an emergency cruise to get over some asshole who broke her heart."

"I probably deserve that term. I let things go for way too long. But you checked on it?"

"I got on her Facebook, and she's posting pictures. She cut her hair. It's a new color."

"That's something women do, isn't it? A breakup haircut?"

"Maybe. I don't know."

"How did you get here at two in the morning?"

"I drove."

"So it's serious."

"You could say that."

She swiped open her phone and spun it toward Rowan. He flipped through her gallery. Lisa's house was trashed. Just like the pictures Lisa had sent earlier from her phone of his own place. "They were looking for something?"

"I doubt it. If they were serious about finding something, they would have cut my wall safe out and taken it with them. Both of our safes were intact and unmolested."

"You called the cops?"

"No, I handed it over to the FBI. This wasn't an ex getting revenge. This was a targeted attack. I told them about your place. I gave them your key and alarm code. They're doing forensics."

"It's got to be work-related."

"My conclusion," she said.

"Anyone else?" Rowan asked as he opened a photo wider to see the details better.

"Just us as far as I can tell."

"When you went to my place, do you think that they followed you home? Is that how they found you?"

"I went from your place, to the gym, to work. When I got home, I found this. It happened in broad daylight. But everyone in my neighborhood works, no one was home. It's actually the safest time of day to attack."

Rowan spun the phone. "This symbol—a heart with a lightning shape striking it—was on my house too. Is that why you thought it was Jodie to begin with?"

"Yup, jumped right to that conclusion despite my training."

"Understandable, though." Rowan studied the symbol. "Have you seen this before? Is it associated with a known group? Does it have street meaning?"

"Think about the hostiles who tried to get to you on your run. Did they seem street to you?"

"No, they seemed to be suburban wannabees." He handed the phone back to her. "Nothing we can do right now. Not our skill set. Let the techs come in and see what they can figure out. They'll want your phone, though."

Lisa wrinkled her nose. "They already have it. This is a new one." She slid the phone back into her pocket. "The FBI won a big one tonight. Have you been playing house, or did you listen to the news?"

"What happened?"

"They arrested a lieutenant in the Coast Guard on drug and gun charges."

"Okay, get to the interesting part." Rowan cast his eyes toward the elevator, wondering if Avery was lying in bed, thinking that his leaving her in the middle of the night was something she couldn't tolerate. He was anxious to get back up there.

"It looked kind of cut and dry, but it turns out he has ties to neo-Nazi groups, white supremacists, he had a hit list and access to HQ. He was planning to check out and make it memorable. He planned to take the whole place down with him."

"Shit."

"And so I made a phone call because it's part of my job to know this kind of thing. And guess what game this guy played almost non-stop, according to his computer data."

"*The Unrest.*" Rowan planted his hands on his knees and exhaled hard.

She nodded.

"Okay. Are you staying here?"

"Just down the block. What does your day look like today?"

"I'll see you get there safe." He stood.

"Hell no, you're not going to see me there safe. Mr. Macho-man. I'm trained by the US Army."

"And this is a big city, and it's the wee hours of the morning. Look, Lisa. I need to sleep. Do you think I can sleep if I'm worried about you?"

"Fine." She stood. "You can ride in the cab with me, watch me walk into the place, and you can have the car turn right back around." She moved toward the door, pulling up the taxi app. "Now, why do you need your beauty sleep? What's going on today?"

"I have a conference call with Iniquus. Prescott signed a contract with them. We're assigned to Panther Force. Their team leader is Titus Kane. Honey and Thorn are on that team. I know them. I'm glad to get this in place. I'll bring Kane in to meet with our task force on the Taylor Knapp case, probably Monday, if he can make time in his schedule. I'd like you to be there. Short notice, but we have a small window to figure this out. I'm hoping that after you talk to Avery tonight, we'll have something actionable for them. Lisa," they pressed through the doors and moved to the sidewalk, "tonight when we're with Avery, keep me out of the FBI talking points. I'm not your wingman on this. I'm Avery's boyfriend."

"That was fast. Zero to sixty in three-point-five seconds."

"Not really." They stood against the wall out of the rain. "We've been friends for years. After Jodie and I called it quits, I reached out to her in a more personal way than I had in the past. We were friends that had writing in common and kept it to that. Anyway, when we met in person, it all clicked into place. It's right. I'm not messing this up." He lifted his chin toward the cab that was heading their way. "And I'm not letting anything that's going on with Taylor Knapp bring crap into her life."

"Okay, Valentino." Lisa grinned. "I'll wear the FBI hat, and we'll see if there's danger on her horizon. We'll play it cool. Well, I'll play it cool, stud muffin. You can play it hot." Lisa cackled.

34

ROWAN

FRIDAY NIGHT
New York City

"Do you remember the time when you were trying to explain to the Twittersphere that stories were a survival technique?" Rowan asked Avery.

They had a cozy corner of the Salty Nomad Lounge reserved and paid for. It was a place that was designed for people who needed to meet casually and publicly, but who wanted their conversations to be private. The walls were padded and covered in velvet to absorb sound. The wait-staff would only approach when you pushed the candle to the edge of the table.

Unless you knew, you'd never know that this was a place that was built to hold secrets. It was a subtle but lucrative business plan. Rowan was glad he'd been able to get the space.

Avery should feel relaxed here.

They sat on the comfy chairs. On the table in front of them, a sampler platter of hors d'oeuvres steamed with delicious spices. Their drinks sat untouched.

"What's this?" Lisa asked, per their strategy. "I don't remember reading that. Survival strategies on Twitter?"

"Oh, it's just that one of the best ways people learn how to survive is through stories that are told to them," Avery explained. "For example, I know that I shouldn't hitchhike, let's say, because I've heard horror stories of what happens to people who do."

"Some of those stories don't bear out," Rowan said. "I never ate an apple from my Halloween bag for fear that there was a razor blade in it. But that whole thing's an urban myth, so I missed out on nutrition all because I listened to some story."

Lisa scowled at Rowan. "Where did you grow up that people were putting apples in your Halloween bag, Lamesville?"

"And what's more," Avery said. "Our brains love stories. *Love* them. The brain wants us to read stories and learn from them, so it dumps feel-good reward hormones into our systems, so we seek out stories, get tangled up in them, live them in our heads as if they are real, so we can assimilate the lessons as our own."

"That seems really dangerous, depending on the story you're reading. A kind of indoctrination," Rowan said, sending a look toward Lisa.

"Can be, I guess," Avery said. "I like to know what folks read. It gives me a lot of insight. Though, it's not always a good indicator. My best friend Lola," Avery stopped and nodded at Rowan to make the connection for him, "reads horror, but she is the kindest, most generous person I've ever known."

"If people already had something going in their lives, would they seek it out in stories? Like, do people in the military choose military thrillers to read?" Lisa asked.

Avery blushed. "Well, I edit romance… I don't know how that lines up psychologically. I've never seen a study. I'd assume it depends. It could be they're reading for affinity. Could be that someone is trying to safely explore their shadow side. Or maybe they're filling a void with the books they choose. Yeah, that's an interesting question. I'll see if I can't find some studies that speak to that. That's actually an important question. Thank you for asking it."

"Does your industry use a lot of psychology?" Lisa asked.

"Absolutely. It's important to engage the reader and keep them turning the page."

"I just read the Taylor Knapp book," Lisa said.

That was his cue. Rowan leaned back in his seat in the corner, moving deeper into the shadows and letting Lisa take over.

"I hate that book," Avery said vehemently.

"Your company published it."

Avery spun her glass in place and looked toward the door.

"I thought it was interesting," Lisa continued. "I was talking to a friend about the themes. They had a completely different take on the book than I did. We had a long discussion about it, and we decided that the author was pretty darned smart and put in little dog whistles for different groups. You wouldn't hear the whistles unless your ears were tuned to those notes." Lisa smiled.

From the way Avery's body was moving, she must have one leg crossed over the other under the table and be kicking it rhythmically. She said nothing, and Lisa plowed on as if she didn't see Avery's tension mounting.

"Bubbles." Lisa laughed. "They say social media is making

things worse. I read an article recently about people getting into their bubbles and having trouble reaching out to others when their different beliefs make them feel endangered. It really has been a huge issue for the world, leading to crazy unexpected outcomes." Lisa had taken a step back. She was a professional. She knew what she was doing.

Rowan hated that she was doing it with Avery.

But Avery, Rowan was now convinced, was up to her neck in this Taylor Knapp shit stream.

"Bubbles?" Avery lifted her glass and took a sip. She spun to check on Rowan. She looked back at Lisa. "How so?"

"Well, take anti-vaxxers, for example. There was a group of people who started spreading the rumor—well, the propaganda really, that immunization was dangerous because it gave you AIDS."

"Autism," Avery said.

"In this case, it was a group that thought it was preferred that African babies died. This group didn't want the babies in Africa to be immunized. So they told the story that the USA was trying to infect the world with AIDS."

Avery laughed.

Lisa looked at her, dead serious. "I'm not kidding."

"And people believed them?"

"Look it up. Put 'Polio vaccines and AIDS Link' into the search engine."

Avery pulled out her phone.

"To this day, it makes giving vaccinations in Africa very difficult. They have a lot of International organizations instead of American organizations doing the meds for just this reason. No one trusts that the US is there helping. They think we're trying to kill their children."

Lisa was quiet as Avery read.

Once Avery put her phone back down, Lisa said, "Propaganda has long tentacles. It has unknowable outcomes. It can be deadly." Lisa waited a beat. "You know Taylor Knapp don't you."

Avery stilled.

"You can't tell me because you have an NDA, and you're afraid."

Avery said nothing.

Rowan knew she'd deny it if this were deniable.

"Has this been difficult for you?" Lisa asked.

Avery furrowed her brow.

"Having an NDA. Wanting to talk about the projects at your publishing house…"

"No one cares about my comma placements in Saving Gloria; A SEALed Fate Romance." She spun around to look at Rowan.

Rowan pretended to be texting. He could feel her anxiety. He was watching her body language tells. And now, he was sure. Avery was on the team for this book. She didn't want to be. She had been threatened. He thought of all the ways they could do that. It wasn't a hard stretch. It didn't take FBI training.

Rowan had been on Twitter with writers for a long time and had always been grateful that he had no aspirations for publishing his work. It was a hard industry that was constantly changing. The biggest change was that with self-publishing, authors were finding that they could get their work in front of readers quickly instead of waiting the year for publication, plus the time trying to find an agent, plus the time for that agent to develop a publishing contract. It could be two years or more from the point where someone typed "The End" to the point where they saw a check from a traditional publisher. That was too long for most. The journey too daunting.

The publishing industry was devolving. Descending into obscurity. Ancient and quaint.

If they had threatened Avery's job, she wouldn't have many options when it came to finding a new one in the industry. If they told her they'd blackball her, she'd have no chance at all.

And Avery wouldn't just be thinking about herself. She'd be weighing her promise to her dying father into that equation. Without a job, how could she keep her mother safe?

It was a very potent threat.

It would feel life-threatening.

Rowan thought about Finley. How easy it would be to fall into that trap of thinking he could be both protector, lover, and information gatherer.

At this moment, Rowan wanted nothing more than to reach out and hold Avery. But that was the worst thing he could do right now. Lisa needed to be the one who forged this new relationship.

"Did you sign an NDA with your initial contract?" Lisa asked. Her voice was calm and encouraging.

"No." Avery focused back on Lisa. "We were given the NDAs two years ago. We were told to sign them or be fired."

"And what do you think precipitated this change?" Lisa asked.

"The industry is in trouble. Authors are finding that it's more profitable and easier all around to publish themselves. We're grasping at survival. I imagine that the NDAs had to be company-wide, so no one felt targeted, but I think that management wanted to protect our internal numbers so that if we founder, we don't look like a sinking ship. If we look like we're going down, we couldn't get prestigious authors. We'd be done if that happened."

Lisa offered a hint of a smile. "What else happened about that time?" she asked gently.

Avery shook her head.

"I read the Taylor Knapp book that your company published, not for pleasure but as part of my assignment as an FBI special agent."

Avery's shoulders came up to her ears.

"I have some pointed questions, Avery, and I need you to answer them. I'm speaking to you as a special agent for the FBI."

Avery looked back at Rowan, and Rowan struggled to keep his head down, typing at a text, seeming to be unaware.

"I have an NDA," Avery whispered.

Lisa leaned in. "Do you know Taylor Knapp's birth name?"

"No, they use a pen name," Avery whispered.

"They, plural?" Lisa canted her head.

"No, 'they' non-gendered," Avery said.

"Have you met this individual?" Lisa was calm, and that should help, Rowan thought.

"Twice. Well, I suppose I have. I met someone who purports to be the author."

"And why would you have met with them? This was a general meeting?"

"No." She picked up her drink and drained it down.

"Are you working on the Taylor Knapp project, Avery?"

"Am I in trouble?" She turned. "Rowan, stop with that stupid subterfuge. I know you're listening to this. Is this why you're talking to me? Is this why we went out? You said you didn't sleep with people for the FBI. You lied to me about that because I was the one you were sleeping with for the FBI." Anger seethed out of her pores. Her fury was palpable.

That time when he was holding Avery in the warm water, and

they had discussed their future together, had been such an important moment in Rowan's life. And now it was stained.

"Avery." Lisa's voice was sharp and pulled Avery's attention away from him. "Avery, look me in the eye. No. Absolutely not. No, Rowan didn't seduce you to get information. If he was doing that, I wouldn't be here. First, that's not who he is. Second, that's not what he does. Third, he wants a relationship with you. Fourth, he's frightened for you. And he wants the FBI to step in and save your ass from the crazy that's sure to come down the pike and hit you full force." With each point, Lisa was jamming her index finger into the table. "Rowan is your knight in shining armor in this scenario. He's trying to find a soft landing for you. To that end, he asked that our hard hitters from the task force not step in, and instead, he got me involved. He thought you'd feel safer since you and I know each other, and I hope you can trust me. *We* hope you can trust me. It's the only way."

Avery had her elbows posted on the table and rested her head in her hands. She was crying hard.

Rowan swallowed. He hated every single second of this.

"Hey." Lisa reached out and touched Avery's arm. "You're not in trouble with the FBI. But this is complicated."

Avery didn't stop her sobbing.

It was almost impossible for Rowan to sit still. He wanted to fix this and make it better.

"I understand. It's pretty scary," Lisa said. "The FBI can help you."

"No. You can't." Avery moved her empty glass off the cocktail napkin, then used the napkin to swipe at her eyes. "I have a contract—an NDA. I have a future, which sounds unpatriotic to put first. But I have to put it first. I read the newspaper. I see what happens to whistle-blowers and informants. Their lives are destroyed. It's not just my life on the line here."

Lisa nodded. "We can help protect you."

"No. You can't." She shook her head at Lisa. "With all the things I've been learning about social media and manipulation in the last week, I'm even more terrified than ever. If my name goes on someone's Get-Avery-List, I will never find peace. I will be trolled and botted, and God knows what else." She flung her hand in the air. "*Doxxed.* I'm not sure if what very limited information I have would be helpful in any way, shape, or form."

"Right now, the biggest help would be figuring out who this person is who is calling themselves Taylor Knapp."

"I *don't* know their legal name."

"But you know how we could find them?" Lisa lifted her brow. "You have an email? A phone number? An address? Because I have a plan."

35

Rowan

Friday Night
New York City

"Avery, how good are you at lying?" Lisa asked.

"I suck at it, to be honest. I get so anxious. I turn bright red. Please don't ask me to lie."

Lisa looked up at the ceiling, thinking, then focused back on Avery. "Okay, let me ask it this way—Avery, I hear that you tell wonderful stories. Are you a good storyteller? Have you ever acted?"

"I can tell stories. I've never tried acting."

Lisa nodded, storing that away, then seemed to change tack. "I wrote a story once, and you sent me editing notes. Well, I've sent you lots of stories, and you've sent me lots of editing notes over the years. I just looked over the notes you sent me on my new short story. You were right about all of that. It was as plain as day the holes I left, once you pointed them out to me. So thank you."

Avery nodded.

"But I'm thinking of a specific story. It was the story about the woman in prison, do you remember that?"

"I'm sorry, I don't."

"It was a pretty long time ago. I remember it vividly because it made a lot of sense to me. You told me to walk through the scene with my body, bend over the way my character did, and when I tried it out on my own, I would see it was impossible. The reader, you said, might not know why they didn't buy into a scene, but the scene wouldn't make sense to their brains. I followed your advice, I walked through the scene, and I learned a lot."

Avery shrugged and shook her head. She didn't see the relevance. Lisa was trying to slow spin this, and Avery's mind moved too fast for the long drag out. Rowan didn't know how to signal Lisa. He had to sit there and hope she had a plan.

"Pretend this is part of a novel. Pretend you're walking through the scene to see how things play out. You're not lying. You're watching characters in an unraveling plot. This is a thriller. The timeline for this is really short. We need to push the pedal down and try to get ahead of this before the new video game drops. As soon as the video game is released, the good guys lose a lot of control."

"Are you trying to stop the release?" Avery asked.

"I can't comment on our goals." Lisa was matter of fact.

Avery breathed in, sighed out. "I don't know what to do." She looked back at Rowan. "What should I do?" she whispered.

Rowan couldn't answer her. There was no right way to answer her. She needed to trust Lisa, and she needed to make up her mind on her own. This was her life, and Avery seemed to understand. Things could unroll very quickly and very badly.

Again, Avery nodded, acknowledging his silence as his answer. "I need to go to the ladies' room and blow my nose." She got up and left.

"We could put a tail on her and see where she goes," Lisa said.

Rowan drummed his thumb on the table. "You heard her using the 'they' form of pronoun. But the way she used it didn't sound like someone from the LGBTQ community using the non-specific gender pronoun. It sounded like she was using it to hide Taylor's identity. We, on the other hand, used the masculine pronoun. That leads me to believe Taylor Knapp is a woman."

"You could be right, which means, if a team tailed Avery, they wouldn't even know what gender subject we're looking for. They're an adult human and breathing, and that's all we've got."

They sat in silence until Avery came back and found her seat, looking composed and very business-like.

Rowan would say she'd gone off to get her head on straight. Could be a good thing. Might just as well be a bad one. It depended entirely on how Lisa played this.

"I'm not here to scare you. I'm not here to twist your arm. I'm here because we need Taylor Knapp's help. That's why we need to get in touch."

Avery reached over to Rowan's scotch, took a sip, and coughed hard.

"In the aftermath of the 9-11 Terror Attacks," Lisa said, once Avery was breathing again, "the CIA came to understand that their thinking might be homogenous. They needed a way to anticipate attacks that they couldn't see coming. We've been looking through our intelligence agency lenses. Sometimes, those lenses can make us myopic. Sometimes, they can be blinders. If a threat hasn't occurred to you, how could you possibly be prepared to thwart it?" she asked. "The Intel Community was blindsided by the airplanes being hijacked."

Rowan moved his chair close to Avery's, and she shifted around, pressing up against him until he wrapped his arm around her. She snuggled in, resting her head back against his shoulder, listening.

"Now that this problem was exposed," Lisa continued, "the CIA decided to form a group of people who could and would challenge the intelligence agencies. They hired out-of-the-box thinkers. People willing, and even delighted, to freak out the higher-ups by shining a light on ideas that might piss off the senior officials."

"Okay, I'm hearing this as a romance editor, and that makes perfect sense to me. This is the frame I've put that in—one of the genres that I edit is military romance. One of the tropes is that the men in these novels are the best of the best. Super-human, if you will. The problem for my authors is how to make them unique and show their individual personalities. In this set of people, they are homogenized by their professions, and their personality differences become more nuanced and less obvious."

Avery shot a "sorry!" glance toward Rowan, knowing that he had been one of these elite soldiers.

"You mean beyond being the best-trained killing machines on the face of the planet, and being the most egotistical, that special operators actually have personalities?" Lisa asked. "I mean, is there really anything else to know? I say, just let me read about how big their muscles are and how they're willing to swim through fire to save the heroine, and I'm good. Personalities are overrated." She winked at Rowan.

Lisa had a girlfriend and less than zero interest in men and their muscles.

"Okay, look, I know you're teasing me," Avery said. "But I'm talking about editing and writing here. I'm talking about this as an observer and not someone who lives the life of a special operator." She squeezed Rowan's thigh. "And I'm using this as a metaphor to show that I can understand how the CIA got into their pickle. People who chose that career have specific personality traits. We know this because there are tests. They have to be of a high intellectual caliber. They have to be of a certain physical capability. They have to be honest. They have to be law-abiding, and so forth. Now, go back to the author writing elite soldiers. The characters enter into the military world, where their egos are stripped down and built back up. The characters train to think as a single unit. Each may have their strengths and weaknesses, but in action, those nuances don't show up as vividly as, say, heroes with different backgrounds—the nice guy who wanders into a cupcake shop in a sweet romance, for example. I'm not saying the military heroes are cookie-cutter characters. I'm just saying that the authors who are writing about operations and missions and what have you, work very hard to portray differences in personalities of their characters while their characters are in stressful situations where they've been trained to act in a very specific way. And those actions, reactions, and thought processes are standardized for the sake of success."

She held out her hands, stretching her fingers wide. "Now, I'm imagining the CIA. People who get to the level that would be calling the shots would have been trained to think and institutionalized to behave in a monochromatic way. It would be far *better*," she stopped and lifted her brows for emphasis as she looked up at Rowan, "to bring in creative thinkers. For example, you could give me any scenario, and without batting an eyelash, I could tell you fifteen plausible ways that this could all go to hell in a handbasket. Why? Because the stories that put characters in life or death situations are the stories that trigger the brain to pay attention, and brains hearing danger stories get that dopamine reward we were talking about earlier. If I get a manuscript in, I'm looking for places where the author got lazy and let the story be too bright and happy. Too predictable. Bright, happy, predictable books are put on bedside tables. We need bad things to happen in the books, so the reader's mind is enthusiastically learning. Those bad things have to be interesting, so readers are hungry to turn the pages. How do you make a story interesting? By finding new and unique ways to twist the plot. And to make the possible outcomes dangerous."

Lisa and Rowan were grinning at her.

"My recommendation would be to get a bunch of authors, good authors, the ones with a vast breadth of knowledge and a curiosity to dive into the depth of a subject. Those are the authors I personally like to work with. Stop grinning at me like that."

"Your mind, Avery Goodyear, is astonishing," Rowan said.

"Good God, Kennedy." Lisa blinked at him as if he'd shocked the shit out of her. "Cupid's arrow pierce you twice? It's kind of nauseating to watch happen," Lisa said and turned to Avery. "No offense. And I would say exactly the same thing about you being astonishing, just maybe not in such a sappy tone." She paused. "The reason we would both say that is because that's exactly what the CIA did. They developed a group called 'Red Cell.' It's a bunch of creatives whose task and purpose is to look at the intelligence and come up with alternative ways of putting the pieces together. Or as you said, hand them fifteen ways that things could go to hell in a handbasket."

"I bet they piss off the analysts," Avery said.

"They do," Lisa said. "But that's their job. If they aren't pissing people off, then they are failing at their mission."

"So who did they pick for their Red Cell?"

Lisa smiled. "As I hear it, it was actually a pretty hard task to find the right people. They wanted writers." She nodded at Avery. "They wanted them to be well versed in history, geopolitics, thriller writers, research-heavy."

"Big names, obviously."

"Why do you say that," Rowan asked. She was right, but why?

"Because one of the superpowers of a writer is that they can walk up to almost anyone and say, 'I'm a writer, and I have some questions for my novel that you have an expertise in, would you help me?' and people will tell you anything you want to know. When I was writing my last story, my heroine had to steal a plane. I went to an airport to talk to their safety officer, and without blinking an eye, he taught me how to steal a plane."

"You're a dangerous woman." Rowan laughed.

"And don't you forget it." She reached for his glass and took another sip of his drink, and coughed equally hard this second time.

Rowan reached out and pushed the candle to the edge of the table, so he could order Avery a drink that was easier to swallow.

"Anyway," Avery continued. "To answer your question, that writer-super-power thing only works but so much when you're a lesser-known writer. The more prestige you have, the more contacts you have, the more interesting places you get to go to see the behind the scenes. If you wanted someone who really knew what they were talking about, you'd need an international political or military thriller writer who was top of the charts, has all kinds of behind-the-scenes access, and has talked to all kinds of people. They know how to ask the oddly detailed questions. The weird little titbit that will twist the plot hard. It's those odd details that creates the interest because it's the little things that are known to few that are the cracks where things can go so wrong."

She wrinkled her nose. "But," Avery said, "there would be a problem with egos, just like with special operators. The only problem is, writers have strong egos, individualized egos, and are not team players."

"Right again. Avery gets all the gold stars," Lisa said, wiggling the candle around to catch the server's attention. "They start the folks on short rotations, so they can see if they play well in the sandbox with the others." She turned to the waiter. "Another round, please."

When the waiter left, Avery leaned her elbows on the table. "What's this got to do with me?"

Lisa grinned. "The FBI would like to start their own Red Cell." She raised her brows and dropped them to show her excitement about the project.

"And you want me to suggest some authors? I do romance."

Lisa mimicked Avery's posture by crossing her arms on the table and leaning forward, closing the space between her and Avery, and whispered, "We want a specific author. Taylor Knapp."

Avery stilled.

Rowan's muscles banded with tension.

"You want me to deliver Taylor Knapp to you. You want to convince Taylor Knapp to work on some newly formed FBI creative team?" Avery looked at the front door again.

Rowan couldn't tell if she thought someone was going to burst through the doors, throwing flashbang into the room, or she wanted to run away.

When she focused back on Lisa, she said, "I bet there is no team. I bet you just think this is the enticement you need to get a special agent and Taylor into the same room."

Again, Rowan found it interesting and curious that Avery was very careful not to use a gender-related pronoun. He doubted sincerely that it was her being PC or that Taylor went by a non-gendered pronoun by choice. Avery wasn't smooth enough with it. Rowan could see Avery editing her words before they exited her mouth. He was almost a hundred percent sure that Taylor Knapp was a woman. Did that change anything about their approach? He'd have Lisa take that back to the team.

"If that were true, that we need an FBI agent in the same room with Taylor," Lisa asked, "would you help us?"

36

Avery

Saturday Morning
New York

THE PLASTIC SEAT was hard and uncomfortable. The sun had hit an angle where it glared directly into her eyes, and there was a tantrum-throwing toddler screaming at her feet. Yet Avery felt only relief. The ticket agent overbooked the return flight, and Avery was one of ten bounced passengers.

All right, she volunteered.

She couldn't catch another plane until one-thirty. She'd already called Fanny with the heads up that she'd be delayed getting home. And Fanny was going to pick up their mom at the end of Sally's shift.

Maybe Avery could finagle it so she could go home and have

some peace and quiet to process before she let Fanny know that she was home.

As a matter of fact, Avery just didn't think it was wise to try to handle Taylor and the FBI on zero sleep. She dialed the bed and breakfast in Warrenton, where she had her reservation, and changed her arrival date to this evening. It was on the Windsor Shreveport bill. There was no reason not to go now, besides ticking off her sister.

Avery's gaze skimmed the waiting area. A handful of restaurants clustered nearby. She checked her watch, 11:20. Lunch would be nice, but every place looked crowded, and Avery was loathed to give up her seat. As awful as it was, at least she wasn't sitting on the floor like many of those around her. And she had the good luck of being positioned next to a wall socket.

Avery plugged in her laptop and booted it up, using her hot spot.

Scanning through her emails, Avery saw nothing urgent. Thank you letters from the authors she'd met over the last three days comprised most of them. She'd asked for the first two chapters from most of the writers. It was hard not to. They were so earnest about their work.

The truth was, not a single plotline interested her. What they needed at Windsor Shreveport was something exceptional—a standout. Something bound to hit the New York Times Best Seller list. If only she could find it, then George might take her off the Taylor Knapp book.

That would be a miracle.

The Uprising—what nonsense. Horrible. And now the FBI was involved. Avery brushed her hair from her face, twisting it up into a knot and sticking a pencil in the bun to hold it secure.

Avery wished Taylor would get finished writing the manuscript so Avery could do her job, then move on. Like swallowing down cod liver oil, she'd pinch her nose and do what had to be done.

Staring past the luggage carts on the runway, where men and women in their florescent green jumpsuits scurried about, Avery focused on the horizon and sighed deeply. She seemed to do that a lot. Lolly thought it was a sign of depression. But Avery didn't feel depressed, just…overwhelmed.

An arctic blast from the air-conditioning system swept the room.

Pulling her suit jacket closer, Avery leaned her forehead against the window and closed her eyes. *The Uprising, can you imagine?* Why was the FBI involved? That's the part that Avery couldn't fathom.

Her phone beeped. Avery looked at the screen: George. Booking issues didn't affect *his* seat. He'd probably already landed in D.C. That's what happens when the boss flies business-class, and she was relegated to the back of the plane, flying coach. George had no idea what a favor he'd done for her by leaving her behind. Avery smiled and turned the ringer to vibrate.

Then she thought about Rowan and his toe-curling, breath-stealing kiss good-bye. He was going to take her to brunch Sunday, and they were going to go for a walk along the river if the weather was nice. She pulled up Twitter. Her hand hovered tentatively over her laptop keys.

Her inbox dinged, and Avery saw it was a file from Taylor.

With a sigh, she opened it.

It was long. Fifty thousand words long. Half the word count for the contract.

Too long, too soon.

There's no way in this world that Taylor could have typed

these many words in the last few days even if she snorted a nose full of cocaine and dictated this into a voice to text app.

Avery changed the zoom level to thirty percent and scrolled through the hundred and seventy pages. These were notes, not prose.

This information wasn't dictated. This was carefully thought through and arranged under chapter headings. Lists.

On this page, the goal is

This character sends message X

This character send message Y

This character contradicts the X and adds Z

In the world of writing, there were three basic ways that authors figured out their plots. "Pantsers" sat at the keyboard to see what came to them. They were as surprised as the reader at how things unfolded. "Planters" were writers who had a good feel for the story and a basic trajectory, but they let the characters develop and unfold as the story took shape. And "plotters." Plotters knew exactly how the story would transpire. They might put their story on sticky notes, or on whiteboards, or Excel spreadsheets. It didn't matter. There were tons of ways to plan. And they could be excruciatingly detailed plans.

But Avery had never seen anything like this. This level of plotting was absurd.

And then Avery remembered Taylor's old college roommate who, for a thousand dollars, sent her notes for *The Unrest.*

A Russian here in America illegally.

A Ph.D. candidate in Germany who wrote code to help Taylor harvest personal data about the players.

Patrick Windsor's wife, Inge Prokhorov, from Bulgaria.

And the FBI.

Avery was assigned to help Taylor put out that book.

Chill bumps raised on Avery's arms, and she felt sweat form on her brow.

She looked through the notes. She looked at the descriptors. While the English was very good, Avery knew these weren't written by a native English speaker. But what was it that Taylor had said about her Russian roommate? She'd been here since she was a baby. She'd lived here until high school. The roommate would speak English like a native.

These notes were from someone else.

And, Avery could show the FBI how she could tell that Taylor Knapp, or whoever she was, was getting the basis of her work from somewhere else. All Taylor was doing was turning bullet points into prose, using the vast wealth of language that she'd developed as a child memorizing poems. Pulling up Milton with ease.

Avery's mind went to the CIA Red Cell, and she juxtaposed that with a conversation she'd had with Rowan about Russia. Rowan had told her that Russia knew it couldn't beat the West with typical military warfare. Long ago, they had taken their military financing and had rerouted it away from bullets and armor and toward psychological operations. Or as Rowan called them 'psy-ops.' The Russians had been working since the end of the Soviet Union to take down America from the inside.

While America had been dancing and patting herself on the back for the victory after the fall of the Soviet Union, getting drunk on the U.S.'s superiority, Russia plotted.

The battleground had shifted, that was all.

Rowan had a Ph.D. in propaganda. Surely, the same kinds of men and women did the same kinds of jobs in Russia. Each country was trying to increase the power and safety of its citizens. Disinformation. "Tech wars" was what Rowan said.

If we had a Red Cell, why couldn't they?

Avery needed to reach out to Rowan, like a touchstone, as she contemplated the fact that somehow, she, Avery Goodyear, a romance editor from the suburbs, had become a player in an international game of psychological warfare.

How terrifying was that?

Avery wasn't at all surprised when her phone buzzed with a text.

Rowan – **Are you home safely?**

She looked at the message for a full minute, wondering how she should reply.

Avery – **It's very odd, don't you think, that whenever I'm about to send you a message, you beat me to it?**

Rowan – **Ha! I've noticed that myself. I guess I'm pulled to your magnetic personality**.

Avery – **That sounds like it might hurt.**

Rowan – **Not so far. Not for me, anyway. Are you okay**? **You don't feel okay to me. Your words feel tired and uncomfortable.**

Avery – **See? You are psychic. I'm stuck at the airport for the next few hours.**

There was a long pause, and Avery's muscles tighten.

Rowan – **No. It's more than that. I'm worried now**.

Avery – **I have a question for you.**

Rowan – **Shoot.**

Avery – **You know what? It can wait. I have a lot to think about. I'm having trouble sorting it out.**

Rowan – **I'd be happy to help.**

Avery – **Thank you. I wish you could. But again, I have that NDA. And I need to decide what to do next.**

Rowan – **Maybe we could find a way to talk about it without actually talking about it? Maybe we could talk about hypotheticals?**

Avery – **Maybe. Let me sit with this. I need to think this through.**

She tucked her phone away. She read through the plotting notes. Avery could see quite clearly how the us-them narratives were constructed. How, whatever you believed, would be supported. And whatever you believed, you were endangered.

These notes were quite genius—evil genius.

Like a Bond film.

Avery wasn't equipped to play on that kind of cliff's edge.

37

AVERY

SATURDAY AFTERNOON
Washington DC

WHEN AVERY LANDED in D.C. at four, the traffic was bumper to bumper. There was no way she could get home by the time that Sally got done for the day. Avery called her sister to tell Fanny she needed to go and sit with their mother until Avery could get there.

Fanny wasn't thrilled. She said she only had this weekend break, and then she was "doing Mom" for the rest of the month.

"I didn't plan the traffic, Fanny."

Until Avery could figure out a better living arrangement for their mom, their mother would be living with Fanny's family.

And when she got home, Avery was going to spring it on Fanny. She would be leaving to stay in Warrenton, Virginia tonight, one point three miles from Taylor. Avery was going to facilitate the project, so she could keep her job.

And she was going to spy for the FBI.

Despite how bad she knew she'd be at the job of being a spy, her mind was made up.

AVERY SEEMED to have magicked her way home. She had no idea how she'd gotten all the way to her house by five o'clock. She pulled in beside Fanny's car.

Curtis and Fanny were holding hands as they walked up the sidewalk.

Fanny's face changed from anxiety to relief as she saw Avery.

That wouldn't last.

The two walked back to their car like they'd just pile in and head out.

"I need to talk to you," Avery called, climbing from her own car. She caught up to them as Fanny was waiting for Curtis to unlock the car door.

Avery left her purse and bag where they were and rounded the car with her keys in her hand. "Late notice, I'm sorry. But I have to grab my bag and go. I'm expected out of town tonight."

"Tonight? But you said Monday. Sally isn't working tomorrow."

Avery shrugged.

"We have church tomorrow. I can't miss service," Fanny said. "I can't take Mom with me. She'd tell everyone they were going to hell for being Baptists."

Curtis laid his hand on Fanny's shoulder. He'd take over the arguments now.

Avery worked to stop herself from rolling her eyes.

"I'm concerned about bringing *your* mother into *my* home. I think it's too dangerous for my children."

"Fanny's mother." Avery crossed her arms over her chest. "Fanny's home. Fanny's children. Fanny's problem. I won't be here to take up the slack. I'm just grabbing my suitcase and walking back out the door."

Avery wondered how Curtis could gyrate his face into that bizarre combination of surprise and fiery brimstone.

"Fine!" he sputtered. "She must stay in your house during the day. Sally must pick up your mother in the morning and bring her back at the end of her shift."

"You arrange that with Sally. And you pay that fee. Because Mom could just as easily stay at your house and have Fanny do the watching like I do on the weekends. Or Sally could watch Mom at your house. All that's up to you. I'm not going to be here."

"Absolutely no to her being at our house around the clock. I draw the line." Curtis lifted a righteous finger into the air. "Can you blame me for not wanting her at my house during the day?"

"Whatever." Avery looked at him like he was out of his mind. "I'm just saying that I'm not paying Sally while I'm away. If you're using Sally, you're paying Sally. I pay Sally because I have to go to work during the day to support Mom and me. Fanny, on the other hand, is at home."

"I am rarely at home," Fanny countered.

"You're at home when you're not having your pedicure done and lunching with your friends. How you spend your time is your choice. You could choose to spend it with Mom. If not," Avery shrugged, "it's your dime, not mine. When I get home, different arrangements need to be made. I can't do this anymore. I'm done."

"And until then, I have to do all the work? You're off to wherever, doing as you please, and you're shackling me to Mom?"

"This is *not* a vacation. This is a pain in my ass."

Curtis sucked in a sudden breath and turned a shocked pink. "Language! And those provisions will not do. I will not allow my wife to persist under such stress. I will not allow my home to become a shambles."

"But it's all well and good for me?" Avery asked, spiking a single brow. She was done with this. What needed saying had been said. Avery stalked to the front door and was confused that it stood slightly ajar.

Cold washed through her system as Avery remembered that her mom had escaped just the other day, heading naked to the grocery store.

She pushed the door open, then stood with her hand on the doorknob and her heart in her throat. She looked in on the chaotic scene. The cushions were off the furniture, slashed, the down stuffing was like snow across the carpeting. Drawers upended, the lamp lay on its side.

It took Avery an agonizing minute to process the mess, then slowly, her brain thawed.

Blue spray paint graffitied the walls. Cuss words spelled out and hearts with lightning bolts.

What had her mother done?

Why would she destroy everything like this?

Where was she? Where was Sally?

Fear dried her mouth as she lifted her cell phone to call 911.

Before Avery tapped the send button, she heard pounding on the basement door.

"Help me!"

38

Rowan

Alexandria, Virginia
Saturday Evening

Avery had texted – **My mother's lost her mind. It's serious. She destroyed everything in the house. There's spray paint all over the walls. I can't see you tomorrow**.

Rowan had tried to call, but Avery wasn't answering.

He tried texting – **What color spray paint?**

Avery –**??? Blue.**

Rowan – **I need to talk to you. Answer your phone NOW.**

He watched as the text said delivered. He waited for it to indicate "read," but it didn't. He called and went immediately to voice mail. She was probably talking to someone else.

Rowan called Lisa.

"Missed me already?"

"I just got a text from Avery. Her house was destroyed, and there's blue spray paint on her walls."

There was a long pause, then, "Well, shit."

"I'm on my way there now. I texted you the address. Can you meet me?"

"Yeah, sure. And you might want to call Iniquus to come, too. I got a report that might shine a light on some of this."

"But they're tasked to the Taylor Knapp case. We can't just bring them in on something because of Avery."

"*Really?*"

Rowan could hear Lisa's fob beep and the door click as she got into her car.

"Thanks for explaining that to me."

"Stop." Rowan was on speakerphone as he wound through the weekend traffic aimed for Avery's house. "I'm sorry I didn't couch that as a question. Let me try that again. If you're telling me to pull in Iniquus, that means that you have a link between the vandalism and the Taylor Knapp case, right?"

"That's better. And bingo. And no, before you even ask for a single detail, I'm not going to talk about it on the phone. My GPS is saying I'm ten minutes out from Avery's, so much for my hot yoga class. What's your ETA?"

"Twenty. I'll call Panther Force now."

WHEN ROWAN ARRIVED, people were hovering outside. Lisa probably pulled them away from the crime scene that they hadn't realized was a crime scene.

Lisa was standing there, her foot resting on the first brick step of a typical nineteen-seventies style split level, a pad out and pen poised.

A couple stood apart, over by their car, looking for any opportunity to jet out of there.

Avery was rubbing the back of a fifty-something-year-old woman with fire-engine-red spikey hair. The woman was dressed in scrubs. That must be Mrs. Goodyear's caretaker.

Mrs. Goodyear was wearing what looked like a pair of her husband's old jogging pants pushed up to her thighs, and maybe one of his tank tops. Her legs were white with blue marbling. Her breasts skipped and swung untethered as she moved about. On her feet, she wore a pair of bedroom slippers.

"You don't know who put the chair in front of the basement door?" Lisa asked.

The red-haired woman shook her head.

Lisa turned his way. "This is Sally."

Rowan held up a hand as he headed over. "Hi, Sally. Rough day. I'm sorry."

"I already told Miss Avery that I quit. I can't do this anymore."

"I wouldn't ask you to," Avery said. Her hand rubbing the woman's shoulder. She spoke in a soothing, supportive tone. "You've been through so much. I'm so sorry." She turned to Rowan. "Thank you for coming."

"Of course." He glanced at Lisa. "Have you been in?"

"Yup."

"Is it what we thought?"

"Yup."

He walked around Sally and up the steps. The door wasn't pulled all the way shut. He tapped it open with his keys. When the door opened, Rowan looked around without crossing the threshold. Same heart and lightning sign. "Did anyone touch anything?"

"They all said no other than when Avery was helping Sally

get out of the basement," Lisa said. "Sally was locked down-stairs, with a chair shoved under the doorknob. She didn't hear anyone else in the house. She didn't think to listen if the noise was coming from two places at one time. She didn't see any strange cars out front today or any other day. But Sally said that this is the second time she was locked in the basement this week. She had her phone with her this time, but it had run out of battery."

He focused on Sally. "Ma'am, has Mrs. Goodyear ever done anything like that before? Locked a door..." Rowan asked.

"Mrs. Goodyear didn't do it this time either," Avery's mom said. "It was the bad men. Hey, I know you. You were talking on the computer with Avery the other night."

"Yes, ma'am, that's right. Did you watch the bad men lock the door on Sally?"

"No."

"Did you see the bad men spray paint the wall?"

"Yes. What else was I going to do besides watch?" Mrs. Goodyear asked. "They told me to sit in the chair. And I did what they asked me to do. I'm just an old woman, and they were young and big."

"How many did you see?" Lisa asked.

The woman standing to the side sighed loudly, crossing her arms and tapping her toe.

"Fanny," Avery rebuked her.

Rowan repeated. "How many?"

"I don't know four, maybe five. Two of them were either the same guy or looked a lot alike."

"Iniquus is here," Lisa said, her focus on the road.

A Hummer pulled up in front of the house. Honey Honig climbed out of the passenger side. Titus Kane rounded the vehi-cle. Titus and Honey sauntered in lockstep toward them.

Rowan's mind went back to what Avery had said about how hard it was to explain the nuance of personality differences in special operators. The special operators, his brothers, were as different as night and day but watching these two striding across the lawn, both simultaneously removing their sunglasses, the same stoic facial expressions, Rowan could see the issue for the layman.

Avery sent the Iniquus guys in their tactical camo pants and their charcoal-gray compression shirts a startled look but focused back on her mother.

"Why did you cut the furniture, Mom?"

"The bad men did it."

"Where did you get the paint, Mom?"

"The bad men brought it with them. Then they gave me the spray cans after they were done. Then they left."

"Were they wearing gloves?" Lisa asked.

"Yeah, the long, yellow, kitchen kind. But just the two of them that had the paint."

Sally stood up. "I'm done. I'm sorry for you and your troubles, Miss Avery. You're a really good daughter. But, no." She turned and made her way toward an ancient turd-brown Buick.

As Sally passed the couple, the man turned to Avery. "I won't bring *your* mother to *my* house. This is just too dangerous."

"Fanny's mother," Avery said, turning back to Mrs. Goodyear. "Mom, please tell me, where did you get spray paint?"

39

AVERY

SATURDAY EVENING
  Falls Church, Virginia

"AVERY, STOP, PLEASE," Rowan said. "Your mom didn't do this. She's telling the truth. Those symbols on your wall have meaning." He looked at Lisa, and she gave a nod. He focused back on Avery. "Do you think your mother needs medical care?"

Avery swept her gaze over her mom. "No, she seems fine."

"All right." Rowan looked over to the man, glaring down his nose at the scene. "Avery and I will go in and get Mrs. Goodyear's medications and things for tonight." He shifted his gaze to Fanny. "It would probably be best if you go ahead and take your mom to your house and settle her in."

"Best for whom?" Curtis stormed. "Not best for *me*, that's for sure."

Avery watched as Rowan's stance changed, his gaze. He transformed from nice guy to what Avery would imagine Rowan would look like when he was on a mission with the Rangers—hard-minded, hard-bodied, a force to be contended with.

As Rowan's gaze bore into Curtis, Avery felt sure that Curtis saw it too, and he crumbled into a beta character, swallowing hard and ducking his chin subserviently.

Fanny smacked him in the chest. "Tell him no!" she said. "We can't take her. I don't want this responsibility."

Rowan sent Lisa a look and tipped his head toward Fanny's car. "Can you get Mrs. Goodyear settled in the back seat of their car? Avery and I will be down in just a minute with Mrs. Goodyear's things."

Lisa had morphed too. She didn't look like the computer-geek girl that Avery had known, now she had the body language of a woman who would be assigned with the Rangers and support their missions. Focused. Muscled. Unswerving.

Avery tucked that into her memory bank for a future plot point. It was very interesting to see it unfold in real life.

Rowan pointed at Fanny and Curtis, shooting them a look that said "behave," then put his hand under Avery's elbow to steer her through the front door.

Rowan probably thought Curtis and Fanny would jump in the car and roar off into the sunset, never to be seen again if Lisa wasn't on guard.

And they probably would have.

But they were intimidated, and Avery reveled in the moment of *schadenfreude* until she moved farther into her house.

"Are you sure Mom didn't do this?" She was bewildered by this information.

"Look at the furniture. Do you think your mother has the strength to flip things over like that?"

"I don't know. She can be surprisingly strong."

"She didn't have any scratches. No bumps or bruises."

"Okay, you've got me there. These symbols have meaning?" She reached out to touch the blue heart with the lightning bolt, and Rowan tapped her hand to keep her fingers off.

Yeah, if this were a crime scene, then she shouldn't be messing anything up.

"Lisa and I had the same thing happen at our houses."

Avery dropped her chin to absorb that information. Processing. "That's why she was in New York at two in the morning?"

"Exactly," Rowan said as he reached the top of the stairs and waited for Avery to show him to her mom's room. Calm. That helped.

"You didn't tell me," Avery whispered.

"We had no idea it would touch you. Lisa says she has some information."

"And the huge men that got out of the Hummer? The ones that look like Rambo's best friends? I didn't even know they made human beings that big."

"Stuff of novels?"

"Apparently not, since they're standing, flesh and blood, in my living room."

"They're going to help us figure this all out and make sure you're safe."

Avery opened the door to her mom's room. It had gone untouched. Everything was where it should be. It took Avery no time at all to scoop up what was needed and head down the stairs.

She handed the things to the big guy with the outstretched hand. "Thank you, ma'am. My name's Honey. My team leader is Titus Kane." He lifted his chin to his partner, who was walking around the corner of the house toward the back yard.

Honey took the suitcase to Curtis, who had to tip his head straight back to look Honey in the eye.

Curtis didn't say a thing. Simply took the bag, climbed in the car, and they left.

Now what?

40

AVERY

SATURDAY NIGHT

Avery's not quite sure where

SHE SAT in the back of the Hummer, sandwiched between Lisa and Rowan. Titus was driving, Honey beside him. Avery assumed they were listening to someone talking to them with some communications device in their ears, because why else would they randomly be saying, "Good, copy," and "That's a go. Take care of it."

Honey had said Titus was the commander. Why wouldn't they send an underling to come pick them up from a vandalized house? Understanding this might come in handy for the next military romance she edited. And understanding her own situation.

Rowan and Lisa sat still and contemplative.

Their houses had been vandalized.

Her house had been vandalized.

What a crazy set of circumstances. Avery almost preferred—okay, she *much* preferred—thinking this had been her mother.

Lisa, Rowan, and she had left their cars behind, their keys under the front seats.

Rowan hadn't been trying to be funny their first Skype talk; he actually drove a Volt. That really didn't fit in with the endangered-hero trope.

Someone who thought they might depend on their vehicle to save their lives would drive something more muscular like this Hummer or maybe something with a lot of horsepower for flying down the road out of the bad guy's grasp.

A Volt didn't say lethal and prepared.

A Volt said responsible and suburban. Avery would give a beta-hero a Volt. But Rowan was anything but a beta. He was pure alpha-male. So, she'd have to rethink character assumptions.

Titus had asked the three of them to leave their vehicles behind. He said someone would move them.

Avery's editorial mind tried to figure out why that would be a plotting point. The only thing she could think of was that they were afraid that GPS trackers were attached to their cars. These Iniquus people didn't want anyone to know that the three vandalism victims were headed toward Iniquus Headquarters.

It was really strange that vandalism would get any attention, let alone this level of attention.

Why didn't Honey and Titus want anyone to know the three of them were going to their headquarters? Maybe they didn't want to give up their location? Maybe they didn't want someone to know they were using Iniquus for whatever it was that they were using Iniquus for?

Keeping her safe, Rowan had said.

That could mean a bunch of things. They could be a close protection team. They could be trying to figure out if there were bad people in contact with her. Okay, there were obviously bad people in contact with her—Taylor and now the group that vandalized her house.

This couldn't be about the vandalism, she decided. It must be about Taylor.

Rowan squeezed her hand. "You're thinking so hard you have smoke coming out of your ears. One-step and then another. Okay?"

"Okay," she said, then went right back to speculating as they pulled up at a gatehouse.

It hadn't been far. Avery thought they were still in Virginia but close to Washington D.C.

Titus Kane lowered his window. After the guard looked around the interior, they were allowed to pass.

They motored up to an enormous building with wide verandas that looked like a country club. One that was exclusive enough to require imposing gates and a security guard with a dog who had run around the vehicle sniffing.

They parked in a visitor's spot.

Honey and Titus escorted their group into the atrium. Men in uniforms, like Honey and Titus wore, walked through the halls, with an air of focused action. The atmosphere had a military quality to it, though Avery knew this wasn't part of the US military. She didn't think so anyway.

Avery wanted to cower against Rowan as they walked the long corridor but decided it would shine her in a bad light. So, she tried to look calm, cool and composed. She remembered her day at the top of the FBI building in New York, the day when she was sure she was going to end up in handcuffs charged with some obscure law. That was the feeling she was experiencing now, creeping doom.

A man walked up to them and asked Avery for her phone. Avery turned to Rowan.

"Diagnostics," he said.

She handed it over, not fully understanding what that meant. She wondered what they were looking for. She noticed they didn't ask for either Lisa's or Rowan's phones.

On the elevator, Rowan looked down at her with a half-smile and sent her a wink. He was obviously distracted, though. His cogs almost audibly whirring. His mind was as busy as hers was.

Now, here they were in a plush conference room. A woman named Margot gestured them in with an open hand. The guy tapping at his computer was introduced as Nutsbe.

Nutsbe Crushed, to be exact, but that was probably more information than Avery wanted to know about the man.

Rowan and Lisa moved over to confer with Nutsbe.

A man with a white waiter's coat brought in a trolley with sandwiches and fruit.

"Have you had dinner?" Margot asked and extended her hand to the cart.

Avery wasn't hungry for food. For answers? Yes, for that, she was starving. "Not right now, thank you."

Margot pulled out a chair. "Why don't you have a seat. They just need to put their oars in the water."

Lisa lifted her head from Nutsbe's computer screen. "I know your anxious, Avery. One step at a time, okay?"

Avery nodded and sat in the seat Margot had indicated. Something upsetting was on Nutsbe's computer screen. Avery could see it plainly on both Lisa and Rowan's faces.

Rowan tucked in and was now scanning through something

on Nutsbe's screen. The three were talking in tones designed not to carry.

Avery had no idea what was going on.

Someone had broken into her house, locked Sally in the basement, destroyed her belongings, and spray-painted cuss words all over the walls. Someone had done that to Lisa and to Rowan. How would anyone put the three of them together? Why would they be targeted for such an attack?

First Rowan and Lisa, then her. Significant?

Two FBI agents and an editor. Significant?

"Is this about Taylor Knapp?" she asked. It was the only conclusion that drew straight lines for her.

Everyone stilled and turned to her.

"If it is, I have some things I want to share."

Lisa, who was hunkered over the computer, slowly stood. "Okay. Thank you."

"Taylor Knapp is a pen name, as you know. But she's working with someone who speaks English as a second language. Some of the things I have learned have led me to believe that this isn't a book. This is a plot." Avery closed her eyes, centered herself. "This is not a book plot. This is a some-thing dangerous plot."

"Okay." Lisa sounded a bit too much like this was light and fluffy girl talk when her body conveyed danger. Her eyes were hard and focused.

Rowan sat out of Avery's view.

"Let's start with the English as a second language part," Lisa said.

Avery looked over to the whiteboard on the side wall. "May I write on there?"

Margot stepped forward and handed her a dry erase marker.

Avery stood and walked over, her whole body tingling. "I

met Taylor Knapp this past Monday and saw her again Tuesday. Both days I tried to get some information from her to give to my boss at Windsor Shreveport, an outline, a character list, anything. She gave me nothing. She told me she'd give me an update on Saturday—today. And she did. It was a big file. Too many words for someone to be able to concoct in three days. It was a file of highly specific notes. As I read through them, they sounded off to me. The English was good, just off."

"Do you have the notes with you?" Lisa asked softly as if she didn't want to stop Avery's train of thought.

"Yes, it would be good if you all could see them to make my point." Avery walked back to the table and pulled her computer from her purse. "Is there a place I could forward these?"

"If you pull up the file, I'll hand your computer to Nutsbe," Margot said.

Avery did that and waited for instructions.

"While he's downloading, do you know Taylor Knapp's legal name?" Lisa asked.

"This is what I know." Avery moved back to the whiteboard and pulled the cap off the marker. "She said that she went to the University of Michigan. She had a Russian roommate who majored in Anthropology and minored in women's studies."

Avery made a list just like she did when she was working on a book, and she needed to make sure the details all lined up.

"That roommate is living in America under the radar because she is afraid to go home to Russia, and her visa has run out. The roommate's name started with the sound Kah or Cah sound."

Avery noted this, then turned to the room.

"Taylor would start to call her by name and stop herself. I don't know what year, but Taylor looks like she's in her mid-to late-twenties. Taylor is the second pen name that this woman has used. Well, I only know of one other."

Avery turned back to the board.

"She also used the pen name, Tyler Krill. She used it when she developed a school shooter video game that was about to go to market but got pulled after there was public backlash."

Nutsbe was grinning hard as he tapped on his computer.

"Those are some good details, Avery," Lisa encouraged.

"I'm an editor. I have to remember tiny details. This leads me to two things that made me particularly worried. One, our publishing house is Windsor Shreveport. Windsor is Patrick Windsor. He's married to Inge Prokhorov, who is Bulgarian. Inge helped Taylor Knapp get her book contract with our publishing company without going through the normal channels in the regular way, which means having a manuscript submitted by an agent. Also, even though I'm a romance editor, Inge Prokhorov told Taylor to insist that I be her editor, and Taylor should stipulate she wouldn't work with anyone but me. There must be a reason." Avery sought out Rowan's eyes. "Don't you think?"

A screen came down. The plotting notes flashed into place.

"Yes, I think," Rowan said.

The room fell silent.

Avery watched the people in the room read through the information on the screen.

After a few minutes, Lisa asked, "Is this what you thought it would be, Rowan? I'd say you hit the nail right on the head."

"Yes. This looks right," he said.

"On Monday and Tuesday of this week," Avery continued. "I met with Taylor Knapp with the goal of producing some indication that Taylor was indeed moving forward with her contract. I asked for anything she could give me. Anything at all. She said to me, 'I'm still waiting.' To which I responded, 'I don't understand.' She said, 'Which is fine. Look, you said Saturday, right?' then, 'You need my outline by Saturday, you'll have it by then.'"

"Which you did," Lisa said.

"Fifty thousand words. From zero to *fifty thousand* focused, systematized words. In three and a half days. I don't care if you're the Forest Gump of literature. That can't happen. These were delivered to her, and she passed them on to me. I can't imagine another scenario. And they were written by someone who speaks English as a second language."

Avery turned to the screen. "Okay, your English lesson for today. Listen to this phrase at the top of the page. The one I highlighted—'Have three people discuss this—choose a bad big man'. Does that seem weird?"

Avery sidled over to the whiteboard where she wrote:

- Quantity or number
- Quality or opinion
- Size
- Age
- Shape
- Color
- Proper adjective ex nationality
- Purpose or qualifier.

"THIS IS how people who speak English as their mother tongue order their adjectives without thought. I once had a woman who wrote beautiful prose, but her mother language was Portuguese. When I edited her work, I had to be hypervigilant about these mistakes. So, this list always holds *except* when there's a repeated sound. Listen to the phrase 'the big bad wolf,' according to this chart, the quality of the wolf that he is 'bad' should come first, but we would never say the 'bad big wolf' like the 'bad big man' in the notes because it's just weird. In words that repeat a sound 'i' typically comes before 'a' or 'o' – zig-zag, hippity hop."

"The person who wrote these notes is not the person you know as Taylor Knapp," Lisa said.

"That's my point, yes."

"Good thing you're an editor. I never would have figured that out," Lisa said.

"Here are some other pieces that I've learned." She turned to write on the board. It's one of the ways she could see a story unfold.

And quite frankly, the intensity of the people in this room was overwhelming.

"Taylor said the Russian roommate had charged her a thousand dollars to write notes for her original concept, *The Unrest* video game, using her anthropology background. These notes were not made by that woman. Well, no. I don't have those notes to look at. *These* notes were not made by that Russian roommate, but she's still significant. I'll get to that in a minute."

"How do you know it wasn't the Russian roommate?" Lisa asked.

"The Russian roommate grew up in America, and so we should suppose that she speaks like a native. She'd never make the mistake of 'bad big.' Taylor told me that her ex-roommate not only gave her the notes for *The Unrest* but software code that was developed by the roommate—this is too hard, I'm just going to call her 'Katya' to have a name." She wrote the name and drew an arrow to Taylor. "Katya told Taylor that she had a Ph.D. boyfriend from Germany. That boyfriend, out of the goodness of his heart, wrote some code that Katya also gave to Taylor."

"What kind of code?" Lisa asked.

"Okay, I'm not a computer person, so see if this makes sense to you. The code was to show Taylor how the game could both collect data from a specific user and use data that had been collected by the Internet about a specific user to help filter that user's experience in the game. The goal was to put those users who had the same world views onto like-minded playing teams."

"Any clues about who this Ph.D. could be?" Lisa asked.

"Taylor said he lived in Munich and worked for or was somehow associated with Fast Forward, the producers of Taylor's video games." Avery moved to a clean portion of the board. She wrote out the name Katya and drew a circle around it. From there, she added spokes: one for notes, one for Ph.D. boyfriend and code, one for Fast Forward and producers, the last one for Windsor Shreveport. "Katya also told Taylor she should present this as a three-pronged campaign of book, music, and video game. To that end, she introduced Taylor to Patrick Windsor." She tapped the board on the name of her publishing house. "Well, no, she introduced Taylor to Patrick Windsor's wife, Inge Prokhorov. Inge Prokhorov took Taylor's manuscript to her husband, Patrick Windsor. Patrick Windsor then gave her a contract."

That had meaning. Everyone in the room leaned forward, and the intensity went up another three notches.

"Oh, one more." Avery drew another spoke and wrote "band." "Katya also knew of a band who then wrote the music."

"Of course she did," Lisa said.

Avery focused on Lisa. "I can't figure out why that's significant."

"Music is often used to indoctrinate the listener with an ideology. It's a new way of branding hate," Lisa said. "Taylor talked to you about her code? How the game is developed?"

"A little, yes."

Rowan looked over at Lisa. "I know that's what excites you,

but we have a lot to debrief Avery about. Can we get to that later?"

"Sure," Lisa said. "Where should we go from here?"

"I'll tell you where I'd like to go from here," Avery said. "Why was my house destroyed along with yours and Lisa's?"

"In a minute, Avery." Rowan looked at Nutsbe then back to her. "First, we need to show you something. I think maybe you should sit down for this."

41

ROWAN

SATURDAY NIGHT
Iniquus Headquarters

TITUS, Honey, Margot, and Nutsbe had been low key, and Rowan appreciated it. They blended into the background, facilitating as Lisa and Rowan directed the conversation with Avery.

Back at Avery's house, Lisa had taken Titus and Honey aside and had given them details about the attack on Rowan during his run, and both of their houses, including the photos, police reports that she accessed from her computer, and the names and contacts for their FBI colleagues who were investigating the case.

They'd sent those details ahead to Iniquus Headquarters.

Rowan knew that Iniquus had computer systems that rivaled the Intelligence Community. He hadn't been prepared for how fast this team could work.

"In our job, lives can depend on seconds, not minutes," Nutsbe had said. "We're geared to work fast and go hard."

No kidding.

Rowan was grateful the FBI had signed this contract. Iniquus didn't have red tape to tangle them up and slow them down. The team just put their heads down and stormed the castle.

In a calculated move, Rowan walked over to sit beside Avery.

This wasn't going to be pretty.

When they had walked in, and Nutsbe had flagged them over, he had shown Lisa and Rowan the video. They needed to tell Avery about this, and they'd come up with a plan. Nutsbe had said he'd be the one to rip off the bandage.

Cowardly, maybe, but Rowan preferred it was Nutsbe who showed her the video. Rowan didn't have the intel or the next steps that Iniquus did, so this made sense.

At least he could give Avery some physical and moral support.

"Ma'am," Nutsbe began. "You mentioned that you're a romance editor and that you were assigned to work on the Taylor Knapp book specifically by Inge Prokhorov."

"That's right."

"One of the jobs that we do here at Iniquus is to protect people. We protect their physical person, their assets—their house, for example. And we also protect their reputations."

Avery nodded.

"In the last few years, this has become more and more complicated. But we have some pretty good ways to mitigate issues that come up."

"Okay…"

"For example, social media. We have ways to search for attacks, track them, and to intercede where necessary."

"Okay…" Avery was shifting around in her seat now. Her brain worked fast, and as she had said it herself, if you gave Avery any situation, she could tell you with a snap of her fingers fifteen ways that things could go to hell in a handbasket.

Rowan was sure that Avery's mind had churned up at least that many.

"When we received your name for this assignment a few days ago—"

"Days ago?" Avery interrupted and looked Rowan's way.

"The Iniquus team was hired to work on a case that includes Taylor Knapp, and you were listed as a possible informant."

"Lisa…" Her voice trailed off.

"Was assigned to talk to you," Rowan said.

Avery focused back on Nutsbe and nodded her head that he should go on.

"I entered your information into my program. And we got a hit this morning. We've already taken action—"

"For god's sake, Nutsbe, spit it out," Avery said. "I'm breaking out in hives listening to you."

Nutsbe reached over and clicked his computer.

The screen changed to a video of Avery and her mother in what Rowan now recognized as Mrs. Goodyear's bedroom.

Avery was dressed in a thin cotton nightgown. She wasn't naked, but with the way the light was shining, you could see a lot. Too much. She leaped into the frame. Her hand came up and slapped across her mother's open mouth. Until this point, there had been no volume. Whatever Mrs. Goodyear had been saying was not included on the video. It looked like she was screaming, or maybe singing. "Don't you dare open your mouth. Do you hear me?" There was another blank space where Avery was saying something, but there was no sound.

Mrs. Goodyear fought against Avery. "Avery Grace Goodyear, how dare you manhandle me?"

"Get up," Avery ordered.

"What? No. Leave my room this instant."

Avery reached for her mother's wrists, planted a foot on the bed, and now, leaning out of the camera view, she yelled, "Get up!"

There was a blip where the video had been edited.

"Here you go, open up." Avery's face was determined, her voice tense, her hands shaking.

Rowan had seen her mother hit Avery in the head with the hairbrush—had seen with his own eyes what that looked like. Had felt sympathy. Having watched the video repeatedly now, he still couldn't believe how volatile, how physical, how difficult it had been for Avery. His heart went out to her.

Mrs. Goodyear sealed her lips in a tight pucker.

Avery reached for her mom's jaw, but Mrs. Goodyear twisted her head to the side.

"I swear to God, Mom, you're going to take these pills and go to sleep if I have to sit on you and force them down your throat."

"Why?" Mrs. Goodyear's voice trembled with emotion. Fear and sadness filled her eyes. "Why are you brutalizing me? Why are you helping them?"

"Take your pills, and we'll both get some rest."

"No!" Mrs. Goodyear put her fists up like she was going to throw punches.

Avery lunged forward, grasped Mrs. Goodyear's face. Mrs. Goodyear's mouth popped open.

Shaking, Avery shoved the pills down the back of her mom's throat then released her.

Ginny was sobbing.

The video ended.

"What? How?" Avery shook her head.

Nutsbe moved his chair to the edge of his desk, where Avery had a better line of sight. "My analytics suggest that this video was taken from your phone when control of your phone was accessed remotely. Did you have your phone in the room that night, do you remember?"

"That's why you took my phone from me for diagnostics?" she asked under her breath. Then louder, "Well yes, I always take my phone into Mom's room with me in case I can't handle my mother, and I have to call 911. I always set it in the same place, and I always put it upright so I can see it and grab it if things go to hell." She held up her hand toward the screen where the video had played. "As you can clearly see, they can."

"Is the video shot from the location where you set your phone?"

She looked from the still frame back to Nutsbe. "Yes, but how did you...?"

Without waiting for Avery to finish, Nutsbe said, "This is posted on different social media sites and is going viral."

"Viral?" Avery shook her head. She looked over at Rowan. Rowan recognized that look, it was called freeze, and it was the moment when the brain felt so shocked and endangered that it failed to function.

Avery couldn't process.

Nutsbe must have seen it too. His voice became louder, slower, so the words could go in. Calm. That should help lower Avery's adrenaline. "It made more sense to me when you mentioned that you were selected specifically as the editor when this isn't the type of book you normally edit," Nutsbe said. "That probably meant that they thought you were the most vulnerable to attack."

"Sex appeal is a major component in making a video go viral," Rowan said.

"There's nothing sexy about that video," Avery protested. "That video is horrible."

"But you're attractive, ma'am, and if you'll forgive me, your nightgown is pretty see-through. A beautiful person means more clicks," Honey said matter-of-factly. "Sexy, even in a circumstance like this, means more clicks."

Avery hadn't stopped shaking her head. "I'm still lost."

"They're getting ready to release the Taylor Knapp video game next week," Lisa said. "The way to make sales is publicity. The way to get publicity is through controversy. They want to brew controversy. Nutsbe's been tracking it."

Rowan said, "I'd imagine that, between the first Taylor Knapp book and the second, they did research on all of the potential editors that could be assigned. You were most likely tapped as the editor for two reasons—you're attractive, and like Honey explained, that gets social media clicks, and you're in a vulnerable place with your mother. Without further proof—"

"Inge Prokhorov had her husband assign me to Taylor to set me up for a fall? They got this video. Obviously, it's been edited to meet their needs, and now the time is ripe to start the controversy? How is this controversial?" Avery looked over to Lisa.

"They show this video to the world, and the whole world sees that you're an elder abusing monster." Lisa did the air quotes. Hopefully, Avery wouldn't feel judged by the people in this room. "They have people up in arms. Then others who pretend to have family members with mental health disorders get on and say, 'That's life. You do what you have to.' They start attacking each other. The bot farms push both narratives."

"Exactly," Nutsbe said. "The bots are clearly involved. Influencers have been purchased to weigh in."

"I don't know what that means," Avery said. "And did you actually tie this to Taylor Knapp, which it would have to be, right? Or you wouldn't care."

"Paid professionals were involved in making this go viral," Nutsbe said. "In all of the posts, they've specified that you're Taylor Knapp's editor."

"And they're trying to push sales by destroying me?"

42

Rowan

Saturday Night
   Iniquus Headquarters

Avery took in a deep breath and let it out. She was shifting gears. And that was a good thing. Putting both feet on the ground and leaning forward, her fingers laced, thumbs pointing upward, she obviously was shifting from an emotional state of mind to her analytical mind, and her body language suggested that there, she felt some level of power.

"Okay. They're going after my reputation." She looked at Nutsbe. "This is associated with me being Taylor's editor. Fine. I'll quit. My mother can't stay with me anymore, anyway. I can get a job as a ghostwriter or something. I'm not going to live this way—trashed in the media. If I'm no longer associated with Taylor, I'm no longer a target."

"We need you to not do that," Lisa said. "Even if this sounds ridiculous, I'm going to say it anyway. Your country needs you to *not* do that. You are our 'in' with Taylor. If you stay in the game, we have access."

"And that's the case that makes me interesting to Iniquus and their reputation protection. If I'm not involved in the case anymore, that goes away too, doesn't it?" Avery asked.

"Yes, ma'am," Nutsbe said.

She looked down at the carpet. "So I have no choice."

"You always have a choice. If you laid low for a few weeks, this would go away," Titus said. "They'd find another victim."

Avery looked over to the corner of the room. She stilled. Her eyes lost their focus as she thought. When she turned back, she said, "I have a plot point I want to have addressed, please. And I say that because this does seem to be some crazy suspense novel I've fallen into. I want to understand why they attacked our houses."

"And Rowan," Lisa added.

"What do you mean, *and* Rowan?" She turned to Rowan, her face creased with concern. "Is that the accident you got into? Is that why you're bruised the way you are? I thought you were overseas when that happened. They tracked you overseas? Knowing me is going to impact your job?" With each sentence, her voice ratcheted up to high-pitched, breathless squeaks. Her eyes were held wide and disbelieving.

Rowan took her hands, sending her a smile that he hoped would take her concerns for him off the table. He'd work through things as they came. And no, even though the Taylor Knap strategy was associated with the Prokhorovs, this had been a project that had been spooling out long before they knew Rowan was in that picture. They shouldn't have made the connection. He didn't think he was exposed. But time would tell.

"If they look for me on Twitter, I followed you as Row_man, and I followed Lisa. Is that how they associated us?" She gasped. "Your picture! If they know who you are on Twitter…Lisa and I had avatars…but it was *your* picture."

Man, her mind was sharp. She could wiggle around and find all the twists and connections. No wonder the Red Cell at the CIA was so effective.

Rowan was definitely going to broach this subject to his task force leader and see if they couldn't get something like that set up for the FBI. "Avery. Stop. I'm fine. No one can search that photo."

Avery's lips drooped; her frown had a ferocity to it.

"You searched, didn't you?" Rowan reminded her. "You said you were trying to find me on the Internet and found nothing, even with my correct name?"

"Yes, I searched for your photo. I thought it might be a stock photo. Neither the banner photo nor your icon came up."

"The banner photo doesn't appear anywhere else on the Internet. It was a gift from a photojournalist, I know. Those pictures were encoded, so they can't be traced. Lisa did them. They're both safe images. And that Twitter account was closed last week before this happened. So no, that didn't compromise me, either. Next." He waited for her to move her gaze from the floor to his eyes. "Next, I told you there was a disturbance in my neighborhood Monday night. Remember?"

"Yes." She exhaled.

"A group of men was trying to ambush me on my jog. They were armed. But I was a Ranger and have plenty of rotations under my belt. They didn't find me. Well, a couple of them found me, and they were incapacitated."

Out of the corner of his eye, he saw Nutsbe lift his chin. Rowan would ask in a minute.

"These men were talking about my running pace, Avery. Other than staking me out for months on end, the only way they might have known what they knew was through the running app on my phone. So the pieces of the puzzle are starting to fall into place." Rowan turned to Nutsbe. "You got something on that?"

"Three of the men were injured. And two of those men had their images captured. The FBI was able to track down the names of the men in the photos you took. Prescott sent me the file when I called over to your office earlier."

Rowan pressed his lips together. He hoped this information would be actionable.

"Some interesting data points, both are young, white, males. They live in Northern Virginia. Both have social media footprints. They've formed a kind of a weekend warrior group that gets together and plots for doomsday. It looks like on weekends, they train with a group out of West Virginia named Sons of the Iron Cross. Again, that information came from the FBI. I'm still compiling a list of their members."

"You have their name?" Lisa asked.

"Patriots Pledge is the name of their group. A skull cut out of an American flag is the symbol."

"You're nodding your head," Lisa said to Rowan. "That seems right to you, based on what you saw that night?"

"Yeah, that stars and stripes skull was on both guys' arm patches. They acted like a bunch of wannabes. Weekend warriors and new at it, too. It was like watching cosplay."

Lisa lifted a brow. "Bet they didn't expect the bullets."

"It didn't seem like they'd thought any of it through. Someone had to turn them on to me." He turned to Nutsbe. "What about the heart and lightning bolt? Getting anything on that?"

He shook his head. "Pictures of the vandalism haven't gone

up on social media. I'm expecting them. Our computers are watching for them. But it didn't look like someone leaving a calling card. That looked like a gang tag. Sort of like counting coup, they want to show someone how big and brave they are. Those images will be up soon if this ties back to Knapp."

Rowan thought of Brussels and making contact with Sergei Prokhorov, the alpha-dog himself. He'd thought in just those terms, counting coup, when you don't kill your enemy, you just take a smack at them to show your superiority and disdain.

The vandals had miscalculated what bravery looked like.

The Patriots Pledge, though, wasn't an act of cowardly destruction. That team had intended an act of violence. Not a counting coup. Something else. Rowan wondered just what it was they had thought they would have accomplished, ambushing him on his run.

"These might be two separate groups?" Avery asked.

"They may all be separate. One, the attack on Rowan by Patriots Pledge," Lisa explained. "Two, the vandals, and three, the viral video maker who co-opted your phone. Unless and until we have something tying them together, they'll be treated as separate attacks."

"What the hell?" Avery swung her head around, looking from one person to another. "This is crazy!"

"I can tell you," Nutsbe said. "The computer found postings from the Patriots Pledge members that let us know they coalesced as a group playing *The Unrest.* So that's an important point."

"I don't understand," Avery said.

"Instead of them being friends who started to play *The Unrest,*" Nutsbe said. "*The Unrest* helped them to become friends, and from that friendship, they developed a group that trains and attacks."

"The game gathered people from the same geographic vicini-ty?" Lisa asked.

"So far, it looks that way," Nutsbe said. "As we do more research, we'll see if that bears out."

"Isn't that terrifying?" Avery asked.

Rowan looked at her.

"A computer that gathers people in the same area," Avery said. "That means they can meet, and plot, and act. The game introduced them like the Russian chick did when this all started as a pretty benign idea in Taylor Knapp's head. Katya put the right people together, and out of their association came this bigger badder plot."

Avery spread her fingers and pressed them to the sides of her head.

"I'm seeing this playing out in my mind. It's like all of these little terror cells. Tribes of people who feel that they are just and right, work to stop people of divergent views. They do whatever they think will advance their cause. Different views clash both in the cyber and real worlds. The violence spreads to the streets. The violence spreads to the neighborhoods."

Avery lifted her hand to Rowen. "People see fighting, hear shots fired, they buy a gun, get a personal arsenal of bullets. They take action to protect themselves. It's a free for all of us-them tribalism."

The room fell quiet.

Tribalism. She was right.

It's what happened in the Middle East.

There was really no reason it couldn't happen here in America.

43

Rowan

Sunday Morning
Springfield, Virginia

Rowan had gone to Mass with Avery that morning. She said it was the first time she was able to receive communion at a service since her father died. Avery couldn't leave her mom alone, and her mom would sing through the ceremony.

It seemed to help Avery.

He was glad they had gone.

Now, they were back in their hotel room with Lisa. Iniquus had come to catch them up on what they'd found. Until they were given the green light. Lisa, Rowan, and Avery would be staying here at the hotel with no outside contact.

"The vandals with the heart and lightning are called Flash-Death." Nutsbe was telling them.

"Oh. That's also a song from Taylor Knapp's new video game," Avery said. She was lying on the hotel bed with a pillow over her eyes. "It's already been released on YouTube. I've met them, the band members. I heard that song when they were playing her new video game, *The Uprising*."

Nutsbe and Titus sat in the hard chairs over at the table, their computers booted up. Rowan was next to Avery on the bed. Lisa had brought chairs in from her room next door. She was perched backward on one, her hands crossed on the back, her chin resting on her hands.

"When you came in, you said you had an update on the Patriots Pledge guys?" Rowan reminded Nutsbe.

"There are arrest warrants out for the guys with the photos. They've gone to ground," Titus said, then looked over at Nutsbe.

"There was a BOLO out for the men you incapacitated," Nutsbe said. "Knowing they would probably seek medical attention. Once we knew about the attack, that was one of the parameters I inputted to our system. An hour ago, the police found a guy passed out in the streets. No I.D. Two bullet wounds in his leg." Nutsbe was speaking directly to Rowan. "They must have been round-nosed bullets. They passed straight through, according to the responder chatter from the paramedics. The wounds were days old and infected. The unknown subject was transported to the local hospital. We already flagged this for the FBI. We're sure the hospital did, as well. It's a little sketchy when you don't seek help after you've been shot. We sent Panther Five over, Margot, she'll get photos. We'll get the patient ID'd and see if this isn't the guy we're looking for."

"Gunshots?" Avery gripped his hand harder as she pushed the pillow off and lifted her head.

"Left leg?" Rowan asked. "Outside thigh?"

"Roger that," Nutsbe said.

Rowan smiled broadly. "Finally, some good news."

"Unless he dies," Lisa said.

"Gunshots?" Avery stammered.

Rowan leaned to the side and kissed her forehead. "I'm fine. Nothing happened to me. I just got some aerobic exercise in a way I hadn't planned. That's all."

"More good news," Nutsbe said. "We're pretty sure that we know how the vandals linked the three of you."

"Have there been police reports of similar incidences?" Lisa asked.

"No, ma'am," Nutsbe said. "And I'm not expecting them based on this data." He turned from the desk to look at Avery. "Thank you for letting us check on your phone. We're going to keep it a little longer if that's okay with you. I brought you another one." He reached into the pocket of his tactical pants and pulled out a phone.

Same brand, this one was black.

"I input all of your contacts. This one should be safer. Your phone number didn't change." He laid it on the table.

"Safer," Avery repeated.

"Avery, what day did you get assigned to Taylor Knapp?" Nutsbe asked.

"Last Thursday afternoon."

Nutsbe gave a thumbs up. "And last Thursday, did you happen to read something from a ShareTogetherApp after the time when you accepted that assignment?"

Avery looked around as Rowen and Lisa groaned. They hadn't warned Avery to turn on the security key.

"It wasn't an option to accept or not to accept the Taylor Knapp assignment, but yes. After," she said as she spun back to look at Nutsbe. "An author from Twitter asked me to read her first hundred words in her WIP, and I said I would."

"Someone you know?" he pressed.

"Not really, just a young English major who recently followed me on Twitter."

"Twitter? What's that name?" Nutsbe asked as he faced his computer and started typing.

"Mary Turner and then a string of numbers."

Rowan and Lisa groaned again. Anytime there was a string of numbers after a name, it was almost a hundred percent guarantee that was a Russia-connected bot.

Rowan climbed from beside Avery and moved to the extra chair by the computer where Nutsbe was searching.

"Got her," Nutsbe said. "Look at this, Kennedy. She's following Avery and two hundred bots. And look at her join date. This sockpuppet was set up just for Avery," he said quietly. He changed the screen as he pulled up a schedule of events, put a finger on a line, then turned back to Avery. "When you opened a ShareTogetherApp file on Thursday at 11:37 p.m. malware was placed on your phone that allowed for the person on the other end to access your phone's microphone, your video camera, and your keystrokes."

"Oh." Avery was sitting with her back to the headboard, hugging a pillow, her legs pulled up to her chest. "They could read my texts?"

"And any passwords you typed in."

She shook her head. "I don't like to use my phone for anything beyond phone calls and the occasional text. I've been so busy this week with my mother, Taylor, and the convention, I haven't been on my phone much at all." She looked at Rowan. "The text when I gave you my phone number, and we arranged a

Skype, then the airport. I think that's it for texts. And Taylor, there's no cell phone service out her way. We e-mail to communicate, or I bang on her door."

"That's an important piece of information," Titus said. "Thank you."

"Right, I can see you didn't have a lot of communications through your phone during that time. You looked at Twitter on Friday. Lisa private messaged you that Row_man was now going as LeGit."

"Oh, yes, that's right. And that's Rowan on Twitter," she said.

"Can I take a look at Mary Turner?" Rowan asked.

Nutsbe spun the computer toward Rowan as he said, "It was a good thing you opened the ShareTogetherApp on your phone and not your laptop."

"It had a virus?"

"Malware. It could look around. And it could gain access to anything you linked by sending a file and opening it. I believe they found Lisa, not because of Twitter, because she was in your phone contacts."

"I opened Taylor's notes on my computer."

"Yes, ma'am," Nutsbe said. "When we were at Headquarters, and I was putting that on the big screen, my security programs scanned the file, and it was clean. So was your computer."

"That's a relief," Avery said. "But about my contacts, I don't have Lisa's address, just her phone number. And Rowan isn't in there," Avery said. "Oh, wait. You know I texted him. But how would someone who sent me malware know where either Lisa or Rowan lived? I don't even know that."

Rowan had been looking into MaryTurner578293401. He pushed the computer toward Nutsbe so he could see. "This bot was out of Bulgaria. They identify each other through this little symbol at the bottom left corner of their banners."

If Sergei Prokhorov had any idea that Rowan was the guy who approached him at the gala, Rowan would be dead.

Or worse, captured.

44

Rowan

Sunday Morning
   Springfield, Virginia

"To answer your question about how they knew where we lived. One way would be through my contacts. Rowan's not only in my contacts, but he's also my ICE—in case of emergency. And I'm his ICE," Lisa said. "The malware could have spread when you sent back the file with the short story I had you read."

"That was a Word document, not a ShareTogetherApp, like Mary Turner's was," Avery pointed out.

"Once your phone had the malware, anything you sent from your phone, that someone opens, could have that malware spread into their device," Lisa explained. "I have programs on my phone to protect me, but it very easily could have just looked around my system to see what apps I had and looked through my contacts list. My home address is listed in the setup."

"That was Saturday," Nutsbe said, looking at the readout on his computer. "10:23."

"I am so confused," Avery said.

"Not to worry," Nutsbe said. "This is all just drawing lines of connection. The take away is that a bad actor planted malware on your phone, and we're speculating about how that information could have been used. One way is by accessing your microphone and video camera, which ended up being put up on social media, and another was to access your contacts."

"Okay. Well, no, not okay," Avery said. "I guess I should have said, I'm still following along."

"Nutsbe, they'd know Kennedy and Griffin are both FBI from their GPS?" Titus asked.

"No," Lisa said. "Rowan and I have an app on our phones that cleans out our GPS files as they're made. They can't be tracked back to FBI Headquarters."

"My phone has been with FBI forensics since the Patriots Pledge, before the vandals. I haven't heard word back about malware. But I don't access files on my phone as a rule," Rowan said, looking at Nutsbe. "I have only one app." He shrugged. "Yeah, I know its vulnerabilities, and yet I still use it. It's used by most of the military community. It's sentimental, I guess. It's for—"

"Let me guess. Running app?" Nutsbe asked.

"Bingo," Rowan said.

"That explains Monday night then."

"It's starting to line up," Rowan agreed. "If someone was good with computers and knew I was a runner. But, man, this is bizarre. Avery and I talked for the first time Monday night. Monday night, after we got off Skype, I was attacked. They had to have that information for at least enough time to form a plan. It wasn't a great plan, so give it twenty-four hours, maybe? I honestly don't know how the Patriots Pledge could tie to Avery."

"I have a guess," Lisa said under her breath.

Rowan leaned back in the chair and crossed his arms over his chest. His brow drew tight.

"Remember the day I told you about the tweet that got erased?"

Rowan felt the blood drain from his face. *Jodie*. "There was more than the one?"

Lisa looked over at Avery then back at Rowan. She tipped her head toward the bathroom and moved that way.

Rowan pointed at Nutsbe, and they both followed Lisa.

After Nutsbe shut the bathroom door, Lisa turned on the water in the sink.

"There were two other tweets that Jodie posted before she linked Row_man to Dark Matters. They were spaced with a bunch of rambling nonsense tweets, over two hours' time, between the earlier ones and the one that doxxed your work account. One was something like, 'Girls, make sure to know your fella's passwords. You'll find out what lying cheats they are in their DMs. You want him @A_Very? You'll see how much that relationship sucks."

"She erased it?" Rowan asked.

"Yup, same time she erased the other. Chances are slim to none that Avery saw it. Knowing Avery, she wouldn't get messed up in anyone else's crap. She has enough of her own."

"Agreed, and the third?" That tied him to Avery, but it didn't put Patriots Pledge on his heels.

"She said, "If you see this @Row_man, make sure you take me off the StrideApp. I'm not your running partner anymore. I'm your nothing partner anymore. Maybe @A_Very wants my empty place."

"If someone put A_Very into the search bar. You'd see those tweets up until they were removed," Nutsbe said.

"Yup."

"So Friday morning, they see that. Someone who is watching knows that A_very and Row_man are now an item." Nutsbe turned to Lisa. "Is that Twitter handle in your contacts, Lisa?"

"Yes. It is. Was. I changed it to his new one, LeGit, a few days ago."

"It's easy to set up a computer search to flag any time that A_Very is mentioned on the Internet. They find out that she has a new love interest via the exes tweet. They already have access to Avery's phone. Saturday, they get access to your phone, Lisa. The phone searches your contacts for Lisa and Row_man and up pops two addresses, yours and Rowans. That person or organization, we label them *Mary Turner*, knows that Rowen uses the StrideApp. That's easily hackable." Nutsbe focused on Rowan. "You have that under your name?"

"Rowan Kennedy, yes."

"Okay, they pull that up and see your running history. The heat ring probably goes in two directions out of your house."

"Yes."

"So your house is easy to pinpoint, and they can see the address in Lisa's contacts."

"And they'd see the ring from Lisa's house. We sometimes run together."

"Bingo. Okay. It's looking like *Mary Turner* handed two groups the information. One over the weekend. One after the attack failed. This data leads to more questions. Let's get out of the bathroom. It's too small in here, and I think we can debate this with Avery present."

They moved back to the bedroom. Nutsbe walked over to a portable whiteboard that Iniquus had brought in. He wrote A_Very ->Twitter->malware->Mary Turner, circled the name, and drew two spokes, one for Patriots Pledge and the other for vandals.

Avery was hugging two pillows now. Tears in her eyes. A big frown on her face.

"Sorry about that, Avery. Lisa was sharing information she thought might be sensitive. I told you that I recently broke up. The night we called it quits, she got drunk on Twitter and doxxed me. We now understand the running app." Rowan couldn't tell Avery everything about his life, but he was darned sure going to be straightforward with everything he could be. Rowan pointed toward the whiteboard. "We were able to draw these conclusions from what my ex, Jodie, had posted on Twitter. Now, we're asking what makes sense if *Mary Turner* is involved with both groups. My guess is that they had a plan for the Patriots Pledge to accomplish something. They failed. *Mary Turner* sent the B-team, these FlashDeath vandals."

"To what end?" Titus said.

Nutsbe held up a finger as he tapped at the computer.

Avery turned to Rowan. "Titus said GPS earlier. Is that why you asked everyone to put their phones on airplane mode at my house?" Avery asked. "They couldn't listen to us or film us. Couldn't follow the GPS back to your Headquarters?"

"Exactly," Nutsbe answered as he looked up.

Avery spun his way. "Everyone in my contacts might get their houses destroyed?"

"It's doubtful," Nutsbe said. "The perpetrators would want more information than a phone number and address. And they probably got what they needed from Lisa and Rowan."

"Which was what?" Avery frowned. "Why attack our houses?"

"I hypothesize that they just needed pictures and a salacious story to drive the social media algorithms with your name, Avery, and a connection to Taylor Knapp. If they hit too many houses, the chances of them being caught go up exponentially," Nutsbe said.

He paused for a moment and clicked at his keyboard.

"Okay. That ping was a computer report landing in my in-box. I have an answer. In the case of FlashDeath, and their vandalism in your three houses," he read. "A new Internet topic was detected this morning. Again bots and influencers are involved."

He had his focus on the computer screen. "This social media campaign is targeting anti-LGBTQA groups. They are specifically identifying religious groups that promote marriage between a man and a woman."

He turned toward Rowan and Avery. "They're saying that you, Avery, along with Rowan, and Lisa are a triangle marriage. You, Avery, are advocating for marriages like those allowed in the Middle East, where a man can take many wives. You want to take down the whole concept of one man and one woman marriages. That's one prong of the attack. Another prong is that now that same-sex couples can marry, your relationship of multiple partners is the next step in the slippery slope to the destruction of the traditional family. A group, which is not being named, set out to punish the three of you. There are pictures of your houses and their tags, so we know this is FlashDeath. The vandals are being lauded as heroes. It's only a few hours old. They're building steam with their bots, and I'm sure that if the Iniquus computers weren't intervening, we'd see the clash later today."

"Clash. That's the counter-narrative?" Avery asked.

"Exactly, and the vehemence of the clash is what drives the social media algorithms to make these things go viral. So far, they aren't naming Lisa or Rowan, just Avery and her connection with Taylor Knapp."

"But you're mitigating it?" Avery asked.

"Yes, ma'am," Nutsbe said. "We have our computers searching and scrubbing the Internet. We should be able to keep the numbers down, so the social media sites don't push it out like we've done for your video with your mother."

"This is because of me—your houses destroyed, Rowan attacked." She dropped her head. "I am so so so so sorry. I will make it up to you." She looked up, catching Rowan's gaze. "I don't know how. But I'll fix it." She turned to Lisa. "I'm sorry."

"Shhh." Rowan pulled her into his arms and tucked her under his chin, stroking his hand over her hair. He couldn't imagine what this must be like for her, to watch her life blow up in a week, and to feel like you were dragging people you cared for down with you. Especially for someone with Avery's sensibilities. "You're not responsible for anyone's actions. We'll find them. They'll be punished."

"They already found you. What if they doxx you?" Avery asked. "Wouldn't that mess you and Lisa up in the field? Wouldn't that put you in danger?" She spun around to look at Lisa.

"Me? No, I'm not out in the field," said Lisa. "I mean, I'd have to lay low, live somewhere else for a while, but this will blow over. The news cycles are fast-moving these days."

Avery spun back to Rowan. "Rowan?"

"Yeah. It could be a problem. But my house is pretty secure. As a rule, we're trained to be no profile. They couldn't have gotten to anything telling at my house. But I'll have to wait and see how this unrolls. Iniquus does this all the time. If there's something out there that I don't want out there, they'll find it." He waited until she had a moment to process that before he added, "Our priority is getting the guys who did this in a room and asking them some questions."

"Okay, I can sit here and feel sorry for myself, or I can help make this stop. Tell me what you need from me. How can I best make sure that Taylor doesn't get to win?"

"Taylor is probably a pawn too. Less so than you. But used. She surely can't be naïve enough to think that what she told you about showing the shadow side of people is what's happening," Nutsbe said.

"It *is* exposing their shadow sides," Lisa countered. "And the manipulation of those shadows is the twenty-first-century version of a nuclear warhead aimed straight at American hearts and minds."

45

Avery

Monday afternoon.
Springfield, Virginia

"It'll be a chess game," Honey said. "And it has to come off as natural."

Avery was in the hotel room where she and Rowan had spent the last two nights.

Yesterday, on her new Iniquus-provided phone, Avery had emailed Taylor to let her know that she was moving to the bed and breakfast and that she'd be there later that day.

"No can do. I'm in writing mode. Come Monday evening, and I'll hand you the first ten chapters. That should make you happy."

That seemed like a reasonable amount of writing to have

done from Saturday until Monday evening, assuming Taylor started writing after she emailed Avery the outline, especially since each chapter was laid out so explicitly.

Avery had looked over at Titus. He'd given her a thumbs up. And Avery had said, "Ten chapters would make me very happy. I'll eat an early dinner and come Monday evening, then."

Now, Monday had arrived. Nutsbe and Honey were here today, going over details.

"We'll be able to hear you at all times." Honey held up a wire. "We'll be able to see in the direction you've focused your head." He pulled a pair of glasses from a case. "Try them on, and I'll adjust them."

"Is this why Margot asked me if I had my glasses with me the other night?" Avery slid the glasses on. "So she could get the prescription?"

"Exactly." Honey looked left, then right on her head, and gently pulled them from her face. "I want these to be comfortable and fit well. If not, you'll keep fussing with them, pushing them up. It's best if you leave them alone, okay?"

She nodded.

"If you're looking at something you want us to be able to read, it's best if you lay it on a flat surface, so your hand isn't shaking. Try to remain very still and take a full breath cycle before you change your focus. When we scroll through your video, we can capture a stop-frame easier that way. I'm going to put the wire into the seam of your blouse along your side. If anyone were to pat you down, they would think it was the stitching."

"Someone would think to pat me down?"

"No." Honey chuckled. "Just part of the spiel. I'm giving you information, in case you're editing something like this in one of your books. You can make it more authentic."

Honey was a good name for this guy. He must be seven feet tall. His voice was husky and rumbly like a bear. But he was as sweet as could be. Avery noticed he had a gold band on his left ring finger. Whoever Mrs. Honey was, she'd picked herself a really nice guy.

While Honey was fussing with her, Avery was trying to listen to Rowan on the speakerphone. The gist of what she got was that the guy with the gunshot wounds had woken up at the hospital. They hadn't been allowed access yet.

It wasn't confirmed that it was the guy Rowan shot.

Rowan had shot a man.

In his neighborhood.

Shot him twice with someone else's gun. How crazy was that?

They'd also run down the names and addresses of the men attached to FlashDeath. The FBI had search warrants in hand.

Lisa leaned toward the speaker. "When you go into their houses with your search warrants, I want their electronics, including their televisions and their gaming consoles. And check their places for blue spray paint."

"That feels fine, Honey." Avery worked at not batting Honey's hand away. "They're fine like that. Thank you." Avery's anxiety was starting to climb. She could feel the welts from hives starting to make her skin prickle.

Avery was right back to the feeling from that horrible day at the New York FBI Headquarters. What a poor excuse of a spy she was.

She was just darned bad at subterfuge.

They'd given her a thumb drive to keep in her pocket. If she could get to Taylor's computer while it was booted up, she was supposed to insert it into the port and wait for the green light before she pulled it back out. Doing that would give the team access to Taylor's computer, just like someone had access to her old phone.

Not the same end-use, Avery reminded herself. Good guys versus bad guys.

"A friend introduced me to a woman while I was in New York," Avery practiced. "She worked for the FBI, and she asked for my help. Have you ever heard of the CIA Red Cell?" Avery cleared her voice. "The CIA red—" She coughed, sniffed, and tried again. "Have you ever heard of the CIA Red Cell? It's pretty darned cool. They asked for recommendations. And you popped immediately to mind. How would you like to help your country?" Avery paused, smiled. "The way it was explained to me is that they give you top secret information, you look it over, and then tell them different story plots that you would develop from the information they gave you. For example, you might have the terrorists attack from the sea or land or air. It's really perfect for you. This is just like the rings that you develop for your games. Choices made and what can be learned from each iteration."

"You're going to do fine," Honey said. "Keep it natural. Let it work its way into the conversation."

"Mention that we'll have to do a background check," Nutsbe said. "That might be the time when you ask her real name."

"From what I told you, did your AI programs figure out who she is?" Avery asked.

Nustbe showed Avery a picture on his screen.

Avery peered down at it. "Yes. Well…I think so. This photo is younger. Plumper. And Goth. She doesn't really look like this now. But she's got that mole there by her hairline." Avery reached up and touched her own head where the mole could be found. "And she has that little cleft in her chin." She touched her chin. "So, what *is* her name?"

"We're not going to give you any information about her that you don't already know, so it doesn't slip out by accident," Rowan said. "We don't want her to have a heads up."

Avery dropped her voice to a whisper. "Do you think she's dangerous?"

"Not at all. She's out in the middle of nowhere. She lives alone, as far as we can tell from our satellite surveillance. It's just you and her. And we'll be nearby. We can hear you and see what you see. You go in and chat, try to find out what you can. See if you can't get the name of her contact and come out."

"Then she'll be arrested?"

"Right now, we won't arrest her. Instead, we'll watch what she does, with whom she interacts. We're hoping to gather more people into our net. To that end, you might want to start by talking about Inge Prokhorov. Think about any connections you've had with Patrick Windsor's wife and see if you can't make that work for you. Lastly, and most importantly, we want to see if you can't get to her computer and plant our spyware in there."

"Not malware?"

"We're the good guys. Ours is called spyware."

"What are the chances that Taylor's computer is encrypted and has self-destructive capabilities?" Avery asked.

"High." Honey handed her the blouse she was going to wear, the wire now integrated into the seam.

"Isn't it illegal for me to do this? Record someone in Virginia without their knowledge and plant spyware?"

"Rowan and Lisa have electronic surveillance warrants. You signed the contracts with Iniquus. We'll provide you with all the necessary legal support. We won't let anything bad happen to you. I promise."

A shiver raked through Avery's body. In books, Avery knew,

if a character ever offered an unsolicited promise, that promise would be broken.

46

Rowan

"We have an ID on bullet boy. He's Bradford Michael Sullivan." That was Lisa over the speaker. She was at Iniquus Headquarters with Margot, working the cases from their computers.

Lisa thought that having three different groups attacking was actually extremely helpful in finding the mastermind. Two groups who performed physical attacks had already been identified. It would be interesting to see if this was the same strategy that Avery mapped out on the Iniquus whiteboard Saturday night.

Avery had charted the Russian roommate as the hub with each spoke that made Taylor Knapp's work into a weapon extending out from that central player. That was significant.

Knowing if Taylor's video game was the hub for this set of crimes would be significant too.

It sucked to be personally caught up in this. It really sucked that this was affecting Avery.

But here they were.

It was time to figure it out and make it stop.

Brad Sullivan, though, wasn't cooperating. Lisa said he'd lawyered up and didn't want to talk. The FBI got a search warrant on his house.

That was fast.

Not fast enough for Margot and Lisa, though. They decided to hack into his computer.

"Ah." Nutsbe chuckled. "Are you finding anything?"

"Plenty," Margot said. "You ready for this, Kennedy?"

"Probably not, but hit me with it anyway." They were sitting in chairs in front of a bank of electronics equipment in a tricked out cargo van a klick down the road from the farm Taylor Knapp was renting. From here, they could provide Avery with a hot spot for her phone and monitor her feeds.

They were there early to make sure that everything was set up and functioning properly. Avery would follow in her own car.

Nutsbe had given her the green light to proceed.

"Sorry about that. Lisa just handed me some new data, and I was looking it over. Okay, The night that Lisa opened the Word file sent from Avery with Lisa's short story edits is the same day that—" Margot stopped. "Let me back up. Patriots Pledge is comprised of upper-tier players in *The Unrest*. Lisa said that from her research, once someone attains that level, they seemed to be attached to a charismatic figure. The charismatic then encouraged them to form bonds. In the group made up of Patriots Pledge members, it looks like their charismatic contacted them off the game via the ShareTogetherApp."

"Oh good," Nutsbe said. "So, none of this was picked up by signals intelligence."

"We still have the files," Margot said. "Brad doesn't clean his computer."

"Or use basic protection on his computer," Lisa threw in. "His password was 'password.'"

"Okay…" Rowan wanted them to get to the good stuff.

"The charismatic goes by Gusto," Lisa said with a laugh.

"Of course he does." Rowan did a mental eye roll.

"Gusto has a Bulgarian IP as one would expect with Inge Prokhorov involved. I'm going to see if I can't find his social media handles. Check out his banners and see if this charismatic happens to have the Prokhorov symbol in the bottom left."

"Yup. That's what I'd be interested in."

"This is how it ties to you, Kennedy," Margot said. "Gusto wrote that he came across some information that Rowan Kennedy, along with your two jihadist brides, Lisa Griffin and Avery Goodyear, are plotting against the United States."

"We're married!" Lisa called out, and Rowan could hear clapping. "I can't wait to tell Sandra. She's going to be thrilled that her girlfriend is married to a guy."

"The charismatic told the Patriots Pledge that you, Kennedy," Margot continued, "were going to shoot POTUS at his speech last Tuesday."

"What?" Rowan looked down at his boots as he processed that thought. If the Patriots Pledge guys thought the POTUS was in danger, why wouldn't they have called the FBI or Secret Service or someone with capabilities? Why would they grab a gun and run to the would-be assassin's house to ambush him on his jog?

"Yup." Margot continued, "Then the charismatic said that something needed to be done to save the POTUS. And, oh, by the way, I know where he lives and, better yet, where he jogs. Then Gusto posted a graphic of both running directions and how long it took for you to get to one of three points mapped in each direction. Gusto said it looks like rain on Monday. And that if he, Gusto, was planning an op, he'd wait for the skies to clear. That it should happen after nine, according to the weather channel. Then he stepped back. The boys on the Patriots Pledge are true believers and one hundred percent dedicated to the POTUS. They decided they'd capture you and torture you until you exposed everyone involved with the plot to kill the president."

"And not take the threat to the FBI," Honey said.

"FBI is part of the deep state," Margot replied.

"Right. So I guess it was up to Patriots Pledge to take me down," Rowan deadpanned. "Did they have my picture?"

"No," Lisa said. "They asked for one and were told that no picture was available. So that's really good news. The Patriots Pledge probably identified you by watching you leave your house. It's a damned good thing they didn't catch you. Margot looked through this guy's Internet search history. He doesn't clean that out either. And amongst the porn sites, there were 'how to waterboard' videos, among other torture tutorials."

"Well, crap."

"Yeah," Lisa said.

"So when they didn't get to me, they just decided to watch and see what happened next?" Rowan asked. "Does that make sense?

Margot's voice came over the comms. "They figured out that another group had targeted you. They were making fun of the spray paint. Like that would stop you from killing POTUS. Patriots Pledge knows you're not home. They're trying to figure out where you work. They're not coming up with anything.

Which seems weird. The charismatic should be able to track your GPS history if they're good with computers, which we have to assume."

"Oh, you weren't there when I explained that at the hotel," Lisa said to Margot. "I designed a GPS filter that Rowan and I are field testing. Besides wiping our histories, in case someone was following real-time when either Rowan or I get near an FBI site, the GPS continues down the road until it gets to the next strip mall and places the car there. It functions again after we're two miles away. It's so if this happened, no one could figure out where we work. Anyway, it's something I'm playing around with, trying to find the bugs in the system before I offer it to others."

"Excellent," Margot said. "We'd like to stay in that loop."

"Avery's in the house," Honey said. "Let's stop the chatter."

The image that Avery was capturing with her glasses came up on the screen. A woman, about Avery's height, slender, hair back in a messy bun, wearing a pair of black yoga pants and an over-sized t-shirt, opened the door.

"Hey there," Avery said.

Rowan could hear the nerves in her voice. "Let's see the picture you have of her."

Nutsbe put it up side by side with a still shot from the glasses. Bingo.

"Did you really move to the bed and breakfast so you could babysit me?" The woman backed from the door and started down a short hallway.

"Does that mean you've identified the Katya-roommate?" Rowen whispered.

"Katerina Sokolov," Nutsbe whispered back without letting his focus stray from the video feed. "We're looking for her."

"Sorry," Avery said. "But, yeah, my boss said he'd fire me if I didn't come. So here I am, keeping my job."

"Men are assholes," Taylor said over her shoulder.

"Nutsbe, do you have the house schematics?" Rowan asked.

Nutsbe touched a button, and not only did a schematic come up, but a red dot that moved with Avery as she shut the front door and followed after the woman.

Avery arrived in a bright yellow kitchen. She moved like she was familiar with the setup and walked straight to a stool, and sat down. "They can be. How's Goose? Does he have a shed out back?"

"He sleeps in the barn. He's fine. I got to ride him earlier. He needed the exercise. I'm drinking. Do you like white Russians?"

"I don't know that I've ever tried one. But since I'm driving, a glass of water would be nice."

Taylor turned on Avery and sent her an "are you kidding me?" kind of snarl. "You're driving a mile and a half up a deserted road. What's going to happen to you? You're going to hit a cow?"

"Just a personal policy." Her glasses bobbled. "It keeps me out of trouble."

"Goody two-shoes like you?" Taylor spun back and mixed her cocktail in what looked like a pretty hefty sized glass. "You've never been in trouble a day in your life."

"Probably because I have this no drinking and driving policy." Avery laughed.

Taylor took a sip from her glass, moved to the counter, grabbed a stack of papers, and handed them to Avery. Taylor pulled out a drawer and handed her a red pen. "You read these. I'm going to take a long hot bath and get changed into pajamas. It's been a tiresome day."

"You know what?" Avery said. "I'd rather just edit them in a

Word program. That way, when you send me the file, I have the track changes." She pushed the pages to the side.

"Good job!" Nutsbe said under his breath.

Taylor took a long sip from her glass. Eyeing her. The goody-two-shoes comment probably meant that she didn't suspect Avery of anything.

"Fine." Taylor reached over to her desk for a laptop. She opened the lid and booted up, found the file, and handed the computer over to Avery.

"Thank you." Avery focused on the first page then looked up to watch until Taylor was out of sight.

"Is that weird?" Honey asked. "Taylor leaving Avery alone like that? Isn't Avery kind of like the boss in this dynamic?"

"She's a creative type," Lisa said over the comms. "Who knows what she's thinking. Could be a prima donna. She took her drink." She and Margot could see everything the men in the van saw from their location in the Panther Force war room back at Iniquus Headquarters.

"You got Taylor's landline phone tapped, though, right, Honey?" Lisa asked.

"We got audio in place to monitor her home and landline Saturday when Avery gave us the farm's address. With no Wi-Fi in the area, Taylor uses a hot spot on her computer. That's probably why she felt safe handing it to Avery. The hot spot's turned off right now. Taylor doesn't know that there's Wi-Fi available, and Avery can make contact."

They watched Avery look up to the ceiling when the sound of water in the shower was picked up. Then she slowly walked from room to room. Probably trying to show them what was there. She carried the computer into a den area and curled in the chair. She pulled the thumb drive from her pocket and pushed it into place.

She typed on the screen: **What do you want me to do now?**
Paused for them to read it from her glass's camera, then erased it.

For someone who was freaked out about being a spy, she was doing a great job. Rowan was really proud of her.

But something had him by the craw, and he wanted her out of that house. *Now.*

47

Rowan

Monday Night
Warrenton, Virginia

Nutsbe texted – **You're doing fine. Greenlight on the thumbnail. Put the thumbnail into your pocket. Edit Word file until Taylor comes back down. Then broach FBI Red Cell. Erase the text after reading.**

They had explained to Avery that they were scrambling the airwaves in a perimeter just beyond the van, and if they texted, the bad guys wouldn't be able to read them. But they needed to keep the contact to an absolute minimum.

When the text dropped into her cell, it buzzed in Avery's pocket. She pulled her phone out and read the instructions. They watched her erase the text and set her phone on the side table.

Avery pulled out the thumb drive and put it deep into her pocket. Then she started editing.

"Chances that Taylor will own up to the fact that she got the research notes from elsewhere if Avery suggests the Red Cell?" Margot asked.

"I can't imagine that she'd cooperate in any way, shape, or form," Rowan said. He didn't like that Avery had left her phone out. She shouldn't be able to use it in that house. It was dangerous to make it buzz with another text, though, to tell her. Avery could probably cover by saying she'd forgotten it wouldn't work or something. "If it's possible to get Taylor to comply, Avery will find a way," he said.

"You don't need to convince me," Margot said. "I'm team Avery."

"Hey, Honey. In Brussels last week, when you and Thorn were at the event. You did me a solid. Thank you. There's some chatter that you guys had a tough assignment after that. Everyone pull out, okay?" Rowan asked. "I didn't see Thorn in the halls."

"Thorn's assigned to a personal protection contract. Panther Force is healthy."

"Good to hear."

"I'm marking the board," Nutsbe said. "Avery has a green light on the spyware. I'm on the computer and behind Taylor's firewall. I'm downloading data. The safest thing Avery can do is keep doing what she's doing."

"While we're just hanging out. I can pass you more information about two of the three attacks this week," Margot said.

"Yeah? What have you got?" Rowan asked.

"Once we identified members of FlashDeath, the group of men who attacked your houses, Prescott handed over the names to the PD. We just got word that the DCPD is getting them rounded up. The FlashDeath guys will be sitting on ice when you get done with Avery's mission." There was a pause. "Yup, I just got a message that the round-up is a go."

"I'll be glad to talk with them," Rowan said.

He had to admit it. Sitting in this van was harder than he thought it would be. His antennae were up and pinging hard.

Avery should be in zero danger. Rowan didn't know if he was picking up on her nerves, if this was what it was like to think of a loved one talking to the enemy, or if this was the early warning system he'd developed in combat. His emotions around Avery were too new for him to be able to make out the differences.

The one thing he knew was this sucked.

"We already know FlashDeath members play Taylor's game," Lisa said. "And have a charismatic cheering them on. It's all in their social media chatter."

"No word yet on who hacked Avery's phone and sent out that video?"

"I got some code samples," Lisa said. "I'm going to see if I can't spot a signature in there. This is too advanced for some wannabe. Whoever did this is top-notch."

"I think all roads will lead through Inge Prokhorov," Rowan said, his heel tapping nervously. "Do you have a family tree? How does she fit in with Sergei?"

"First cousins," Margot said. "Sergei's mother is Inge's aunt. Was. Sergei's mother is deceased."

"Are you following that thread?" he asked.

"Roger that," Margot said.

Suddenly, monitors went black except for the glow of the computer Avery was working on.

"What the heck?" Nutsbe leaned forward.

"Rowan? Rowan, what's happening?" Avery's whisper sounded panicked. "Rowan, the lights went out."

"Honey," Nutsbe said.

"I'm on it."

"Take comms."

Honey pulled a plastic box from a cargo pocket on his pants and put his earpieces in place. "Testing. Testing. Testing."

"Good copy, Honey."

"We're seeing this," Margot said. "I'm checking now for closest available operators to respond to your location. Just in case."

"Copy," Nutsbe said.

"I'm going."

Nutsbe reached around to a drawer and pulled out a comms packet. "Tonight, you'll be 'Foxtrot,' Kennedy." He spun to the wall and pulled down two helmets with night vision. "We own the night."

"Foxtrot. Roger that." Rowan geared up.

After slipping his comms into his ears and doing a sound-check, Honey handed him body armor and a rifle.

"What the heck is this?" Rowan asked, looking the weapon over.

"Stun rifle," Honey said. "Use it if you can. If you can't, I'm assuming you came strapped."

"Always," Rowan growled, jumping out the back of the van. As soon as his feet hit the ground, he pulled his night vision into place and took off running. "Move!"

48

ROWAN

THE CRASH WAS FOLLOWED by glass shattering and a high-pitched scream of terror through their comms.

"Nutsbe. What have you got?" Honey's voice was combat steady.

Find the fire, put the fire out.

It was what Rowan had lived throughout his years in special forces. But he was not prepared to tamp down the kind of feral savagery that expanded through his system. He wanted to rip any hostiles apart. How dare they endanger Avery.

"Avery's got the computer. It's the only source of light. Not sure if I want her to drop it or keep it on so I can see. Okay, she's put it on the chair and stepped back from it."

"Want to call her cell?"

"I have it ringing. But she's got it set to vibrate. She's probably got tunnel vision, so all thought processes are out the window. She's scanning, trying to figure which way to go."

Another shrill scream.

"Nutsbe. I've got shadows. Two, maybe three."

"Honey. What's that crashing?"

"Avery's throwing shit at the shadows," Nutsbe said. "We have a 911 call going out to the Warrenton P.D. from the house. She's not giving her name. It must be Taylor."

"Panther Five." Came Margot's voice. "I hear a ten-minute police ETA on the scanner. You need to jump on that before the police go running in guns a-blazing."

"Honey. Copy."

"Panther Five. I'll let PD know there's an FBI special agent on site."

Honey lowered his voice. "Honey. Command, be advised we have two hostiles at the front door. They have weapons brandished. We're going to dispatch them."

"Nutsbe. Copy."

"We need to clear this silently," Honey whispered. "Choose your guy."

"I've got right."

"Zip ties in your front right pouch. I'm thinking we just give them a hug and let them go night-night." They stood in a copse of young trees just before the yard opened up. Honey had his mouth up to Rowan's ear. "We don't want to get their buddies excited. We'll clear this one hostile at a time."

Rowan moved his gun from his ankle holster to the chest holster, ready to grab and shoot if need be.

"Nutsbe. Two hostiles have hands on Avery. One on either side. She's struggling with them."

"Honey. Moving."

On silent feet, Rowan and Honey slipped forward. The men on guard had their backs to the road and were focused on the windows. Poor training, or maybe they got cocky because they assumed that they'd be alone, getting the drop on the farmhouse.

Which made this next move easy.

Honey held up count down fingers—three, two, one. They pounced.

Rowan got an elbow around the hostile's neck and clamped down tight before he could make any noise. He walked backward as he tightened down on the guy's carotid so he couldn't use his legs to manipulate himself out of Rowan's grip.

The hostile slapped at Rowan's arm and tried to keep his feet under him. But Rowan had done this a thousand times before. This was second nature to him.

Once the guy passed out, Rowan spun him onto his stomach, zip-tied his hands and feet, then left him there in the tall grass to jog over to Honey.

"Honey. Front clear. Door's locked. We're going to make our way around the back and see if they have any other sentries."

"Nutsbe. Third guy in the room with Avery. Be advised, he has a high lumen flashlight that he's shining in her eyes. She's going to be blinded when you enter. And you'll want to watch your night vision."

"Honey. Copy."

"Foxtrot. What are they saying to her? Who are we dealing with?"

"Nutsbe. He's asking her where her husband is. She said she's not married. She thinks he has the wrong house. She might have sputtered when the breech first happened. She's firing on all cylinders now. They're spouting some shit about saving the POTUS."

Through the window, Rowan heard the man yell, "Do you think I'm going to let a crazy jihadist come into my country and put their scope on my president?"

"Nutsbe. We can hear him now. I don't know if that's drugs or just crazy."

Rowan reached his hand in front of Honey with two fingers up, then pointed into the tree line.

Honey used hand signals to tell Rowan to circle to the man on the right. He'd take the guy on the left.

As long as the guy was just yelling, it was better to take down the crew outside. Rowan slipped along the shadow of the house and into the woods. He came around behind the guy and was reaching out his arm when his boot caught a stick, and it snapped loudly.

The hostile spun around to see what was behind him.

Rowan yanked the gun from his chest holster and bashed the tango across the temple. The guy dropped like a sack.

"Hey, you okay?" a tango called over.

Then the grunts.

Honey had him.

Rowan could focus on getting this hostile trussed.

"Honey. Two hostiles disabled."

"Nutsbe. Copy. The P.D. called up a SWAT team, and they've been directed to gather two klicks from the farmhouse at a convenience store. They estimate their roll-up to be twenty minutes. They sound pretty excited about the possibilities of getting to play tonight. I'd make sure this is taken care of well before then."

Honey and Rowan were up at the house, looking in the window of the room where Avery had been sitting. The computer was on the ground in the corner, and the man's flashlight shone in Avery's face.

There were four figures in the room. Not three. One stood back by the door—arms behind his back.

Rowan tapped four fingers on his arm to indicate the Patriots Pledge patch on their jackets and make sure Honey saw the unexpected player.

Honey gave him the thumbs up.

The two slid under the window panes and hunkered down to plan a course of action.

"I say we just walk in with the stun rifles," Honey whispered. "Hit the two touching Avery. The noise and lights will be unexpected. We'll grab Avery and get her to safety. Take the others down. You can take them into FBI custody. And Taylor Knapp. We need to scoop her up in this too."

"Sounds good to me."

"Honey. You get that Nutsbe?"

"Nutsbe. Copy Lima Charlie." —loud and clear.

As the two rose, there was a scream.

"Nutsbe. Abort. Abort. Abort. Fourth guy just shoved a gun in Avery's face. He's up in Avery's grill and sweating. He's got poor trigger control. No surprises."

"Honey. Copy."

They stepped away. Rowan was frantic. This was what he did, day-in and day-out, for years on end. And even if you had experience and skill under your belt, brains and bodies did crazy things. Counterintuitive things.

He just needed Avery to remember that they were there.

They knew what was happening.

They were coming.

"Okay," Honey said. "Danger level just escalated. They must have gone in the back door. You slip into the back hall. I'll watch from the window. The moment he drops the barrel, I'll signal over comms. You throw flashbang. I'll break the window and throw mine. Let's see if we can't get them out of there without shots fired." He reached over and pulled a canister from Rowen's vest and handed it to him. "That should put them on the ground. I'll get the weapons while you get Avery out of there."

"Got it," Rowan said.

"Honey. Nutsbe, how about you start sneaking the van up the road and get yourself behind the trees. As soon as Avery's out of there, I'll secure the last four tangoes, then I'm going after Taylor to bring her with us. We'll rally at the van. We'll exfil with Plan B."

"Nutsbe. Copy."

Rowan skulked to the back porch, making his way to the door.

Tucked low, he reached for the handle and pushed the door wide enough to move in, his head on a swivel looking for any other Patriots Pledge idiots who wanted to play war games.

He'd gladly take them down.

Rowan depended on his training because every fiber of his being yearned to race into the room where Avery was being held and eliminate the threats. Doing so would put her in terrible danger. Honey must know that would be Rowan's instinct, and that's why he was sent to the back rather than be the man with his gun against the windowpane and a tango lined up in his sights.

Rowan pulled up his memory of the house schematic. He rounded out of the kitchen and sidestepped down the hall, then crossed over once he got to the door to the den. "Foxtrot in place," he said under his breath while the tango in the room yelled about how he'd never let a jihadist wage war in America.

"I don't even know what to tell you," Avery said. "Since I'm not married. And I don't have a sister-wife to hand over to you. I'm not sure what to do to help you."

"Help me! Help *me*? What do you think would *help* me? Do you want to convert me?"

"Uhm. Roman Catholics don't really do a lot of converting. I guess I could say a rosary with you." Avery's voice sounded very small.

Rowan hated every nanosecond of this shit.

"Shut up! Shut up! Tell me what the plan is. If you don't tell me right now how your husband plans to kill the president, I'll have to torture the truth out of you. Do you want me to have to do that?"

"Are you crazy?" Avery yelled.

Rowan swung around, so he had as much of the room in his field of vision as possible. A tango shifted his weight and hit a table. A vase crashed to the ground. The tango who had a gun on Avery slid his head in that direction, and his finger curled reflexively on the trigger.

BANG!

The shot rang out.

"Now." Honey's voice in Rowan's ear had not even finished the sound when the flashbang left Rowan's fingertips. He covered his ears and hunkered against the wall, protecting his eyes.

The explosion was followed by the crash of glass breaking and the flashbang that Honey threw into the mix.

Rowan twisted and ran into the room. Avery was in the fetal position on the ground. The guy in front of her was reaching out, patting the ground for his gun. Rowan shot him with the stun rifle. His unholy scream filled the room.

Rowan focused on the man on the ground who lay still. Blood pooled beneath him, shot by his own guy. Rowan grabbed up the shooter's gun and shoved it into his belt against his back. Crouching, he rolled Avery into his arms. At first, she flung out, not knowing who had her. She'd be blind and deaf for a while yet. But as he rolled her to his chest, even in her survival-mode, she must have realized it was him. He lifted up from his squat and ran out of the smoke to get Avery to fresh air.

He didn't stop running until he was at the back of the van.

"Nutsbe. Precious cargo secured and is receiving first-aid," he announced, moving away from the opened van door, giving Rowan room to set Avery down. He handed Rowan an oxygen mask and a bottle of water to minister Avery, then turned back to his bank of video feeds.

"Foxtrot. Honey, do you need me?"

"Negative. Four hostiles secured. I'm going after Taylor."

"Panther Five. Taylor told 911 she's unarmed and in the guest bathroom closet. But still, exercise caution."

"Honey. Copy. Wilco."

Rowan cradled Avery in his arms as he flushed her face and held the air mask.

"They're crazy," Avery said. "Those are the people that jumped you on your run, aren't they?"

The sirens from SWAT sounded.

Nutsbe picked up the radio. "Nutsbe. Panther Five, advise the good men and women in blue that we have an agent securing the scene, and he's still inside."

"Panther Five. Good copy. Wilco."

"Same guys," Rowan told her.

"And they really believed that someone was after the president. This is crazy. Taylor was in there. Is Honey getting her?"

"He'll get her out."

"And what will you do with her?"

"I'm going to put her under arrest. After what you've told us, I think we have a pretty clear picture of her conspiring to incite hate crimes."

Avery lay in his lap, pushing away the air mask. "She'll be in jail. That's going to make a lot of people angry."

"If they find out about it, yes, it will. What will end up happening is that she'll turn State's witness to stay out of jail. We'll be able to use her to help us understand who and what's involved here, so the good guys can round up everyone who's dead set on destabilizing America."

"Are they going to come after me again?"

"We'll protect you. I'm sorry this happened, Avery. I had no idea that this might have been dangerous."

"Taylor must have told them that I was going to be here and what time I'd arrive. It was too convenient, too precise for that not to be the case. If the guys were told how to get to you before, on your run, by a charismatic, then that means that the charismatic must be connected to Taylor somehow. The charismatic must have told them to come here after me. And Taylor must have known too."

"Why do you say that?" Nutsbe asked.

"Because she knew what time I was coming. She settled me with the chapters and went to take a bath. Who does that when a business person comes for a meeting? No one. It's crazy. I was sitting there trying to figure out why she removed herself from the room when the lights went off."

"Your mind, Avery, is astonishing. You should be writing, not editing," Rowan said.

She lifted herself up and kissed Rowan on the lips, and he closed his eyes to focus on the sheer bliss of having her safe.

He leaned his forehead against hers and blew out a heavy breath. "When Nutsbe said you had a gun to your face, that's the worst thing I've experienced in my life." He lifted up to look her in the eye.

"It was pretty scary, I have to admit. My ears are still ringing.

I can barely hear you. That's pretty nauseating…that flashbang stuff. " Rowan handed her a water bottle, and Avery took a sip.

"Yeah. I need you to consider a safer job," Rowan said. "I don't know if I can go through my day, thinking you're putting yourself in dangerous situations like this."

"Oh, now stop. You told me you shook hands for a living and didn't throw flashbang."

"I did, didn't I?" He gathered her tight to his chest and squeezed.

"Air!" she gasped to make him let go.

"Honey. The P.D. has taken custody. They need each of us to give them statements. We have permission to go to the hotel and get cleaned up before we do that. Avery, those were trying circumstances. You did great."

"Thank you," Avery called into the air for Honey to hear.

"Honey. Foxtrot, I pulled Avery's car to the side of the road. I put her phone and keys in the front seat. Nutsbe and I will meet you back at the hotel. We'll wait here for FBI transport to come pick Taylor up. I'm going to hold her here in the house until you pull away with Avery."

"Foxtrot. Copy."

Avery scooted to the ground. She reached out her hand and laced her fingers with Rowan's. Together, they walked toward her car.

"I'm imaging, Avery Goodyear," Rowan released her hand to wrap his arm around her and tuck her tight, "that life together with you is going to be full of excitement."

"A whole life, huh?"

"At the FBI, we're taught to speak in an individual's vernacular." He dropped a kiss into her hair. "When I write, I'm a *planter.* I have a trajectory for the story, and I know the ending. But I like the story to naturally unfold and surprise me."

"Ah, and what kind of story is this? You usually write thrillers."

"Not this time. This is a straight-up romance."

"You know I'm a romance editor." They stood beside her car, his arms wrapping her tightly, her cheek resting against his chest. "There are certain elements that are absolutely necessary for writing a romance. There can be no wiggle room."

"Yeah? Like what."

She leaned her head back, and their gaze met. Held. "In romances, it *always* ends with a happily ever after."

"That works for me." He bent to kiss her. "We'll do the happily ever after then."

EPILOGUE

WEDNESDAY AFTERNOON
Washington D.C.

THE LAST TO SLIDE INTO a seat at the table at FBI Headquarters, Rowan looked around at the task force members. They all had that sizzle of excitement that happens when they got their teeth into a case.

Amanda Frost sat at the head of the table. Prescott sat to her right.

"Good," Frost said. "And now we're all here. Let's get an update on players and actions. Let me start with Taylor Knapp. Her real name is Tara Michelle Hollinsworth. She remains in our custody. We are charging her with a laundry list of crimes, including conspiracy against the United States and being an agent of a foreign government. We're hoping to get her flipped

and thoroughly debriefed. We're working on that with her
lawyers. So far, this has stayed out of the news cycle and off
social media, which is helpful in being able to scoop everyone
up." She turned to the man next to Prescott. "Talbott, what have
we got on Katerina Sokolov, Taylor Knapp's—well,
Hollinsworth's—university roommate?"

"We're looking for her."

Frost turned to Carmichael. "And the band members?"

"We have names and addresses. We've filled out search
warrants and are waiting for signatures."

"Good. I'll be interested in who actually writes their music
and how they're connected to Sokolov. Are they all United States
citizens? Were they at university with Sokolov and
Hollinsworth?"

"We're running that down," Carmichael said. "I'll submit a
report later today or first thing in the morning."

"All right," Frost continued. "One of the interesting connections that Avery Goodyear was able to make for us was that
while Inge only used her married name for legal documentation,
Patrick Windsor's wife used her own name, Inge Prokhorov,
routinely. Finley, where are you going with that?"

Finley leaned forward. "Inge Prokhorov is in Paris with
Sergei Prokhorov's wife, Irenka Orlov Prokhorov. Sergei is plan-
ning to join them in a few days. We've filed FISA warrants on
Inge to see who else she's in contact with."

"And you're scheduled to fly to Paris, Kennedy?" Frost's
brow furrowed.

"Yes, Friday morning. That has to do with another aspect of
this case, not connected to this task force," Rowan replied. "I can
try to put eyes on her and make sure she's there."

"As for Patriots Pledge." Frost turned a page on her notes.
"We have all the members that we've connected to this group,

except for their charismatic, in jail for the attempted murder of a federal agent. It was a small enough group, but they trained with SIC—Sons of the Iron Cross—in West Virginia. I've sent that information to our West Virginia office to look into. Griffin, you accessed their electronics. What are you finding?"

Lisa shifted in her seat. "From Patriots Pledge members' interactions and their gaming history, I can see that they were funneled into a group that was geographically within a half-hour drive from each other. It looks like they all share a psych profile for individuals who are susceptible to being indoctrinated on the web. The interesting thing I learned was that each was added to a group that consisted of ten players. All of the original group members were out of Bulgaria. As an American player became a 'true believer,' one of the Bulgarians left the group, and another American was added until the group was comprised of the single Bulgarian charismatic leader. I saw a similar system unfold when I looked at the FlashDeath group. Though that group only had five American members when they were encouraged to go do the vandalism. I perceived the FlashDeath members as lower on the IQ range. Their charismatic—and it does look like a single individual was tasked with the whole Taylor Knapp strategy—walked them through the process step by step, while the Patriots Pledge members were given information that they then planned and acted out on their own. Tactics apparently change by group."

"They have the FlashDeath members under arrest?" Carmichael asked. "We can talk to them?"

"Yes," Frost said. "None of them has lawyered up. They don't have the money. They'll be using public defenders."

"Good, we might be able to get something from them," Carmichael said.

"Right now," Lisa explained, "I have a team that's using all of the suspects' computers to play as Patriots Pledge and Flash-

Death. I'm posting as them on their social media accounts. We'll see if any more directives come through."

Finley swiveled toward Rowan. "How's Avery doing?"

"Avery's got some post-traumatic issues, nightmares, and heightened startle reflexes... anyone would after they had a gun to their face and flashbang thrown in the room. Iniquus has its crisis therapist involved."

"You two are living together now?" Frost asked. "I saw that you are both listing the same temporary address."

"Both our houses need to be repaired, and new furniture needs to go in after the FlashDeath attack. We're each waiting on insurance checks to get going with that. In the meantime, we have an Airbnb for the month."

"So that's not permanent?" Frost asked.

Rowan hoped it was permanent. Waking up with Avery in his arms was such a great feeling. "We haven't discussed that. I'll keep my relationship and housing records up to date."

Frost turned to Lisa. "How are you doing? Your house was hit as well. Where are you staying?"

"I'm staying with family. I'm doing fine. It's inconvenient, but it'll be okay."

"Good then." Frost looked back at her notes. "Iniquus is working this case from their end and with their contacts. The liaisons between the Panther Force and our team is Rowan Kennedy, and Steve Finley will take over when Kennedy goes out of the country." She gave him a nod. "All communications flow through them, so we aren't repetitive or missing something. And the last thing I want to bring up, Kennedy, is that you and Griffin had planned to use the idea of the CIA Red Cell as a means to entice Tara Hollinsworth as Taylor Knapp to come and talk with us. Since then, you have both shared with me your conversation with Avery Goodyear on the subject, and you both voiced that you think the CIA Red Cell might be something that the FBI should replicate. To that end, I have set up a meeting with the CIA officer who heads that program. I think that Avery might be helpful in giving insight as we feel our way forward. Rowan, can you ask her if she'd be willing to help us with this project?"

"I'll check with her tonight."

"Very well." Frost's voice changed timbre, letting the task force know she was wrapping up. "Things are getting clearer. We have names. We have arrests. We have the chance of turning Hollinsworth and getting even more information as we let her out to operate as Taylor Knapp again. We're making progress. One step and then another. This is an important means for us to understand how deeply Russia and Russian proponents have wormed into our society and how they are influencing and changing Americans as a people. Figuring out at least this game plan and learning how to counter their manipulation is no small undertaking. And it is of vital importance. As Madeline Albright said, 'It is easier to remove tyrants and destroy concentration camps than to kill the ideas that gave them birth.' We still have hope of stopping them, but it's going to be the fight of our lifetimes."

WEDNESDAY EVENING

"AND TWO GLASSES OF CHAMPAGNE, PLEASE," Avery added to her dinner order.

"We're celebrating?" Rowan asked.

She smiled. "I'll tell you when the champagne flutes arrive."

They were sitting across from each other at a small corner table in a dimly lit restaurant that catered to the romantic crowd. Their fingers were laced as they held hands across the crisply starched white linen tablecloth.

"This is our first traditional date," she said. "I don't usually move in with men who haven't taken me out for dinner."

"How many men have you lived with?"

"Just you," she said.

Rowan leaned across the table to kiss her. Her soft smile was just too enticing to resist. Rowan was doing a lot of resisting right now. He much preferred their first date, where they'd gone right to his hotel room and satisfied their appetites before they ate dinner.

"Were you able to make it over and see your mom? How is she doing?" Rowan asked, just to get the images of Avery in her purple lace panties out of his head.

"She looks so much better. She seems so much better. I think this is the best possible move for her. I childishly trusted my dad when he said she would wilt on the vine in an institution." She shook her head, and Rowan could see self-recrimination in her eyes.

"Stop. You did the best you could every day. I saw you trying. Please don't beat yourself up."

She pulled her lips into a fake smile and looked at her lap.

Rowan wiggled her fingers. "What about Curtis and Fanny? Are they comfortable with the move?"

"Are you kidding?" She looked up and gave him a real smile this time. "Ecstatic! They are just so thrilled that they didn't end up stuck with her, and they don't have to worry about me going out of town anymore." Avery turned her head as the waiter approached with their champagne. "You know, as much as I am uncomfortable with Curtis and his ethics, he did say something that actually helped me during my decision making."

"How's that?" Rowan leaned back as the champagne was placed on the table with a bowl of strawberries.

Once the waiter left, Avery continued, "Curtis said, 'Inaction is the same as action. If you are not dynamically opposed, then you are propagating Taylor Knapp's sins.' And as I weighed my situation, I found that he was right. Silence and inaction allow the bad guys to get away with bad things. Fear is a tool that bad people wield like a spear." She took in a deep breath and looked over to the empty wall, then released that breath slowly. When she turned to focus on Rowan again, she blinked and frowned.

He took her hand between both of his. "You were and *are* incredibly brave. And incredibly smart. And here you told me that you would be a terrible spy. And yet, look what you were able to accomplish."

Avery's cheeks flushed pink, and Rowan loved that about her.

He let go of her hand and lifted his flute. "Champagne. What are we celebrating?"

"You helped me fill out the paperwork for human resources on threats against my job, threats of violence, and sexual harassment by my boss, George Pratt. I handed those in, and before the day was done, George was walking out of the building with his belongings in a cardboard box, a security guard at his heels."

Rowan felt relief wash through him. He had been afraid that if this didn't work, that he might find himself banging on George's door one night. And that wouldn't be good for anyone involved.

"Then I was called into Mr. Shreveport's office. Mr. Windsor, by the way, is apparently out of the country with his wife. I'm assuming the FBI has a plan concerning them?"

"You assume correctly."

"Good. Well, as to the champagne, you, Dr. Kennedy, are about to drink champagne with the new head of the EverMore label. That's the Windsor Shreveport's label for romance, women's fiction, and chick-lit. George's old job."

"Wow!" Rowan grinned. "Well done. Well deserved."

They clinked and sipped.

They sat in silence, looking at each other, and feeling contented.

Rowan had never been this satisfied in his life. Like this was right and didn't need fixing. A complete revelation. He'd never felt like this in a relationship before, like a key that slid into the right lock.

She waggled their hands. "Now you know about the high-lights of my day. How about you?"

"Apparently, the idea of a Bureau version of the CIA Red Cell is getting attention. I was asked to reach out to you and see if you might like to work with them as they set things up." He tipped his head and paid close attention to her body language as her muscles contracted.

"Does that include getting wires and video glasses again?"

"No. No. This would just be chatting with folks at the office."

"Okay. Yes, I think that's okay." She nodded, but there was still some stress there. And there probably would be for a long time to come.

"I talked to my team about my having to go out of town on Friday."

"So soon," she whispered.

"And I was asked about our living arrangements."

Avery tipped her head.

"For security's sake, they keep track of our home lives. They want to know if our living together is permanent. I didn't have an answer for them yet. I wanted to tell them yes. But, we've not had that discussion."

The stress that Avery had held a moment ago sifted away. Her face was soft, her eyes warm, he read love in their depths and found himself grinning like an idiot at her.

"Yes," she said. "We should turn the page from this Taylor Knapp mess. I think moving in together should be permanent. I'm ready for a new chapter to begin."

The end

Thank you for reading Avery and Rowan's story.

The next book in the FBI Joint Task Force Series is
COLD RED

**They might survive the madmen trailing their every move...
if the elements don't kill them first...**

Readers, I hope you enjoyed getting to know Avery and Rowan. If you had fun reading Open Secret, I'd appreciate it if you'd help others enjoy it too.

Recommend it: Just a few words to your friends, your book groups, and your social networks would be wonderful.

Review it: Please tell your fellow readers what you liked about my book by reviewing Open Secret. If you do write a review, please send me a note at FionaQuinnBooks@outlook.com so I can thank you with a personal e-mail. Or stop by my website www.FionaQuinnBooks.com to keep up with my news and chat through my contact form.

Turn the page for some delicious recipes!

LOLA'S TO-DIE-FOR CAKE RECIPE

Lola Zelkova can do little to make her friend Avery's life any easier. Lola's solution? A sinfully rich chocolate cake. It can cure almost anything that ails you. Here is her recipe:

I will warn you at the outset:

- This cake takes forever to make (but I'll give you options along the way)
- This cake is HIGHLY ADDICTIVE
- Once you make this cake, no other cake will ever be good enough. Yup, this cake will ruin you for all cakes from here on in.
- If you share this cake with others, they will insist on this cake to feel loved.

So hand out the slices with caution.

Start with the chocolate mousse because this is a lovely dessert in and of itself. If you only get this far, it's all good - just pipe this into a martini glass, add a garnish, and call it a day.

NEXT STEP...

RUM CHOCOLATE MOUSSE

Ingredients

    1 3/4 cups heavy cream

    12 ounces quality semi-sweet chocolate chips

    1/2 c dark rum

    4 tablespoons butter

    1 teaspoon flavorless, granulated gelatin

Directions

The colder, the better:

1. Chill 1 1/2 cups heavy cream in the refrigerator: chill the metal mixing bowl and mixer beaters in the freezer.

2. In top of a bain-marie, combine chocolate chips, rum, and butter. A bain-marie is when you put water into a large pot and simmer it and place a smaller pot inside with your ingredients. This lets your ingredients warm gently and evenly.

- Melt over barely simmering water, stirring constantly.
- Remove from heat while a couple of chunks are still visible.

- • Burned chocolate is nasty and ruins the mousse.
- Allow to cool to room temperature.
- Pour 1/4 cup heavy cream into a Pyrex bowl and sprinkle in the gelatin.
- Allow gelatin to "bloom" for 10 minutes.
- Carefully heat by stirring in the top of the bain-marie.
- Do not boil, or gelatin will become a gloopy mess.
- Fold into the cooled chocolate and set aside.
- In the chilled mixing bowl, beat cream to medium peaks.
- Fold some of your whipped cream into the chocolate mixture to lighten it.
- Fold in the remaining whipped cream in two batches.
- Do not overwork the mousse.
- Stick your bowl in the fridge.

NEXT STEP...

RASPBERRY DRIZZLE

This, too, can be an excellent dessert addition. Once made, you can spoon it over brownies, ice cream, what-have-you.

- Mix one small jar of raspberry jam and a mini bottle of Chambord.

- Tah dah! Wasn't that easy?

NEXT STEP…

CHOCOLATE RUM CAKE

THE CAKE

- Ingredients

- 1 cup room temperature butter
- 2 cups granulated sugar
- 4 large eggs
- 1/2 cup dark rum
- *2 cups all-purpose flour*
- *1 cup unsweetened cocoa*
- *1 teaspoon baking powder These five dry ingredients get sifted*
- *1 teaspoon baking soda*
- *1/2 teaspoon salt*
- 1 cup hot water
- 1 teaspoon vanilla extract

- Beat the butter at medium speed with an electric mixer until fluffy; gradually add sugar, beating well.
- Add eggs, beating until blended after each addition.
- Add rum; beat until blended.

- Combine flour and next 4 ingredients sift into sugar mixture
- Add hot water and vanilla
- Beat at low speed until blended.
- Prepare pans by spraying with non-stick spray, then dust with
-     Cocoa powder.
- Pour evenly into 2 - 9" pans, then give a shake to smooth tops and
-     release air bubbles.
- Bake at 350° for 27 minutes (cake will be slightly underdone).
- Cool in pans on a wire rack for 10 minutes.
- Remove from pans, and cool completely on wire racks.
- Whew! Almost there. Did you give up? Slice the cake, drizzle with raspberry sauce, and add an ice cream scoop of mousse, garnish with chocolate shavings.

But if you're still hanging in there...

You need to make sure your cake is cool, and you work quickly to keep the mousse firm.

1. You have 2 cake layers. Slice each one in half to form what will be

four layers. You can use a serrated

knife or dental floss if you don't have a cake cutter.

2. Place one of the layers smooth side down spongy side up on

your cake plate.

3. Use strips of waxed paper of aluminum foil around the edge so

your plate is clean when you're done icing.

4. Stab your sponge side with a fork and spread 1/3 of the raspberry mixture onto the cake. Stabbing your cake means the Chambord will step down into the cake and infuse it with moisture and flavor.

5. Add 1/3 of your mousse spreading it to the edges.

6. Repeat until you place your top layer sponge side down smooth

side up.

CHILL - to firm up your mousse

RUM FROSTING

1 lb. confectioners' sugar
   1/2 cup unsweetened Dutch-process cocoa powder
   1/4 teaspoon salt
   12 ounces cream cheese, room temperature
   3/4 cup unsalted butter, room temperature
   18 ounces bittersweet chocolate, melted and cooled
   1 1/2 cups sour cream
   2 tbs rum (you knew I'd have to do it)

DIRECTIONS
   Sift together confectioners' sugar, cocoa, and salt.

- With an electric mixer on medium-high speed, beat cream cheese and butter until pale and fluffy.
- Add sugar mixture
- Mix in melted and cooled chocolate and sour cream
- Beat until smooth. Leave out on the counter, so it is room temperature.

FROST...

Please note: This is not a smooth pretty frosting. It is more a thick layer of chocolate deliciousness that wants to look a little wild and free. The kind of cake that you can slice right into and don't need to remark of its beauty. Nope, this is just a decadent gluttonous cake that needs to lay on your plate and be spooned into your mouth.

It's like crack. One taste, and you'll be addicted. This is your warning. Make this cake at your own risk.

And if you do.

Well, you are entirely welcome.

Now that your sweet tooth is satisfied, ready to read?

THE WORLD of INIQUUS

Chronological Order

Ubicumque, Quoties. Quidquid

Weakest Lynx (Lynx Series)

Missing Lynx (Lynx Series)

Chain Lynx (Lynx Series)

Cuff Lynx (Lynx Series)

WASP (Uncommon Enemies)

In Too DEEP (Strike Force)

Relic (Uncommon Enemies)

Mine (Kate Hamilton Mystery)

Jack Be Quick (Strike Force)

Deadlock (Uncommon Enemies)

Instigator (Strike Force)

Yours (Kate Hamilton Mystery)

Gulf Lynx (Lynx Series)

Open Secret (FBI Joint Task Force)

Thorn (Uncommon Enemies)
Ours (Kate Hamilton Mysteries
Cold Red (FBI Joint Task Force)
Even Odds (FBI Joint Task Force)
Survival Instinct - Cerberus Tactical K9
Protective Instinct - Cerberus Tactical K9
Defender's Instinct - Cerberus Tactical K9
Danger Signs - Delta Force Echo
Hyper Lynx - Lynx Series
Danger Zone - Delta Force Echo
Danger Close - Delta Force Echo
Cerberus Tactical K9 Team Bravo
Marriage Lynx - Lynx Series

FOR MORE INFORMATION VISIT
WWW.FIONAQUINNBOOKS.COM

ACKNOWLEDGMENTS

My great appreciation ~

To my editor - **Kathleen Payne**

To my cover artist - **Melody Simmons**

To my publicist - **Margaret Daly**

To my Beta Force - who are always honest and kind at the same time. Especially E. Hordon, M. Carlon, V. Makosky.

To my Street Force - who support me and my writing with such enthusiasm. If you're interested in joining this group, please send me an email. **FionaQuinnBooks@outlook.com**

Thank you to the real-world military and FBI who serve to protect us.

To all of the wonderful professionals whom I called on to get the details right. Please note: this is a work of fiction, and while I always try my best to get all of the details correct, there are times when it serves the story to go slightly to the left or right of perfection. Please understand that any mistakes or discrepancies are my authorial decision making alone and sit squarely on my shoulders.

Thank you to my family.

I send my love to my husband and my great appreciation. T, you are one of my life's greatest miracles.

And of course - thank YOU for reading my stories. I'm smiling joyfully as I type this. I so appreciate you!

ABOUT THE AUTHOR

Fiona Quinn is a six-time USA Today bestselling author, a Kindle Scout winner, and an Amazon All-Star.

Quinn writes action-adventure in her Iniquus World of books, including Lynx, Strike Force, Uncommon Enemies, Kate Hamilton Mysteries, FBI Joint Task Force, Cerberus Tactical K9, and Delta Force Echo series.

She writes urban fantasy as Fiona Angelica Quinn for her Elemental Witches Series.

And, just for fun, she writes the Badge Bunny Booze Mystery Collection with her dear friend, Tina Glasneck.

Quinn is rooted in the Old Dominion, where she lives with her husband. There, she pops chocolates, devours books, and taps continuously on her laptop.

Visit www.FionaQuinnBooks.com

COPYRIGHT

Open Secret is a work of fiction. Names, characters, places, and incidents either are the product of the author's imagination or are used fictitiously, and any resemblance to actual persons, living or dead, business establishments, events, or locales is entirely coincidental.

CPSIA information can be obtained
at www.ICGtesting.com
Printed in the USA
LVHW050708151021
700519LV00001B/14